SLAYING WITH SYLPHS
HAVEN EVER AFTER - BOOK SIX

HAZEL MACK

COPYRIGHT

© Hazel Mack Author 2025

EBOOK ISBN: 978-1-957873-59-6

PAPERBACK ISBN: 978-1-957873-67-1

All rights reserved. No part of this publication may be reproduced, stored or transmitted in any form or by any means, electronic, mechanical, photocopying, recording, scanning, or otherwise without written permission from the publisher. It is illegal to copy this book, post it to a website, or distribute it by any other means without permission.

This novel is entirely a work of fiction. The names, characters and incidents portrayed in it are the work of the author's imagination. Any resemblance to actual persons, living or dead, events or localities is entirely coincidental. However, if I get the chance to become Ever's newest resident, I'll take it!

I don't support the use of AI in book, book cover or book graphic creation. If you love human generated books, please feel free to learn more at my website at www.annafury.com/ai. I do not approve the creation of derivative works based on this book or series without consent.

Editing - Krista Venero at Mountains Wanted

Cover - Anna Fury Author

Cover Art - Linda Noeran (@linda.noeran)

❀ Created with Vellum

AUTHORS ARE NOW FACING AN UNPRECEDENTED CHALLENGE - ARTIFICIAL INTELLIGENCE (AI).

AI-based "books", which are computer written, rather than human, are flooding the market and reducing our ability to earn a living wage writing books for you, our amazing readers.

The problem with AI as it stands today? It's not capable of thinking on its own. It ingests data and mimics someone else's style, often plagiarizing art and books without the original creator or author's consent.

There's a very real chance human authors will be forced out of the market as AI-written works take over. Yet your favorite authors bring magical worlds, experiences and emotions to life in a way that a computer can't. If you want to save that, then we need your help.

LEARN MORE ABOUT THE HARMFUL EFFECTS OF AI-WRITTEN BOOKS AND AI-GENERATED ART ON MY WEBSITE AT WWW.ANNAFURY.COM/AI

SYNOPSIS

Lou

I came to the hidden monster town of Ever for one reason—my nieces. I definitely didn't expect Connall, the quiet, authoritative shifter male whose intense stare follows me everywhere I go. And I sure didn't move for the hilarious, snarky elemental who floats outside my bedroom window at night. Is cozy stalking a thing? Because that's what Dirk does.

But it turns out my nieces are thriving, those badass bitches. They don't *need* to be saved. So when Dirk asks me out on a date and casually mentions we should *also* be dating Connall, I surprise everyone by agreeing. Really, though, who could say no to that?

One steamy date turns into another, and before I know it I'm living the double-teaming life of my dreams. Things aren't all hunky dory, though…I've never been *that* lucky. First I start seeing a dead guy nobody else can see. Then someone starts attacking my friends, leaving them paralyzed and unhealable by even the brilliant local doctor.

I worry that I'm somehow the genesis of what's happening. Yet my quest for answers leads me in circles that have me wondering if I'll get to keep my happily ever after, or have to deny Dirk and Connall in order to protect them.

Slaying with Sylphs is a cozy but very steamy MMF monster romance. Come for the snacks but stay for the happily ever after.

GET THE FREEBIES

WANT SPICY EPILOGUES?

Sign up for my newsletter to access the FREE bonus epilogues to every Hazel Mack book I write.

www.annafury.com/subscribe

CONTENT NOTICE

While this book is very sweet and lighthearted, there are a couple heavy themes to mention. In particular, there's reference to past involvement in accidental death (off page), light violence, grief and PTSD.

If you have any particular questions, feel free to reach out to me at author@annafury.com!

CHAPTER ONE
LOU

"Now drop the amethyst in slowly, so it doesn't hit the bottom of the pot too hard." Malik's instructions sound simple, but I know from attempting this potion three times this week, it's not that easy.

Relaxing my jaw so nervous energy doesn't filter through the quartz, I stir as I reach down with the amethyst in my fingers. Malik's steady, huge presence should be a comfort as he hovers by my side, but instead, I worry I'll fuck up the potion a fourth time in a row.

Three times was not a charm, as it turns out.

Come on, Lou, get it together.

I release the crystal into the pot, continuing to stir the blue mixture carefully as I listen for it to land on the bottom. Instead, it hits with a thunk, my heart sinking just as fast. The edges of the cast iron pot begin to vibrate as the mixture simmers wildly, purple sparks shooting up out of the liquid. One hits me in the face, singeing my left eyebrow as I sigh and step back.

Malik slings a pale muscular arm over my chest, curling his fingers into my skin. His left wing, covered in pale purple feathers, curls around me, shielding me from the sparking pot.

I sigh and cross my arms, infuriated by my fourth failed attempt at finishing his signature sleeping potion.

Glancing up at my new friend and boss, I sigh again. "It shouldn't be this hard, Malik. At this point, I'm costing you more money than it's worth for you to have an assistant."

The big pegasus tsks, pale pink lips curling into a smirk as he looks down at me. "When Richard suggested you become my assistant, I knew it would take time to impart my knowledge to you, Lou. But I also knew it was a task worth doing. You'll get it. It took me decades to get to where I am."

I snort. "It helps that you're a warlock, I'm sure."

"Of course." He dips his head in agreement. "And it helps that I put in thousands of hours of practice at the academy when I was younger. And then spent decades honing my skills to get to this point. A sleeping potion sounds simple enough, but making a good one is like creating any work of art, my friend." His fingers leave my side, his wide wing retracting backward against the white horse half of his body.

"You'll get it, Lou, and we will practice until you do." He winks as he nudges me with his elbow. "In the meantime, you get to clean up the mess you made, mineirah."

Mineirah. The pegasi word translates loosely to "deep friend," almost like the pixie concept of a soulfriend. I know what Malik means. From the moment Richard, the pack alpha of the shifters, introduced us, I liked Malik. More than that, I respected him.

Malik gets me.

Even now, he stares, luminescent blue eyes sparkling. Something about the way Malik looks at me makes me feel like he's looking right into my soul. I'm as transparent as a piece of glass in a window frame, and Malik's got both hands over his brows, peering inside.

His assessing gaze moves back to the pot. "Give it a few minutes to cool, then dump it out back."

With the other failures, he means. There's a nice gooey pile of unusable sludge behind Malik's potions shop, Alkemi.

When I acknowledge his directive, he clip-clops toward the front of the shop and begins to unpack a box of crystals that arrived this morning from another monster haven.

Blowing out a frustrated breath, I uncross my arms and lean against a table covered with crystals and gems of all sorts. Most are familiar to me from my time working in a potions shop back home in upstate New York, but many are specific to the monster world.

I glance at a transparent black crystal at the center of the table. It's something called pegasite, a crystal that only comes from a haven on the far side of the world where most pegasi originate from. Pegasite grows in the depths of a volcano there. Every century or two, the volcano erupts and spews the beautiful onyx crystal out onto black sand beaches. A small community grew at the edges of the volcano, and when the beach is full of crystals, they harvest them and send them to potion shops all throughout the monster haven system.

My gaze travels from the pegasite to a sprinkling of amethyst and aragonite. The beautiful varied colors never fail to amaze me. It's easy to get lost in those sparkling, angular depths. I like to imagine that every crystal is its own unique, magical world. One day, if I learn enough about them, maybe a magical portal will open up and pull me inside. It'll be like *Journey to the Center of the Earth*, except my real life.

Then I consider how living in a hidden monster town is pretty much the same thing. The tiny haven of Ever is protected by magical wards, ensconced in a gorgeous valley in Massachusetts. No human could ever find it unless specifically called here by the town's magical homing beacon map.

That's how I got here, thanks to my nieces and the town's previous Keeper, the mayor of sorts, if monsters have a mayor.

I twirl my strawberry blonde braid around my finger as I

consider my dramatic arrival. It turns out all monsters aren't nice, and I got firsthand knowledge of that on my way here. Thinking back to the bites I sustained trying to get into Ever, I scratch at the back of one arm, grimacing at how tender yet itchy the skin still is.

As soon as my potion pot is cool to the touch, I unhook it from its spot over the fire and walk-rush to the back door, trying not to let it slosh up over the pot's thick cast iron sides.

At the back door, I shoulder my way through and set the pot down on a patch of moss. It's beautiful behind the long row of shops Alkemi is part of. Like a magical monster strip mall, backed by gorgeous, dense forest. Trees as wide as cars soar above my head, blotting out the sky, ferns growing thick and lush at their bases.

I grimace as I glance down at an oily, sticky-looking puddle outside the back door. Sighing, I push the potion pot over, frowning as the ruined potion joins its predecessors, forming an even deeper pool.

Movement at the building's edge draws my eye. A pointy red hat appears, followed by the tiny face of its owner.

"Messed up again?" His voice is impossibly small, like a mouse, as he jumps around the edge of the building and crosses his arms.

I resist the urge to reach over and splash sludgy potion on him with my shoe. "Yeah, Bellami. As you can see, I messed up again. Thank you."

The tiny gnome male snorts. "You're not great at this, Lou."

I breathe deeply through my nose. "Obviously." I wave my hand dismissively in his direction. "Don't you have something to do? Malik told me you're expanding the gnome village. You should get to that."

The gnomes are horribly straightforward. Last time I had a bad day, one of Bellami's brethren asked me if I actually ate shit or just looked like I had.

Case in point. Bellami uncrosses his arms to straighten his hat with a grunt. "There's potion all over your hands."

I look down, turning my hands over to see what he's talking about. After a second, I get it and loose an irritated breath. "Those are freckles, Bellami. They're permanent. It's part of my skin." *And I happen to like them, thank you very much.*

He gives me a blank look. "Whatever you say. Anyways, I'm not here for that. I came to ask for your help. Your niece, Wren, told me you were good with organizing. I'm thinking you should try helping us for a while since your career in potion-making looks like it's gonna be short."

"Jesus, Bellami," I snap. "I've been at this for all of two weeks."

"Precisely," he says with a snort. "If you were gonna get it, you would have. My people could use help from someone—" his eyes rove over my much taller figure, "—broader."

Damn. How rude can this diminutive male be in a two-minute encounter?

"What kind of help?" I hedge.

He glances at the black puddle where I've been dumping my potion. "Hauling plants and small trees. Moving rocks. Lifting mushrooms. You know. Gnome village stuff."

Lifting mushrooms.

It's on the tip of my tongue to deny him help simply because the gnomes are so…bossy. But then I consider that I, too, am very bossy. It takes a bitch to know a bitch. That being said, if I can do something to help, I will.

"Okay."

Bellami gives me a clipped nod. "Good, just show up whenever you have free time, and we'll put you to work."

Before I can answer, he turns on a heel and stalks back around the side of the building, his tiny legs moving at super speed. The gnomes are always so purposeful, so quick to go wherever they're going. Damn, the one time they offered to help me learn how to throw an ax at Bad Axe, a half dozen of them crawled all over me shouting directions. They don't do anything in a relaxed way.

I wonder if they're into potions like most of the other monster residents of Shifter Hollow, outside of downtown Ever. Now that I think about it, I haven't ever seen them in the store during my shifts. Some calming tea is what they need. Or a chill pill.

"Everything okay?" Malik's soothing voice echoes from inside the doorway to my right.

I turn and force a smile. "Bellami was just here commenting on the state of my potion, and then had the gall to ask me for help after insulting me."

Malik snorts, stamping one of his horsey forelegs as he crosses his human arms. "You know what you need, Lou? Another kind of potion." His expression goes a little devious, elegant pale nostrils flaring.

"Let me guess. Milkshake?"

He plants both hands on his hips with a huge grin. "Milkshake. Get on, friend."

It's always an odd feeling for me to climb onto Malik's broad back. It feels personal, like something a mate might do, and I am most certainly not his. In fact, I'm pretty sure he's got the hots for Alba, the centaur who owns the Galloping Green Bean diner up on Main Street. So, when he takes me for milkshakes, it's an excuse to visit her at work.

Even so, I smile as he bends his left foreleg, curling his fetlock so I can use his hoof as a step. I grab a thin fabric handle sewn at the bottom of the back of his vest, using the leverage to haul myself onto his broad back, careful not to kick his wings.

"Settled, Lou?" He glances over his top half's shoulder as I tuck my feet between his sides and his beautiful big wings.

"Don't know about settled," I mutter, "but I'm on."

Malik turns and clops carefully out his back door, his white wings tucked tightly over my legs. Like always, I have to resist the urge to stroke the beautifully detailed feathers. Up close, they're iridescent, each one bursting with tiny rainbows of color.

He steps into the small clearing behind Alkemi and spreads his wings wide. He's stopped telling me to hold on at this point because he's flown me so many times. Flying seems to be Malik's answer to everything wrong in the world. Stomach issues? Go for a flight. Feeling down in the dumps? Soaring through the treetops will fix it.

And honestly, he's sorta right. I always feel better after flying with my friend slash boss. It's a different perspective on the tiny monster haven that's my new home.

His incredible muscles bunch underneath my thighs, and then he takes off into the sky, soaring between two enormous trees. I press into his muscular back, having learned the first time we flew that he is utterly unconcerned about being whipped in the face with branches. And he forgets that I am *highly* concerned about it.

When wind drags my hair behind me, I look around. We're above the treetops, Malik's wings beating the sky in steady, bird-like movements. I never took much time to stare at bird wings before I started riding Malik, but his are so large, it's easier to see the full range of motion.

First they curl up into an inverted U, then they press forward straight ahead, and finally they swoop down and back up again into a U. Flight is such a wild and weird thing, but I often get lost in the movement of his wings when we fly.

Down below, the dense forest surrounding Shifter Hollow moves lazily by. Malik swoops low over the lake. From this altitude, the mermaids' city below the surface is partially visible despite being set deep along the lake's bottom.

We leave it behind as tiny gusts of wind dance over my cheeks and hair, tangling it into a knot that's always a bitch to get out. I close my eyes and let my head fall back, loving how the wind kisses my skin, its temperature cool in comparison to the warmth of the sunrays that filter through Ever's bubble-shaped protective ward.

The flight is over too soon, Malik descending gently out of the sky to land in the middle of Sycamore Street. His feet touch down, and he folds his wings back, as cautious as ever not to jostle me. I stay seated on his back for a moment, sad as the wisps of wind that always follow me disappear.

Malik shifts from one foot to the other, swishing his tail from side to side. I pop my eyes open to see him staring over his shoulder at me. "Everything alright, Lou? We're here."

"Yeah, I know," I murmur. "I was enjoying the perfect sunny weather."

He snorts. "Seventy-eight percent of havens pick a weather pattern and stick to it year round. That's why it's always the same here within Ever's wards. But just under twenty percent of havens opt to follow the weather patterns of wherever they're located. It's fascinating to me. Can you imagine living in a haven where it was sunny one day and a blizzard the next?"

I match his disbelieving sound. "Uh, yeah. I lived in New York state when I was in the human world. I can absolutely believe that. The sun is what's so nice of a change though. Normally in winter in New York, the skies are gray for a few months straight."

"I feel so bad for humans," Malik says on a sigh. "Not being able to control the weather, not having magic." He crosses his arms and sighs again loudly.

"Thank gods we had potions and crystals though," I remind him. "You'd love the little shop I worked in before I came here to be with my nieces."

I slide off his back, brushing horse hair off my jeans. When I look up at my boss, he's staring at an adorable red, white and turquoise retro-style diner in front of us. A flashing neon sign on a tall pole tells us it's the Galloping Green Bean.

I elbow Malik in the side. "Did you see Alba through the window?"

He snorts like a horse and stomps a foreleg, his tail lashing against his sides. "Not yet. Perhaps she's not working today, or her nephew, Taylor, is covering for her."

"Well," I say with a laugh, "let's go see, friend."

Ten minutes later, we're seated in a colorful booth on the far back wall of the Galloping Green Bean. I'm on a red bench seat, and Malik rests opposite me on one of the long, curved centaur benches they use in lieu of chairs. It seems like it should be awkward watching someone with four legs and two arms "sit," but he makes it look graceful. If I glanced quickly, it would seem like a hot human guy was sitting across from me.

He sips at his water, glancing around surreptitiously, blue eyes roving the room. I know he requested this booth so he could look for Alba without having to glance behind him.

"See her yet?" I whisper over my menu.

He shakes his head, disappointment obvious on his handsome, angular features. Honestly, Alba's missing out if she doesn't take him up on it when he finally asks her out. He's like Legolas and a centaur smashed together, with better style. The fitted vest he wears accentuates his broad shoulders and thick, muscular chest.

"She's probably not here," he murmurs. "I could have asked Taylor. I saw him this morning. Gosh, I'm an idiot."

Reaching across the table, I place my hand on top of his. "Malik, just make the move. The worst that can happen is she says no."

He visibly pales, reaching up to wipe a bead of sweat off his brow.

"Malik!" a brash female voice echoes off the shiny metal roof.

His worried expression falls, a broad smile replacing it as he rises from the bench.

I turn as Alba trots to our table, stopping next to our booth with a scratch pad in one hand and a purple pen in the other. She's usually gruff and sarcastic—love that—but she beams at Malik. Only for Malik, I've noticed.

Gods, they're so fucking cute.

He shifts on the bench and runs a hand through his hair, his fingers getting stuck in his manbun. Blushing, he rolls his shoulders and crosses his arms over his chest. "Alba, how are you?"

"Busy," she says with a smile. "But glad you're here. Do you need a few minutes with the menu?"

I resist the urge to kick his back leg under the table. We've talked so many times about him asking her out. The attraction is obvious. I try not to be the third wheel as he and Alba make small talk.

Movement outside the wall of front windows catches my eye. The shifter pack alpha, Richard, walks past with his Second, Connall. Time slows as I watch how Connall's jean shirt pulls tight over his impossibly broad barrel chest. He runs a hand through auburn waves, green eyes flashing as he responds to something Richard says.

My heart rate kicks up when he reaches for the door to the diner and pulls it open. Both males disappear from view, blocked by the building, and then reappear inside the door. Shocking green eyes flash to me before a half smile tips Connall's sensual lips upward.

I resist the urge to fan myself. I've always found him insanely attractive. It's more than that, though. He's such a comfortable, grounded presence. He should be, I guess; he's the pack's version of a therapist. I'm so much the opposite—I crave steadiness like he has. What would it be like to date someone who's such a rock?

But then the door opens again, and a blue-skinned elemental sylph comes through, an absolutely wicked grin on his face. Electric blue lightning streaks jaggedly over his pale skin. He claps

Connall on the back as I consider the rollercoaster of my thoughts.

Richard, the shifter alpha, sits at a table. Like clockwork, the sylph and Connall both look over at me.

And there's the crux of my problem. Because Dirk has made his interest in me known from the day we met. But when I look at the two of them together, I find myself just as drawn to Connall. Seeing them looking at me like they both want me tears me up inside. How can I say yes to either of them? How could I ever say no?

It's not like I can have them both.

CHAPTER TWO
CONNALL

Fading sunlight filters through the singular window above my pack omega's head, illuminating the tiny crown she occasionally wears. I don't think she loves wearing it outside of her home haven of Santa Alaya, but our pack here in Ever adores seeing our princess all "gussied up". It's such a stark contrast to her rocker chic style.

And all of that's a stark contrast to the laid back, feminine vibe of the human woman who seems to take up most of the space in my brain these days. It's been hours since I saw Lou at the diner, but I seem to have left most of my thoughts behind with the pretty little human.

"Oh, this is interesting!" Lola's dark fingers move down a page of text in a language so old, nobody alive can even read it. Nobody except for her and my pack alpha, Richard. Or do I address him as king now...I'm not sure.

Lola and Richard are newly mated, and the Luna bond they share is the first in thousands of years. The text she's holding is ancient, but because of their bond, she can now read our goddess Alaya's words.

My queen practically vibrates with excitement, seated in a

chair in what used to be the potions shop, Alkemi's old location, but is now an office for Vikand, our resident bookworm and scholar.

"The Luna bond's strength grows over time, its powers broadening depending on the needs of the community." Lola glances over at me. "Technically, since I'm now the queen, every shifter community belongs to me. Do you suppose this means my powers will extend to everyone in all havens?"

It's a rhetorical question, I'm sure. There's no possible way I could know the answer. But I lean against a stack of dusty, smelly old books and consider it. Or I try to. The reality is that my mind is never far from Lou Hector, even when I should be focusing on my pack. Seeing her earlier at the diner just cemented that for me. She's beautiful, kind, fierce and loyal. Everything I've ever wanted in a mate. And, gods, I want to make a move.

Lola seems oblivious to my straying thoughts.

I try to focus on her and not be rude. "Well, so far, you can shift into any animal you want instead of just a wolf. Then, this week you started reading shifters' wolves' sentiments like an aura. I think you'd have to go back to Santa Alaya to test if that works there. Actually, if you traveled anywhere other than Santa Alaya, you'd know. But since Santa Alaya was your home, and Ever's your home now, your bond might consider both of those places your technical pack."

Lola smiles up at me from the confines of the weathered leather chair, her grin growing wide enough to reveal tiny twin fangs. "Connall, Richard and I are lucky to have you by our sides. Have I mentioned that this week?"

Her compliment causes my wolf to preen, rolling onto his side as he stares at our queen through my eyes. "You've mentioned it," I say with a smile.

"We will always need you," she says, her smile falling as her gaze grows more serious.

And there's the heart of why she continues to remind me that my pack leadership needs me. Technically, I'm Richard's Second, meaning I rule if he's not around. He can count on me for anything the pack needs. I'm his sounding board, his partner, his closest confidante. But the Luna bond between them is new, and we're still figuring out what it means. I mostly feel like a third wheel, because Lola and Richard are so powerful in their own right, I'm not sure they even *do* need me.

"We do," she whispers.

I curl an auburn brow skyward. "You reading minds now, my queen?"

She scrunches her delicate, ski-sloped nose upward. "Eww, let's don't use titles, *so* gross. But, no, your wolf looked despondent for a moment, and it's not hard to imagine why that might be. We've talked about this topic several times, and you know how Richard and I feel. If you decided to leave Ever, for instance, I would be absolutely distraught." She levels me with a very queenly look that has my wolf crouching down, dipping his head in deference to her. "I'm serious as a heart attack, Connall."

"And it's appreciated," I murmur. The sentiment of unease doesn't dissipate in my gut, but that might have more to do with the pretty little human who works next door.

The moment I think about Lou, my wolf perks up and whines in my mind. I can't talk back and forth with him like Richard can talk to his wolf—very few shifters get that ability—but I push understanding through our bond.

"Connall? Connall?" Lola's gravelly voice breaks through my train of thought.

When I glance at her, she laughs and closes the book in her lap gently. "I totally lost you there for a minute. Let me guess... Lou?"

This is when I hate being a redhead, because the blush hits hard. My cheeks are on fire, heat radiating from them as my queen's grin splits her face even wider.

"Mhm." She stands—since the Luna bond, she's grown taller.

Now she's almost eye to eye with me as her pitch-black eyes travel over my face, down to my neck and back up. "Tell her, Connall. Isn't that the advice you'd give one of your clients if they came to you in this exact situation?"

I smile. She's not wrong. "I wouldn't encourage a client to enter into a love triangle scenario. Dirk has expressed his interest in Lou regularly, and *loudly*," I tack on, my tone bitter. "And we all know that, despite the way she needles him, she likes him too."

It's more than that, though. *I* like Dirk. He's fiercely loyal and intensely interesting. We could be friends. I don't begrudge him his interest in her. Any smart single male would be interested.

Lola nods, dark eyes focused on mine. It's been like this since she developed the ability to read auras. She stares so deeply, I can practically feel her in my soul, poking around and exposing all the wounded, tender parts of me. Can she see how badly I want to ask Lou out and how conflicted I am, knowing Lou cares for Dirk?

"She's never actually gone on a date with Dirk, despite him trying for months," Lola hedges.

"Has Dirk ever actually *asked* her on a date?" I give Lola a look. "Because it seems to me that he follows her around like she's his queen, and he can't wait to be of service."

Lola throws her head back and laughs, the sound bright and joyous despite a topic that has my heart shredded. My queen wipes at her eyes, tears rolling down her cheeks. "Moons, Connall, do you even know how fucking funny you are?"

I cross my arms and scowl, but she reaches forward and rubs her cheek against mine, purring softly. "I'm not laughing at you, bestie; I'm picturing Dirk in medieval knight gear carrying a glass slipper on a pillow."

"What does that even mean?" I whisper as I rub her cheek with mine, telling her we're all good, that there's no discord between us or our wolves.

Lola pulls back. "Ah, it's a human fairytale where a girl loses her shoe, don't know why, and the guy rides around on a horse to find her and give it back."

I snort. "That's weird. She didn't notice she lost it?"

Lola shrugs.

"And she couldn't just...find it immediately? What kind of monster is this girl?"

Lola laughs. "Not monster. Human."

I curl my nose up. "Are other humans not like the triplets and Lou?"

The queen's eyes drift up as she considers that. "You know, I've met a half dozen humans at court over the years, and they've all been very interesting and intelligent. I can't see anyone losing a shoe and not noticing. So, now that you point it out, what kind of dumbass was this prince chasing?"

We share a knowing look, and then one of Lola's black brows rises in a devious fashion. "You know who would never lose a shoe and not notice?"

"Don't say Lou."

"Louanna." Lola giggles. "Louanna would never lose a shoe and wait for you to bring it to her."

"Don't I know it," I mutter. My imagination immediately runs wild, envisioning crawling up the trellis on the outside of the Annabelle Inn to Lou's room with a random shoe in one hand. I could slip through the window and eat her alive until she woke up and begged for my knot. I could—

"Rein it in, lover boy," Lola says with a laugh. "Your aura is red-hot."

I blush again and turn to focus on the nearest stack of books, pretending I want to learn something new, I suppose.

Red hot.

Cool blue.

Dirk and I are opposites in every way.

Do I want Lou? Absolutely—but I don't think I'll ever get the chance to have her.

CHAPTER THREE
DIRK

I walk up Main Street in the tiny monster haven of Ever, Massachusetts, admiring the red and white awnings over every shop. Flower pots dangle from the street lights, overflowing with blooms in every possible shade. Monsters stroll in pairs along both sidewalks, enjoying the perfect weather.

The idyllic small town has everything a monster could want: movie theater, historical society, candy store, ice cream shop, coffee shop, fine dining, general store. The list goes on, and that's just the downtown area.

'Tis a beautiful day. I could easily have gone to Shifter Hollow on the other side of town and spent time with the wolves or centaurs, perhaps visited the potions shop to sneak a peek at a certain someone. Or maybe taken a trip to the shifter pack therapist, Connall, to chat something through.

Of all the havens I've visited in my role as a hunter for Hearth Headquarters, this is my favorite. Not just because it can get a little wild here—thrall attacks and warlock wars and such—but because I met Louanna here.

"Hey, Dirk!"

I glance to my right to see a darling teal-haired pixie standing outside the candy shop, its red and white awning floating on a soft breeze.

Stopping to lean against the doorframe, I smile. "Hello to you, Miriam. How's the candy-making business going?"

She grimaces. "Iggy's in the back with Alo working on a new recipe for red-hot lollipops. Needless to say, there's a lot of burnt candy in the kitchen, but Iggy absolutely insists—"

Just then, the tiny gargoyle in question zooms past her, barreling out of the sweets shop door and circling around my head.

"Aye, little man, got the zoomies, do yeh?" I laugh as Iggy cackles and flips onto his back, still zipping around me.

Moments later, a muscular gargoyle ducks through the door and wraps a three-fingered purple hand around Miriam's waist. "On your way to see Lou, Dirk?"

It's no secret I stand outside Lou's window at night and stare at her. I'm relatively certain she knows I do it. Alo and Iggy caught me once, though, which I suspect is why the big protector gargoyle mentioned it just now.

"It's not creepy if we're mates," I say.

Alo gives me a look. "If Lou tells you to stop, you're gonna stop though." His tone brooks no argument, but I don't bother to remind him that I'm the most powerful air elemental in recorded history. I could blast him to bits with that power if I chose to.

It's just that I prefer being charming. And funny.

"Noted, giant strong male," I joke.

"He's making fun of you, Dad!" Iggy shouts, stopping between us, his tiny wings flapping slowly.

"Nope." I poke him in the chubby belly. Why is he shirtless? "Why are you such a tattletale, anyhow?"

Iggy slaps my hand away with his long tail, the spade-shaped end thwapping against my arm. Just for funsies, I call the jagged rays of lightning that cover my blue skin, giving him a tiny zap.

He screeches and zooms up to Alo's shoulder, alighting there with a vicious wee look.

"That hurt, Dirk!" he shouts, pointing a finger at me in accusation.

Alo glances at his young son. "Ig, what have we said about touching others without asking?"

Miriam stifles a laugh behind a fake cough as Iggy rolls his eyes.

"You said don't do it, especially Dirk, because his lightning can hurt."

"Right." Alo draws the word out long. "Dirk's lightning is—"

"A weapon," Iggy grinds out. "I forgot." His gaze goes thoughtful. "If your lightning is a weapon, how are you ever gonna hug Lou? Won't you zap her to bits?"

My nostrils flare as my grin grows broad and devious. Alo gives me a warning look, and Miriam leans against the doorframe as the laughter finally escapes.

"Zapping her to bits is exactly what I'm gonna do, Iggy," I say, "the moment she allows it."

"You better not!" he screeches, balling his tiny fists as his tail snaps wildly in the air. "'Cause I'll protect her with my life! If you so much as—"

"Easy, killer." I give him a serious look. "I dinnae wanna hurt Louanna. I was just joking." There's no way I can explain to this tiny gent what I want to do to her.

"See that you don't," he says viciously, crossing his arms over his tiny, puffed-up chest. When he and Alo give me matching irritated looks, I can't hold back a laugh. Grumps, the both o' them.

Two minutes later, I've extricated myself from them after reassuring Iggy a half dozen times that I have no intention of killing my Louanna. Seems six-year-olds struggle with jokes and innuendo. I suppose I should get used to that, living in Ever full-time.

Well, technically, I'm only using my vacation days for the next few weeks. Hearth HQ will call me back to my headquarters-based office soon, but that's a problem for another day.

I walk up Sycamore Street, absorbing the beauty of the Community Garden to my left, and the gingerbread pink and white Annabelle Inn to my right. The Inn waves white shutters at me as I walk up the pathway toward her front entryway.

"Hello, darling Annabelle," I say, leaving the path to walk around the back of the Inn.

Her siding ripples playfully, so I stroke my fingers down the wooden planks. The Annabelle has a sense of humor, I've come to realize. Once, when I was staring at my Louanna, the Inn whacked me in the arse with a plank of wood. The Annabelle might have a crush, come to think of it.

"Don't be jealous, darling," I whisper. "Yer always in my heart, Annabelle."

She preens mightily, all the planked siding rippling and waving as if delighted.

"Knew yeh had a crush," I say on a snicker, tickling the section of wall closest to me as I round the corner.

Behind the Annabelle is a gorgeous rose garden with a giant pedestal in the middle. Technically, it's behind both the Annabelle and Alo's cottage next door. The roses are in full bloom as always, helped along by magic, I assume. They've been blooming since I arrived in Ever months ago.

The sun has dipped low behind the trees, casting the garden and Inn in pale, muted light. It's my favorite time of day, the time when wind plays through the air, diving and dancing like it's calling to me. I glance up at the giant bay window to the room my Louanna is currently staying in.

Reaching to the crisscrossed leather straps over my bare chest, I slap a giant sapphire gem in the middle. Immediately, my physical body dissipates, and I become the wind. Like this, it's nigh impossible for anyone to see me, a fact that's made me incredibly popular with my boss, Evenia. Being invisible does lend itself to hunting rogue monsters—criminals and misfits and the like.

Rising through the chilling air, I pause outside the bay window, looking inside.

Louanna stands in front of a tall mirror, unbraiding her incredible strawberry blonde hair. It's so long, it reaches her arse. Gods, I would give my right arm to fist that hair around my hand and use it for leverage to do naughty, naughty things.

I can't groan or speak in wind form, but, gods, I can fantasize with the best of 'em.

Louanna's pale, freckled fingers move deftly through her hair. I get lost, watching the long strands tangle and be untangled by her. When she's done, her hair hangs in a glorious sheet at her back while I resist the urge to crawl through the window and muss it.

That done, she turns to the ornate wooden desk in her room, seating herself gracefully as she tucks her hair over her opposite shoulder. She's wearing a long nightgown with ruffles on the edges and shoulder straps. I've never seen anything more womanly than this fookin' nightgown she wears.

She opens a box on the desk and brings out a single sheet of blank paper. Like always, there's a pen next to the box. She reaches for it and begins writing. If this is like other nights, she'll write for hours.

And this is where I wish I had a shifter's hearing, because Louanna mutters while she writes, but I cannae hear her through the thick window. I'd consider using my wind to open it, but then she'd certainly know I was here, and I adore the thought of spying on her. Because, one day, she's gonna pace to the window, say, "Hello, Dirk," and invite me in.

My mate.

Even though she hasn't acknowledged it yet.

I'm playing the long game with Lou. She arrived at a time

when her triplet nieces needed her. Thralls, soul-sucking monsters, chased her into town, scratching and biting her. Instead of turning into one, she remained human.

Maybe the first being ever to do that. So far, nobody's been able to explain it.

And then she was intimately involved in the accidental death of one of the shifters from the other side of Ever.

Louanna's had a hellsuva time since she arrived.

So, the long game it is.

Which is fine for me, tae be honest. I'm a long game sort of male. I love a good tease. Because when Louanna finally unleashes with me, we'll be hot enough to burn alive.

I float quietly, watching my mate scribble a letter to…someone. I haven't invaded her privacy far enough to read the letters. But I know she'll follow the same pattern as every other night. She'll write it, reread it, maybe have a good cry, and then she'll tuck the letter into the box and never take it out again.

I've a theory about the letters. Her dead sister Caroline was the Hector triplets' mother. She'd have been far older than Lou, because Lou is only a few years older than the triplets. But I surmise she and her sister were close, and it's my theory that Caroline is the recipient of those letters, and it's some sort of human trauma process to write to a woman who can never read them.

Louanna. I ache to enter the room and pull her into my arms, to ask her to let me shoulder some of her burden. But she has a dozen layers of walls built around her heart, and so far, her nieces seem to be the ones who are allowed into the inner circle. I reckon I've got about eight layers of walls left before she lets me fully into where all that pain and hurt thrives.

Lou's door swings open, slapping the wall with a bang. The Annabelle Inn lets out an angry groan as Iggy zips through the door with a box under each arm.

Scratch my earlier thought. Iggy barged directly through

Lou's walls right to the center of her soul, even though she grumbles about how impossibly direct and meddlesome he is.

"Ignatius," she says with a warning, pointing to the door as it swings closed. "That was too hard. What if you put a hole in Annabelle's wallpaper?"

Iggy shrugs and flies to the bed, settling himself in the middle. "I could fix it if I put a hole in it. Dad says I should be more careful too, but I was excited to bring you snacks."

My woman rises from her seat and joins Iggy on the bed, lying flat on her stomach as she looks at the boxes. Movement at the door draws my eye. A black hellhound lumbers in, pregnant belly swaying as her tongue lolls from her mouth. Rivers of fire run under her inky fur, her red eyes glowing like twin embers. I watch in amazement as my former hunting partner pads across the room to the foot of Louanna's bed and drops to the carpet with a pained-sounding huff.

Minnie girl.

Hard to believe she hunted criminals with me for years and abandoned me the moment she met Iggy. But she and I never had that permanent bond that hellhounds sometimes form. She has that with Ignatius. When he grows up and goes off to the protector academy, she'll go with him. He'll become a powerful guardian one day with a hellhound by his side. In the meantime, she's a very pregnant, uncomfortable-sounding presence at the foot of the bed.

I float outside the window, invisible to the room's occupants. For twenty solid minutes, Iggy talks Louanna through the snack boxes, shoving bits and pieces of baked goods in her mouth when she opens it for him. They have such a pure friendship, and I'm appreciative of the tiny protector's care for her.

O' course, it's built into his DNA to protect and serve the monster community. Nearly all haven protector teams are led by, and primarily composed of, gargoyles.

I watch for a while as they laugh and talk, but when Louanna slips off the bed and heads for the window, I resist the urge to morph back into monster form. She says something over her shoulder to Iggy as she reaches for the window and pushes it up. The momentary vacuum of the window opening pulls me into the room—or maybe I just tell myself that—as I swirl in wind form around the foot of the bed with Minnie and the dust bunnies.

Minnie raises her head and whines at me, flame-red eyes wide. Her black furry tail thumps a slow, happy rhythm against thick carpet. When I rustle over her fur, she harrumphs and lies flat once more.

My Minnie girl.

She dropped me in a moment for Iggy, but it's just as well. My focus is elsewhere these days.

Floating across the room, I settle into an empty chair in front of the fireplace. Gods, I'd love to half-morph and be seated here as my wind form but in the shape of my human form. I bet Louanna'd get a kick outta that.

As it is, I don't want to shock the group. So I stay invisible and watch as Iggy goes sugar crazy and passes out in Lou's arms. I watch as she strokes his back and wings and dark hair. Eventually, she calls Alo to come get his son. A minute later, the gargoyle himself shows up in the open window and slips in, carefully taking Iggy from Louanna's arms.

"I know he acts like he's taking care of you, Lou," Alo says gently, "but hanging with you is his favorite time of day. Thank you for that."

My love smiles at the big gargoyle. "You and Miriam are raising an amazing young man. He's so refreshing, honestly. I should be thanking you."

Alo smiles as he rubs his son's back. He gives Lou a final look before glancing in my direction with a frown, then slipping gracefully out of the window and into the sky.

And then it's just us, because Minnie pads away the moment Iggy and Alo are gone.

Louanna returns to the bed and flops in, letting out a sigh that sounds bone-deep. She lifts her wrist as if she'll call someone, but seems to think better of it.

Call me, I silently urge. *Call me, Louanna, and I'll rush to your side.*

Disappointment rises when her wrist falls to the pillow. She curls onto her side, shoving a pillow between her knees and clutching another to her chest. Like every night I spend watching over her, I float above, kissing her cheeks and hair with my currents. Within minutes, she's asleep.

And still I don't leave.

I will never, *ever* leave.

CHAPTER FOUR
LOU

"Lou, you alright?" Malik's voice breaks through the cloud of nothing in my brain.

I rub at my eyes as a yawn escapes me. "Didn't sleep well. I had weird nightmares."

My niece, Morgan, rubs my back as Malik clip-clops past a half dozen tables covered with moss, potions, mushrooms and bottles to join us. A pale finger comes beneath my chin and lifts, forcing me to look up into worried eyes and scrunchy eyebrows. He chuffs, swishing his tail against his furry sides. "The same nightmares as before?"

I nod. Morgan lets out a displeased little noise. She's gotten downright motherly since I arrived in town. I was hell-bent on protecting the triplets from evil monsters, but these days, it seems more like they're protecting me.

Malik sighs. "It's not unusual after someone goes through what you went through. But—"

"You mean after accidentally killing someone?" I pull my chin from Malik's hold, familiar grief welling up inside for my part in the accident that took Leighton's life. My heartbeat flutters wildly, stealing my breath as I consider that I might be having an actual heart attack.

"It wasn't your fault," Malik murmurs.

"For real, though," my niece repeats.

"It wasn't," I repeat, too, even though it feels rote to say it.

"We keep saying that to you for a reason, Lou," he continues. "Have you considered talking to the pack therapist about it? Connall is absolutely lovely. I see him once a week, in fact, for braintenance."

"Braintenance?"

"Brain maintenance," he says with a laugh.

"You made that up," I say with accusation. Next to me, Morgan chuckles.

"Yeah, but Connall inspired it," he responds slyly.

Connall.

Just the mention of the handsome shifter makes my body even tighter than before. I wipe the back of my hand across my sweaty brow.

"Lou, shall we go for a flight?" Malik asks.

I shake my head, my eyes moving around the store. It's far better if I can focus on the tasks at hand rather than the grief. It's like, if I stand in place for too long, I might just expire right there from the overwhelm.

"It takes time." It's another common response I've started to use. I've got a handful of them now when people ask me how I'm doing.

It takes time. I'll be fine. I'm taking it slow. Thanks for your concern.

What people don't realize about grief is that it comes in waves. One minute, I truly am fine, and the next I want to hide under the table and never come out again.

I can't remember if Malik asked me a question I haven't answered or what, so I look up. He wears a kind expression, his hands clasped at his front. With his elegant tailored vest, he looks like a hot monster professor. I glance between him and Morgan, but she gives me a soft smile and goes back to helping organize the crystals. She doesn't even work here, but I know she's hanging out to keep an eye on me.

Just then, a bell dings, the sound muffled by the root-bound roof above us.

I know who it is before he announces himself. Wind ruffles my hair, stroking it away from my face and over my shoulder. Turning, I hold back a smile, 'cause it'll just egg him on.

"Hello, Dirk," Malik calls over his shoulder as the tall blue sylph struts into Alkemi with his typical devious expression.

"Louanna, my darling," he comes to a stop beside Malik, "I've a proposition for you as soon as yeh're off work." He glances at my niece and winks playfully.

"Hello, Dirk," she says with a laugh. Giving me an expectant look, she jerks her head toward the door. "I'm gonna head home, Lou. Call me later?"

When she waggles both dark red brows, I resist the urge to stomp on her foot for being so obvious.

"Get outta here, bitch," I command, shoving her toward the door.

She swats my side and leaves. Dirk watches her go, but once the door closes, he returns his focus to me.

My heart clenches and tightens, fluttering again when he reaches out and brushes his knuckles along my cheek. His skin isn't as warm as mine. Neon zips of blue lightning travel across it as navy eyes alight on me and crinkle at the corners. He's so striking, but I try hard not to stare too much—it just encourages him.

"She's done for today," Malik says. "Take her out for some fun, would you?"

Something inside me tightens. This feels precariously close to a date. My mind drifts to Connall. If I take this offer, I'm effectively closing the door on ever starting anything with the big shifter.

And this is one of the many reasons I've kept Dirk at arm's length. I don't want to make that decision.

But then Dirk's smile goes broad, revealing twin rows of conical teeth. "Fun I can do. Shall we, Louanna?" His hand drifts to mine, his fingers interlacing in a loose grip.

I war with my thoughts. But realistically, going on one date doesn't have to be serious. "Are you sure, Malik?" I glance up to see my centaur boss frowning. "Okay, okay, I'll go."

"That's my girl," Dirk praises, winking at me.

Reticent, I allow him to pull me past Malik toward the front of Alkemi, but I can't resist a glance over my shoulder to see if Malik opens all the boxes that arrived yesterday. It's so much product, and he'll have to put it all away himself. But—

"Stop worrying over Malik," Dirk whispers in my ear the moment we get outside the potions shop. "He had no helper at all before you, Louanna. He'll be fine until tomorrow."

I pull my fingers from his grip and cross my arms. "What is this proposition you've got for me?" I look way up into his bright eyes, trying not to get distracted by the flashes of lightning that spark over his skin.

"Yeh're staring at my body, Louanna," he murmurs. "Would you like tae touch it?"

Heat flares through me, my cheeks heating. Gods, they must be pink as shit. Whenever Dirk talks dirty to me, I blush, and then I resist the urge to tug at my collar. He'd just smirk and keep doing it.

We're in a weird place. He's always made his interest in me known. And gods know I'm attracted to him. But apart from the random touches and innuendo, he's never actually attempted to kiss me. So I guess we're super flirty friends? Maybe that's fine.

Dirk jerks his head toward the treetops. "I'd like to take yeh flying, Louanna. How do yeh feel about that? I'll take another date tomorrow, as well, now that we're discussing it."

I snort at his presumptiveness. "Why are all the men around me constantly trying to fly me places?"

His grin grows impossibly big until he looks like a shark. Pressing forward, he brings his lips to my ear and nuzzles the curved edge.

"Perhaps we all want to touch that beautiful body, love. To feel those thighs wrapped around us. To be close enough to scent yeh. I know that's what I want."

Without thinking, I reach up to place my palm on his shoulder. At the last minute, I worry about the lightning—it's a deadly elemental weapon that can flatten buildings and flood towns—but when I touch his skin, it zips toward me and sunbursts away from my palm.

Fascinated, I remove my hand, and his lightning goes back to normal. I'll admit I've stared at him long enough to know there's actually a pattern to it, kind of like how Minnie's fire runs underneath her fur in rivulets.

Curiosity gets the better of me, so I place my hand in a different spot on his trap muscle. Just like before, his lightning redirects to gather under my palm, then bursts outward, zipping its way over his skin.

"No shock."

He straightens enough to look at me. "I would never shock yeh, Louanna." He winks. "Unless yeh wanted me tae do it, o' course, in a sexy way."

I cock my head to the side. "If I wanted you to? So…you're like a giant vibrator? Is that what you're saying?"

He laughs and slings an arm around my waist, pulling me close. Immediately, tiny tingles of electricity kiss my skin, pebbling my nipples as Dirk grins like the heathen he is.

"Exactly, Louanna," he whispers. "Don't tell me a little tingle doesn't fascinate yeh."

It's on the tip of my tongue to tell him he has no idea what fascinates me, but that's probably not true. Since the day I arrived, he's been a steady, near constant presence by my side.

And, without meaning to, I've become accustomed to that.

I resist the urge to rub at my hard nipples. And I definitely ignore the wetness between my thighs. I've been reading up on sylphs at the historical society. Dirk likely has above-average senses of smell and sight, part of what makes him a great hunter for the monster world's governing body, Hearth HQ. Most elementals are solitary, unfriendly and they can be dangerous.

I never could resist a red flag. Or a blue one, I suppose.

"Okay, I'll go."

Dirk's hand slides up my back until he can grip my neck possessively, pulling my body tightly to his. "I've got some fun planned, Louanna. Are you ready?"

Yes.

No.

Sudden worry hits me like a lightning bolt. "You won't drop me, right?" It's an irrational fear—of course he won't—but it still overwhelms me every time I think about flying. Malik's vest has a handle on the back. That feels safe. I've seen Dirk become his element. There's no corporeal body left. Nothing to hold on to.

Dirk presses a kiss to the top of my head. "I'll never drop yeh, Louanna. I will never, ever let you fall."

Joke's on him though, because I've already fallen as far as a person can possibly go.

CHAPTER FIVE
DIRK

I recognize the shadows in Lou's gaze, the way her lashes flutter and her breath becomes short when she's worried or nervous. It's not difficult to read the grief, which is part of why I want to take her flying for the first time. My approach to Lou is the same way I'd approach an injured hellhound—carefully and ideally with snacks in my pockets.

Letting go of her neck, I grab her left hand and spin her around so her back is to my front. She stiffens when I wrap an arm around her waist, curling my fingers against the curve of her hips.

"I love this spot," I whisper in her ear, tickling her side.

She giggles nervously and squirms, although I don't let her get away from me. Looking up at me over her shoulder, she glares, but there's no malice to it. No, my Louanna uses those frosty looks and her sense of humor like armor and a weapon.

I get it. I've done the same. I'm no stranger to grief.

"If you tickle me while we're flying, I'll thrash around and get dropped to my death."

"Never." I lean down and lick a stripe up the side of her cheek to her hairline.

"Dirk! What the hells, man?!" Lou wriggles again, wiping a hand over the wet trail.

I chuckle and hold her tighter to me. "Keep wiggling like that, my sweet, and you'll be flying with a poker in your back."

She whips around in my arms. "Gods, Dirk, could you be any less appropriate?"

"O'course," I say with a wink. "I've been a wee angel since we met, but I'm done with that, Louanna."

A pink blush travels up her chest and neck to those high, elegant cheeks. Her nostrils flare as her mouth drops open. "What do you mean?"

I pull her flush with my body again, leaning down to hover my lips above hers. "I mean we both know I've been pursuing yeh, and that I've been givin' yeh space because of everything that's happened. But I'm making it official, Louanna. It's my goal to make yeh mine in a more permanent way."

Her eyes widen, her chest rising and falling rapidly against mine. Gods, it feels good for her to rub those barely-covered tits on my chest. I roll my eyes playfully, releasing a soft groan. "Keep going, my sweet." I reach for the end of her braid and twirl it between my fingers. "I'd happily get indecent right here."

Lou grumbles and tries to cross her arms, but we're too close, so all it does is squash her breasts upward, drawing my eye to the soft-looking globes.

Without thinking, I lick my lips. I can't wait to taste those luscious tits for the first time.

"Earth to Dirk," Lou snaps. "Can you stop ogling my tits?"

"Never." I shake my head. "I will be ogling every inch of yeh, thanking the gods for making yeh until my very last breath. Look at yeh," I say more forcefully, wrapping my fingers around her throat just enough for her eyes to flash. "You're a wonder, Louanna. Fiercely loyal, endlessly brilliant and kind, beautiful within and without. I'm locking yeh down as quickly as yeh'll allow it."

"Locking me down, huh?" Humor enters her voice as one auburn brow travels upward.

"I want you to want that," I whisper, rubbing her throat with the pad of my thumb. "I want to pursue yeh in such a way that yeh can't help but want to be mine."

Her expression goes soft and thoughtful. "I don't know if I'm ready, but I'm still happy to be here."

"It's a start," I agree jovially. "Now, I'm going to smash my gem, and you'll become wind with me."

One of her arms wraps around my waist, and the other comes to my forearm, gripping it tightly. Does she notice how my power streaks over my skin to get closer? It aches to play with her, to connect with her in every way.

When I reach down to depress my gem, Lou squeaks and squeezes her eyes closed.

I'd laugh, but she looks a bit terrified. Holding her tightly to me, I press the gem that helps activate my power, and we disappear into a swirl of wind.

CHAPTER SIX
LOU

The scream I release gets lost in the vicious swirl of wind that whips around us. My braid gets sucked into the vortex of air, slapping me in the face until it suddenly *doesn't,* and the wild sound stops.

I hadn't realized my eyes were closed until I blink them tentatively open to find the treetops far below us. A scream attempts to burst from me as I grasp for Dirk, only to find I can't move anything. And when I look down, there's nothing but what I can see far below me.

I have no arms, no legs. There's nothing but wind and the trees below.

And even those are getting farther away by the moment. Struggling to wrap my brain around what's happening, I think about Dirk. Can we talk like this? Are we technically still touching?

The treetops disappear as we move up through the clouds. Terror and panic grip me until I realize I can't actually feel my heart threatening to beat out of my chest. Confusion swirls as I catalog my feelings, only to find that I feel...lighter.

A faint squeezing sensation at my back sends reassurance

through me. It's Dirk; it must be. But he says nothing, of course, and when I try to glance over my nonexistent shoulder to say something to him, I can't.

This is the strangest experience, being noncorporeal. Is this what he feels like every time he flies?

As I think that, there's the phantom sensation of someone grasping my wrist and stretching out my arm. We drift upward, and though I have no visible fingers, the clouds' chilly moisture gathers on my fingertips.

It's weird to smile and know my smile doesn't exist. I'm invisible to everyone. There's something kinda freeing about that, if I'm honest.

We shoot up through the clouds, moving faster and faster until we come to the faint green bubbly ward that insulates Ever. But somehow, my worry fades.

Then we smash into the ward, and I think about screaming, but there's no way I can. We spin and twirl in the air, zipping alongside the ward ceiling, which is when I realize I can see a current of wind traveling fast along the ward. And when I focus more fully on what's in front of us, there's a maelstrom of currents in hundreds of different blues.

Aqua. Sky blue. Navy. Royal.

The shades are stunning, twisting and spiraling around and through and over each other. We're in the middle of a current the color of cotton candy. It goes as far as I can see, skirting the ward bubble.

It occurs to me that my niece Thea's gargoyle mate, Shepherd, has mentioned catching the currents when he flies. Is this how he sees them?

Gods, this is exhilarating.

So, I let it go, everything I've been carrying in my heart and mind. I stare in awe as Dirk guides us, somehow, along the cotton candy current, barreling beneath the ward. Then he hops us to a current the color of a midnight sky. It spins us in circles until I'm dizzy and breathless, and then we sprint to a current the palest shade of cerulean.

I lose myself to the air, sensing Dirk at my back even though I can't feel him. His presence is a warm mental hug. But then we dive through the pale current and pick up a current so dark, it's nearly black. It zips us down, down, down out of the clouds until we're flying through the forest near Ever's singular gas station.

Except we blow past that, through the woods until the current darts past Hel Motel. Something behind me shifts, and we hop out of the wind. It's like a rollercoaster ride but backward. One minute we were flying downhill, but now we're just spinning around lazily in the air like two dust motes.

I don't wanna be done flying, though. That was the most fun I've had in a really long time.

But Dirk spirals us up through chilly air, past black wood siding and black paned windows. I try to get a look inside the infamous wraith motel, but all I see is a faint blue figure before we pass the window and head toward the black tiled roof. We alight on it, and then the wind whips my phantom hair into a frenzy again.

When it dies down, warm lips brush the shell of my right ear, tickling me. "How'd you like my version of flying, Louanna?"

I look up over my reappeared shoulder at him. His lips brush my cheek, and he doesn't move. It should be awkward, but I'm lost in the navy depths of his eyes. This close, they're not just navy. Sprinkles of pale gray and pitch-black ring the outer edge of his iris. When I don't immediately answer, he smirks.

"You look ready for a kiss, Louanna." He presses his lips to the tip of my nose.

My body tightens and tenses, ready for something. We've danced around attraction, and I lied to myself for a while. I said it was a bad time, and the triplets needed my attention and support. But all three of them are mated and happy. They're fucking thriving, my badass bitches.

There's no reason I couldn't kiss Dirk right now.

"I brought you to this place for a reason." He leans back just enough for me to see him better and jerks his head toward the forest. "Wanna know who runs a path around Hel Motel twice a day?"

Confusion fills me, and I scrunch my brows together.

"Connall Blackwater, that's who," he says. "It's part of his rounds. And I've noticed when he does the rounds alone, he stops in that grove down there, the one yeh can see at the edge of your vision." He points over the trees to a spot where grass is visible. "He does naughty things out there, on occasion."

Something inside me flutters until a blush heats my cheeks.

Dirk laughs. "I love how I can read every emotion on that beautiful pale skin, Louanna. Shall we wait for him to pass and then do a little spying?"

I spin around and slap his chest, ignoring how all the lightning on one arm streaks toward my violence. "You can't go around spying on the entire town, Dirk. Why would you do that to him?"

He rolls his eyes as if I just did something intensely sexual. "Yer givin' me sexy schoolteacher vibes. I can just imagine yeh sayin', 'to me office, Mister Zefferus. I'll deal with yeh after class.'"

I level him with the rudest expression I can summon. "It's a violation of his *privacy*, Mister Zefferus."

"Oh fook," he groans, grabbing at his crotch. "I just came in me pants a little, Louanna. Say it again. Anyhow," he grins, "are yeh jealous?"

I narrow my eyes and shake my head, despite the fact that he's partially right. We've never talked about how he floats outside my window at night and stares. Well, I'm pretty sure he does. It's always windier outside my window than anywhere else, and somehow, I sense it's probably him. Honestly, if anybody else did it, I'd find it creepy. But, with Dirk, it makes sense to me. It feels safe even though he's a stalker. Is there such a thing as cozy stalking? Because that's what he does.

The idea of him floating outside Connall's window doing the same thing makes me want to flip tables. Or join him. Gods, I'm not sure.

"What do you think about what I shared?" Dirk questions me softly.

What do I think? I think I *knew* but hadn't absorbed how serious he was. And now? I'm not sure what to do next. I'm saved from answering by faint footsteps that reach us from down below. Dirk lifts a finger to his mouth, indicating I should be silent. I shake my head, but he grabs me and pulls me carefully to the edge of the roof. Gods, this is bad.

We're spying on a nice guy. A *really* nice guy I sometimes think about when I'm alone in my room. Does Dirk stick around long enough to be aware of that?

Steady breathing drifts up, and despite what I told myself, I creep to the edge of the roof and lie flat next to Dirk. He glances at me with a saucy grin, then points toward the forest.

Every bit of breath in my body leaves on a whoosh as a shirtless Connall comes jogging up a path through the forest. His tee is tucked into one of his belt loops, his jeans doing nothing to hide enormous, muscular thighs. He must have a solid fifty or sixty pounds on Dirk. He's thickly built and covered chest to belt with wolfish tattoos.

They still don't hide the dips and valleys of every ab, or the puffy, thick pecs coated in auburn hair. His eyes, luminescent green, cut left and right as he scans for anything amiss.

Guilt hits me like a Mack truck. He was Leighton's friend. I killed Leighton. And now I'm Peeping Tom'ing like a real bitch.

But then he pauses and reaches down the front of his pants, adjusting a large bulge.

"He runs and gets hard," Dirk whispers. "And then he goes to that glade and fucks his hands, Louanna. Shall we watch?"

This has gone too far. It's too much. I force my gaze from Connall as he disappears up the path toward the glade.

"We should go. This isn't right. And the fact that you spy on him like you do me? So rude. No points in the 'should I go out with Dirk' category. You're in the red, Mister Zefferus."

But instead of even acting remotely concerned by my statement, his grin broadens. He rests his head against three fingers, beaming at me like the cat that got the cream. "Wanna know a secret, Louanna?"

Fuck. Do I? How many does he have? Because everything about Dirk screams secrets and layers. He's the embodiment of the ogre onion explanation from *Shrek*.

I scowl back at him. "Does it explain why you think it's okay to be a Peeping Tom?"

He shrugs as best he can with his head in one hand. "Don't know what the fook that is, Louanna. Must be a human thing. But I'm gonna let yeh in on my secret, my sweet. I spy on you because you're mine." His grin grows absolutely feral. "And I spy on him—because he's *ours*."

CHAPTER SEVEN
DIRK

The color drains from Louanna's face, her mouth dropped open to form a perfect, delicate O. "You must be shitting me. Are you for real?"

I play with the end of her long braid, smiling. I know this is a shock for her. And I've seen her stare at Connall. She wants him. As she should.

"Serious as a fookin' heart attack, my love."

"I'm not your love," she grumbles.

Well, I cannae have that, so I grab her hand and shove it against my chest, above my gem nestled between my pecs. My power streaks across my skin to gather under her palm, sparking and flashing as it connects with her.

"If you were anyone but *my* woman, this would shock the shit outta yeh, Louanna, as I've said. It doesn't shock Connall either."

Her fingers curl against my skin as her amber eyes land on mine. "You've touched him?"

I grin. "What do yeh think about that, my sweet? Me touching him. Him touching me. Both of us touching yer beautiful self."

Pink dusts her cheeks. "I...I don't know. I haven't considered it."

"No?" I reach out to stroke my fingertips down her jawline. "Pretty sure that's a lie, my sweet."

"Well," she hedges, "are you planning to drag him up to a rooftop sometime soon to have this same convo? Shall we turn it into a mating production line?"

I grip her chin and force her gaze not to waver from mine. "I may be all charm, my darlin', but the love? That's only for the two o' yeh."

Her pink cheeks flush to red, but when she opens her mouth to say something, I jerk my head to the forest. "We're gonna miss the show, Louanna. Shall we get going?"

It's clear to see her struggle with the concept of spying on Connall.

"Don't think of it as spying, my sweet," I say. "I'm a hunter, so let's go hunt."

Louanna nips at her lower lip. "I don't know if I'm in a good headspace to date anyone, much less this idea you have of all three of us. I just…I'm dealing with a lot right now. And if you think he's your mate, you should be pursuing him, not acting creepy."

"Mmm." I stroke the shell of her ear as I don't agree or disagree. "We'll take it as slowly or quickly as yeh like. Just know that yeh've got my full attention, Louanna. Let me prove how good I can be. And don't worry about me telling Connall. I will."

Amber eyes flicker with an emotion I read as uncertainty, but she nods.

"Let me hear yeh say it with a playful wink: 'Yes, Mister Zefferus.'"

She slaps my chest again, pulling her emotional armor back on. "I'm not repeating that. Once was enough; it'll just encourage you."

"Tae be honest, Louanna, there's no stoppin' an elemental male when he sets his eyes on his prize."

She rolls her eyes. "Well, perhaps you should start by

explaining more about that. What do elemental mating traditions look like? Is it *all* spying and secrets, or is there some part of dating you that would feel normal to a human and a shifter?"

I snort and grip her hand. "Normal? Not in the slightest, doll. But I can't wait to show yeh what that means for us." Glancing to the forest where Connall disappeared, I rub my gem. "I don't need my gem tae fly. It does help to cement and strengthen my power a bit, but I can fly without it in my current form. Otherwise, it works the same way, so we'll just step off the roof intae the air."

Lou glances over the side of the roof to the ground two stories below us. "Umm, are you—"

"Sure? Yeah. Trust me for the second time tonight?"

She nods and stands, reaching for my hand. "Kind reminder that I am terrified of being dropped."

I spin her in my arms and pull her against my front again. "Never, my sweet." And with that, I step backward and pull us into midair.

～

Lou screams as we fall, but before we hit the ground, I take off into the trees. Gods, I hope Connall didnae hear that shriek.

Lou grabs at the arm wrapped around her middle and threads her feet through my legs, gripping me tightly. We fly quickly through the forest, past beautifully aging pines with ferns growing thick around their bases. Minutes later, we come to the clearing, and, like always, Connall's stopped on one side, leaning against a tree, just hidden in the shadows of its broad branches.

I stop far enough away that he cannae hear us, alighting on one of the lower tree limbs. It's broad enough for me to sit on it with Louanna caged between my thighs. I position her there, keeping one arm around her middle. Her heart flutters wildly, her pulse pounding just under her skin.

"Keep quiet," I murmur in her ear. "We're just outta range of his hearing, but a lively shout would call his attention."

"Maybe I'll do that, then," she snarks. "Something like, 'Hey, over here! Dirk wants to fuck you!'"

"Good. Do it." I grab her braid and pull it over her back so I can lift it to my nose and breathe in. "I'm gonna mightily enjoy this."

Across the clearing, Connall glances at his comm watch. I don't know what he's looking for, but he drops both hands to his waist, staring around. A time or two, I've thought he knew I was here, but like Louanna, he's never said a word. And I've watched. A lot.

Lou hisses in a breath when Connall reaches for the button of his jeans and opens it. He slides the zipper down, his heavy cock falling thick and hard from the opening. I've stared at it a million times, but I'm certain Louanna hasn't had a chance to see how gloriously perfect it is.

"I've gotten close enough to see the veins," I whisper in her ear. "When I'm in wind form, I can hover right beside him, spin his hair up a bit while he touches himself."

"Getting creepier by the minute," she hisses.

"Not creepy when yeh both belong tae me," I remind her. "I mentioned this earlier, but it bears saying again, Louanna. There are no lengths a sylph male won't go to to claim his mate or mates. No *lengths* whatsoever."

"So you've said."

Like always, Connall rubs the mushroom tip of his cock first, wetting his fingers with his tongue. And like every time I watch him jack off, I imagine wetting those fingers myself, or dropping tae my knees on the forest floor and helping.

Soon.

He plays with the tip for a long moment, rubbing and squeezing. I hold back a groan as my cock responds, hardening against Louanna's back.

"Oh my gods, Dirk," she mutters as she elbows me in the side.

"We can play this one o' two ways, Louanna," I say, brushing my mouth along the soft skin below her right ear. "I can touch yeh while he touches himself. Or I can whisper filth in your ear and not touch yeh at all. What's yer preference?"

When she doesn't answer, I chuckle, my eyes still on Connall across the glade.

We watch together as he strokes his cock with slow, measured movements. If I could get closer, I'd see that his cheeks are flushed pink, his mouth open and eyes rolling back in his head.

Louanna is stiff between my thighs, her heart racing.

"He moans your name when he comes," I whisper into her ear. "Sometimes it explodes from him in a great bellow while he coats his fingers with seed. Louanna," I say on a low groan, mimicking words I've heard from Connall, "get on your knees, woman."

Her heart rate speeds up.

"He's got jest as filthy a mouth as I do, my sweet."

"Dirk, stop," she whispers. But she presses harder against me, slinging one arm around my thigh as if I'm her lifeline.

"Never." I press a tender, teasing kiss to the base of her neck. Then another just above it. "I'll never stop lavishing you with praise, with attention, with whatever yeh need, Louanna."

She's silent, but her fingers curl around my knee, tightening as Connall continues fucking one hand. But when he cries out, her name audible from even this far away, Louanna moans. Connall brings his free hand to his cock and fucks hard through both fists, his cries rising and rising until he comes with a roar, back arching as cum spurts from him.

And her name falls from his lips like a godsdamned prayer, his body jerking as his spend coats the forest floor. In my arms, Louanna pants as she covers her mouth with her left hand, her body hard and hot against mine.

"Yeh could be comin' now too, my sweet, if yeh'd allowed me to touch yeh."

A muffled, frustrated groan is my answer. I nip playfully at her neck, following the bite with the barest hint of tongue.

"Imagine this mouth between yer thighs. Or between his. Or both of our mouths on yer sweet pussy. I cannae wait to do that with yeh."

This time, she doesn't chide me or remind me why it cannae happen. She presses harder against me, her muscles quivering with need.

I've always read monsters well, something I have tae do to perform my job duties. Which is how I know to give her a moment of space. I've teased enough for now. Jest like I'll tease him soon.

Across the long, thin glade, Connall wipes both hands down his handsome, angular jaw. He tucks that gorgeous cock back into his jeans and zips them up, shaking his head. He turns for the forest and jogs away, leaving Louanna and me alone in the tree.

She watches him go, but once he's gone, she spins in my arms and cocks her head to the side. "You're serious about this, aren't you? About us? And him?"

I nod, stroking her collarbone toward her shoulder. "I am, Louanna. Consider this our first date. First of many."

She gives me a wry look. "And you plan on letting Connall in on this when?"

"Immediately," I confirm. "But just like with you, I've been playing the long game with our wolf. He's a little flightier than you are."

She snorts. "Flighty, huh? He seems about as grounded, loyal and reliable as they come."

I smile. "He's never been with a man, Louanna."

Her expression softens. "How do you know?"

"I listen to his therapy sessions sometimes, and one of the other wolves brought up being attracted to a friend."

The red in her cheeks grows deeper. "Dirk! You can't fly around spying on people all the time!"

"It's literally what I get a paycheck for," I remind her, curling one brow high.

"When you're investigating crimes. In the human world, we have laws about this."

"Well," I say with a snort, "all laws have nuance, Louanna. And in the elemental world, there's almost nothing you can get in trouble for if it's done in pursuit of your mate. Even murder." I let that sink in for a moment.

"Murder?" Her brows go straight to the top o' her forehead.

"Yep," I confirm with a pop of the P. "Elemental mate bonds are undeniable. For one of us to pursue someone when a mate bond has been identified is a capital crime in my culture, punishable by death. It's typical for a mate to deliver that punishment."

Lou opens her mouth as if she'll start asking me questions. I can almost see her mind spinning around what I've jest shared. Sylphs are secretive, living often solitary lives in a singular haven on the opposite side of the world. Not many have experience living in a haven with one. Which is why me and Minnie dog showing up to hunt criminals is always an invigorating experience. I love to surprise monsters.

I can't wait to keep surprising my two.

"Let's go, Louanna. I want to tell him how I feel right now."

Her eyes go wide and she sputters in shock as I pull her off the branch, depressing my gem at the same time. We disappear into the wind, gusting after him.

CHAPTER EIGHT
CONNALL

Coming doesn't relieve the frustration building and churning in my belly. It's against every shifter instinct I have not to pursue Lou. Within our shared mind space, my wolf grumbles and rolls onto his side. Usually, he likes to be let out during a run so he can stretch his legs and keep his senses sharp. But since Lou arrived, he's morose, pitiful and irritated that I'm not actively pursuing her.

I'm sorry, buddy. I'll figure this out soon, I promise him. I've been considering for a few weeks what I'd tell a client in this exact situation. And while it's true I wouldn't encourage a friend to enter a love triangle, I'd encourage good communication.

If I knew Lou was my mate, it'd be easier. But I haven't had a chance to get that close to her, so I can't be sure. Plus, if she were mine, she wouldn't pursue Dirk…right?

Or maybe she doesn't take it very far with Dirk because she *is* mine.

But then, if she's mine, and she's dating Dirk, then what?

I've been considering all of that, doing what I tell my clients to do and looking at all the angles. Trying to be rational. Attempting to infuse logic into an emotionally fraught situation.

And I can only see one way through it.

I'm going to ask her on a date. I'll say I know Dirk is interested, but it's unclear to me what's going on there. If she doesn't want to go, she'll tell me. But the thing is, I can't be her therapist like he's asked me to several times. It's a conflict of interest. Even if she wanted that, it would be hard for me to be purely professional with a woman I'm interested in romantically. She'd distract me with that sharp wit and soft looking skin.

The truth is, I ache to know what she smells like, to bury my face just below her ear and kiss and suck until I find a spot that makes her squirm. A mental image of her straddling my lap in my office chair, smiling up at me, rushes to the forefront of my mind.

And just like that, I'm fucking hard again. I've literally blown through every toy in my closet trying to fuck my way out of being obsessed with Lou.

It's no good. That alone is enough to make me suspect my attraction to her is more than a passing fancy. I don't want a fling with her. I don't want something casual.

I want *time* with her—a lot of time. I want to know her favorite ice cream, how she feels about living in a monster haven. I need to learn how she takes her coffee. I want all those small moments that collectively form the soul-deep knowledge of another person.

Pumping my legs, I move from my usual jog to a full-on sprint. Can I burn the need away if I run fast enough?

I'm gonna find out.

I barrel forward until the trees are a blur, ferns whipping at my legs and sides. Brown and green swirl together as I struggle to focus on patrolling, which is what I'm supposed to be doing. Soul-sucking thralls often congregate outside of Ever's wards, and while the wards protect us, we like to stay alert for anything sneaking through. I've never actually found anything dangerous when I patrol, which makes it easier for my mind to wander.

Long minutes pass, my heart rate speeding up to help me

push through, but it's no use. I can't get her out of my mind, and I'm still hard.

Irritated, I return to Shifter Hollow and head for Biergarten to sit on the porch and grab a mead. Stalking inside, I pray for the sweat to dry fast as I head for the bar. One of my clients is behind the wide wood countertop. She smiles and gives me a wry look.

"Book?"

"Book," I confirm.

She sets a beer glass down and reaches under the bar, withdrawing a book I leave here for when I come to read.

I take it with a nod of thanks and head for the back door to the patio. Exiting the dark, sensual bar, I relish the light airiness of the outdoor area. Richard's bar, Bad Axe, is great for a rowdy good time, but I love Biergarten for a more laid-back feel. I sit in the far back corner and order a mead.

Ten minutes later, the patio door opens, and Dirk sails through, holding it open. Lou exits and gives him a kind smile. Amber eyes flick to me and flash.

Goddess, she's so fucking pretty.

I stop breathing as Dirk guides her in my direction. Half a dozen empty tables sit between us, but they're coming to me. Shifting forward, I set my book down.

They're on a date; it's clear from the way he has his hand on her back. She's not snarking at him to remove it like I've seen her do in the past. She's allowing it, although she looks…concerned.

I resist the urge to leap over the table and rip into him. Except, when I think about it, I don't really want that. I like Dirk. I consider him, well, almost a friend. I respect and admire him.

They stop in front of my table. Lou rubs at the back of one arm, glancing up at the sylph. He smiles at me. "Mind if we join yeh, Wolf?"

Wolf. He always calls me that. And every time he does, my wolf sits up and pays attention. It's…disconcerting.

I settle back in my seat. I don't understand what's happening, but the chance to sit and have a beer with Lou is too compelling for me to say no. Without thinking, I stand and pull out a chair for her. When she steps toward it and sits, I blanch. Fuck. But when I look sheepishly at Dirk, he's smiling at me.

This is getting stranger by the second. I'm off-kilter. I want to cater to her—even with Dirk right there.

The centaur waiter takes their drink order so I guess they're planning to stick around for a minute.

We look at each other awkwardly. Well, Lou and I look at one another awkwardly. Dirk stares around the patio, seeming to admire its beauty and completely ignoring the fact that he brought his date to sit at a table with me.

When their beers arrive, he takes a sip and smiles, licking the rim of his glass. Somewhere inside, where I don't want to focus too hard, something stirs. Interest. Heat. I will my still-there erection to fade.

Lou lifts her hand and nibbles at the edge of her thumb.

Something's up.

Dirk's smile grows broader as he sets his drink down and looks at me. "I'm officially pursuing Louanna—because I believe she's my mate."

My heart sinks into the pit of my stomach. Why is he telling me? Why even involve me? I'll admit, I thought he might be aware of my interest, but this is a level of directness I was unprepared for. I sit forward and force a smile. "I'm happy for you both." When I risk a glance at her, I can't read the expression on her face.

Dirk leans forward and stares at me. "I'd like to do the same with you, Connall, if yeh'll allow it."

Lou's mouth drops open, but she quickly zips it closed.

A moment passes.

And another.

And another.

I blink and try to process what he just said.

My brain seems unable to put his words into any meaningful order.

I clear my throat, glancing between them. "What do you mean?"

Lou begins fidgeting in her chair.

Dirk's grin is practically feral at this point. "I want to pursue yeh both formally. I believe yeh to also be my mate, Connall, and I understand if—"

"I don't date men," I say evenly. "I've never been interested in a man in my entire life.

But Dirk's smile goes soft at the corners. "Savin' yerself for me, I see. Love that."

"That's not what I meant." I run both hands through my hair.

"O' course." Dirk lifts his beer glass and takes another long sip. I watch his throat bob as he swallows, and heat flushes through me again. Goddess Alaya help me process this.

"I need to think," I blurt lamely. "This is all very sudden."

"Take all the time you need," he says quietly. "Well, until tomorrow, because tomorrow I begin my formal pursuit of you, Connall. Same as Louanna."

"Dirk, chill out!" Lou snaps. "This is a lot to absorb, okay? Jesus."

"Och, Louanna, things will work out," Dirk vows. "Let me get yeh home, my sweet. Tomorrow's another day and another date." He rises from his chair, winks at me, and heads toward the door.

Lou stands and gives me a shy look, something I'm so unused to seeing on her elegant features. Reaching down, she places her hand on top of mine. "He sprang this news on me today, too. What a weirdo." A soft smile tips her plump lips upward. "I don't know where it'll lead but I think you and I might be feeling some of the same things, mostly shock and probably a degree of uncomfortableness. But now that I've had a minute to sit with it, I hope you'll consider it. Maybe just a date to see?"

Heat flares through me. Is she saying what I think she's saying?

I flip my hand over, and she strokes my palm gently. Amber eyes come to mine as she gives me a genuine smile. My wolf is fascinated, pressing forward to stare at her.

She removes her fingers and clasps her hands at her waist. "Enjoy your book, Connall." Her scent explodes across my senses, and I can't help but rise and bring my cheek to hers to rub affectionately.

"Oh," she says, a strangled noise coming from her throat. But after a moment, she rubs back.

Dirk is quiet, but when I glance at him, he points to his cheek expectantly.

"Ugh, dude!" Lou shoves him toward the door. "Give him some damn space, you rude-ass Peeping Tom."

It's not until they leave and I pick up my book again that I think back on what she said.

Peeping Tom? What the hells is that? I resolve to go home and search it on the internet in case it's important.

CHAPTER NINE
LOU

A shiver travels down my spine as I stock empty potion bottles in the back storeroom at Alkemi. I lose myself to the work, my mind spinning over how Dirk spilled the news to Connall. Poor Connall looked so shocked and discombobulated. Then he rubbed his stubbly cheek on mine, and I nearly combusted.

Dirk put the damn idea in my head of all three of us together, and it just won't leave.

Out of nowhere, something hits my ear, and I jump, knocking into the shelves as my arms fly sideways. Eyes wide, I whip around as bottles tumble off the shelf and fall back into the box.

At my feet, a red and white mushroom stuffie rolls across the floor. What the fuck?

A snicker at the door draws my attention. Fucking godsdamn Bellami stands in the doorway with his tiny arms crossed, a mischievous grin on his round face.

"Scared the shit outta you, didn't I?" His voice is so small, I have to focus crazy hard to hear him.

I bend down and grab the mushroom, launching it back at

him. He ducks, but I nail the top of his hat. It goes flying, along with the mushroom, out of the room.

Bellami scowls. "Hey now, that was rude. A mushroom is nothing to you but could seriously injure me!"

I plant both hands on my hips as the heat of being terrified drains from my face. "You know what, Bellami? We humans have a saying, 'Don't start no shit, won't be no shit.' You should really, *really* take that to heart."

He snorts and ducks out of the room, returning a moment later with the hat back on his head. "I like that. I'm gonna use that. Except, as you know, gnomes are great lovers of starting shit."

"I'm aware," I mutter, turning back to the bottles.

Out of the corner of my eye, I follow as he crosses the room. When he taps my shoe, I scowl down at him. "Yes, Bellami?"

"We need your help in the gnome village, Lou. Remember?"

I slap my forehead. I'd forgotten, what with stalking Connall like a creep and all.

Bellami climbs onto my knee and uses my shirt for leverage to pull himself up. After hopping onto my forearm, he uses it like a bridge to get close to the shelf. He crawls onto it and stands there, looking at me as I debate whether to remind him that it's not all that polite to crawl up a girl's boobs like a ladder.

"Can you help us tomorrow night?"

I snort. "I work here until eight, but then—"

"Eight's perfect," he interrupts. "Our best work is done at night once the moon comes out. It helps us identify where to place all the toadstools and moss, et cetera. They prefer nighttime, as you know."

I sigh. "Eight sounds fine. What exactly is it you need me to do? And why do you even need a new village?"

He grins. "Haul logs, move houses, dig holes. The heavy stuff, basically, as I previously mentioned. While we're industrious, it'll go a lot faster with your help. We've been living in the tree trunks, but we've outgrown them, so it's time for a formal village. It's a big deal for us."

I glance down my nose at him. "You know, there are a million other monsters in this haven who could also help you."

"Gotta be you," Bellami says in a final tone. "We trust you, and we don't allow most outsiders into the village."

Cocking my head to the side, I absorb his words. "Why on earth would you trust me?"

Bellami's usual scowl falls, replaced by the tiniest of smiles. "You have a beautiful aura, Lou, a gentle, loyal aura surrounded by a circle of fierce protectiveness. You're basically a gnome at heart."

"I don't find you all that gentle," I say with a laugh. "You think gnomes are gentle?"

He shrugs tiny shoulders. "Do we look that way to outsiders? Probably not. We have to be fierce and act big and loud, or else nobody pays us any attention. But that's not who we really are. It's just who we have to be because of the world we live in. You'll see tomorrow when you help us."

Something pangs in my heart at his words. I was always a nerdy kid, way more into plants and magic than people. And then I was a nerdy, witchy teenager far more interested in the occult than anything I learned in high school or college. And now I'm a grown-ass woman with three nieces who're witches, trying to find my place in a monstery world that's far too cool for me.

The front door bell dings, announcing a patron.

Bellami tips his hat at me before leaping onto my arm and army-crawling down it to my elbow, where he executes a dainty little flip onto the floor. "Eight p.m., Lou, don't forget!"

"I won't," I return, standing to follow him out of the storage room.

I pick my way past chunky wooden tables piled high with specialty mosses and crystals and potions of every kind, and I avoid looking at the new batch of sleeping potion Malik made when I couldn't complete the recipe.

I'm not surprised to find Dirk standing at the front, leaning against the tall wooden checkout table with his elbows propped on it. His feet are crossed at the ankles, blue lightning moving over his chest and arms. I take it in like I always do. I've never told him because he'd be insufferable, but I find his lightning beautiful. Especially now that I touched it, and it came to me. That was so…cool.

"I like the way you stare at me, Louanna," he rumbles, his voice going low, navy eyes hooded.

I cross my arms and stop next to him. "So you've said."

His grin becomes a lascivious beam as he licks his lips, dark eyes traveling down my body and slowly back up. Lightning sparks across his chest, moving in fascinating rivulets over his smooth skin. If I tell him I've stared enough to notice he has tiny blue freckles, I'll never hear the end of it.

"Louanna," he draws my attention.

When I look up, he wears the most serious expression I've ever seen on him.

"Yesterday was an emotional rollercoaster, my sweet. Do you want to talk about it?"

A harsh chuckle leaves me. "Oh, you mean spying on Connall like creeps? Or how you blurted out that you wanted to pursue him? Or maybe how he looked totally horrified?"

"All of it." He reaches out with his right hand, curls his fingers through mine and pulls me flush with his chest. When our bodies touch, he drops his hold on my hand and tucks my ever-wayward bangs behind my ears. Dark eyes scan mine, as if he can see how I'm feeling simply by looking. Perhaps he can. Despite his effusive charm, Dirk's the most observant male I know.

He waits silently for me to answer. After a long moment, I sink into him. "I'm stressed." It's hard to admit it. I've tried so hard to be strong for the triplets with all the shit they've had to deal with. I don't cry in front of them. I wait to get to my room before I fall apart. But sometimes, I wish I didn't have to hold myself together quite so well.

Dirk says nothing but slides his warm hand up the back of my tee to stroke. Shivers of electricity kiss my skin everywhere he touches. It should be shocking, but somehow, it just feels good. Without allowing myself to overthink it, I turn my head sideways and press my cheek to his chest.

A happy sound leaves him, but he holds me, rubbing slow, comforting lines up and down my skin. It feels so incredibly good. His heart beats fast like a bird's, an insistent flutter that seems right for someone who can turn into the wind.

"Louanna, my sweet," he says after long minutes of simple touch. "Let me shoulder some of this burden. Please." His voice is soft, soothing. "Give me some of yer stress, sweet girl. Let me handle some things so you dinnae have to."

"That's a nice offer," I muse, allowing myself to take comfort in him for just a minute. "But maybe handling burdens is something we should reserve for some time after the first weird date."

A little sigh leaves him. Reaching down, he tips my chin up so I'm forced to look into wide, beautiful blue eyes.

"There's nothing about dating you that I want to put off, Louanna. I want you tae be fully you when yer around me. I need the good, bad and ugly, as the triplets say."

When I say nothing, he grips my chin a little harder. "I'm serious, my sweet."

I fall back on humor because it's an easy way to defuse real feelings. "What about Connall? Maybe he's got baggage too. You might be in for a lot of big feelings, Dirk."

He smiles. "I intend to pursue the both of yeh. Nothing that happened yesterday will halt that pursuit. I told yeh he'd come around, and he will. There is no amount of baggage either of yeh could hold that would stop me."

If he keeps repeating that, I'm in real danger of believing it.

Looking up, I give him a wry smile and pull away slightly, although his hand on my back flattens, not allowing me to move far. He wears the same serious expression he did when he came in.

"Is your pursuit going to involve anything other than spying on him?"

"Yes."

"Like what?"

"Conversations. Invitations. Touching. Romantic dinners."

Heat flares through me. Gods, the idea of Connall and Dirk touching is exhilarating. The truth is, Dirk is so intense, he scares me a little bit. I've imagined what he'd be like in bed, and I bet he'd be wild. But add Connall to the mix? He's got to be three hundred pounds of solid muscle. Quiet strength and dominance exude from him.

Dirk sucks in a deep, ragged breath. "Ah, Louanna. You've imagined it, then, haven't yeh? The way your scent blossoms when yer hot under the collar does things to me, my sweet."

A hot blush pinkens my cheeks. I've always held Dirk at, well, not quite arm's length. But away from me a little. I've never let him fully in. And despite my reticence, he's never stopped being there. He's as constant as the earth beneath my feet.

"Are you sure you're not an earth elemental?" I ask with a lilt in my voice.

His nostrils flare. "Why, Louanna? You achin' tae feel my rocks, pretty girl?"

I slap his chest. "Can you sexualize *anything*?"

He snorts. "O' course. You cannae do it?"

When I can't hold back a smirk, his own wide-mouthed smile grows insufferably huge. For long, heated moments, he stares at me like I'm the center of the universe, dark gaze roving over my face and neck before landing on my eyes again. It's the gaze of a lover, someone who knows all of your secrets and wants to help you make new ones.

For the first time ever, maybe, I stare back, not telling him to stop, not slapping his chest or playfully pushing him away. I just let him. And it feels nice.

Better than nice.

Malik's old cuckoo clock chimes from the depths of the store.

"Nearly closing time, my sweet." Dirk is still smirking at me.

I groan. "I'm not done with everything. I was still putting inventory away in the stockroom when you got here."

Dirk waves the comment away. "No matter, Louanna. Put me to work. The sooner I can get yeh out of here, the sooner I can take yeh on that date I mentioned yesterday."

I blink my eyes. Date?

Dirk's smirk grows bigger, eyes wrinkling at the edges as he plants both hands on his hips. "Louanna, you don't mean tae tell me yeh forgot our date, do yeh?"

I straighten. "I was distracted."

"Oh, Louanna," he murmurs, stepping forward into my space, his chest pressed to mine. He grabs the end of my long braid and twirls it around his fingers. "Good thing yeh have me here tae remind yeh. After I assist yeh in yer closing duties, we'll be headed to Herschel's Fine Dining for a lovely dinner. He's prepared something especially for us, at my request."

Worry and awe fill me in equal measures.

"Are we really doing this?" My question comes out so softly, I'm not sure he could even hear it.

His grip on my braid tightens. "Yes, my sweet. You deserve a happily ever after and I want to be the one to give it to yeh." He dips down, gripping my chin with the fingers of his free hand. His lips are so close to mine, he could kiss me.

I stand frozen, staring into eyes as dark as the deepest parts of the sea, both terrified and praying he takes this tension a step further.

"Oh, Louanna," his lips pull wide to reveal double rows of conical teeth, "when I kiss yeh for the first time, it won't be at yer workplace, my love. I want yeh to think about it every second until I do it, too."

Irritation sparks and sputters, and I move to pull away, but Dirk laughs and holds me tight, dipping lower. His lips brush faintly against mine, his gaze locked onto me. The soft touch of his mouth nearly has me screaming at him to kiss me already. But he holds the position as we breathe the same air.

Dirk drags his lower lip along mine, teasing me before he takes an abrupt step back. He spins and heads into the depths of the store, calling out over his shoulder, "Come, Louanna. Let's get yeh closed up."

Fuuuuck me.

I refuse to grumble about his intense teasing, so I force myself to zip my lips as I follow Dirk to the storeroom.

It takes the better part of an hour to get everything put away, but Dirk is a dutiful helper. He stocks shelves and organizes bottles and refills potions, all without complaint. As we head to the front door to lock up, it's on the tip of my tongue to thank him when the bell rings and Connall steps into the store.

CHAPTER TEN
DIRK

Louanna freezes as our big wolf steps into Alkemi. Bright green eyes flash, his wolf's electric shade glowing faintly as his focus flicks from her to me and back again. He schools his features into neutral, his wolf's green disappearing as he closes the door softly behind him.

"I didn't mean to interrupt," he starts. "I came for a sleeping potion for a client."

"You're not interrupting anything," Louanna says quickly. "What kind can I get for you? We've got a few for falling asleep, and some are meant to help you remain asleep through the night."

Connall shakes his head, eyes moving to me once more. "You know what? I can come back another time."

It's plain to see he didn't expect to find me here, and he's about to run. We can't have that.

"Don't let me stand in yer way, Wolf," I say, grinning at Connall. "I jest came to help Louanna close up."

He nods curtly, stepping around me to a chunky wooden table piled high with tiny vials of potions. Intelligent eyes scan the labels until he finds what he's looking for. I take the time to drink him in, those gorgeous auburn waves, the hint of freckles that dust his cheeks. He's a vision, and I am going to have so, so, *so* much fun playing with him when he gives in to us.

"We're going to dinner after this," I say as he grabs a vial. "Come with us."

His bright eyes meet mine, emotion flashing through so fast, it's hard to catalog what he's feeling. He glances over his shoulder at Louanna. "I...can't. I've got something to do."

"Do yeh?" I take a step closer to him. "Come with us, Connall."

His cheeks go pink, then red, and he shakes his head. "Have fun. I'll just pay for this and be on my way."

My poor, sweet wolf. He's never been with a male; The topic comes up from time tae time in his sessions, and he's open about sharing his personal life with his patients. I cannae wait to be his lover, his instructor, and, gods, I hope the recipient of the weapon between his thighs.

"I insist," I say a little more forcefully. "It'll be a good time. We can chat."

Connall's eyes go full blue, his wolf pressing forward to get a good look at me. I stand tall and proud, staring back at the predator that lives inside my mate.

"Come out and play, Wolf," I whisper to him. "I'm right here."

A soft growl leaves his throat, half warning and half...something else.

A scent soaks the air, pulling Connall's focus from me.

Louanna's arousal is the sweetest of essences. When she's turned on, the air smells of the climbing honeysuckle vines from the meadow I grew up in.

Connall and I turn as one to find my sweet Louanna's mouth open, eyes hooded as she watches us. Her chest rises and falls rapidly, both hands flat on the checkout counter's surface.

Next to me, Connall sucks in a deep, ragged breath, another soft growl tumbling from his throat. Louanna's scent explodes, drenching the air with her need. Connall strides to the checkout counter and sets the vial down so hard, I'm shocked it doesn't break.

"Just this, please," he grits out, his voice rough with his wolf's deeper tone.

"O-okay," she says, eyes wide as she rings him up without even looking, her fingers still on the keys. "Connall…"

I stand silent, watching them, getting hard as he breathes heavily. He can't pull his eyes from her, and with his incredible sense of smell, I'm certain he's struggling not to yank our Louanna over the countertop to fuck her.

"Do it," I encourage. "Whatever yer thinking about…do it."

He ignores me and reaches into his pocket, withdrawing a fistful of cash and slapping it on the counter.

Lou sputters, "This is too much; it's like four times what the—"

"It's fine." He spins in place.

He's gonna run. I can feel it.

"Louanna, my sweet," I urge, "come find the key, my darling."

She rounds the checkout counter with an exasperated sigh. "Are you kidding me right now?"

I glance down at her, then back at Connall where he stands frozen next to the checkout. His eyes are planted firmly on Louanna's ass. I'd pay good money to know his exact thoughts.

"Give me the key," she commands, scowling up at me.

"Gods, I love it when you get bossy," I admit, crossing my arms. "Yeh'll have to find the key, Louanna."

"Stop it," she hisses. "Hand it over. You're making this weird. Again."

"Weird. Hot. Sexy. Plenty of names for it," I joke. "Go on, my beauty, find it."

She lets out a string of expletives to make a sailor blush, then grabs my chest straps and looks underneath them.

"Not there, Louanna," I say with a laugh, bending to bring my lips close to her ear. "Look lower."

Connall stands there, eyes roving the both of us as Lou reaches a hand into one of my pockets, grumbling about how the key isn't there. When she rounds me and feels in the other pocket, I roll my eyes and let out a soft, sensual moan.

"Yes, Louanna, keep going in that direction," I say.

Connall grits his jaw but can't keep his eyes off o' her as she checks both of my back pockets. I grin at him, loving how he can't bring himself tae leave.

"Come with us to dinner," I say again. "I want yeh to. She wants yeh to."

Lou stops her search of my body and looks at him. "Please, Connall."

Green eyes flash again, but he shakes his head. "I shouldn't."

"C'mere, Connall," I command. "Why don't yeh help Louanna find the key?"

His brows shoot skyward, but he licks his lips as she slaps my stomach.

"Dirk, it's not in your pocket. Where the hells did you put it?"

"Check inside the pants, my beauty," I encourage.

A scrambling noise pulls my attention back to Connall, whose back is the last thing I see before he shuts the front door quietly behind him and leaves.

He's a runner, I'll give him that. But I'm nothing if not devoted to the chase.

∾

Hours later, Louanna rubs her full belly, staring at an empty plate as we sit in Herschel's Fine Dining.

"That was amazing, but I ate far too much," she groans, amber eyes flicking to mine and softening at the corners. "This was lovely, Dirk."

"But what?" I question. "I can hear the 'but' in yer tone, Louanna."

She leans forward over the table. "I feel bad that Connall didn't come. He ran off." Her eyes flash with command. "I think there's a super solid chance he's not as into this as you hope. You laid it on pretty thick yesterday at Biergarten."

I grin. "I haven't even begun to lay thick things on you, my sweet, but I told yeh he'd come around, and he will. He needs time to think, to see I'm serious about him."

I rest both forearms on the table and lean close, noting how our knees touch and she doesn't pull away. Scanning her face, I look for signs of lingering discomfort.

"What do *you* think about this whole thing?"

She looks away from me, scanning the room as she considers my question. When she looks back, I worry she's still reticent about me, and us.

"I thought it might be too much, too soon, but I'm having fun," she admits.

Pride blossoms through me. I can work with slow and steady. I just need a chance to prove to her that I can be a good mate. I need to unpack those walls around her heart to get close.

"Tell me if it's ever too much." I grip her knee and squeeze gently. "I want yeh; I've always wanted yeh. But yer comfort, and his, are my priority."

She reaches down and lays a hand over mine, curling her fingers into my palm. "Some days I feel like my mental state is two steps forward and one step back. You might be getting damaged goods, Dirk, but somewhere underneath all of that there's still a badass bitch."

I snort out a laugh. My sassy, confident female is self-aware. I love that.

"Yer right, o' course," I say. "And I'm attracted to every facet of who you are. I want yer good days and the bad, my sweet."

Her half-smile grows a little bigger.

Glancing down at my comm watch, I decide it's time to get her home. We made good progress tonight, but I don't wanna push my luck. Squeezing her fingers with mine, I pull her closer.

"I'm going to walk yeh home, Louanna. And, on the way, I'd like to hold yer hand."

Pink dusts her cheeks and neck, traveling to full breasts forming soft mounds underneath her wrap dress.

"My eyes are up here, Dirk," she says in a laughing tone.

"Thank fook." My gaze trails down to her waist and slowly back up. "Imagine if yer eyes were somewhere else. I'm just appreciatin' every one of yer curves. Does watching me stare at how stunning yeh are not make yeh hot?"

She shifts on the bench seat next to me, her long hair brushing against my forearm where it rests on the bench behind her.

"It does," she says so quietly, if I wasn't a monster, I doubt I'd be able to hear her.

Fraught emotion furrows her brows, her expression tense.

"What is it, Louanna?" I stroke the knuckles of my free hand down her jaw.

"I don't know how to navigate all of this with everything going on."

A soft smile tips my lips upward. "Yeh'll not be navigatin' it alone, my sweet. Yeh've got Connall and me by yer side."

She leans in like she'll tell me a secret. "I hoped he'd come to dinner with us."

"I would have liked that." I glance around the formal dining room, filled to the brim with monsters.

Amber eyes move back to me, her lips still close to mine. "I prefer the vibe in Shifter Hollow. It's so much more…peaceful out there."

I brush the tip of my nose along hers. "Shall we move you into a guest cottage, Louanna? Perhaps Connall's house?"

She slaps my shoulder half-heartedly. "Don't be ridiculous."

Little does she know, I'm not being ridiculous at all.

CHAPTER ELEVEN
CONNALL

The following afternoon, I run both hands through my unruly waves as I consider what Dirk told me. I haven't been able to stop thinking about it since he dropped the bomb on me. And then seeing him and Lou touch?

Goddess Alaya, I'm still processing the whole thing.

"Everything okay with you?" Richard's eyes swirl green and amber with the color of his and his mate's wolves. He sips a beer as he stares. Thank fuck Lola isn't here to read my aura and tell me it's red-hot again.

I stare deeply into his eyes, still fascinated by how Lola's wolf can enter Richard's mind and just...be there. So weird.

"Hey, Big Daddy," I croon to his wolf. "How's it going in there?" I'm pointedly ignoring his actual question.

"Fucking fine, Second," the wolf's tone laces through Richard's as Richard grins. My pack alpha takes another sip of his beer, his expression going thoughtful. "You're an amazing Second, and I'm goddess-blessed to have you by my side through all of this. But don't forget that, where your duty is to me, I also have a duty to be a good partner to you. You seem distracted, and you might not want to talk about why that is.

But I've got a better than good guess, and I'm here if you want to discuss it."

I roll my shoulders, letting my head fall back. I told him once how I felt about Lou, how badly I wanted her and how determined I was not to shove my way between a happy couple. But—

A knock echoes through my treehouse, and somehow, I know it's Dirk before Richard even trots to the entryway and lets him in.

A bracing wind brushes past my cheeks, ruffling my hair as Dirk enters the room with a grin. Is he ever *not* grinning?

"Hello, boys," he says in that same charming tone he uses on practically everyone. "I jest came to have a word with Connall, but I can come another time if yer busy." I swear his blue eyes drop to my dick before he focuses on Richard.

Richard gives me a quizzical look. He knows how I feel about Lou, but I didn't share Dirk's bombshell. Dark eyes flick to Dirk and back to me. "I'm gonna head home. Lola's cooking a late dinner."

"Tell yer princess hi fer me," Dirk says with a grin.

"Queen," Richard corrects with a wicked grin. "I'll tell my *queen* you said hello."

They share a smile that looks secretive, and for the millionth time since they returned from rescuing Lola from being kidnapped by her father, it rankles. Dirk was the one to use his security clearance to get Richard through the series of security portals between here and Santa Alaya.

I couldn't do it. I couldn't even stop the king when he alpha-barked at me and dragged his daughter through Ever's portal and away from her alpha.

"Stop," Richard commands. "I can see your thought train headed off the tracks. There is no finer Second than you, and I've had a fair few in my life. I've said it once, and I'll keep saying it. I need you, Connall. Lola needs you. We couldn't run this pack without your contributions."

I nod, but I can't force myself to look at my pack alpha, truthful as his words may be.

As a therapist, I start picking apart my own behavior and reactions to what's happening around me. I can tell myself all the logic in the world, but emotion can be hard to overcome. Drawing in a steadying breath, I finally look at my alpha. "Let me walk you out."

He gives Dirk a quick nod as he rises and turns for the door. I walk him to it and hold it open.

"Good night, Second," Richard murmurs.

"Night."

When I swing the door closed behind him, I half expect to see Dirk right behind me, ready with a quippy comment. But he's not there. When I return to the main living area, he's seated on the sofa with a full glass of whiskey in one hand, sipping the amber liquid.

"Made yourself right at home, I see." I cross the room and pour a whiskey for myself, sitting on a chair across from him. Nerves clang in my belly, knowing what he probably came here to discuss.

"I came to speak with yeh about Louanna," Dirk says, "and what happened last night."

Nerves spark and sputter in my chest.

Dirk's eyes drop before traveling a leisurely path back up to my face. "Yeh rubbed her cheek, touched her."

I set the whiskey down and lean forward, both elbows on my knees. "I'm not trying to step on your toes, Dirk. I'm s—"

He continues with a sly smile, "Did yeh ever stop to ask yerself why Louanna and I were right there at Biergarten after you arrived?"

Suspicion wars with something else, something instinctual in my mind.

Pieces click together as I pick up what he's saying. "You were following me?"

Dirk nods. "All the way from Hel Motel. Know what we saw, alpha?"

Confusion and horror fill me in equal measures. I jacked off in the woods, bellowing Lou's name as I spilled hot seed into the dirt. Is he saying they saw that? Oh fuck. Goddess help me, I'm going to die of embarrassment.

Dirk sets his glass down and rounds the table, dropping to both knees at my feet. "Yes, we followed you. And I teased her while yeh touched yerself, alpha. We followed you because you belong to us. Yer our mate, Connall."

I fly back in the seat, eyes wide as the sylph by my feet grins.

"That's it," he murmurs. "Let it sink in, Wolf. You belong to me, and I to you, and the both o' us to her. Better to rip off the Band-Aid, as the humans love to say. I told yeh last night, but I'm here to reiterate how very serious I am."

Blinking rapidly, I try to remember any time I could have picked up on this. I've always read Dirk's smiles as somewhat victorious, considering he was already pursuing Lou. But maybe there was more, and I missed it?

"I took her on our first date tonight," he says softly. "I invited you fer a reason, Connall."

My heart flutters so fast in my chest, it feels like it'll burst out and fly away. Hands trembling, I look at Dirk again.

He sits on his knees, rocked back onto his heels. Now, he leans forward and places a hand on either arm of my chair. "Yer shocked, alpha. I've been bidin' my time with yeh, knowing yeh've not been with a male before. But that's okay. I'm an excellent, excellent teacher."

Heat flares through me. Oh my gods, he's suggesting that he, that we, with Lou... My thoughts scatter onto the breeze as I struggle to wrap my mind around what he's insinuating.

"How do you even imagine this working?" The words come out of my mouth like tumbling boulders, rough and sharp and clanging together as they crash downhill.

"Well, I shocked her with this news last night, too, and then she yelled at me for spying on yeh, as I do it quite a bit. Then she—"

"Wait," I bark. "Spying on me? You spy on me?"

Dirk shrugs. "I'm a hunter, Connall. I hunt things for work, and I hunt things I want for myself."

I bristle, shooting forward until our faces nearly touch. "It's a violation of my privacy, Dirk."

His gaze goes thoughtful. "Hunters and elementals in general aren't fussed about privacy, Connall. But if yeh ask me right now tae stop, I will."

"Stop," I command.

"Done." His tone is assured as he remains on his knees in front of me. The dominant side of my nature rears up, my wolf pleased at seeing the slightly smaller male below us.

"I don't believe you," I snap, concerned and filled with horror. But heat flushes through me too, because the thought of him—of them—watching me jack off gets me fucking hot, and I didn't know that until he said it just now.

Dirk drags in a slow, deep breath. "Gods, yeh smell good when yeh're aroused, Wolf. Shall I call Louanna to come over so we can do something about it? I haven't kissed her yet because I was waiting until we were all together."

Oh goddess. Oh fuck. The mental images that slap me at the idea of Lou between us are lascivious and filthy.

"Speaking of which, to answer your question, I imagine us all dating together and separately. You and her, me and her, all of us together." His focus intensifies. "You and me."

Before I can say anything, he continues, "Imagine it, Wolf. Us on our knees before yeh, taking turns pleasing you. Her between us, taking us both. Gods, I can see it now."

My chest heaves as I struggle to pull in enough breath for my lungs to function.

"Do you have questions for me?" Dirk's voice is soft, thoughtful.

"How do you know?" my voice comes out as a whisper. "How could you possibly know? Wolf mating bonds are…"

"I'm not a wolf."

"I know."

"Touch me," Dirk says, nodding at my hands. "And I'll show yeh how I know yeh're mine, just like I know Louanna is ours."

Hands trembling, I lift one. Am I doing this? Am I touching a male sexually for the first time in my life? The idea of it isn't as shocking as I imagined it to be. I lay awake last night thinking about it, and I'm coming around.

Dirk's hand comes to mine, his fingers slightly cool to the touch.

Like the wind that brushes across my face when he enters a room.

Like the chilly breeze that follows me when I run, keeping me cool.

Oh, my fucking moons. It's been him from the start.

Navy eyes stare deeply into mine as he draws my hand toward his chest, slipping my fingers under the straps that crisscross his muscles. Even his pecs are a little cool. I watch in shock as the lightning on his skin zips toward my hand. I try to jerk it away, but Dirk holds me there.

"Easy, Wolf," he says quietly. "I won't shock yeh."

But from what little I know of elementals, his lightning is dangerous. Yet when it connects with my palm, all the blood in my body rushes to my dick, hardening it until it feels like it'll break off.

"Fuck," I grit out.

"We will," Dirk says with a grin. "But I want to woo yeh before we get tae that, Wolf."

I move my hand over his chest, fascinated by the way the lightning follows my touch. No shock, just that barest hint of electricity vibrating up my arm and pooling down low in my balls.

Pulling my hand away, I stare at Dirk in surprise. Running both hands through my hair, I sputter, "This is a shock, Dirk. I didn't know, and I—"

"Look like yeh're about to run again," he says quietly. "But this is your *home*, so I'll make yeh this promise. I'll give yeh space now, as I can see it's needed. But I'm always around, Connall. Call me, and I'll come. Call me, and I will be there. And as yeh asked me not tae spy anymore, I won't without your knowledge. But jest know that, when I leave, and yeh touch yerself thinkin' about us being with Louanna, I'll be doin' the same thing."

A groan leaves my throat unbidden, my cheeks flaming hot as Dirk's hands move to my knees. He beams at me as he licks his lips. "Or I could stay, Wolf, and do something about that beautiful erection. What do yeh think?"

"What would you do?" I croak out before I can even stop myself. I'm in shock. That must be what this is.

"Shall I show yeh," he questions, "or simply tell yeh?"

"Tell me," I manage, chest heaving as Dirk presses my knees outward and slips between them, his upper body brushing my inner thighs.

"I'd unzip yer jeans, Wolf, until that gorgeous cock and knot sprang free. And then I'd lean in like so—" he shifts forward, his mouth hovering just above my obviously hard dick, "—and I'd take yeh into my mouth, all the way to the back. I'd suck," he says confidently, "and lick and stroke until yeh spilled yer seed down my throat."

I'm going to combust, just explode right here into tiny Connall bits that someone else has to clean up. My cock throbs in my pants. It's close, so close to his mouth, straining to get to that heat. Or would his mouth be cool?

"Allow me tae do it." His eyes scan my face. He's waiting for my consent, my approval.

"I'm surprised you don't just do it, given how little you've cared for my permission in the past." I attempt to look pissed about it, but the reality is I'm too oversensitized by this entire experience to be mad. Maybe I'll be mad later.

He leans down, dragging his open mouth along my cock through my pants. "Don't be upset, mate. I'm drawn to yeh in the deepest ways of my people. I could no sooner stop following yeh than I could stop following Louanna."

I gasp as his mouth closes over the tip of my dick, biting through my jeans. My hips jerk, back arching as pleasure zings through me like an electrical storm.

"Fuck!" I cry out. My mind is going haywire, shooting off scattered thoughts.

Lou between us, head on my chest as Dirk fucks her.
Dirk on his knees in front of me, his head dipped between her thighs.
Making out with him. Right here. Right now.

My wolf shoves to the forefront of my consciousness as I let out a soft growl.

Dirk stares seductively up from my lap. "Whatever yer thinkin', tell me, Connall."

Even the way he says my name is like a hand fisting my dick. At my pause, he shifts upright and rolls his shoulders back, straightening his spine.

"I'll tell yeh the same thing I told Louanna tonight when I dropped her off at the Annabelle Inn. I want yeh, Connall Blackwater, the same way I want our Louanna. And I cannae wait to have the both of yeh together. I know this is a bombshell, that you likely haven't considered me in that way. But I'm askin' yeh to consider it now." His expression goes soft. "Yer everything I ever wished for in a partner. You and Louanna, yer my gifts, and I will treat yeh as such until the end of my days. And one day, when yeh move on from this earth, I'll go with yeh."

A million questions spring into my mind, but I can't find my voice to utter a single one. I'm still planted in shock against the back of the chair with a dripping erection, staring at Dirk as he all but professes love.

"Good night, my sweet wolf." He shifts to a stand. "Call me if yeh're ready to voice the questions I see on the tip o' yer tongue."

And with that, he slaps the jewel in the center of his chest and disappears on a gust of chilly wind, leaving me with a tornado of thoughts and one hellsuva hard-on.

∼

The following morning, thoughts still tumble like rocks in my head as I walk up Sycamore Street from Shifter Hollow toward downtown Ever. I think I'm imagining Lou's humming as she walks along, but when I round a bend in the road, she's there, walking along with a bouquet of wildflowers in one hand.

At my footsteps, she turns, a bright smile faltering slightly as pink crawls across her cheeks and down her chest.

"Morning, Lou." I'm painfully aware of her physical reaction to me. She doesn't technically perfume like an omega of my people would, but her arousal is no less potent. Gods, the ideas Dirk planted in my head last night rush right back as my cheeks heat, probably matching hers in their intense shade.

"Umm, good morning," she says, crossing her arms over her chest.

Does she know Dirk planned to come to my place last night? She flew through the forest with him. She watched me jack off and scream her name. Goddess Alaya, help me find the strength to not be weird about that.

The truth is, I find the idea of it all incredibly hot, now that the initial shock has worn off.

"So," I manage, eyeing the bouquet, "where are you headed this early in the morning?"

Her awkward expression becomes a scowl as she drops one

hand to pick at her elbow. "Oh, I'm just going over to Doc Slade's for him to check on my thrall bites."

My heart sinks, and without meaning to, I push her sleeve up enough to see the bites she received when she first arrived in Ever. She should *be* a thrall by now, but somehow, she's not.

I run my fingers over the slight indentations from the thrall's teeth. Lou holds still while I do it.

"You're remarkable," I murmur, even though I'm worried for her. Looking into her eyes, I force a smile even though I can't understand how she managed to fight off the monsters and not become one. It's well known that a thrall bite turns any monster into a thrall, the soul-sucking creatures who try to burrow into havens to turn monsters into more thralls.

Lou lets out a wry laugh. "I don't know how remarkable it is, but I'm really fucking pleased not to have turned." She smirks up at me. "I wouldn't look great as a zombie."

I force a laugh, but I'm still worried.

She cocks her head to the side, her arm still in my hands. "Do you want to come with me to see Doc Slade?"

"Yeah," I manage. "I'd love to." I want his take on this, because the mental vision of Lou getting sick makes me want to flip tables.

"Connall," her sweet voice breaks through my thoughts, "you're squeezing me kinda hard."

"Oh, moons, sorry," I blurt, dropping her arm.

"It's okay." She laughs. "I can see you about to get all alpha protector on me, but I'm fine, I swear."

I shove my hands into my pockets to avoid touching her again.

"So…" she says, drawing out the O. "Dirk mentioned he might drop by to see you. Did he?"

Fuck. Oh fuck. Here we go.

I clear my throat. "He did."

Her cheeks turn redder, if that's even possible. "Oh, and did he, umm, say anything...interesting?" She clears her throat too, and the noise slaps me out of my shyness. This is getting absolutely ridiculous.

I straighten and nod. "He did, yeah. He reiterated that he believes the three of us to be mates. And he's convinced of it because his lightning doesn't shock me."

She drops both hands to her sides, mouth open. "So he...did he make you touch him? He did that to me at Alkemi! And the lightning zinged toward my hand and, well, it kind of—"

"Felt good?" I ask wryly.

She grabs her braid and starts twisting it around a finger absentmindedly, but her eyes are wide.

I step closer to tilt her face up to me. "It was a shock, and I lay awake all night thinking about it. At Biergarten, you asked me to consider it, and I am."

Her voice is so soft when it comes out, I'm thankful for my extra-sensitive hearing. "And what do you think?"

This is it, my chance to tell the female I've been agonizing over that I want to see where it goes between us.

"I was surprised, Lou, but I've been wanting to ask you out for a long time. Since the moment I saw you, really."

And there it is, my greatest secret.

Her mouth drops open, and she sinks naturally against me, my finger still under her chin. Whiskey-gold eyes flash with emotions so fast, it's hard to catalog them all. But it's a particular skill of mine, reading people.

"I wasn't aware of his feelings about me. I thought we might be in sort of a love triangle situation, and I didn't want that." I keep my voice deep and low, an alpha instinct. "Allow me to take you both out tonight. We can talk about what this might look like, what the ground rules are. There's been none of that and honestly, it's needed. But like you said, we'll try it and see what happens."

"I—I can't," she sputters, sinking a dagger into my heart. At my look, she shakes her head. "Not because of this. Bellami the gnome asked for my help in the gnome village, and I'm doing that tonight at eight."

My brows travel upward in shock. "The gnome village?"

"I know," she exclaims. "I was so surprised."

"It's an honor to be invited," I say. "Nobody in Shifter Hollow has ever been into the gnome village, not even Richard."

She makes an impressed face as I drop my hand by my side. I itch with the need to put both hands on her and draw her to me. The need to wrap her safely and securely in my arms is nearly overwhelming.

"I've been meaning to ask you something else." Lou's soft smile returns. "Dirk has suggested this a bunch, so it's probably just meant to be sexy because that's all he thinks about, but I know you've been reticent to do therapy sessions with me. But… will you?"

I sigh, withdrawing my hands from my pockets to cross my arms over my chest. "Here's the thing about therapy between us. It's a conflict of interest, although I understand why both you and Dirk might believe I'm the right person for it."

She nibbles at her lower lip. She must think I'm rejecting her request.

"I'll do it," I say quietly, "but let's not call it therapy. Let's just get together and talk. It'll be a good chance to get to know one another better and to help give you some coping skills for what you've dealt with. We can take it easy. Let's not put pressure on it. We could never have a true therapist and client relationship. Not if we're dating."

"I understand." She straightens and rolls her shoulders. "I just…you've always seemed like such a rock to me. Confident and friendly, and I think I could talk to you about things I can't talk to anyone else about." Amber eyes move up to mine. "So I agree, let's keep the expectations light."

"Good idea," I say. "I promise to be completely professional when we're in therapy mode, Lou." Even as I say it, I'm drawn to look at that long, gorgeous braid and the way her amber eyes flash in the early morning light.

Her exposed throat bobs, calling my attention to smooth, sun-kissed skin. "Is this what you mean by professional? Or is this more like date-mode Connall?"

A chuckle leaves my lips as I bend down to breathe just beneath her ear. Goosebumps cover her skin as one of her hands comes to my left side. Possession rages through me.

"It'll be a fight for me not to be distracted by things I shouldn't let distract me, Lou. Date-mode Connall is a little more forward, Lou, a little more aggressive. I've likely come across as quiet, even shy. I've been trying not to step on Dirk's toes, and you seemed interested in him. We should try to keep date-mode Connall out of our sessions, if possible."

"Agreed," she whispers. "But if date-mode Connall happens to pay me a visit, I don't think I'd be too upset."

Fuck. This woman.

"We need to talk all together," I reiterate. "We need ground rules for our sessions and dating in general. There's nothing more important than having consent around what's happening." Her scent strengthens, imprinting on me, drawing me to her by a tether that's as real and tangible as a leash.

Reaching out, I grip her throat softly, running the pad of my thumb up the elegant column. "We need those ground rules because, to be honest, it wouldn't surprise me if Dirk showed up right now, or if he's been here the whole time, although he promised not to spy on me anymore if I asked him not to, which I did."

Lou's eyes flash with indignation. "I told him spying on you was an uber-creepy move, and I'm just as bad. I went along with it when you, umm—" her eyes flash to mine, "—well, you know."

"Yeah, I know," I say with a grin, trying to dissipate the tension. Taking a step back, I release my hold on her. Wolves tend to go hard and fast when we believe we've identified our mates. It's been a surprising twenty-four hours. I should probably take things a little more slowly.

I jerk my head toward downtown. "Shall we get to your appointment?"

Lou nods and turns to walk by my side, tucking her hands behind her back. But all that move does is highlight her soft-looking breasts.

"You and Dirk," she mutters, elbowing me playfully in the side, "you must both be boob guys because it seems like you can't look anywhere else."

I laugh, because she's right. Running both hands through my hair, I admit, "It's not that I'm a boob man. I'm an all-the-things man, because they're yours."

She smirks up at me like the cat that caught the canary. "Are you a sweet talker, Connall? You gonna be my Romeo, writing love letters and whispering sweet nothings in my ear while Dirk cheers you on?"

Goddess, this woman. I've seen bits and pieces of Lou's snarky, bratty side, and I fucking love it. Because what comes next is me teaching that pretty mouth a lesson. I want to put my hands all over her, to get rough, to spank and disrespect in the most respectful way possible.

Wolves in general love bratty, back-talking women.

"I'm generally romantic, yes, but that doesn't make me any less alpha in other ways." I give her a look I pray says what I'm thinking.

When she holds back a grin and nips her lower lip, I know she read between the lines. She doesn't respond though, which, I suspect, is because this sexy playfulness is a new dynamic for us. I've been holding it back since I met her. And she's been going through so much.

She falls quiet, and we walk in peaceful silence to Doc Slade's. The dark elf waits by the front door, arms crossed as he leans against one of the porch posts. He gives me a quizzical look as I trail Lou up the walkway toward the front porch.

"Connall? Something wrong, son? Do you need an appointment?"

Lou loops an arm through mine. "Nope! He's accompanying me today."

Slade looks at me, the tips of his black lips curling into a smile. "Alright then, come on in, both of you."

We follow him into one of the cottage's small exam rooms. I hold my breath the entire time he examines Lou's bites. But he confirms what she told me. They're healing, and there's no explanation for it. On the one hand, I'm relieved. But the fact that our brilliant doctor can't explain why Lou's fine is deeply concerning.

More than that, it scares the shit out of me.

CHAPTER TWELVE
LOU

My first therapy session with Connall is tomorrow.

With a male who wants to pursue me romantically.

And all of this has been orchestrated by the other male pursuing me romantically.

He was right to suggest we not consider it like typical therapy. But if there's anyone in this entire haven besides my nieces I can talk to, it's Connall.

I consider my current situation as I attempt Malik's sleeping potion for the millionth time. Dropping the last ingredient in, I hold my breath as it sparks and sputters and a pale purple mist hovers above the cast iron pot.

Slow clapping drifts from somewhere in the depths of Alkemi.

"Well done, Lou." Malik appears in the storeroom doorway with a wink. "I was peeping from here. I thought perhaps hovering over you wasn't doing you any favors."

Victory fills me with frenetic energy as I resist the urge to hop up and down. I did it! Finally!

Malik clops out of the storeroom and carefully rounds the

long table that separates us. He cocks his head to the side, putting a finger beneath his chin as he examines me.

"You seem different today. Lighter. Has something happened?"

I resist the urge to tug at my nonexistent collar as my cheeks heat.

"Ohhh," Malik draws out the word. "Something *has* happened. You know I'm an excellent confidant, so spit it out. I must know what put that sweet smile on your face."

The usual guilt at finding happiness in anything rears up, but I do my best to shove it aside. I'm allowed to find peace. I'm allowed to be happy. I'm allowed to be enthralled with the concept of dating two people, all of us together.

It's *okay* to be happy. Sometimes I need to remind myself of that.

"Well," I start. "I went on a real date with Dirk, and it was wonderful."

Malik's eyes flash, and he starts swishing his tail lazily from side to side. "Tell me everything."

I fill him in on the meal at Herschel's Fine Dining, but I leave out the whole throuple thing. Connall, Dirk and I haven't had that conversation all together yet, and it seems like something that should happen before any of us tells the world about our connection. Although, knowing Dirk, it wouldn't surprise me if he announced a haven-wide meeting just to make sure everyone knows. Dirk is the type to put that shit on a billboard.

Oh god, that is terrifying.

"I lost you," Malik murmurs. "Are you going out again?"

I snort. "Is the sky blue? We didn't make a specific plan, but you've seen how Dirk is. He could show up out of thin air any moment."

"I've noticed," Malik says with a soft laugh.

No fucking sooner have I said it than the bell hanging over

the front door chimes. When I scoff, Malik raises a brow, and we turn as one.

Sure as shit, Dirk stands in the doorway, an innocent look on his face as he slips both hands into his pockets. "Yeh look like yeh were expectin' me, Louanna."

Malik and I share a look before he snorts out a horsey laugh and turns for the storeroom.

I shoot Dirk a meaningful look, glancing at the clock. "I'm here for another two hours, Dirk, and I've got a date with the gnomes after that."

"I know," he chirps. "I'm off to find Connall to see if he'd like to grab a beer."

Oh fuck. He's taking Connall on a date? I want to go with an intensity that steals my breath.

Like always, Dirk practically reads my thoughts. "Don't worry, Louanna, I'm jest killin' time between his last session and yer time with the gnomes. Once yeh're done assistin' them, I'm stealing the both of yeh for a bit."

A muffled sneeze echoes from the storeroom, pulling my attention from Dirk.

He glances over at the storeroom door, where Malik's tall shadow darkens the floor.

Dirk's fingers trail along my jawline and then into my hair, canting my head slightly backward. "See yeh later, Louanna." He brings my free hand to brush his lips, nuzzling softly along the back of my hand.

For a long moment, I'm lost in the depths of his intense, focused gaze. As quickly as he came, he spins to go, and then I get lost in staring at his fine ass and the way dark leather pants hug his muscular thighs.

I stare until the door swings quietly shut behind him, and then I stand in place for a moment, wondering if the gods are finally smiling down at me after a super shit six months.

"Ahem, Lou," Malik's voice echoes from the storeroom as he

peeks his head around, concern on his face. "Your sleeping potion is boiling over."

"Oh fuck!" I shout, spinning toward the cauldron.

~

Two hours later, I've cleaned up the boiled-over cauldron and bottled all of the sleeping potion. Every table is fully stocked and cleaned, and the store looks amazing. I've been tackling deep cleaning projects one at a time because, while Malik is an amazing potion maker, he's not that great at cleaning. Moss is adorable in a cottagecore potions shop. Mold, not so much.

I push the cash register shut and wipe down the checkout counter as Malik joins me, slipping a bag over his broad chest. "Best of luck tonight with the gnomes, Lou." His voice is wondrous as he grabs the front door and holds it open, gesturing for me to go through. "What an honor."

"Everyone says that," I say on a laugh, "when the reality is they literally want me to do hard labor. I'm not sure how honored I'm going to feel here shortly."

Malik smiles as he locks the front door, handing me the ornate metal key since I'm opening in the morning. "Well, I can't wait to hear about it. To be honest, word has gotten around, and it wouldn't surprise me if you find half of the Hollow standing in the street watching."

I scoff and slap his furry shoulder. "Are you telling me you're turning this into a watch party?"

His cheeks go faint pink. "If you mean, am I making popcorn and inviting Alba to stand in the street with me and drink while you lift logs for the gnomes? Yeah."

I halt and pinch his side playfully. He stomps and swishes his tail at me.

"You sneak!" I whisper-hiss. "You didn't tell me you asked her out."

He arcs away from my pinchy fingers and swats at me with one hand. "Well, you've been busy."

"We worked together all day, Malik!" I shout, pinching him behind his horse elbow where he's extra ticklish.

"Ouch!" he hisses, but there's no anger in his tone. He's the most low-key, chill monster I've ever met. "Fine. I asked her out for a late dinner, but we're coming to stare at you before."

"How romantic," I deadpan.

Someone hails Malik from across the street. He squeezes my shoulder and then takes off at a trot across the wide fairway.

Grumbling at his nosiness while also not revealing his own secrets, I cross my arms and walk up Sycamore toward Biergarten. The new gnome village is on the left tucked between Biergarten and a newly vacant building. The space is about fifty feet wide and the same distance deep before the giant trees in this part of the forest take over. Although, if this is anything like Rainbow, the only other monster haven I've been in, the gnomes will take over parts of those trees as well to create tiny column-shaped shopping malls and hotels for visiting gnome families.

A tiny figure stands in the middle of the sidewalk, waving with his red hat tipped back as he stares up at me.

"You're here and right on time too! Good! Come on, Lou!" Bellami waves me toward the gnome village. A wide sand pathway weaves from front to back, tiny clusters of building materials scattered throughout the space. The far back corner looks like it's nearly complete. Seven or eight layers of logs topped with giant mushroom-shaped homes are arranged artfully at an angle. A singular tall streetlight illuminates the gorgeous corner.

"That's what it'll all look like when we're done." Bellami grabs my jeans leg and uses the fabric to haul himself alllll the way up my body until he can sit on my shoulder.

I glance at him with a scowl. "Hello, Bellami. Seems like the last time you crawled all over me, I reminded you that my body is not a ladder."

"Pfft," he snorts, crossing his arms. "You'll survive. It's not like I grabbed your nipple or anything."

I slap my arms over my chest. "Oh my gods. Why would you even say that?!"

He thwaps me on the tip of my ear with his hand. "Lou, can we get moving or what? This will go a lot faster with your help."

I eye the sand path. It's well known about gnomes that no one is allowed within the boundaries of their village. Even though the first monster I ever met was a gnome, I never went in his village. I'm sure hitting him with my car didn't help.

Gods, now that I think about it, I have a history of accidental monster injury. That thought in the forefront of my mind, I eye the pathway again. Gnomes protect their villages with an ancient magic to keep big monsters from stumbling into their villages and wreaking havoc.

"It's okay," Bellami says more gently. "We already coded the magic to let you in."

I give him a final tentative look. "You sure you don't want to ask more monsters to help you? I know Dirk would be happy to help, for instance. Anyone would."

"Nope!" Bellami says with a pop of the P. "Just you, Lou. We don't want anyone else."

I don't know if he means for those words to sound so heartwarming, but they do warm something inside me that's been painfully cold for a while now.

"Okay," I finally say, urged forward by Bellami kicking at me like he's coaxing a wary horse over a jump. I place a tiptoe on the sand, wincing just in case he was wrong about the magic. If he was, I'll get shocked and thrown backward into the street. But when I place my foot flat on the path, nothing happens.

"Told ya." Bellami sighs like we've been standing here for hours.

I take another step, and when nothing happens, I walk along the path, glancing at the stacks of lumber, siding and miniature shingles.

"Okay, let's get started at the back," Bellami directs, pointing to the finished section. "Over there. I'm tonight's foreman, so I'll be your boss for the next hour or so."

Gods, I guess we're doing this.

CHAPTER THIRTEEN
CONNALL

Dirk comm'd me earlier to ask if I'd like to grab a drink. Lou's working in the gnome village tonight, but he wants to get together while she's working. He positioned it as killing time until she's off, but we both know he wants to talk about us.

I kept myself busy with Richard and Lola all morning, doing the rounds of our pack. Checking on everyone, making sure the pack is good and strong. Then we had our regular pack leadership meeting to discuss upcoming initiatives. Lola's leaving next week for a short concert tour, starting in her home haven of Santa Alaya. Richard will join her, so I'll be in charge in their absence.

I'm considering that as I clean up my office after my last patient. The pack is still reeling from my friend Leighton's violent death, and that's been the topic of many of my sessions lately, although most of the pack isn't aware of Lou's involvement. That was a personal request by Leighton's parents before they left Ever to return to their home haven. That was a wonderful bit of kindness on their part.

A knock at the door pulls me from my reverie, nerves coiling tight in my belly. My wolf sits up and focuses, pricking his ears as I stride for the door. When I swing it open, Dirk stands there in tight jeans, his gem straps crisscrossing over his chest like always.

His expression is as devious as ever when he smiles at me.

"You always look full of secrets," I say with a laugh, opening the door for him to come in.

"Och, Connall, a hunter *is* full of secrets. That's sorta my thing." He glances around the room as he steps inside. "Lovely little space yeh got here."

"It's meant to be homey and inviting." I point to the kitchen. "I was just cleaning up. Would you like to grab a beer here, or go somewhere?"

Goddess Alaya, I don't know what I'm doing. The topic of us dating seems crouched between us like a coiled serpent, ready to strike.

"A beer here's fine," he says quietly. He rounds me, not touching me as he heads for the kitchen.

After opening the fridge, he grabs two beers and uncaps them. Setting them on the countertop, he stares at me. And that stare flays me open. It's like he's looking right at my wolf and every innermost desire that has surfaced since he mentioned wanting to pursue me.

I pull in a deep breath and call on years of training. Crossing the room, I sit on a barstool and grab one of the beers. Dirk shifts forward onto his forearms, leaning over the bar toward me.

"So…it's been a minute since I shocked yeh, Connall. How do yeh feel about things?"

I take a deep gulp of the beer, willing my nerves to dissipate. My wolf drops to his belly and watches the smaller male with intense interest. He's not put off by the thought of dating *this* male. Not at all.

"It's not common for wolves to mate in throuples," I offer. "This is very new for me. But after thinking about it, I'm open to it."

Dirk's smile broadens, revealing both rows of conical, shark-like teeth. "Thought yeh might say that. Well, I hoped yeh would."

I set the beer down. "We still need to have this conversation all together, though. It's critically important to lay a foundation for good communication. I've counseled monsters who attempted this, and without rock-solid communication to begin with, it can be hard. And consent. No more of the spying, I'm serious."

"O' course," Dirk says. "Tae be honest, I thought it might take yeh a while to come around to the idea. I knew you hadn't been with a man before."

I gulp. "You know because you've spied on me."

"Hunted," he corrects. "I hunted yeh, Wolf."

"The spying has to stop," I say again. "We've discussed this before, but I want to be very clear. It doesn't start us off on the right foot."

"I've stopped," he confirms and lifts both hands in the air. "I swear on my gem, Connall. I haven't peeped on yeh a single moment since yeh asked me to refrain."

"What about Lou?" I give him a wry look.

"Ah, well." He runs a hand through his blue waves. "She didnae ask me tae stop, so…"

I shift on my seat. "You should clarify if she wants that or not."

"I will."

The moment stretches long, and he shifts onto his forearms again, playing with the label on his bottle. "So we've confirmed you're willing to try dating me. How do yeh feel about the physical nature of that?"

Heat flushes through me, and my wolf stands, pressing to the forefront of my mind as his focus intensifies. His tail swishes lazily in the mental dirt.

"Och," Dirk says. "Yeh're interested, if the gleam of yer eyes is any indication. Am I right?"

I rise and round the island, stopping to lean on it next to him.

"I'm interested. But take it slowly with me, let me lead on the physical front. I don't know what I don't know, and I don't know exactly what I want. Can you do that?"

He shifts upright enough to mirror my stance. "I can do that, but I'd like to give yeh opportunities from time to time, Wolf. I can't sit around and wait for yeh to decide to touch me. It's my intention for us to date in the same way we'll date our woman."

I let out a soft growl. "I'm a Dominant, Dirk." My eyes flash to his. "I can't be dominated. At least, I don't think I'd enjoy that. But again, this is all new."

Dirk's eyes roll playfully into his head, then he levels me with a lascivious grin. "Good. Toss me around. Use me up. Take yer needs out on me."

He's saying words I like to hear.

"I want to touch you," I admit. "But I don't want to do it for the first time without her. I want her there. I need her to be part of it from an emotional and physical perspective."

"I understand." Dirk sets his beer bottle down on the counter. "When we snatch her up after work, I want us to have this same conversation with her. I'll tell yeh the same thing I told her at dinner the other night. Yer comfort is important to me. I'm in this for the long haul. However quickly or slowly we need tae take it is what we'll do."

I nod, focusing on the soft bob of his throat. He's muscular, slightly shorter than me. He's not built as thickly, but corded muscle shows how strong he is.

"Yer welcome to touch," he says.

Steadying my breath, I reach out and bring my fingers to his throat, gripping him lightly. His eyes flash with something intense, something needy. I squeeze tighter, marveling at how much bigger he is than Lou. Taking another step forward until we're almost touching, I rub my thumb over the side of his neck, imagining biting him. Will I claim him one day the same way I'd typically claim Lou? Toss him into a shifter nest, service him and then keep him?

Neither of them are shifters, though. Would they even like a typical nest?

Licking my lips, I let the idea of that run through me. "What would it be like to mate a sylph and a human?"

Dirk's throaty laughter rumbles beneath my fingertips. "Glorious. We can make our own traditions, keep what we like from each other's cultures, and discard what doesn't serve us. We can do anything we want."

I smile, dragging my hand down his neck, fingers curling into his cool skin. "What would you do on our first date?"

"Och, easy," Dirk says on a laugh. "Cook for yeh and then watch a movie. I know how wolves love food, and it's a relaxed date. Nothing too fancy, or too public."

I frown. "Is public a problem?"

His smile falls. "I just meant since this is new, it would be easier to take things slowly until yeh feel more comfortable with me."

"That's thoughtful. What about what you want?"

He presses forward until his naked chest brushes mine. "If I had exactly what I wanted, yeh'd be fucking me against this counter right now, Wolf. We'd be filthy together. That's what I want. But I've got the benefit of fantasizing about you for quite some time now."

His words have my wolf pacing behind my breastbone, eager to get out. Instinct tells me to let him.

I take a step back and look at Dirk. "I'd like to let my wolf out. Are you alright with that?"

He grins. I swear nothing shocks the sylph. "I'd be delighted, Connall."

After pulling my shirt over my head, I toss it on the counter, watching as Dirk's eyes rove hungrily over my chest. His breathing goes shorter when I slide my jeans down my legs and step out of them, cock swinging against my thigh. He's seen it; I know that. But having his focus on it now is riling me up.

Stepping out of the kitchen, I let my wolf out. The transition happens fast, and then I'm standing in wolf form on the opposite side of the island.

Dirk looks at me, a smile on his face. He rounds the counter and comes to a stop in front of me. "Hello, Wolf." He reaches out with a palm, offering his hand for me to smell.

Shifting forward, I press my nose into his palm and snuffle. He smells good, like the wildest winds of my home haven of Arcadia.

He strokes his fingers along my snout, moving them beneath my chin to scratch it. Preening, I cock my head to the side as he moves along my head and neck, touching and talking in low tones.

My wolf is relaxed and welcoming of the affection. As Dirk strokes up my forehead, I stare at him in wonder.

I'm going to date him and Lou. And what's more? I can't wait to get started.

CHAPTER FOURTEEN
LOU

Forty minutes after beginning work at the gnome village, I regret ever meeting Bellami the effing gnome. I've hauled at least five enormous thick logs from pretty far in the forest back here via rope and sheer gumption. Then, of course, they have to be pulled into gnome village and placed *just so* at some specific fucking angle the gnomes swear is important.

Five degrees to the west, or is it the east? I don't even care anymore. I'm coated head to toe in sweat. I bet I stink, and my shirt is plastered to me, soaked through.

"Okay, Lou," Bellami shouts. "Shall we do another log tonight, or are you ready to start stacking?"

"Oh my fucking gods," I shout. "Are we putting logs on top of these ones?!"

Bellami turns and looks at the stacked log village to his left, then meaningfully back up at me. "Uh, yeah? Obviously?"

I groan and let my head fall back when the first shout rings out: "You've got this, Lou!"

I whip around to see Connall and Dirk standing on the sidewalk, clapping. Fuck me, they look kind of tipsy, grinning and elbowing each other. Dirk stands close to Connall, close enough that their bodies brush together.

Now my panties are wet too.

"Lookin' good, Louanna!" Dirk shouts. "Way to go, girl!"

Oh my gods, he couldn't possibly sound like more of a weirdo than using human sayings.

I choke out a laugh and shake my head, planting both hands on my hips as Bellami and I turn and head for the forest again. No sooner do I leave the bounds of gnome village than Dirk appears, grinning at me.

"Hello, Dirk," Bellami shouts up.

Dirk pops down to a knee and dips his head at Bellami. "My friend, how's my Louanna doin'? I see yer workin' her hard."

I have to physically hold myself back from gathering the sweat at my brow and flinging it at him.

"Connall and I'd be honored to help yeh, if yeh'll allow it."

Aww. His sweet words warm my heart. Maybe I *won't* throw sweat at him.

Bellami looks at me, tiny eyes falling to my soaked-through shirt, then moving to Dirk. "Okay, that's fine, you can help move the logs, but just to the boundary. Don't attempt to come through, or—"

"Technically, I've got diplomatic immunity," Dirk says with a wink.

"Do you?" Bellami snarks right back. "'Cause after that stunt you pulled with Richard and Lola, I'm surprised Evenia didn't snatch that right back."

Dirk's smile falls slightly, but he purses his lips together and jerks his head toward the forest.

Connall appears then, jogging along the back of the building. He halts next to Dirk, who glances up at him with a smile. Connall's cheeks are pink, and he's breathless. But he's in fucking good shape—I watched him run.

Oh my gods, I'm desperate to know if they went for a beer

and what happened, and why do they look so guilty, and did they touch?!

Dirk elbows Connall softly, although he doesn't look away from me. "We're allowed to help drag logs to the village barrier. Wanna manhandle some wood with me for a bit?"

Connall's cheeks turn bright red as I muffle a laugh behind my hand. Okay. Dirk is never changing. I don't know why I expected anything else.

"Lead the way," the big shifter says with a soft laugh. "Anything for Lou."

"Yeah, boys," I tease. "How much gnome wood can you handle?"

Bellami spins in place and glares at all three of us. "What are you three talking about? Why are you laughing? I don't get jokes, and this feels like one."

I zip my lips and shrug.

"We're flirting," Dirk offers with a wink.

"Yuck, I'm not interested." With a final grossed-out look, Bellami spins in place and jogs off into the forest.

I stare in shock, trying to process his response.

Connall clears his throat. "Well, hmm. There go all my dreams of being fucked by a gnome."

Dirk and I burst into laughter at the same time as I risk a glance at the two males to my right. They look happy, so *happy*, laughing together.

As our laughter fades, Bellami's clear mumbling drifts to us from the path he disappeared along.

Dirk gestures for me to go on. "Go ahead, Louanna. Connall and I wanna stare at that beautiful peach while yer hauling wood."

I mutter but jog to catch up with Bellami. For a creature who stands eight inches tall, he's shockingly fast. Behind me, Dirk and Connall must be shoving one another off the path because there's a series of taunts and then a crashing sound.

I spin in place as Connall leaps out of the underbrush, winks at me, and crashes into Dirk with a mighty roar. Dirk slaps the jewel on his chest, and they disappear on a gust of wind, appearing right in front of me in a heap, legs tangled together.

But Dirk is definitely, one hundred percent, on top of Connall like he's riding him. I skirt them both with a grin. "Don't let me get in the way," I tease.

Connall's muscular chest heaves as his beautiful green eyes flick to mine. "Never," he murmurs. "You could never be in the way, Lou." He stares at me like a man starved.

"Gods help me," Bellami shouts. "Do I need to let Lou go so you three can run off and roughhouse somewhere else? We have shit to do, you know!"

Dirk lifts gracefully off Connall with a little smirk. When he stands, he reaches a hand out to help Connall up. When Connall takes it, I almost swoon at how romantic it is. But then he yanks Dirk down in a smooth move and flips him over his head, slamming Dirk to the ground on his back.

They burst into delighted laughter as Bellami and I share a concerned look. I round the giggling males and join Bellami. It's hard not to laugh right along with them at how lighthearted they're being. For some reason, it reminds me of my best friend trio in high school. How we were always silly, always laughing, all together.

And I might have that again. Connall comes up behind me and slings his big arm around my waist, his huge body dwarfing mine as I try not to fan my face at having him so close.

"Which log is next?" I question Bellami as he looks disapprovingly from one male to the other. It's hard to keep a straight face. Any moment, they're going to start play fighting again or making wood jokes. Connall's fingers play at the edge of my tee as if he can't stop himself from touching me.

Makes a girl feel pretty damn good, if I do say so.

Bellami shakes his head and points at the log to his right.

"This one's next. It'll go on top of the first one you put down tonight, at a precise fifteen degrees to the southwest, so we ca—"

"Got it," I mumble, picking up one of the many ropes he must have laid out for this project.

The moment I struggle to wrap the rope around the log, Dirk and Connall are by my side. Connall grabs the end of the log in both hands and squats down, lifting it as if it weighs nothing. Dirk slips the rope around a knot in the log and ties it off, then winks at me and Connall.

"Giddyup, Wolf," he says with a lilting tease in his tone.

"Work it, Connall," I cheer as Bellami ignores us and takes off back up the path.

Connall grins and throws the rope over his shoulder, walking up the path with the log dragging behind him.

"Gods, he makes that look easy," I mutter.

Dirk slips his fingers through mine. "Or maybe it's just so fookin' easy to look at him that it wouldn't matter what he was doin'."

I glance up to see a familiar smirk.

He pulls me up the path, along the tracks from where we've dragged all the logs. "How much longer have yeh got, Louanna?"

"I don't know," I grumble. "But I'm going to be so sore. I've already dragged so many logs, and now I have to lift them."

"I'll ask them again to allow me in." Dirk slips our intertwined hands to my lower back. "Yeh shouldn't have to lift those logs on. They tend to build eight and ten stories tall."

I groan as the gnome village comes back into view. Connall drops the rope and rolls his shoulders, muscles popping in stark relief beneath his dark tee.

He turns and grins at us, eyes dropping to where Dirk holds my hand at my lower back. Plush lips part into a sensual smile.

Bellami stands by the rope, giving me his best foreman scowl. "C'mon, Louanna. This is the last one tonight. I can tell your attention is—" he eyes the two males, "—flagging."

"More like my muscles are flagging," I correct, stepping over the log.

Connall gives me an apologetic look and bends down to grab the rope and hand it to me. "I'm so sorry," he says with a soft smile. "You've got this, and we'll reward your hard work with a drink after. And maybe a massage," he tacks on, reaching out to stroke my long bangs back behind my ear.

His offer sends a thrill zinging through me as I shoulder the rope. When I pull the log over the barrier, a cheer goes up from in front of me. Glancing up, I realize half the fucking Hollow has now gathered on the sidewalk, staring at me. There's Malik with Alba standing shyly by his side.

As if it's not weird enough to see Alba looking shy, my fucking nieces stand there with their mates, grinning at me. They've all got milkshakes in their hands. Bitches. Just teasing me with all that creamy goodness while I haul shit around like a draft mule.

"Get it, girl!" Thea shouts.

"Crush it, Lou!" Morgan shouts right after her.

Laughing at the ridiculousness of it all, I turn to Bellami with a smile. "Okay, friend, tell me exactly where you want this to go."

CHAPTER FIFTEEN
DIRK

Connall and I jog around the long line of shops to the corner and back around.

He laughs as we join up with the crowd, all focused on Louanna and her work in the gnome village. He stares around at the gathered wolves, centaurs; even most of the pegasi herd is here. Not to mention Louanna's nieces and their mates. Thea and Shepherd cheer wildly, louder than the rest of the crowd combined. Ohken holds his mate, Wren, while she claps excitedly. And Abe rests his cheek on top of Morgan's head as she shouts for Lou.

My family. These monsters are my family. They don't really know it yet, haven't comprehended it the way they will. But they're Lou's favorite people in the world, which means they're mine too.

I glance up at Connall, who's staring at Lou, green eyes hungrily eating her up. When I step closer, our thighs brushing against one another's, his smile grows wicked, barely withheld behind a smirk to rival mine. We made progress tonight in our conversation.

Lou roars as she drags the log around under Bellami's gruff

directives. Connall rears back and howls for her, his wolf's deeper tone laced through the noise. Other wolves take up the call, their howls echoing off the glass fronts of the homes built above the shops in the Hollow.

The noise brings goosebumps to the surface of my skin, watching my mate yowl for our woman. When he drops his hands by his sides, his fingers brush mine. He said he wanted to instigate physical contact with me…is that what he's doing?

Was it purposeful? I was careful tonight to be flirtatious but not romantically touchy in public. I'm not embarrassed, not by a long shot. I long for the day when I can hold both their hands and walk them around to show them off. But it surprised Connall when I initially shared my interest in him. I can't rush too quickly with him.

I curl the tips of my fingers into his palm, still focused on Lou. He shifts to the foot closest to me, his hand curving around mine.

He's holding my hand. He's holding. My. Hand!

I resist the urge to crow in victory or slap my jewel, turn us to wind and snatch Louanna from the gnome village. I could. Despite Bellami's earlier comment, my boss hasn't rescinded my portal override access yet. She will; she's jest waitin' for the right moment to do it in an embarrassing way. I know Evenia well enough for that. But I don't worry about it. No.

Instead, I shout for my hard-working mate as she, with a bevy of gnomes beneath the log, manages to drag it on top of the first story. She bends in half, looking exhausted as she flops over the log, only to be shrieked at by Bellami and the rest of the crew. He quickly shoos her away as the crowd shouts in triumph for her.

Connall pulls me up the sidewalk, but we drift apart as the crowd jostles around us.

I ache to touch his warmth again. But there's time. Tonight, I'm moving us another step forward. And then another. And another. Until they're both fully mine and one another's. I won't rest until it's done. This is the most important hunt of my life, right here.

Lou drags one foot in front of the other until she reaches the edge of the new village. Stepping carefully out, she raises both fists high in victory, laughing as her nieces crowd around her and crush her in their embrace.

Amber eyes close as she hugs her girls, then open again and move around the crowd until they land on Connall and me. I shoot my woman a quick wink as Connall backs up a step until our thighs are touchin' again. I can't hold back a smirk as Lou's pink-dusted cheeks grow a darker shade of rose.

Her boss, Malik, high-fives her when she parts from the Hector triplets. The crowd begins to slowly dissipate, the gnomes still hard at work behind Lou. Connall and I move with the crowd until we're reunited with her.

Thea glances up at me from her mate's embrace. "Dirk, what a surprise to see you here." Her deadpan tone always makes me laugh. Ever the detective, this woman.

"Jest here for my woman, as yeh know, Althea."

She rolls her eyes but laughs at me. The Hector triplets have been front and center to my pursuing antics for a bit now.

Morgan rubs Lou's back, playing with the long end of her lovely braid. "Lou, honey, we're headed to Bad Axe to get nachos. Abe challenged me to an axe-throwing competition, so I obviously have to win that. Come with us?"

Lou's eyes flick to mine. Ah, my woman needs a rescue.

"I'm stealin' Lou for the night," I say with a wicked grin. "Got a special somethin' planned fer her."

"Oh," Morgan says with a sly smile. "Well," her eyes flash at Lou, "I can't wait to hear all about it later."

"I promise to provide excellent fodder for yer next girlie Green Bean date." I reach for Louanna through the crowd, and without hesitation, she places her delicate hand in mine and allows me to pull her to me.

"Green Bean for breakfast!" Lou shouts to the triplets as I grab Connall's hand and slap my gem, dissolving us into pure, beautiful element. We whirl away from the crowd and off into the night.

I dance them through the clouds and up along the ward ceiling, grabbing current after current until we come to a tiny wildflower meadow tucked in the rolling hills behind Abemet and Morgan's castle. He already knows we'll be coming here tonight, so we'll be undisturbed. Nobody else comes to this part o' the woods.

Twisting through the clouds, I skirt us underneath them, marveling at the sentiment I read from both mates. Connall's aura in wind form is all bright, steady joy, where Lou's is unfiltered shock and awe. I never knew wind dancing with them would be so thrilling. Nothing could have prepared me fer it. But spinning along with their auras held close is a pleasure I'll never stop thanking the gods for.

I guide us slowly away from the clouds, grabbing a pale blue current as it spirals down toward the meadow to rustle the flowers. When I shift us back into monster form, Lou sways off her feet, but Connall catches her easily around the waist, holding her to his much larger body.

Her hands move to cover his as she looks up and back at him. Her position highlights her elegant neck, freckles dotting the smooth skin. I cannae help myself. Reaching out, I brush my fingertips down her throat to a spot that's just begging for a gift I made her and haven't given her yet.

I don't realize I'm staring so hard until Lou brushes her fingers over mine. "You alright? I've never seen you so serious-looking."

I nod and beam at them both, tapping the spot with my forefinger. "I've a gift for yeh, my sweet. This is the perfect spot for it."

Connall's brows go straight up as he looks over Lou's shoulder, brushing his fingers over the same spot.

"I have one for you as well, Wolf." I smile. "Soon, I'll give yeh both the first of many gifts, and it'd be my honor for yeh both to wear them."

His cheeks and neck go red, but he nods.

Stepping close, I press Louanna between us as I lift my hands to touch the same divot at the base of Connall's throat.

Lou rests her head against his chest as his eyes find mine. A soft smile turns his plush lips upward. I can't wait to taste those lips.

"Is there a significance to this specific gift you have planned?"

Connall's question is fair, so I take a step back and gesture to the picnic blanket and spread of snacks I brought here earlier this evening.

Nodding, I sink onto the blanket and reach for them. Lou takes my hand, Connall positioning himself next to her.

"To an elemental sylph, it means yeh've been identified as someone's mate."

"I see," Lou says, "this is the sylph version of putting a ring on it."

I cock my head to the side. "A ring?"

Connall saves the day with a smile. "Humans often gift rings to their intended when they formally ask to become mates."

"This confuses me," I admit. "Yer mates or yer not."

"Humans aren't like that," Louanna says with a shake of her head. "While we believe in soul mates, it's different for everyone. Plenty of humans marry, which is our version of a mating ceremony, but about sixty percent divorce, or split."

Horror and revulsion streak through me as I shake my head. "That'll no' be happenin' here, Louanna. This isn't a test to see if we work. We're fated, else my—"

"Easy, Dirk." Connall's tone is soothing and deep. "We both know Lou was always meant to be in the monster world."

She glances at him, her smirk falling into a thoughtful smile.

I struggle to wrap my mind around the concept of finding yer mate and then splitting from them. As it is now, playing the slow an' steady approach with them is a struggle. Mostly, I want to move Louanna into Connall's treehouse and spend all my time learning more about them.

I want to feed them, cuddle them, love them, support them. I am going to be an absolute menace of a mate, constantly in their business. I want to know every fookin' thing there is to know about them so I can memorize it forever.

"Dirk, you look distraught." Louanna's throaty voice breaks through my rushing thoughts, bringing me back to the present.

I blink away the bad thoughts, focusing on my mates. Connall sits with his big legs crossed at the ankle, leaning back on his hands. Lou sits next to him, legs tucked neatly under her body, her braid hanging like a rope over her shoulder.

"I brought us here to have a wee chat," I share. "There's mead and cheese in the basket as well. But now that my intentions are fully in the open with the both of yeh, I'd like to hear your thoughts on the subject."

Lou snorts out a laugh. "How many times did I tell you to stop following me over the last month, Dirk? Are you finally going to listen?"

I scrunch my nose. "If yeh mean I should stop staring at yeh every night while yer sleep, or appearing to help yeh with closing time at Alkemi, I could, but why would I? You love it."

Her smile stills as she glances at Connall. "Perhaps we don't like being peeped upon." Yet I sense no real anger in her words. She's simply making a point and playing with me.

I glance between them. Connall's silent, ever watchful.

"What do yeh think, Wolf? Yeh asked me to stop spying on you. How does it feel?"

His cheeks go pink, the blush spreading down into his dark tee. I want to rip the fabric open and see how far that pretty tint extends.

"It's good when I'm in therapy sessions. Those are designed to be private. But every time the wind blows, I wonder if it's you."

"'Tis not," I say fervently. "I promised yeh I wouldnae continue after our last chat. I can be...respectful."

Lou grins. "The monster world works a bit differently from the human world. For both of you, there are mating rituals and fated mates, and when you know, you know. It's not quite like that for humans. We could believe we know someone is our person, and that could turn out to be wrong. It's not foolproof, not at all. And spying is *highly* frowned upon."

"Yuck," I blurt out without meaning to. I quickly tack on an apology as Connall laughs.

When Louanna looks slightly affronted, I lean forward and place my hand on her knee. "I jest mean, I cannae imagine not knowing with absolute certainty that yer mine, Louanna."

"Oh, I don't know," she says with a haughty lift of her chin. "You could be wrong. I'm very bratty. You might hate that."

Connall lets out a soft growl, turning his attention to her. "As it turns out, I'm a fan of bratty."

Her cheeks go pink as she turns to look at him.

Shifting forward, I get in her space, hovering my mouth just above hers. "Are yeh worried we'll have no sexual chemistry, Louanna? Because I can assure yeh, it won't be an issue."

She looks between Connall and me, her voice soft when she speaks. "Are we doing this? Trying to figure out the whole throuple thing?"

"I think so," Connall states simply. "We're gonna talk more about it before anything else happens, though."

She and I wait patiently as he looks between us.

He leans back onto his hands and focuses on Lou first. "I want to date you, Lou," he says confidently. "Take you out, spend time together. I'd like to have time alone with you as well as time for all of us together. How do you feel about that?"

"Definitely," she says. "Makes sense. I assume it would be the same for all of us...right? Dirk and I will date separately too. But what about..." her voice trails off as she looks between us.

"We'll date too," Connall says confidently. "We talked about it earlier."

"Oof, to be a fly on that wall," Lou says with a huffy laugh.

Connall grins at me, then refocuses on her. "Does the idea of us together do things to you, Sweetheart?"

"Yeah," she says breathlessly. "It always has." She glances shyly at me. "It's part of why I held you at length for a while, to be honest. I wasn't sure I was ready, but also..."

Connall's nostrils flare. "You were drawn to me too."

When she nods, he crooks a finger at her. "Come here, Lou."

To see them together will be the ultimate pleasure.

She hesitates, looking from Connall to me and back again, uncertainty obvious in the furrow of her brow and the way she nips her lip.

"Go, Louanna," I encourage, "or I'll put yeh on him myself."

The heady scent of arousal saturates the air as she gives me a last look, then shuffles closer to Connall.

"Right here," Connall encourages again, patting his lap.

Lou moves delicately, lifting a leg to straddle Connall's tree trunk thighs. His eyes eat her up, moving from her face to her neck and chest and lower. Finally, they move to me as his smile becomes a wicked smirk.

"Dirk, would you like to tell me what I should do to her?"

Oh. *Oh.*

My wolf is invitin' me to direct them. Good, he senses what I like, then, which is to be bossy.

I crawl forward on the blanket until I'm seated with a good view of them. Lou squirms in Connall's lap, looking between us as she grabs her braid and starts twirling the end of it.

"Kiss her," I command. "Put that pretty mouth to good use, Wolf."

Green eyes move to Lou's. "I'd be delighted to. Lou, may I?"

She glances at me again. She's nervous. It's obvious in the way she sits tensely in his lap. This is new and different, and it'll take some work for her inner brat to fully show. She needs gentle, thorough encouragement. Very, very fucking thorough.

"Lou, I need your consent." Connall's deep voice is like a calm, cool river running between us. If I'm the fiery spark of our trio, he is undoubtedly the bedrock of our foundation.

"Umm, that's fine," she says after a moment, placing her hands on her thighs. Her fingers tremble, but Connall chuckles.

"Too many fookin' clothes," I grit out.

Connall grins but keeps his focus on Lou, green eyes scanning her face. "I agree. Take your shirt off."

She spins to face me, chest heaving, but Connall places a finger under her chin, redirecting her to him. "Take your shirt off, Lou."

"Why?"

"Because I want to scent you."

Heat flares through me as she grinds against his lap. It takes everything in me not to straddle his legs behind her and rip the fabric from her shoulders so he can smell every inch of our woman. I want her to experience him, the soft drag of that pretty mouth and sharp teeth.

Lou's chest heaves, but she grips her tee and pulls it over her head, revealing a soft-looking lace bra.

Another groan leaves me. I fookin' love lace.

Connall's eyes eat her up. The hand under her chin drops to her shoulder as he sits upright, bringing their upper bodies closer together. He pulls her arms up around his neck. I hold back a groan as her fingers curl into the hair at his nape.

His fingers trail a path along her exposed collarbone to her bra strap. He tugs it down her shoulder as his left hand slides up her back to the base of her neck.

She pants softly when he dips down and presses his mouth and nose to her collarbone, breathing in quietly. They let out matching groans that make my dick throb, precum pooling on the tip as I watch our mate explore her.

Lou's head falls to one side as Connall drags his mouth along her collarbone and to the hollow at the base of her throat. I watch in rapt fascination at the way his lips move over her skin, teasing, taunting, enjoying. He cocks his head to the side, closing his mouth over her throat, biting and pulling. That move pulls a groan so needy, so desperate from Lou, I spurt in my pants at the sound of it. Connall grins into her skin, eyes flicking to mine as he nibbles a torturous path up her throat to a spot just below her ear.

"Delicious," he murmurs. "Your scent is heaven, Sweetheart."

Oh my fuck, that nickname. I want to be called the very same thing. I've jest decided.

I shift onto my knees, getting closer as Connall's lips trace a path up Lou's neck to her chin. She practically vibrates in his lap, her need so tangible, I drop my mouth open to taste her arousal in the air.

Connall wraps his right hand around Lou's throat and squeezes, forcing her to look into his eyes. He scans her face like he'll never get enough time staring at her, like she's the most beautiful thing he's ever seen. Then his eyes shut, and his mouth closes around her lower lip. He sucks the plump thing, parting just long enough for me to see his pink tongue swiping over her lip.

Lou cries out, but in a rush of movement, Connall swallows the noise, slanting his mouth over hers. He devours her, his lips demanding as he holds her to him, his mouth claiming every inch of hers. And Lou goes wild, panting and groaning at every pass of his lips over hers.

Their kiss grows frenetic, out of control, until she's tearing at his shirt, ripping it open to reveal a broad chest covered in tattoos and auburn hair. She digs her fingers in, clawing at his pecs as he growls, his wolf evident in his tone. His eyes snap open as he parts from her, big chest heaving with his wolf's emerald shade glowing.

"Oh my gods," Lou murmurs, both hands flat on his pecs. "That was...I have no words."

"Hot as fook," I offer. "Delicious to watch. Please don't stop."

Connall grins and bends forward, kissing Lou more slowly. His lips make a tender, soft exploration of hers, as if he has all the time in the world and intends to learn every inch of that sinful mouth.

His hand slides to her bra, and he plays with the clasp, thrumming his fingers on her back. Green eyes focus on Lou. "May I?"

She tosses me a fiery, teasing look over her shoulder.

I move behind her, straddling Connall's knees as I slide my hands up her back to meet his. "Allow me." I press a kiss to her freckled shoulder.

Her scent explodes across my senses, sharpened by her obvious arousal. I'm too hot to move slowly, so I brush my mouth along her shoulder and up her neck, nipping at the spot Connall just kissed.

"Fuck," she grits out, throwing her head to one side to grant me better access. My lips have a mind of their own as I bite, taunt and tease my way back down her neck. I kiss every beautiful, freckled inch I can reach as my fingers expertly unclasp her bra. She gasps when it comes loose.

My eyes drift over her shoulder to Connall's face, his wolf's luminescent shade shining as he licks his lips, focusing on her chest.

"This is a little unfair," I admit, sliding the other bra strap down her shoulder and off her arm to tease him. "I've been spying at her bedroom window for a while. I've seen these breasts dozens of times, and they are fookin' glorious, Connall."

He shakes his head but grins at me. "You are something else, Dirk."

"Mate," I correct. Here in this meadow, we can be free to

behave how we want. I need them both hooked and in love, and then we'll do all of this publicly.

I don't push Connall to respond, to call me what we are to one another. Instead, I drop Louanna's bra around her waist, exposing her firm, bounteous breasts to him.

He sucks in a ragged breath, hungry eyes exploring every inch of her as I kiss a path along her neck.

Bringing my lips to her ear, I nibble tenderly at it. "Look at him, Louanna. I told yeh he'd be enthralled, that he'd be besotted with yeh. I was right. Can yeh feel his wolf's focus? What if he put that pretty mouth on yer body?"

Connall's lips curl back into a soft snarl, mouth dropping open as his hands run up Louanna's back, pulling her flush with his chest. I nearly groan watching her soft body smashed to his. His rough hands explore her skin, running down one arm and up her neck to grip it. It's like he can't get enough of holding her, and I know how that feels. I wanted her in my arms long before she agreed to be in them.

Connall uses his grip on her to tilt her back enough that he can bend down and suck one peaked nipple between his lips. They moan at the same time, all ragged lust as he explores her with patient, thorough intensity. Her head leans back against my chest as I watch our wolf. A soft-looking pink tongue laps at Lou's nipple until it's swollen and flushed, then he moves across her chest to the other one, giving it the same treatment.

"Does he feel good?" I growl into her ear. "Like you could come just from his tongue, Louanna?"

She bites her lip and moans, arching to press her neck to my mouth.

She wants more.

Gods, I've waited so long for her to ask me to touch her, to invite me to play with her. I've schemed and planned, and it's working out.

I hover my open mouth over the side of her neck as Connall

bites his way up to the other side. Teasing her with my tongue, I close my lips around her skin and suck. We're pressed so tightly together with our wolf at her front and me at her back.

Yet I'm not pushing my mates any further tonight. This was about getting somewhere private so we could explore new things and discuss our foundation. They're doing so well. Shifting, I stare as Connall bites his way along her shoulder, rubbing her arm. His brows are furrowed with pleasure; he's intensely focused on her.

But out here where there's nobody to see, I want him focused on me too. So I dip down and bite a spot right next to his mouth. For a moment, we're practically breathing the same air as I swirl my tongue over Louanna's skin. She moans, writhing between us. She fits so perfectly there. I flick my eyes to his, and he's full green, staring intensely at me. He removes his mouth from her shoulder, head cocked to the side. I consider leaning forward to kiss him, but decide a tease is better.

Licking a path down to Louanna's shoulder, I swirl my tongue over her skin. Nipping softly, I watch my wolf. His focus falls to my mouth, nostrils flaring. Is he tantalized? Jealous? Getting hornier by the moment?

I have my answer when he dips his head and follows my trail, his mouth so close to mine.

My wolf is very, very interested.

CHAPTER SIXTEEN
LOU

The morning after our date, I have no words. I'm officially out of words. Words don't even exist to explain how amazing last night was. I throw my braid over my back as I leave the Annabelle Inn to head toward the Galloping Green Bean to meet my nieces. I need a girl date stat.

Because last night? Last night was crazy fun and insanely intense.

By the time I get to the Green Bean, I'm a bundle of pent-up nerves. Pulling the doors open, I step inside the retro-themed turquoise and red diner. Looking around, I find my nieces and Lola in a booth at the far end. I wave to Alba, holding back a wink. She and Malik have been on at least one date now, and I can't wait to see how their story turns out.

When I slip into the booth next to Lola, she leans down and sucks in a deep breath. She pulls back with a satisfied-looking smirk.

"I ran across the girls on the way over and they dragged me here to get the details." The shifter princess' smile goes feral.

Across the table, my niece Thea makes the "what gives?" gesture, rolling her shoulders, her blue eyes wide. "And?"

Lola bumps me with her hip. "I'm guessing things happened. Am I right?"

I turn to look at my friend. "Are you telling me you just sniffed me to see if things happened?"

She grins. "Your aura's a very lazy red this morning. Usually means sex."

Thea leans across the table with a wicked grin, waving her fork at me. "Spit it out, Lou. Every damn thing."

"I bet Dirk was an absolute gentleman," my niece Wren says kindly, lifting a coffee cup to her pink-painted lips. She's fucking glowing. Love her so much.

"Well," I hedge. "They both were."

Lola takes a sip of her coffee with a little chuckle.

Thea and Wren pull in matching shocked-sounding breaths.

"It's everybody with everybody," I confirm. "Dirk and Connall." Thea and Wren stare at me, open-mouthed.

Thea makes heart eyes at me. "Aww, Auntie," she says, "that's the cutest thing I ever heard of! You came here to rescue us, and now you're gonna get double-teamed by two hotties. Things have a way of working out."

My mouth drops open, and then a hilarious giggle erupts from me and Lola at the same time. The laugh breaks the ice, and the entire story comes out from start to finish. It feels so good to share with my girls and my friend my thoughts and feelings, and how on board with this I am.

So far.

"Mama would have been happy for you," Wren says quietly when I finish. She sips her latte, bright eyes wrinkling at the corners as she smiles over the cup at me.

Thinking about my sister Caroline sends a rush of emotion through me. She would have *loved* Dirk and Connall. I go misty pondering that. Next to me, Lola puts her arm around my shoulder and pulls me closer to her.

"I never had the privilege of meeting her," she says quietly, "but if she was your sister and the girls' mother, I bet she was a real badass."

"She was," Thea confirms, looking at Wren who's still smiling at me. After a moment, Thea snort laughs. "And she'd have been hellsa proud of you for locking down *two* hotties."

That makes me chuckle. I don't know if proud is the right word, but Caroline would have understood. She was the only person in my life growing up besides the triplets who *got* me.

"Breakfast" runs until nearly lunchtime. Eventually, Alba stomps back and forth, letting us know she has other customers who "wanna eat sometime this century."

I stand in front of the Green Bean and watch my nieces leave. Thea's headed to meet her mate, Shepherd, to do security rounds of the haven. Wren's off to meet her mate, Ohken the troll, to work a shift at the General Store. And Morgan's probably off to have sex with her hot vampire husband, if I'm being honest. I've barely even seen him since they got mated. I don't think she lets him leave the bedroom.

Nerves fill me as I consider my afternoon appointment with Connall—our first appointment for not-therapy therapy.

Half an hour after I parted ways with the girls, my hands shake as I knock on the solid wood door to Connall's office. He's tucked behind Pack Gem, the shifters' jewelry store on the main thoroughfare. This is likely a terrible idea, going to therapy with the wolf I kissed last night, who carried me home and tucked me into bed. That's the last thing I remember—Dirk standing watch as Connall pulled cushy blankets up to my neck.

Am I seriously pursuing two men? Or, rather, allowing them both to pursue me? The reality is I always wanted to be part of a mystical, ethereal world. It's why I've always worked in occult shops and been drawn to that lifestyle. Now I'm living in a hidden monster town, and a wolf shifter and elemental sylph are my…mates?

It feels too good to be true.

I'm pondering that when the door swings open, and Connall's seductive scent hits me full force. My cheeks heat at the knowing smile on his face. Today, he's wearing a tee that's fitted around his chest and arms but hangs loosely over his abs.

I saw those abs last night. All million of them, covered in sexy wolfish tattoos.

"Lou, everything okay?" His tone says he knows exactly what I'm thinking about.

When I manage to drag my eyes to his face, his smirk is a full-on grin.

"This is probably a terrible idea," I blurt out. "The therapy, I mean," I tack on before he thinks I mean he himself is a horrible idea.

He reaches out and grabs my hand, pulling me over the stoop and into the front room. "It's alright to be nervous about therapy, Lou. Our track is certainly unconventional."

"You can say that again," I mutter as I drop his hand and stare around in wonder. His space is one giant room with a retro turquoise and cream kitchen on the left side. The right side has a sitting area with mismatched plush chairs of all sorts and a tall brick fireplace. Windows along the back wall look out onto an enclosed porch area. I think I see the corner of a canvas, but it's hard to be sure at first glance.

"Come to the kitchen," he says, turning and padding into the depths of the space.

I follow him into a bright kitchen full of pale turquoise retro-style appliances. He opens the fridge door and retrieves a tray of cheese, crackers and a few spreads. When he withdraws two chilled glasses and a bottle of something pale that looks like wine, I laugh, shooting him a wry look. "Is that champagne?"

He smiles. "Therapy and drinking don't really go hand in hand in the monster world. If they do in the human world, I'd love to know more about that. But, no, it's not champagne. It's a special nonalcoholic mead Ohken makes for me. It's been proven that having a drink while at therapy can help soothe your nerves. The snacks serve the same purpose. And I've discovered as a therapist that sometimes the best sessions are the ones where we don't sit awkwardly in chairs staring at each other."

"Are you gonna take notes about me?"

Connall's laugh echoes in the small space. Gods, it's so deep and delightful. I could jump into that laugh and get lost. I've never heard a manlier laugh in my entire life.

"Yeah, but I take them between sessions so that, during our session, I can give you my full attention."

I tug at my collar. The mental image of Connall sitting there scribbling notes about me makes me simultaneously anxious and horny. What if he wore glasses? Gods, that's hot.

He places a piece of cheese on a cracker and hands it to me.

"I want to reiterate that we can in no way consider this real therapy, Lou. I couldn't date a client. So let's just eat and drink and talk about how you're feeling. I want to help, if I can, even if I'm only able to give you coping mechanisms."

"Agreed." I munch on the cracker as he grabs another and tosses it into his mouth.

It's companionable being with him like this. Easy.

"How are you feeling today?" he questions.

"About any specific topic?" I slide my eyes to his.

"Whatever's top of mind," he encourages. "We can talk about Leighton if you like, or about your nieces. We could even talk about last night." His smile returns as heat flares through me.

"Not last night," I say in a rush. "Not that it wasn't lovely, I just think I'd feel awkward talking about it like I need therapy because of it?"

He laughs. "Noted. Then what would you like to discuss?"

"Coping mechanisms."

He pushes his glass to the side and leans over the pale aqua countertop onto his forearms. "To cope with what?"

I hunch over the countertop, wondering if it would be weird

to slide my hands across it and hold his. "Guilt," I finally admit. "I can logically tell myself that what I did to Leighton wasn't my fault, that I was a victim too. But Leighton's gone, and I'm here, and I don't know how to get my emotions in line with the logic part."

He keeps the soft smile, even though I just brought up his dead friend. "Lou, are you familiar with the concept of moral injury?"

I shrug. "Sounds familiar, but I'm not sure I could explain it."

"Essentially, it's applied to any number of emotions or sensations that result from having done something that's contradictory to your moral code, in this instance, your part in Leighton's murder."

Murder. Oh my gods, he thinks I'm a murderer.

"This concept is common among soldiers who've gone through war," he continues. "Even if they signed up to fight, going into battle and killing is another thing entirely. The number of monsters I've counseled who fought in various wars is too high to count."

I blink away errant thoughts as I process what he's saying. Looking up into those green eyes, I try to understand.

Connall rounds the island and grabs my hand. "Come with me. I want to show you something."

Twisting my fingers through his, I allow him to pull me through the room and down a short hall into a sunny porch-like area. A singular canvas sits on a stand in one corner. Buckets of paint cover every surface with giant containers full of brushes.

"Are you a painter?" The words croak out of me as I imagine Connall painting.

"I am," he says, "but it's also a therapy method that works really well for some. That's not what I wanted to show you though." He leans down to a half bookshelf and grabs a thick leather tome. When there's nowhere to set it down, he grabs three buckets of paint and moves them somewhere else, balancing them precariously on top of others. This entire room is one painty disaster waiting to happen.

I love it. I never want to leave.

Connall drums his fingers along the book's cover. "When Hearth HQ designed the haven system, they knew we needed a place for those monsters so scarred from all the wars that happened before, they needed extra help. There's a haven called Shadowsurf, named by its occupants, for those monsters."

Immediately, I picture a leper colony. Or that scene from *Firefly* where the crazy people-eating monsters swarm the town and drag everyone away.

"It's a wonderful place to be and visit," Connall offers, opening the book. A black-and-white photograph of a variety of monsters stares back at me. Their arms are slung around one another's waists, and they're all smiling.

"In order to gain access to Shadowsurf, you must have experienced moral injury—an accidental death, wartime, something like that. And the whole concept of this haven is being around those who can understand what you went through. I've referred many clients there."

I flip the page to see an array of images, all depicting monsters in groups. Talking, playing skyball, sitting in a group with eyes closed like they're meditating.

Glancing up at Connall, I frown. "Do you think I need to go here?"

He smiles back at me, reaching out to tuck my braid over my shoulder. "I'm not suggesting you need to do anything, Lou, just that it exists, because, what you're going through? Others have been through it before. If they can get through it, you can too."

Tears prick my eyes. I want to hug him. Scratch that. I really *need* a hug. Before I can talk myself out of it, I push into his arms and bury my face in his chest.

Connall's purr is immediate, deep and rolling as it envelops me in comfort. Big, warm hands come to my back. One slides all the way around to hold my waist. The other moves up into my hair, gripping the base of my neck.

I've never particularly loved being manhandled. I think I'm just so bratty and independent, and I never had a partner I trusted to take care of me. And thinking about it now, trust is something people have to earn from me.

But I trust Connall. Implicitly. Completely. I've never met a steadier, more calming person. So I sink into his pecs and say nothing as he purrs and holds me tight. The rolling warmth of the sound relaxes my muscles one by one. I never want to leave the comfort of his embrace. Eventually, I glance at the clock and realize we've been standing here for nearly half an hour, and my session is just forty-five minutes long.

"Gods, I'm sorry." I pull away from him. "I didn't realize I needed a hug that badly, and I almost used up our whole time."

Connall smiles at me. "Hugging is an essential part of wolf culture, but not at all for any other type of monster therapist. So, consider yourself a wolf, Lou."

"Wish I were," I mutter. "Being just a human is so boring. I'm jealous of the triplets actually being witches."

The moment I say it, I realize how catty that sounds. I adore my nieces, would give my life for them any day. My loyalty literally knows no depths. But I *am* jealous of their power. Not that I don't want them to have it. I just want it too.

"Sounds like something we should discuss very soon," Connall says with a gentle smile. "You're perfect to me as you are, Lou. Being who you are is magic enough."

I risk a glance at him as tears fill my eyes again.

I want to kiss him. Stepping closer, I press my body to his, glad he insisted we not call this therapy.

"I want to kiss you," I admit.

"A lovely idea, but most decidedly not therapy," he says with a laugh.

I shrug. "I dunno. It might not be your typical therapy, but that doesn't mean it can't be therapeutic." I look up at him. "We should try it, for science."

His mouth drops open, then zips shut as his wolf's brighter green shade overtakes his eyes.

"It might get out of hand," he warns.

"What does your instinct tell you to do?" I'm pushing him a little. But I want to see that side of Connall that's not so professional. Therapy shmerapy.

"It might be rough," he says softly. "And I don't know if you need rough right now."

Heat sizzles through me, my pussy clenching around nothing as I imagine Connall getting rough with me.

His nostrils flare, and he sucks in a deep, slow breath. "Maybe I'm wrong, and rough is exactly what you need."

"We should find out," I manage, my heart beating like a drum.

His lips tilt into a delicious smile. Then he moves so fast, I can't even track him.

In a heartbeat, he has me flipped against the bookshelf, pinned there by his body. His fingers close around my wrists, and he plants them on the book in front of us.

"Don't move your hands, Lou." His breath is warm and ragged against my ear.

He's so much bigger than me, so much taller. On instinct, I let my head fall back against his broad, warm chest. His hands come to my waist and lift me off the ground, bringing me up high enough to slide onto my knees on the top of the low bookcase.

"Better," he grits out, splaying his fingers over my stomach. He moves them up between my breasts until he reaches my throat. His grip is unforgiving, tiny stars dancing behind my eyelids as he pulls my head to the side and buries his nose just beneath my ear.

"Dirk asked me to work with you for weeks, and this is why I said no." His tone is full of his wolf's deeper bass. "Because I want you with a desperation that claws at my insides. I want to be a caveman, Lou, and fuck you right here on top of my books. Then I wanna feed you and drag you to my home and fuck you again. I put together a treatment plan of things for us to discuss, and it did not include playing around like this. This is in no fucking way anything remotely resembling therapy."

"We're complicated," I wheeze as his teeth close softly around the side of my neck. "Give me my fucking kiss."

He bites harder, but all it does is send heat flaring between my thighs, my clit throbbing in time with my heartbeat.

"Now," I demand, trying to rock my ass against Connall's body.

"Or what?" he growls, raking his teeth down the line of my neck. "You didn't give me a timeframe for it."

I gasp and clutch at the hand still holding my throat. "I wanted it the moment I asked!"

Connall laughs, and it's then I know what he means about being dominant. He won't give me what I want without the words. He's getting off on this fucking edging. My first instinct is to be bratty about it, and he said he loved bratty women, so I snarl and shove him away. "If you won't give it to me, I'm leaving."

He laughs again, but his fingers only tighten. "Good, Lou. Get mouthy so I can punish you like the brat you are. Throw my paints around. Make a fucking mess. Taunt me. Because what happens when you're in trouble will be so fucking delicious."

Anger and heat war inside my mind. But I almost laugh at the idea he gave me. Grabbing one of the open cans of paint, I toss it at the wall. It hits with a clang, paint splashing across the white surface.

Connall's fingers tighten as he growls in my hair, "I was kidding about the paint, Lou."

But I'm fired up now. He pushed me, and now he's gonna get me in full Lou form. Plus, we sell a cleaning potion at Alkemi so I can sort this out pretty quickly once we're done. I'm just gonna have fun making a damn mess.

I lash out and grab another can. Before I can toss it, his hand comes to my wrist, closing around it. But he's not quite quick enough, and the paint sloshes down the side and over both of our hands.

Snarling, I shove us both backwards and slip off the bookshelf. Connall matches my snarl, staring at me with eyes full of heat. Purple paint drips from his hand and the flecks of the first color spatter across the bridge of his nose.

I give him a superior look as I whip a hand out and brush three cans onto the floor. "Oops." Batting my eyelashes, I step into the paint and stomp my feet, sending splashes of it all over the books and floor.

Connall slips both hands into his jeans pockets, watching dispassionately.

I shoot him a taunting look. "The paint was your idea, Connall. How far do I go?"

His lips curl into a wicked grin. "As far as you like, Lou. You seem to be having fun, and every can you drop is an extra punishment. The more, the better. I'll have my fun when you're done having yours."

I grin. "You keep saying punishment, but so far all I see is—"

Paint-covered hands are around my throat before I even finish the sentence, green eyes flashing with lust. "Drop another, and another, Lou. Please. Because the punishment I have in mind is gonna be so fuckin' beautiful."

I reach to my left and grab a small can of yellow, tossing it right at his shirt. It hits and splatters. He straightens and pulls the shirt over his head, revealing miles of taut abs and pale skin dotted with tiny freckles.

"Actually, that's enough," he commands. When I reach for yet another can, he squeezes my throat so hard, black stars fill my vision. "I said, that's enough, Louanna."

His use of my full name has my pussy clenching on nothing.

Delicate nostrils flare as he pushes me downward. We sink to the floor in a heap. Connall rocks back on his heels, still holding me tight.

"Get on your knees, Lou. You're gonna suck me off, and when you think you'll choke, you're gonna take another inch for every can of paint you tossed."

I stare in surprise, my mouth falling open as he reaches down with his free hand. He unzips his jeans and pulls out his dick, and, fuck me, he's hard. The thick knot at the base is partially swollen, his tip dripping with precum.

"Good, stare at it, Lou. Because you're about to give me the best head of my life."

When I falter, he strokes his cock languidly. "Pick a safe word, pretty girl."

"Red," I offer. It's easy to remember. Gods help me because I didn't come here for this kind of therapy. But right now, this sort of thing feels like *exactly* what I need.

He drops his grip on my throat. "Good. Now lean forward and take me into your mouth, Lou."

Gods, I can't resist the temptation. It occurs to me to brat it up one more time and deny him, but I think he'd just wrap that big hand around my braid and make me.

Leaning forward, I plant both hands on his muscular thighs and hover just above his bobbing cock. "What do you like?" I ask at the last minute.

"Licking, sucking, nuzzling, biting," he says, a muscle in his jaw working overtime. "Just touch it."

Grinning, I surge forward and take him to the back of my throat, sucking hard around his thick length. He's huge, and I can't fit much of him, but he doesn't seem to notice or care about that as a deep, desperate groan falls from his lips.

I pull off him and lick playfully around his tip, bringing one hand to his knot. The paint makes for a good lubricant, so I swirl it around the bulbous area, tightening and loosening my fingers. Connall snarls at me, precum dripping onto my tongue.

"Time for your punishment," he croons. "Take me to the back of your throat, Lou, and then we'll start counting inches."

Wait, is he fucking serious?

But he is, because he lifts off his heels long enough to bring my mouth down on his cock. He hits the back of my throat and grins. "You dropped six cans of paint, Lou. Think you can swallow six more inches of dick?"

I try to shake my head, but I'm stuffed too full.

There's no fucking way.

"One." His nostrils flare as black overtakes his iris. His hips work as he goes deeper, hitting the back of my throat and going just a bit farther. When I start to gag, he pauses. "Breathe, my bratty little female. In through your nose and out through your nose."

I do as he says, and the need to gag passes.

"Five more inches, Lou." He strokes my bangs away from my face.

His hips move again, teasing my throat as he fucks my mouth. I choke on dick as he slides farther in, growling softly.

"Naughty little girl," he murmurs. "Throwing your alpha's things around. You need a lesson. Take another inch."

I shake my head. I can't even speak around the mouthful of cock.

"Do it, my sweet girl," he commands. So I surge forward, lips and teeth inching closer to his knot.

"Mmm, Lou." His voice is ragged, husky with want. "I don't think today's the day you make up for all six paint cans, but look at you, you're taking your punishment so well."

I could cry with distress when he pulls his thick cock from between my lips. But when he grabs it and slaps my mouth with it, rubbing his tip along my sore lips, the brat in me rushes back. I nip at the tip, pinching it between my teeth.

The effect is immediate. Connall jerks and roars, and precum spurts onto my lips. "Fuck, Lou. You don't know how much it turns me on for you to get rough with me."

I feel powerful. Desired and beautiful and *powerful*. Surging forward, I take his cock into my mouth once more. But this time, I drag my teeth carefully down his length.

"Yes," he cries out. "Again, don't stop."

Opening my mouth, I slip him farther inside until I choke. In a flash, he flips us so my back is to the floor. His thighs come to either side of me as he bends down. I'm encased beneath him, and I've never felt lighter or safer than I do right now. Connall's eyes go wolfy green as he stares at me, his dick bobbing against my upper thighs. I shift onto my elbows, and he reaches one hand beneath my back to hold me up.

"Kiss me," I demand.

His smile grows wicked, something I need to see a lot more of from Connall. Because Connall's bedroom smile is utterly breathtaking.

He leans down and takes my mouth, his kiss rough and punishing. I'm still in trouble. And I love it.

The first swipe of his tongue is possessive and raw, like he's learning every inch of mine with his. He growls and deepens the kiss when there's a knock at the door.

Connall parts from me, glances down, and groans, pulling away. We look around the room and at each other as another knock echoes from the front door.

"Louanna, are yeh done?" Dirk's voice is muffled.

"Dirk," I manage. Thank fuck it's him and not Connall's next client, because I don't know how we're gonna clean up this mess.

Connall nods and helps me out of the pool of paint. He shoves his still-hard dick back in his pants, zips them, and then pads through the space to the front door. When he opens it, Dirk stands there with a serious expression. But the moment he sees Connall, it morphs into a wicked, wicked grin. He eyes the big alpha.

"Well, what do we have here?"

CHAPTER SEVENTEEN
CONNALL

This is a first for me. Sexually dominating a client only to be caught in the act. Paint drips down my body, my knot swollen, hard and uncomfortable. My wolf paces behind my breastbone, panting with the desire to get out and do something with all of this heat.

Our session went exactly where I worried it'd go, yet somehow I can't find it in me to be too concerned about that. It was what Lou wanted, and the way she reacts to me is so perfect, so natural.

She is perfect. Beyond perfect.

And maybe physical affection and interaction is at least *part* of what she needs along her healing journey.

Lou joins me in the doorway. Paint mats the hair on one side of her head, and her cheeks are flushed. Not to mention, she smells delicious, like she was just fucking around with me. It takes everything in me not to bury my nose in the crook of her freckle-covered neck and inhale. She smells like strawberry lemonade to me normally, but all riled up, the strawberry takes on a burnt, sugary edge that makes my mouth water.

Dirk beams at her, eyeing her paint-covered clothes and

hands. "Louanna, my sweet. I thought I might pick yeh up to find yeh'd spilled yer heart out to Connall and had a great session. Seems like yeh spilled something else."

She lifts her chin, that bratty nature rearing its head. "We were just doing some painting. Therapy and all that."

I can't hold back a grin. "Not therapy. Let's not call it that."

Dirk beams at her, rubbing one hand along his jawline. "Painting. Hmm. Last time I saw Connall paint with a client, his dick wasn't hard, my sweet."

Irritation snakes through me until Dirk turns to me with a serious look. "That was before I agreed to stop spying on yeh, Wolf. I haven't spied since that promise."

It's on the tip of my tongue to tell him "good boy," but I shouldn't have to thank him for *not* spying on me. His dark brows curl mischievously upward.

"Well, Wolf, don't let me stop yeh from tossing paint around. I'll happily stand in the corner and watch."

For a second, I think Lou might agree, based on a deepening of her strawberry lemonade scent. It goes hotter and silkier at the edges, spiked with pepper, caressing my senses. But she shakes her head, slapping Dirk on the chest with a paint-covered hand. Purple paint splatters his gem, but he beams like he couldn't be more thrilled.

His eyes flick to me. "Och, Connell. I can see why this woulda been fun. Perhaps I need therapy as well, if this is what we can do during it." His smirk becomes a full-on smile, his sharp teeth showing as he grins at me.

But his offer reminds me of something I've been thinking about.

I return his smile, then glance between him and Lou. "Would you both come to dinner at my place tonight? I'd love to cook for you, and for us all to get to know one another and talk a bit more. Last night, we didn't do as much of that as I'd have liked."

Lou's scent explodes hard, saturating the air. I glance at Dirk.

Can he scent her like I can? I'll admit to not knowing that much about elementals before him. Not that many of them elect to live within the haven system. Based on the desirous look on his face, he's reading her the way I do.

I shift from one foot to the other, trying to ease the pressure between my legs.

Lou looks up. "I promised Bellami I'd help him for a few hours this afternoon, but dinner sounds great." When she glances at Dirk, his lips split into a lascivious grin.

"I'm always available to the two o' you. So, whatever your question is, my answer will always be yes."

Lou rolls her eyes, but pink dusts her cheeks. Chuckling, Dirk swipes his fingers through the paint dripping down his chest. He reaches forward and scribbles on her neckline as she shifts backward, trying to see what he's writing. I can't stop looking at the way his long fingers move over her soft skin. When he's done, I chuckle.

Lou frowns. "What did he do? What does it say?" She glances down again but can't see the writing from her angle. It's tucked at the base of her neck.

"Mine," I say on a growl, my wolf's tone threading through. He's at the front of our consciousness, watching for her reaction when I say it.

On cue, she blushes, the pink traveling over her cheeks and neck and, gods, down into her shirt. I want it off, want to see how far that pink shade goes.

She lifts her chin and crosses her arms over her chest. Doesn't she realize all that does is highlight how soft her large breasts look? Before I can think too hard, I lift a hand above her in the doorframe, backing her against the wood surface. She purses her lips and stares up at me as Dirk comes to my side, caging her in.

"Mine," I say again, nostrils flaring to drink her scent in. The way she smells caresses my mind. Not for the first time, I wonder, if I bit her, would we develop a bond the way wolves do? She has no wolf…so what does that mean for us?

She lifts her chin higher. "This sure is a lot of alpha male posturing. I'm human, you know, maybe I don't even like this." She waves her free hand between us.

A laugh rumbles out of me. Bending down, I bury my nose in the base of her throat and drag it up to her ear. "Your scent's calling you a liar, Lou."

Throaty, soft noises leave her lips.

"Yer made for this, Louanna," Dirk continues. "Made to take us separately, together, all in a tangle. Best to give in now, my beauty."

The moment he says "give in," she tenses and tightens. My woman's competitive, and giving in equals losing, in her mind. Breaking her bratty nature down in the bedroom will be so fun. That final submission is a beautiful thing. And it'll only happen if and when she trusts us—trusts me—enough to surrender control.

Parting my lips, I nibble a gentle, teasing path to where her neck and shoulder meet. When I reach that spot, the spot I'd bite to claim her, I nip harder. Lou jerks and gasps, head falling against the doorframe as she seeks to give me better access.

Now is the perfect time to pull away, to leave her wanting, to edge her so, when she comes to dinner, she'll be aching for more of me.

Of us.

She's soft and pliant against me, eyes fluttering closed as she waits for my lips.

Pulling my shirt over my shoulders, I step backward and smile at Dirk. But his eyes aren't on my face. No. They rove my chest and stomach and…lower. When he drags them back up, his grin is bigger than I've ever seen it.

"Beautiful," he sighs.

It shouldn't feel good for another male to call me that. But my wolf preens and drops to his belly, fully focused on the other male. Wolves are pure instinct, and where normally he'd assess a non-packmate male in a critical way, he's interested in Dirk, searching for a wolf who isn't there. I bite my lip to hold back a smile and turn to Lou, wiping the paint from her upper chest.

"Aww, that was a lotta work," Dirk grumbles playfully.

Lou and I say nothing, but her amber eyes flash in the afternoon light as I brush my shirt over her skin until all the purple paint is gone.

Dirk nudges me in the side. "Wolf, let's go drag wood for Louanna so she doesn't have to do it herself, shall we?"

Without pulling my eyes from hers, I smile. "I'd be delighted to pull wood for her but I have another client soon."

Her eyes flash and narrow, then she dips out of the cage of my arms, her bratty side rearing its head. Muttering under her breath about dudes always needing something from her, she tosses her long braid over her shoulder and heads up the street toward the gnome village. Before she disappears, she turns around and shouts something about returning with a cleaning potion.

"I've got one, Sweetheart. See you soon?"

She beams at me before spinning on her heel and continuing on her way, hips swinging as she walks.

Dirk and I stand companionably in front of my office, watching her go. When she disappears into the village, he turns to me with a grin. "Looks like you two had fun, Wolf. Shall I help you clean up?"

I think he's offering more than cleanup help, but I've got another client in ten minutes, and I'm still feeling out what it means to be in this sort of relationship. Being alone with Dirk feels different now, knowing what he imagines our future to be.

"I've got it," I say softly, hoping he doesn't feel like I'm rejecting him as a monster. "I've got another client coming in ten minutes, and somehow I feel like your cleanup might take a little longer than that." I jerk my head toward the kitchen. "I've got a cleanup potion to make it relatively quick, but…"

He straightens, rolling his shoulders back. The leather straps across his chest tighten, accentuating his cut musculature and the lightning that flashes across his pale skin. "Och now, Connall. I can be quick when the occasion calls for it." His smile grows dark, a tongue the color of the sky peeking out to run suggestively along his lower lip.

My cock kicks in my pants, still hard from playing with Lou and touching her. But this? I don't know what to do with this. But despite that, I'm curious.

"Tonight." I let my eyes drop to his chest again, admiring him. I thrum the backs of my fingers over one of his leather chest straps. "Does this ever come off?"

Dirk's nostrils flare as his hands fall loosely to his sides. His body is tense, poised as his gaze locks onto me. "Only for you 'n' her. I've not taken it off since I was a teen."

Goosebumps cover my skin, and I can't help but take a step closer, bringing my face closer to his. "I'd like to learn more about that tonight, on our date."

Goddess, I'm going on a date with another male.

"I'm an open book." Dirk tilts his chin up as he gazes into my eyes.

"Good," I return, reaching down to rub my cheek along his. It's an affectionate gesture that's common among shifters, but at the rough scratch of my stubble against his smoothly shaven cheek, he tenses.

I nuzzle my way along his skin, testing how he feels about this sort of touch. But to my surprise, he sighs and lets his head fall back, inviting more. I'm standing in the doorway to my office on Shifter Hollow's main drag, but for some reason, I can't stop touching the male in front of me. I tell myself it's the affectionate cheek rub I'd give anyone, but as the edges of my lips touch his neck, I know that's a lie. I recognize it, sit with it for a moment, then let the thought float away.

Dirk's skin is colder than mine and Lou's, refreshing and calming against my much hotter temperature. Realizing I'm standing there with my mouth hovering above his neck, I pull back and straighten.

He stares into my eyes, his look almost a challenge. *Do it*, he seems to encourage as his mouth pulls up in one corner.

"I'm looking forward to tonight," I share. "I'm excited, Dirk."

"Good, Wolf," he barks. "Because I cannae wait to put my mouth all over that gorgeous body."

Fuck. I don't know if he's talking about Lou or me. But either way, I think I'm down.

CHAPTER EIGHTEEN
LOU

"Right there, Lou," Bellami directs as I lift a mushroom the size of a throw pillow above my head. I hold my breath as I set it down on the top layer of logs. Somehow, the gnomes managed to place three additional "stories" since I helped them a day or two ago.

Bellami appears on the top log and brings out a compass, checking something. Shaking his head, he turns to me. "Nah. Move it so the door faces that way a little more." He points toward the sidewalk outside gnome village.

I don't bother grumbling anymore about his obsession with directions. It's important to the gnomes, and they asked for my help, so here we are. Reaching high above my head, I grasp the mushroom by the front door hole and tug it slightly to the left. Bellami waves his hand for me to continue going until it's far enough.

"Right there, that's it! Stop!" He beams at me with a tiny thumbs-up. His gaze softens at the edges. "You're doing a great job, Lou. Thank you."

I feign shock, throwing a hand over my heart. "A compliment, Bellami? I don't think you've ever given me one of those."

He rolls his eyes, crossing his chubby arms over his broad chest. "Enjoy it. I won't make a habit of it." Without another word, he hops off the top story and onto my shoulder.

I've gotten accustomed to the gnomes assuming my taller frame is a ladder. It seems like the second I agreed to come into gnome village, that was a given. Another tiny male crawls up my leg to join Bellami on my shoulder. The snarky comment on the tip of my tongue dies as they stare at the mushroom.

"It's perfect," the second male, Penn, says. I resist the urge to look over at them and see what they're doing. So I stand quietly while they stare at the mushroom. Bellami uses my ear like a handle, holding himself steady.

"It's the perfect spot for a family," Penn continues, his tone soft.

"It really is," Bellami returns, his tone thoughtful and tender.

The next sound is definitely a kiss. The second it sounds spicy, I whip my head toward them. "Are you two making out on my fricking shoulder?"

Bellami removes his tongue from Penn's mouth and gives me a superior look. "Just celebrating with my husband, thank you, Lou."

"I'm gonna have to put my foot down," I bark. "I put up with y'all using my body like a ladder, but I have to insist I not become a mattress."

Bellami pinches my ear and hisses like a cat. Then he grabs Penn's hand as they leap off my shoulder and land on the flat part of the log next to where I placed the mushroom. He slips an arm around Penn and levels a glare at me. "We weren't gonna have sex on your shoulder, Lou, it was just a kiss. Geez, are all humans so…" He waves his hand dismissively at my body.

I lean forward, matching his expression. "Choose your words carefully, Bellami. I might not lift the next mushie, you teeny little terror."

Penn beams at me while his husband and I have a little standoff. After a beat, he clasps his tiny hands together and releases a happy sigh. "Gosh, it's so fun watching you two together. Lou's just a big ole overgrown gnome at heart. The banter, the sarcasm. I absolutely love it."

"This is the strangest conversation I've ever had," I admit, planting my hands on my hips. My sarcasm is a protective barrier I use to keep my heart safe. I think humans sometimes find it too much, although my nieces love me despite it. And my sister Caroline did too.

My heart pangs thinking about her and the box of letters in my room. One day, I might give them to the girls to read.

Penn smiles at me. "I heard through the gnome-vine that you've got a date tonight. A double date, if my sources are correct."

I snort. "The gnome-vine? Is that like the grapevine?"

He chuckles. "Yeah. Gnomes always have the best gossip because we're so small, we're practically invisible to larger monsters. It's a benefit of our size. Also, we're not gossipy anywhere but amongst ourselves, and you are, well, among us."

I grin and lean forward, hoping he'll ignore how I haven't answered his question. "So you've got the hot goss about everyone in town? Is that what you're saying?" When his smile grows wicked, I gasp. "Oh my gods, Penn. Tell me everything."

"I'll make you a deal," Penn says with a sweet smile. "Come back and tell us how your date went, and I'll tell you something shocking about someone in town."

Damn. That's a trade for sure because I have no idea how to navigate a dinner date with two monster males. Much less if they'd care if I tell the entire gnome village about it. Ultimately, I decide I love secrets, and I want to know them.

"Fine, but I will not be answering twenty questions." I wag my finger at the diminutive males. "Understood?"

"That's fine," Penn says as Bellami rests his head against his husband's shoulder. "Have a lovely evening, Lou."

"Get outta here," Bellami barks, pleasant as ever.

I reach out and thump his pointy hat off his head. He gasps and sputters as Penn laughs.

"Bye, boys." I wave.

Turning, I make my way cautiously along the gnome village path, admiring how cute the whole thing is turning out. Crews work diligently to bring more mushroom homes and supplies into the space. The way they work together is fascinating, and despite their generally grumpy nature, I feel at home here.

Smiling, I step onto the sidewalk and head toward the Annabelle Inn to get changed for my date.

～

"Yes, girl," Morgan says with a slow clap as I execute a spin in my wrap dress. Her gray eyes flash with excitement. "Those boys are gonna lose their minds. Your tits look amazing in that dress."

"Thanks for letting me borrow it," I chirp, turning to the mirror to admire the look. Morgan's right, the pale dress is made of the creamiest fabric, and I look hot as hell.

I didn't bring any date-appropriate clothes to Ever. I got the text from my nieces that they'd come here, and I knew what they'd found—a monster haven. I threw four outfits in my bag and rushed to get to my girls. I haven't been willing to part with them long enough to go back to my apartment and grab stuff. Since time passes more slowly outside the wards, if I left for a day to grab my shit, I'd miss a whole month inside the haven.

Date-night clothes aren't worth losing time with my people. But this dress? Oh yeah, this is worth something.

Morgan hops off the bed and grabs my hand. "Okay, Auntie, you're ready. I'm gonna walk you to Sycamore and then meet Abe at the Green Bean for burgers."

I snort and pinch her side. "You finally let that male out of the bedroom?"

Morgan laughs and pulls my bedroom door open. "I need to eat sometimes, and Alba makes the best burger I've ever had. Shepherd said that when we first came here, but it's true. She must put butter in it. I can't tell. All I know is I have to have one."

Together, we leave the Annabelle. The Inn ripples her siding and waggles her white shutters at us. Waving goodbye, we walk past the Community Garden and head toward Main Street. I drop my niece off at the Green Bean. But just as I turn up Sycamore to head for Shifter Hollow, an appreciative whistle stops me in my tracks. Prepared to shout at whoever it is, I whip around to find Lola fanning herself as she walks up behind me.

Inky black eyes drift to my feet and back up again as berry-red lips split into a grin. "Lookin' hot, Lou. Let me guess, you're going on another date?"

I lean in, not sure how I feel about the whole street hearing about my date plans. Plus, I don't know if Connall has even told anyone about our current state of affairs, even though I secretively-ish spilled the beans to the girls already. It sort of feels like tonight's the night where we'll discuss that, because everything else has happened more privately.

"Yeah." That's all I say.

Lola crosses her arms and cocks one hip to the side. "Girl, you're gonna need to give me more than that. Spill it. You look gorgeous, and I'm just going to needle you to death about it if you don't tell me now."

"Okay, okay." I gesture for her to keep her voice down. "I'm headed to Connall's place, but keep it to yourself. We still haven't told a lot of people."

"His place is super cute; you're gonna love it," she says. "It's the perfect blend of masculine and pretty. He's got a great view, too, because he opted for one of the higher-up locations."

My mind spins with ideas, wondering what his place will look like.

"Earth to Lou." Lola rubs my shoulder. "I'll let you get going, but I better get the rundown. I'm dying to know everything about this—" she waves a hand at me, "—arrangement."

My mouth goes dry as I consider what I could possibly say. I don't know if polyamory is common among wolves. Even in the human world, it's not a new concept, but it's not super commonplace in my experience either. I've never been in a polyamorous relationship, although I had a couple friends who were in one. And then I have no idea what's normal for sylphs.

I bump her hip with mine. "I'll plan breakfast with my girls again tomorrow or the next day, like before. Come with us again? I'll spill all the beans."

"Oh yes," she says with a grin. "Just call me when you know which day."

"It won't even be breakfast," I say with a laugh. "We don't go until like ten a.m. because Morgan's not an early riser."

She winks at me. "Bet not with all the shenanigans she and Abe get into." She smiles and waves goodbye, turning to walk back up the street toward Bad Axe, the bar her mate, Richard, owns.

She doesn't know half the shenanigans my niece and her mate get into. Some of the stories Morgan's told me are shocking even when one does know about sexy vampire habits.

Shrugging all that aside, I head up Sycamore Street until I reach the last crescent-shaped street that leads off Sycamore. I follow it to the right until I get to the very end. Connall's the last house on the left, and beyond that is pure, deep and verdant forest. I smooth my wrap dress down again, wiping my sweaty palms on my hips as I stare at a front door wide and tall enough for a centaur or pegasus to go through.

As I lift my hand to knock, the door swings inward. Connall appears in the empty space with a slight smile. He throws a navy rag over his shoulder and reaches for me with his free hand.

I allow him to pull me into the entryway, but he spins me around. When our eyes meet, his flash with his wolf's emerald shade, his wolf so close to the surface.

"You look stunning," he growls, his voice rough. The lower-than-usual tone makes everything in my body tighten.

Connall cants his head to one side and sucks in a deep, slow breath. "So good," he breathes.

For a long moment, I stare into his eyes, wondering what his wolf thinks of the puny human standing in his doorway. Except Connall has never said a single thing to make me feel less than for not being a wolf, or at least some kind of other cool monster.

"Does it bother you that I have no wolf?" I blurt out the thought before I can even stop myself. Gah. Why the fuck did I say that?

Connall takes a step closer, sliding his hand along my hip. He uses the touch to push me back against the curved inner wall. Dipping down, he brushes his mouth softly against mine.

"I haven't been as direct as usual with you because of the way this came about. Let me be direct now." His free hand slides up my chest, his fingers curling around my throat. When he talks, it's like he's breathing the words right into my lips. "I couldn't possibly want you any more than I do. There is no deeper level of desire or excitement I could feel to pursue you. And while some of this is new to me, I'm absolutely on board, Lou. With all of it. I want to know everything about you, to learn everything about you."

My chest heaves, breath coming in stilted gasps at having his soft lips so close to mine. Gods, I need to be kissed.

The moment I think it, he bends lower and takes my mouth. The first swipe of his tongue is slow, languid, just a tease that reminds me of our so-called therapy session.

But his next pass is dominating, his tongue licking along mine as he slants his mouth over my lips. His lips are rough, and when he slides both hands to my ass and parts my thighs, pulling me into his arms and slamming us against the wall, I groan into his mouth.

My groan unleashes him, the kiss growing heated and wild as my hands roam his chest, his neck, up into that gorgeous wavy hair. He ravages my mouth, big hips pistoning against me as one hand slides to my ass and squeezes fucking hard.

I gasp. He nips my lower lip and pulls, growling into the bite as I pant and rock my hips against him. I need more than this. I need all of it. I desperately, desperately need to know what Connall's like in bed. Because, I'll admit, the thoughtful, kind, quiet male I've seen doesn't quite line up with this godsdamn kiss.

Fuck, was I wrong. Because Connall said he was dominant, and he is, based on how he's treated our interactions. I don't know for sure if monsters think about Doms and subs the way humans do, or if they even have the same names for those roles. But when he pulls back, licking a soft path along the bite on my lip, I decide it's one of the many things I want to ask during our get-to-know-each-other date tonight.

"More," I whisper. "Give me more."

Connall lets out a hard, ragged groan and pulls back, brushing his thumb over my lower lip. It's tender from his bite. "If I don't stop now, we'll never make it to dinner."

"Screw dinner," I state simply, leaning down to rub my open mouth along his palm and fingers. I suck the tip of his forefinger into my mouth, biting as I swirl my tongue around the thick digit.

Green eyes flash a darker color as Connall watches me, nostrils flared, big chest rising and falling with deep breaths. He looks on the verge of combusting, or demanding something. But then he smiles and sets me on my feet on the ground.

"Sassy females don't get what they want the moment they ask

for it." He leans down until his mouth hovers just above mine and places his finger under my chin, tilting my gaze up to meet his. "I like teasing you, Sweetheart. Not to mention, you still owe me a few inches, but I think I'll let you pay up a little later."

My pussy clenches on nothing, desperation clawing at me. But I shove it down. I'm not gonna beg a man for dick.

But then the side of my personality that loves to challenge and win rears her ugly head. I lift my chin away from his touch and slip around him so we're a few feet apart.

I smile wickedly. "I know someone who'll give me what I want, if you won't."

Auburn brows travel skyward as he straightens, rolling both beefy shoulders backward. He regards me for a long moment, then the corners of his mouth turn up into a grin that matches mine.

"You sure that's how you wanna play this, Lou?" He slips both hands into his jeans pockets, accentuating the bulging erection between his thighs.

But I'm not a quitter, and I don't back down. "Absolutely, Connall."

He takes a step closer, then another, backing me against the wall once more. His body is hot against mine, the faintest tease of his chest hair peeking out from the top of his shirt.

He slips a hand out from his pocket and grabs mine. After pulling it down between us, he rubs my palm over his rigid length. I hold back a groan at how fucking thick and hard he is, his knot tangible even through his jeans.

He leans down and brings his mouth to my ear. "You're gonna beg for this, Lou, and I'm not gonna give it to you until you apologize for being a brat."

"Never," I state, even as my fingers curl around him to stroke. Playing with Connall is exactly as fun as I thought it would be. The bratty dynamic suits us. Hot *damn* does it suit us.

He lets out a rough laugh and removes my hand from him,

placing it by my side. Turning from me, he pauses just long enough to glance over his shoulder. "C'mon, pretty girl. I need to finish dinner."

Without another word, he stalks up a short ramp from the round entryway.

Grinning, I follow, staring at his gorgeous ass the whole way.

I deserve that ass. I really, really do.

And I'm gonna get it, no matter what.

CHAPTER NINETEEN
DIRK

It's against my nature not to spy on my mates. Every instinct tells me to go windy and fly up to the glass front of Connall's home to stare at them. Will they touch without me there? I'd like to know. But…I made him a promise.

So instead of spying on them as Louanna entered his home, I gave them a few minutes to themselves. Then I forced myself to wait another few minutes before flying up to an open living room window and slipping through.

Lou stands in the middle of the room, mouth open as she stares around. I brush around her, teasing her hair up as she crosses her arms.

"Dirk, come out this instant," she demands.

Reappearing in human form, I tug her braid and flash her and Connall both a ravishing smile.

Connall smiles at me. "I'm glad you're here, Dirk. I was just about to give Lou a quick tour."

"Bedroom first, I hope," I say with a wink.

He shakes his head. "Actually, Lou's in trouble. She challenged me, said she'd go to you for what I wasn't willing to give just yet."

Her mouth falls open as she scoffs. "Are you freaking kidding me? Tattletale!"

I tsk as I move to Connall's side in solidarity. Oh, I like this game very much.

"Louanna, my beauty. Did you think having two males meant yeh could play us against one another? That's not how it works, love."

She crosses her arms and lifts her chin defiantly. "I'll get my way eventually. I always do."

Connall chuckles and glances at me. "See what I mean?"

I smile back up at my big wolf. "Perhaps yeh can give to me what yeh won't give to her."

His smile goes soft and lax at the corners as he bends down, bringing his mouth to the shell of my ear. "Maybe, Sylph. If you're a very good boy."

Oh fook. Oh godsdamn fook. I hold down a groan as I beam at Lou. "I'm a star fookin' student, Louanna. Might wanna take a lesson from my excellent behavior."

Connall laughs low in my ear, a soft growl tumbling from his lips. It brings me back to how he brushed his cheek along mine before, so I turn just enough to rub my cheek along his mouth now.

At the touch, he bristles, then growls again, but there's no malice to it. It's all heat as our sweet Louanna stands before us, practically panting at the sight of us together.

Gods, this is fun.

"How about that tour?" I ask roughly, staring deep into her flashing eyes. It's a challenge, a dare for her to give in to our playful teasing.

"Follow me," Connall commands when the moment passes and Louanna says nothing.

I reach for her hand, and to my surprise, she places her palm in mine without complaint, comment or sass. I've broken past another of her walls, making my way to that sweet, gooey center where she allows me to care for her. I just know that, deep inside, she's a sticky, caramel-filled croissant of deliciousness.

Connall leads us past a black marble kitchen with wood accents. It's masculine and elegant all at the same time. All black appliances, black cabinets and countertops. We pass through an arched doorway and down a short hall. Doors on either side reveal a few bedrooms and a bathroom.

When he doesn't open the door at the end of the hall, I grin. "Bedroom?"

He smirks at Lou. "Yeah. Think I'll save that for another night, though."

"Asshole," Lou mutters. "I don't even care about your bedroom."

He and I share a look.

"What a brat," I say. "A spanking would do nicely, Connall."

"Edging would do better," he returns. "Maybe we should lick her pussy until she's ready to come, then stop and send her home."

Lou gasps, and my cock goes ramrod-straight in my pants. "Gods, yes, let's do that. I want that," I all but beg.

Connall licks his lips but passes us both by, heading toward the main living area again.

I give Louanna a faux shocked look. "Who knew our wolf was such a tease?"

She mutters something but follows him back into the living room, slipping onto a barstool as he moves to a pot simmering on the stove.

He grabs the pot by the handles and shoves it to the back burner. As he turns the stove off, I slide onto the barstool next to my Louanna. Leaning into her space, I nudge her carefully with my elbow. "Beautiful home, isn't it?"

She leans into my space. I wonder if she even realizes she's done it. Spreading my legs wide, I pull her stool between them so I can settle her body against mine. She doesn't protest but looks around the room. It's exactly how I'd imagine Connall's home would look—masculine, peaceful, dark, comfortable.

Connall leans over the black marble countertop onto his forearms, stretching a hand toward us. When I spin us to face him, he smiles. "What can I get you both to drink? I've got mead from Biergarten and Ohken's personal stores, whiskey, tequila from Santa Alaya. Plenty of mixers too."

"Surprise me," Louanna says, her tone playful. There's an undercurrent of challenge there too. Gods, I love the way she pushes our wolf. He's a rock, though, confident and a classically trained therapist. He won't let this slip of a girl push a button he doesn't want pushed.

I grin at him. "Same, Wolf."

He rises tall and turns from us, stalking to our left where a giant built-in holds all sorts of drinkware, plates, cups and a myriad of alcohols. A mirror on the back wall lets us see him as he grabs three glasses. Next he pulls two bottles of something clear off the shelf.

When he begins mixing them together, I bring my lips to Louanna's ear. "Can we get yeh a little drunk, my beauty? I would dearly love to see yeh wild and free."

She spins just enough to shoot me a sassy look. "If you're lucky, Dirk."

"I make my luck," I growl back, nipping at her earlobe.

She jumps between my legs, elbowing me in the gut. "Ouch, that hurt."

"Did not."

"Did too. I bet I'm bleeding."

I lick her earlobe, then suck it between my lips. When she giggles, I nuzzle below her ear with the tip of my nose. "Not bleeding. Jest delicious, Louanna."

Connall joins us, setting three short glasses on the island. He opens the fridge and grabs a decanter of what looks like cherry juice. Dropping a splash into the glasses, he adds an orange twist on top and pushes two glasses toward us.

"My take on what the triplets tell me is called an Old-Fashioned. I'll admit I comm'd Morgan to ask what you like."

Lou reaches for the glass as I resist the urge to lift it to her lips myself. Instead, I reach for mine and take a tentative sip. Orange, cherry and the deep, oaky flavor of whiskey burst across my senses.

"How about a toast?" Connall smiles at us both, leaning over the counter and lifting his glass.

We clink ours together as his eyes rove between Louanna and me. "To surprises. To new beginnings. To delicious food and delightful company."

"And hot sex," I add. "Don't ferget that, Wolf."

His nostrils flare. "Thought I was covering that with delicious food."

Louanna chokes on her drink, sputtering as she laughs at his comment.

He gives me a superior look and turns to the fridge once more, withdrawing a tray covered in filets. He sets it on the countertop and looks between us. "I thought filet, salad and mashed potatoes was a pretty good start. Any allergies or dislikes among those foods, though? It's easy to make something else."

"This looks amazing, Connall." Louanna reaches across the counter to rub the back of his hand.

I lock my gaze to his. "I'll eat whatever yeh give me, Wolf."

Louanna slaps my stomach. "Jesus, Dirk, do you make everything sexual?"

I snort, pretending to be affronted. "I'm not a picky eater, Louanna. I've no allergies. I'll eat anything."

"Grab your drinks." Connall lifts the tray of steaks and grabs a spatula from a drawer. "Let's go outside."

When he turns, he calls out a command to the treehouse. The entire back wall of the living room goes clear as glass, giving us an unobstructed view of the verdant green forest at the edges of Shifter Hollow. Lou gasps and runs to the door, stepping out onto a wide deck with simple wooden rails. She holds the door for Connall as we follow her outside.

The deck is gorgeous, running the full length of his home, nearly fifty or sixty feet long. At the far back end, it bumps out, and there's a covered hot tub. Up against the wall stands a built-in grill with a countertop running five feet on either side. The deck is deep, stretching maybe fifteen feet out into the forest. Comfortable-looking chairs and sofas form a half-moon shape around the grill area. A glass table in the middle has a tray of fruit, cheese, and crackers on it.

"Dig in while I cook," Connall says, setting the tray of steaks down. "Make yourselves at home."

His words send something painfully tender stabbing through my guts.

Home.

A word that's always been hard for me. Elementals don't have homes the way other monsters do. We have home territories, but nothing like this. I've never lived in a house. Even during my hunter training, it was hard for me to live inside, and I never did well at it, preferring to spend time outside in my elemental form.

But the idea of a home with my mates is something I've dreamed of my whole life.

Clearing my throat, I lift my eyes to find Louanna staring at me. She's fookin' observant, but when she opens her mouth to say something, I make her a cracker and offer it to her instead.

"You okay?" she mouths.

"Never better," I answer truthfully. Once my plan is complete and I have my mates locked down, Connall's home will probably become *our* home. House Zefferus. Would they take my name? It'd be my honor if they did.

I cast my train of thought aside. I've wanted all of this for so long, but Connall invited us here so we could get to know one another better. My mates aren't as far down the path toward claiming as I am. They likely haven't been imagining the three of us together for ages like I have. I'd do well to remember that.

Lou takes the cracker and nibbles on it, staring at the wonder around us. When she's done, she glances over at Connall. "This is absolutely beautiful. How long have you lived here?"

He smiles as he turns the grill on and waits for it to heat. "About ten haven-years. I spent most of my life in my home haven of Arcadia. That's where Richard and Ohken are both from too."

She tucks her knees to her chest and rests back in the chair. "Did you know them there?"

He leans against the countertop next to the grill. "No. Arcadia is pretty spread out, unlike Ever. The trolls primarily live in their villages deep in the mountains. The shifters stick to the forest in the foothills. We didn't cross paths often. A lot of havens are like that, disparate communities."

"Ever's a little like that," I offer. "What with shifters, pegasus and centaurs living down here in the Hollow instead of in downtown with everyone else."

"I love it, though," Lou says quietly. "It feels more peaceful to me out here."

Connall gestures around us. "When I came here, Richard gave me the pick of what was available in Shifter Hollow, and I knew it'd be this treehouse the moment I set foot inside. You can't beat this view. In the evenings, I get to watch the pegasi court in the meadow on the other side of the house."

"Court?" Lou gives him a skeptical look.

"Yeah," he says with a laugh. "Pegasi are very public in their courtship, and it involves a lot of sky dancing. They love an audience."

She looks over at me. "You sure you're not half pegasus or something? Sky dancing sounds like something you'd do."

I laugh and take a sip of my drink, leaning forward to rest my forearms on my knees. "I've taken yeh both into the sky, yeh might remember. We danced on the currents, my beauty. That's how an air elemental courts, partially. And it's true I don't mind an audience. I'd court yeh both in front of the entire haven system, if yeh wanted that."

Connall blushes slightly and takes a sip of his drink. Am I pushing him too far? Dinner in his home is private, secretive. We can do whatever we want here without it feeling like an announcement. But maybe saying it aloud is still shocking for him.

He turns and throws the steaks on the grill, checking how we like them cooked. As he grills, we talk about everything and nothing. Simple things like how he feels about being Second to the shifter queen's mate. How Lou feels about her work with Malik, which she loves. I give high-level answers about their questions regarding my work as a hunter. I don't have to go back just yet. That's a problem for another day, and it's sure to be a problem indeed.

Once the steaks are cooked, we help Connall plate everything. Then I insist on feeding my Louanna every bite of food. She protests but allows it as Connall laughs at us. He likes it, though, seeing us together. I can tell in the way he observes whenever I touch her.

By the time he brings dessert outside—a strawberry shortcake —I've refilled our drinks twice, and Louanna's getting a touch tipsy. Her cheeks are flushed. Elementals don't absorb alcohol. I couldn't get drunk if I tried to. And shifters run so hot, it takes a boatful of booze to bypass their metabolisms. So, Connall and I are stone-cold sober as Lou begins to laugh more easily and touch us when we touch her.

It's so perfect being with her like this—having the both of us focused on Louanna is a dream come true.

I hold her in my lap, seated sideways on a sofa with Connall at our feet. He holds a forkful of drippy strawberries.

"Open wide, Lou." His wolf's green flashes through his beautiful irises as he leans forward, reaching for her mouth with the fork. When she snaps at it but misses, strawberries and cream coat her lips, and she falls into a fit of giggles.

"Well," I tease him, "you gonna clean her up, or shall I?"

He licks his lips. "Allow me." Leaning forward, he crawls up our bodies until he's hovering above us. We're dwarfed beneath him. He's so fookin' big.

Lou's head falls back against my chest as he dips down and licks a slow, sensual path along the seam of her lips. They fall open as he makes his second pass. It's a steady, commanding perusal of her mouth as he licks the cream from her, wolf-green eyes flashing to mine. For a moment, I think he'll growl out a challenge. But instead, he licks her again, focus returning to Lou's pretty bow mouth.

He's teasing me, testing this new thing I put into his brain. The idea of me. Of us. Separately from Louanna but also together with her.

"Ouch," she complains, shifting against me. "Dirk, this gem thing is poking me in the back. Can you take it off?"

Connall's eyes flick to me. He already knows it's a big deal for me to remove it. When I sit upright, he pulls her toward him to give me space. Reaching underneath the gem's housing, I unclip it and shrug the straps down my shoulders, my fingers trembling.

I want to share the same story with her that I mentioned to Connall. Mostly I want to give them both insight into me. "I haven't taken this off since I was a teenager," I admit. It feels awkward as I remove the gem and straps and hold them in my hand.

Lou spins and leans back into Connall's arms. "Tell us about it. When did you get it? What all does it do? I want the full story."

I sit back against the arm of the sofa, clutching the gem tightly in one hand. "Feels so odd removing it." I stare into the blue depths that signify my power, then look up at my mates.

They look so comfortable at the other end of the sofa. Connall's thighs are spread wide, Lou relaxing between them, the fingers of one hand rubbing circles on his thigh. It's perfect, seeing them like this.

"I wasn't a powerful elemental child," I share. "I was small, overly confident but powerless. I got picked on a lot. Well," I say quietly, "'twas more than that. Elementals are solitary as adults but tend to stick in groups when there are young ones. We're a harsh race, though. Lack of power isnae tolerated. I got roughed up a lot by the more powerful younglings."

Lou stiffens in Connall's arms, her amber eyes flashing as her nostrils flare. "Roughed up how?" Her tone is full steel.

I shrug. "They'd use their power against me. Trap me beneath a rock in the river or steal my starter gem so I couldnae focus my power. When we're young, we're not so good with our power. We're first given small gems to channel the power until we can sense it well enough to use it. I could never quite seem to grab the wind, so I was a disappointment to me folks. I know that."

Connall and Lou say nothing, but Lou looks ready to fly off the handle on my behalf.

"For years, I tried until I was all but shunned from my community. My parents left the group for the wilds, as is my people's way. They left me to fend for myself. Looking back, they shoulda done more. But they couldnae think of anything to try. I simply wasn't blessed with the kind of power they expected." I wink at my mates, despite their shocked, sorrowful expressions.

"I was as plucky then as I am now, though. I left the wilds and went to the protector academy. I joined and learned more about elementals in general. One day, I had a breakthrough during a session with a kind mentor. My power came in, finally."

I lift the gem. "Turns out, I'm the most powerful air elemental ever recorded. I can harness the wind to topple buildings and control the weather, although I've got to be careful with it. It jest took me some time to figure things out." I place the gem and holster carefully on the table to my right. "Evenia herself gifted me that gem when I graduated and she headhunted me into Hearth HQ. I've nae taken it off since. That's been, och, something like ninety haven years I've worn it."

"And your parents?" Lou's voice dips lower, her tone furious.

I shrug. "No idea. It's uncommon for elemental families to stay together once the children come into their power. It's likely they didn't keep up with who I became."

"And where are they now?" Lou delivers the question with violent intensity, her eyes narrowed as she looks at me.

"Och, Louanna. 'Twasn't all bad, my sweet," I reassure her. "It turned out fine in the end. Although I love how you look ready to do violence on my behalf. Warms my cold, black heart."

She lifts her chin. "I'm absolutely ready to do violence." She glances over her shoulder at Connall. "You'd help me homicide some dickheads and hide bodies, right?"

He plants a kiss on top of her head as she grabs my gem and holster and pulls it to her chest. She sinks back against Connall's chest. "Sounds like elementals are pretty solitary. So how would that work with us?"

"'Tis true," I offer. "But I'm the oddest elemental ever. I crave belonging, family, connection. It's not common for my people, but it's what I need."

Connall reaches around Lou and takes my gem, bringing it closer to study. His wolf's sheen shines through his eyes as they look deep into the gem. After a long, silent minute, he glances up at me.

"You've achieved so much," he says. "But I'm sorry you had to deal with lack of support in your childhood."

"Och, Connall," I tease. "I'm a might distressed about it, sharing my sob story with yeh now. You could make it feel better though, with a kiss."

His immediate blush has me preening. I love how easy he is to ruffle despite his dominant nature.

Between us, Lou's scent explodes.

"Put our woman between us if yeh like," I encourage. "But allow me my first kiss."

When he stares hard, I feel pressed to continue, "If yeh hate it, we don't have tae try again."

He's teased me plenty, but an actual kiss? That's real. It's new. I can't wait, and yet I cannae push him either.

"Alright," he says after an eternity of silence. "Inside, though, where we have space." He stands and pulls Lou up into his arms, then stalks to the door and opens it.

Goosebumps cover my skin as I follow, watching him deposit Louanna on the sofa. She scoots to the back and nips at the edges of her lip. Connall crawls onto the sofa and sits next to her, their thighs touching.

"Come here, Dirk." He pats his thigh then glances at Louanna. "I want you to watch, Lou."

Her mouth falls open as I crawl onto the sofa and seat myself in my big mate's lap, a thigh on either side of his hips. I can't resist touching my Louanna, though. Reaching for her hand, I pull it to my mouth and suck her fingers between my teeth.

Nipping playfully, I wink at her. "I'm taking *our* first kiss next. One right after t'other. I've been ever so patient."

Amber eyes move between us as I return my focus to Connall. He stares deeply into my eyes. "May I touch you, Dirk? Is there anything you don't like in terms of kissing?"

"Yes and…no." I grab one of his hands and plant it in the center of my chest. It's by turns exhilarating and shocking for him to touch the sensitive skin my gem typically covers. His hands are warm, his fingers curling as he strokes a line down my chest and over my abs.

My entire stomach tenses, muscles rippling as his fingers trace the dips and valleys. I fight for control of my breath when his free hand slips to my throat, fingers curling possessively around it. I don't mean to rock my hips, but I can't stop myself as he uses his grip to pull me flush with his chest. We breathe the same air as his lips halt just in front of mine.

I need my woman, too, so I grip her thigh and hold onto it, risking a glance over to find her staring at me, rapt.

I always thought, in this moment, I'd be cheeky and teasing and in control of the experience, but I'm lost to this version of Connall who touches me like he's more experienced with males than I know him tae be. And having my Louanna right there with me to bear witness? That means everything to me.

When I look back at him, he dips forward, capturing my lips softly, and all rational thought evaporates.

Because his lips are so fucking hot, so soft, so rough. He sucks my lower lip between his then slides his tongue across it. Lou lets out a strangled sound as I fight not to devour him. I don't know how he feels about this first kiss.

When he deepens the kiss, big hips bucking beneath me, I have my answer in the form of the thick evidence between his thighs.

He grips my throat harder, his kiss turning rough, ragged. I respond in kind. I'm lost, utterly lost to him as the kiss grows frantic. His right hand roams up my back, and he uses it to hold me tightly to him as the kiss becomes more. We're on the precipice of something here.

When I break it first, sitting back just enough to stare in wonder at my wolf, his eyes are full wolfy shine. "Mine," he growls, his wolf's tone evident in the way he speaks.

"Always," I say back. "Yers and hers, Wolf."

Connall turns to Lou. "Your turn, pretty girl."

To my intense shock, she shifts onto her knees and sits by our side, eyes locked on Connall.

Connall releases his hold on my throat, dragging his claws carefully down my chest and stomach, raising red lines in their wake. "Kiss her, Sylph. Make it a good one. I want to watch you two."

"Finally," I murmur. "I've been waiting ages for this, Louanna."

She stares as I slide my left arm around her body and pull her close. She's off-kilter; the only thing holding her up is my much larger frame.

"Louanna," I whisper, slanting my mouth over hers. "My beautiful mate."

When her mouth drops open, eyelashes fluttering against tan cheeks, I take her mouth for the first time. Her scent, her taste, they wrap me up as my whole body tenses. She sinks harder into me as we pause, breathing the same air as I marvel at the perfection of my woman. But then my Louanna moans, and I lose my fookin' mind.

Growling, I nip at her lips, her tongue, biting and sucking as she responds to me. It's no less frantic and desperate than my kiss with Connall. But when she parts us to cry out in pleasure, I halt, surprised. Looking down, I see Connall's slid the top of her dress down, exposing her pretty breasts. His mouth is locked on one, his cheeks hollowed as he sucks her nipple between his lips.

"Yes, Wolf," I encourage. He smiles with his mouth wrapped around Lou's breast.

"Oh gods, oh fuck," she moans, one hand slipping into Connall's waves. She grips his hair, a groan tumbling from her throat. He bites, and I go harder than granite watching him attack her breast as zealously as he kissed me.

I stroke his jawline until he looks up at me. "Shall we tease our woman, my sweet wolf?"

A ragged growl is my answer as he pushes Lou against the back of the sofa. Big hands come to her wrap dress and yank, breaking the soft belt as he opens the dress and unveils her beautiful body to us. She's wearing a pale pink lace bra and matching panties, and I didn't think I could get hotter. But her sexy lace sets me on fire.

Connall slips a hand behind her back and expertly undoes the bra, then pulls it and the dress off. When he tosses them down, I take a moment to admire the perfect roundness of her breasts. Pretty pink nipples tip them, hard and aching. Our mate dips forward and snarls, latching onto her breast as she arches to meet him.

I can't resist. Moving forward, I lick a stripe up her belly to the underside of her breast. Then I meet Connall at her nipple, slipping my tongue between him and it to lave roughly.

Lou blurts out a stream of unintelligible words as our play turns into a rough kiss between him and me, followed by a hard bite to her breast by our wolf. His chest heaves as the hair rises on the back of my neck.

Bright eyes come to mine, narrowing. Bones shift and crack, and he grows bigger, taller, his ears tapering long and thin as he begins to shift. "Too much," he growls, his voice nearly all wolf. "Too hot."

Bones crack and clothing rips until a half-shifted wolf with luminescent green eyes hovers poised over Lou, his long, curved tail lashing from side to side.

Lou sinks into the sofa, eyes wide with fear as I put myself between them.

"Hello, Wolf," I croon. "Allow me to show you more."

CHAPTER TWENTY
LOU

One second I was getting the best teasing of my life, and the next, I'm staring at a half-shifted Connall with eyes like twin police lights. He doesn't seem entirely in control, and I don't know how much of Connall remains when his wolf comes out.

And his wolf is freaking *enormous*.

"Dirk," I whisper. "What should we do?"

If Connall's still in there somewhere, it doesn't seem like it. I thought shifters controlled their shift, but it felt like he just lost it.

"Lie back, Louanna," he suggests. "You're so godsdamn hot, our wolf cannae help himself. He'll be alright, and we would never put yeh in danger."

Sinking slowly against the sofa back, I pull my discarded dress up around my body to cover it, but Connall growls and takes a step closer, close enough for me to see the green flecks of Connall's eyes within his wolf's. He brings his nose to my cheek and chuffs softly as my heart races.

"Scent her a little lower," Dirk says in a teasing tone.

"What are you doing?" I hiss, fear rising as Connall's focus moves down my neck to my breasts.

"Showing him what belongs to him." Dirk removes my hands from the dress. He opens it back up, exposing my tits and belly to them both.

I should be terrified, and part of me is, but another part of me is fascinated at the way Connall's green eyes rove appreciatively over my figure. This is Connall. *My* Connall. He'd never hurt me.

I hold back a squeal when his warm breath caresses my body. But gods help me for thinking it, he feels good. Dirk reaches for my knee, pulling it toward him, splaying me wide open.

Connall's sparkling eyes drop from my tits down…there.

Elegant nostrils flare, his elongated wolf ears twitching as his muscles grow and expand, his wolf pressing further to the surface. Like this, halfway shifted, he's massive, dwarfing Dirk and me both.

And I can't stop staring at how fucking beautiful he is, now that I'm past the shock of him shifting. His fur's the same auburn shade as when he's in full human form, slightly wavy and just as soft looking.

Dirk gently grabs the dress and pulls it out of the way, exposing my lace undies. My breath becomes rapid panting when fingers come to the crotch of my underwear and tug it to the side.

Connall lets out an otherworldly growl that raises the hair on my nape. When I move to snap my legs closed on instinct, Dirk murmurs to me, "Let him see, my beauty."

Forcing myself to relax, I let my legs fall wide, watching Connall's muscles bunch.

He lurches forward and dips low, his features elongating as his nose becomes a snout, eyes set farther back on his head. He's nearly full wolf.

Oh gods.

He growls and bends forward, burying his nose in my pussy. I jolt at the cold, wet sensation. But when it's immediately replaced by the swipe of a huge, warm tongue, I cry out.

"The two o'you are hotter than a forest fire," Dirk says. "How does he feel, Louanna?"

But I can't talk, can't even think as Connall's claw-tipped, fur-covered hands come to my thighs and yank me flat on my back. He shifts backward, hanging off the sofa as he licks again. His tongue is so big and rough, licking a hard path from my ass to my clit and back again.

Pleasure builds explosively between my thighs. But when Dirk bends over me, sucking my nipple between his soft, cool lips, I lose it. My body jerks and jolts, hips thrusting to meet Connall's tongue as Dirk chuckles around a mouthful of tit. The sensations overwhelm me; I can't tell where to focus. On the slow, playful build of Dirk's mouth or the rough, ragged drag of Connall's huge, worshipful tongue.

Between my thighs, he starts growling, and then it becomes a purr-growl mix that sends vibrations through my entire body.

Orgasm hits me out of nowhere, back bowing as my pussy clamps hard on Connall's tongue. And some-fucking-how he curls it inside my channel, licking my G-spot until one orgasm turns into two, maybe three. I can't tell because they don't stop. And the entire time, Dirk sucks my nipples like a godsdamn champ.

I come until stars begin to dance across my eyelids. Pleasure begins to recede, leaving me washed up and blissed out. Connall slips off the sofa and stands, shifting fully back to human form. I'm too exhausted to even sit up, so I stare at him in wonder.

His clothing is ripped to shreds, hanging off him in tatters. His muscles seem extra huge, pumped up with his wolf's power.

A chuckle from Dirk pulls my attention to him. He's scooted to the back of the deep sofa, an arm on either side as he grins at Connall.

He eyes his tattered shirt and the state of me and drops to

both knees at the foot of the sofa. "I couldn't help myself. Lou, are you alright?"

"It was crazy hot," I offer with a laugh. "Ten out of ten. No notes."

Dirk's fingers slide over my mound and down to my pussy. He rubs along my outer lips, opening me up as Connall stares. "Let's not forget about all that talking we were supposed to be doing."

"What's your favorite color?" I blurt out when Connall's rough lips come to the inside of my knee and nuzzle.

He stares at my pussy. "Pink."

"Blue for me," Dirk teases.

"Did you always know you wanted to be a therapist?" I'm desperately trying to think of questions, of things I *should* know about them, but I'm rapidly losing control.

"Yes," Connall breathes, licking a flat path up my inner thigh to the spot where it meets my sex.

"This isn't a conversation if I get one-word answers," I bark.

But when Connall's lips close over my clit and pull softly, I give up. I give up on driving the conversation or learning more. Because there's no room left in my brain for anything but pleasure. I only know one thing with any certainty at this point—wherever this is going, I am all-fucking-in.

～

The following day, I check my comm watch and realize it's nearly noon. I've got a date with Iggy. It's more of his "check on Lou" plan, but it's so cute, I don't have the heart to tell him he doesn't need to baby me.

I take a left on Main Street and walk past Scoops and Miriam's Sweets. Eventually, I get close to Town Hall and cross over to the movie theater. Iggy hovers in the air in front of the door, a single rose in his hands. When he sees me, his blue eyes go wide and bright, a smile splitting his adorable face.

"Lou! You're here! Are you ready for our date? Well, not a date like Dad and Miriam have, but you know what I mean!" He zooms toward me and flies in dizzying circles around my head.

"Of course I'm here," I sass, pinching at his hip as he barrels by.

He yips and executes a flawless spin and stop, zipping the other direction.

"Damn, Iggy, you're getting good."

He laughs and slows down, flapping to my shoulder and settling on it. Like always, his long tail curls around my neck, the spade-shaped tip slipping into my shirt to rest over my heart.

He wraps one chubby arm around my head. "Your heart beats so fast, Lou. Faster than anyone's."

I reach up and lay my hand on his haunch, rubbing gently. It's easy to act like I don't need Iggy to fix me, and the reality is it's not his job or responsibility to sort out the turmoil in my brain. But I love that he makes the effort anyhow.

When we enter the movie theater, I smile at how retro and adorable it is. Black and white checkered tiles lead to three different theaters, all playing movies from vastly different points in time. Since time moves faster inside the haven system, I thought they'd have new movies every day, but it seems like whoever owns this place randomly picks. Today, they're playing *Terminator 2*, *Practical Magic*, and *Inside Out*.

Iggy opts for *Inside Out* and orders a soda, despite the fact that the movie theater doesn't allow him to drink it. I laugh when he asks me to hold it for him until we find our seats. Minnie, his hellhound, lumbers loudly after us, moaning and groaning. She's got to be close to having her puppies, as miserable as she sounds.

When we reach our seats and I hand Iggy the soda, the seat immediately flips up, knocking him backward. The soda goes flying, drenching the row behind us.

"Godsdamnit!" Iggy shouts, raising a fist at the roof. The movie theater creaks at the same time I pinch his leg for cussing.

He settles in his seat, his tail wrapped around my upper arm. Minnie lumbers up onto the seat next to him and drops her head into his lap, her eyes closing the minute the movie about a young girl's emotions starts.

When we get to the part where the kid's mental Family Island begins to fall, Iggy snuggles up against me and speaks loudly over the sound of the movie.

"Don't worry, Lou. Your family island is like, super strong, and I won't ever let it fall down. You can count on me!"

Minnie chuffs as I reach over and kiss the top of his head.

"I know, kiddo. You're the best thing ever."

He sighs and smiles up at me. "I am." Quick as a flash he leans over and tries to take a sip of my soda.

The effect is immediate. His theater seat completely inverts, tossing him over the heads of the monsters in front of us. He cackles as he tumbles head over tail. Someone shushes him as he zips back and settles in my lap, kissing at Minnie. She looks at the still-flipped seat and lumbers off of hers, choosing to lie on my feet instead.

Iggy's tiny little chuckle is the last thing I hear before Riley's Family Island completely crashes into the abyss in the movie.

As I watch it fall to bits, I think about how well things are going for me right now. Ig is right—my family island feels so good right now. My girls are safe and sound and happy. I've got wonderful friends and I'm dating two males who make me feel more alive than I've felt in a long time.

I just hope it doesn't crash and burn.

CHAPTER TWENTY-ONE
CONNALL

I prep a short canvas stand for Lou as I wait for her to arrive at my office. Our second session is today after her "date" with Iggy. Last night was wonderful. We talked, and then I got a chance to touch her, to taste her, and all I know is I'm absolutely certain she's mine.

It doesn't matter that she's not a wolf. I can't imagine wanting someone any more than I want her. Every new fact I learn about her just makes me more obsessed. I want to make her a nest, even though she's not technically an omega. I still think she'd like it, all covered in pillows and blankets. Dirk and I can stand together outside it, saying the formal words to be allowed in. A smile curls my lips as I consider how I never want to stop unraveling Lou, my sassy, bratty, perfect female.

A knock pulls me out of my thoughts. Jogging into the main area and to the front door, I swing it open. Like always, the sight of her steals my breath. She's wearing thigh-hugging jeans and a black V-neck tee. Bracelets adorn the arm with the thrall bites.

Without thinking, I rub my fingers along the healing indentations, familiar worry rising at how she was able to heal from something nobody has *ever* healed from.

Lou laughs and pats my stomach. "Still fine, big guy."

"I worry about them," I murmur. "Nobody's been fine like this. Nobody." I bring my gaze to hers, memorizing every freckle as I stare at her.

Lou shrugs. "Guess I'm just something special."

"You are." While we've established this isn't like real therapy, I still aim to make it purposeful for her. My treatment plan is meant to give her lots of opportunity to talk and take action. Priority one is identifying her emotions and giving her some semblance of control.

"Come on in." I pull her into the room, then shut the door behind her. Pointing toward the porch, I grin. "Food's back on the painting porch already. We'll be out there today."

Her grin goes mischievous. "Are we actually painting this time?"

"Yeah," I say with a laugh. "I'm avoiding sexy times if at all possible."

"Aww," she whines.

Rubbing her arm, I chuckle. "We seem incapable of keeping our hands off one another, but I put together a treatment plan to work through at whatever pace you like."

She slips forward and presses her body to mine. "And if I get distracted and need another kiss?"

I wave her toward the porch, attempting a serious look. "Then you'll get it, Lou, if that's what you want. But we should try to stick to the plan."

She lifts her chin, playfully defiant, and winks at me. "As long as I get what I want, we'll be fine."

Chuckling, I head to the fridge and grab a couple drinks as she spins and walks out onto the porch. I join her there as she sits on a stool in front of the shorter canvas.

I hand her one of the drinks and set mine down beside my canvas. "Alright, we're co-painting today. "I want you to focus on painting what your emotions feel like when you're alone with your thoughts, alright?"

She nips at her lower lip. "Okay." Amber eyes flick to my canvas. "What are you going to paint?"

Smiling, I pick up a long, chunky paintbrush. "I'm going to be painting how last night felt to me." I point at my timer, which is set for half an hour. "We've got thirty minutes to do what you can. There's no need to 'finish.' Just paint what you feel. We'll spend the last quarter hour going over it."

"Do I have to be quiet?"

She asks the question in such a huffy tone, I resist the urge to laugh and smother her with kisses.

"Not at all. Talk as much as you want."

She picks up a skinny paintbrush and sticks it between her teeth so it pokes out of either side of her mouth. Grabbing the black paint, she deposits a glob in one of the mixing trays. Much to my surprise, she's silent for the first fifteen minutes or so.

I keep an eye on her as I paint in broad brushstrokes. I've developed an obsession with her gorgeous strawberry blonde braid so I paint generous swirls of it on the canvas, interweaving the strands. I'm going to hang it in the house so I can see it all the time.

For thirty minutes, she says nothing, utterly focused on the painting. She seems to lose herself in the activity, switching between paint colors and brushing them over the canvas in confident, brash strokes. I don't know if she has ever painted before, but she appears to be a natural.

Then again, she injects confidence into everything she does. Why should this be any different?

I keep half of my focus on my canvas, and the other half on her. Her muscles are relaxed, her scent filling the air with strawberry and tart lemon. My wolf sits calmly in my mind, interested and focused on Lou's actions. On her scent, on how peaceful she is painting out here on the sun porch. She doesn't even stop for snacks, despite the overflowing charcuterie tray between us.

Thirty minutes passes quickly, and when a small timer rings on my phone, she doesn't notice. I set my brush down and take my mixing plate to the sink to clean up. When I return, Lou's still painting feverishly on her canvas.

I tap her shoulder, and she jumps, whirling around with a fierce look. It softens when she sees me, and she laughs.

"My gods, Connall, I was in the zone, man."

I want to correct her calling me "man." I might look like a man from her world, but I'm all male, all wolf. I've gotten used to her mannerisms, and I love the human sayings she uses. Even when they don't really apply to me.

She glances at the canvas, nipping at her lower lip as a smile turns her plump mouth upward. "How'd I do, from a therapy perspective?"

I take a step closer, focusing on her art. It's all swirls of black and every possible shade of blue. Dashes of red punctuate it at random intervals. And every few inches, there's a white square with black swirls across it.

"These almost look like letters." I smile at her. "Want to elaborate?"

She nods. "Yeah, I write them to my sister, Caroline, every other night or so. I miss her so much. She'd have loved Ever. And she'd have been so proud and amazed at the lives her girls are living now. All she wanted for them was safety, health and happiness." She looks up with a wink. "Maybe I'll let you read them one day."

"The triplets definitely got two of those three things," I say with a laugh, reaching down to rub the thrall bites on her arm. "And I'd love to read the letters one day, if you want me to."

She places her hand over mine, looking up at me fiercely. "I promise I'm fine, Connall. Truly."

"I'll try to stop worrying." I rub her arm again, then stare at the canvas. "Talk to me about any meaning behind the colors you chose."

She shrugs and turns, staring at the canvas. Her scent changes, growing harsher. It's almost tart on my tongue.

"Honestly, I just grabbed whatever colors came to me. And then I got lost in the painting. It felt good to focus like that."

I smile, knowing I'm about to give her homework.

"Think about what you drew," I advise. "Next time we get together, I'd like to dive into the specific colors and shapes and talk about why you think you did them that way. Spend some time this week considering it, and I'll do the same. We'll compare notes."

"Alright," she says quietly, amber eyes moving to my painting. "What'd you paint?"

"Your hair," I say with a laugh, reaching down to tug on the end of her long braid.

"You're obsessed. You're being obsessive and I've already got one stalker." She pinches my side playfully, laughing when I curl into the touch instead of away like she probably thought I would.

"It's beautiful and varied." I tip her chin up so she stares into my eyes. "Your hair is every shade of blonde and red mixed together. It's as diverse as you are, Lou."

She smirks. "I knew there was a hopeless romantic somewhere in there."

"I'm serious," I add on. "There's a metaphor in here somewhere about how you can be strong and vulnerable, light and dark. You can be opposite things all encompassed within one beautiful Alaya-blessed soul."

Her smirk becomes a real smile with no sassy edge. "You think your goddess blessed me?"

"I know she did," I murmur, stroking the side of her neck down to her exposed collarbone. "You haven't had an easy time of things, Lou, but you're still here. And what's more, I believe you can still thrive despite what you've endured."

She glances at her painting then back at me. The first tear falls, but she brushes it quickly away. "I hate crying."

"Let it out." I pull her to me and wrap my arms around her. "Let it *all* out, Lou. Let me shoulder it with you. Let Dirk shoulder it. We want you to be able to let the weight of your hardships go sometimes. You deserve that."

We stand for a long time, long past the end of our "session." She cries, and I purr, and when she finally pushes out of my hold to flash a watery smile, I suspect we've made real progress.

∼

I spent all morning with Richard and Lola, prepping for them to be out of town next week on Lola's first tour as queen. Of course, leave it to my queen to plan a few concert appearances while they're traveling. I wish I could be there to see her play, but having her in town most of the time means I hear a lot of impromptu electric guitar. She's a regular karaoke appearance at Bad Axe.

I'm not worried for them to be gone. In fact, I'm looking forward to it. Them being gone and me being in charge makes me feel useful, something I've struggled with lately. As a therapist, I remind myself that I have high expectations for my role, that I need to put less pressure on myself. Richard and Lola remind me constantly that they value my contributions. I need to take their praise to heart.

I mull that over as Dirk and I jog through the underbrush surrounding the lake, the only sounds our rapid breathing as he accompanies me on my daily rounds. I suspect it's his way of hanging out without it being an official date. Either way, he's been quieter than I expected, but it's given me time to think.

The cool scent of water fills my nostrils. We're nearly back to the lake after a long run. I slow to a walk as the trees thin out, rocks littering the familiar path, then emerge from the trees onto the rock-strewn waterline. The mer-king doesn't like a lot of activity on the beach. Running would be highly frowned upon. It's always struck me as odd—they're a playful bunch as long as he's not around.

Then again, of all monsters, mermaids have the most rigidly structured society. I'm thankful shifters aren't quite that bad. Well, not in Ever anyhow.

Dirk is an unusually quiet presence at my back. I wonder if he's lost in thought about last night the same way I am. We continue along the path, moving away from the water's edge when I get an idea.

I stop, and he runs into me. Spinning in place, I level him with a stare. Sweat drips down his muscular frame, his chest rising and falling as he moves both hands to his hips.

"Run outta energy, Wolf?" His deep voice hits me square in the chest. Before I even knew how he felt about me, I liked his teasing. Liked the way it made me feel, the way he'd look at me and Lou both. I realize that now. It's why I never hated him for pursuing her, because I liked him, even then.

I stalk forward until I can plant a hand on his chest.

He looks up, shocked. But I push until his back hits a tree. And then I bring one hand up above his head, leaning in the same way I do with Lou. I'm testing something I haven't tried yet. But the reality is, the moment Dirk told me how he felt, I haven't been able to stop thinking of ways I'd like to touch him.

He lifts his chin, giving me the same bratty smile Lou does when I play with her. "What are yeh do—"

I silence his snark with the slant of my mouth over his, tongue sliding deep to curl around his. Then I suck, pulling his tongue between my lips as lightning flares between my thighs. This is hot for me in a way I could never have expected.

Shoving forward harder, I force his head back, bringing my hand to cup his jaw. I grip him hard, forcing his mouth open as I move the other direction, taking his lips with rough, ragged nips and bites as I battle the need to do something else, something more.

He groans and breaks the kiss, eyes flashing with heat as I bring my thumb up over his plump lips. When I slide it between his teeth, he swirls his tongue around it, and precum spurts from me.

"More," I command, pushing my digit all the way into his mouth.

When he hollows his cheeks around it, I grunt from the heat. "Dirk," I moan.

He shifts backward, licking a path up the bottom of my thumb as he cocks his head to the side and gives me a wicked look. "Nobody out here to see us if we take this farther, Wolf."

I know what he means, but I want to be clear that I'm not afraid.

And I'm not ashamed.

"I don't feel the need to hide you," I say confidently.

"Are yeh an exhibitionist, Wolf?" His grin is practically feral.

"Not really," I admit. "I didn't want you to think I only wanted to touch you when nobody would find out."

He smirks and reaches down, cupping my dick through my jeans. "Know why that is, Wolf?"

I bend down and hover my lips above his again. "Say it. Remind me."

"Because you're mine," he hisses, fingers clenching playfully around my sack.

I throw my head back and growl. He feels so fucking good. I could come like this, from nothing more than a kiss, a tease and the hint of something more.

He reaches down and rips my jeans open, shoving his hand down them.

A gasp bursts from me at his cool touch. He rolls my sack in one hand, leaning forward to lick a hard path up my neck as I marvel at how different his touch is from Lou's. More forceful, more demanding. She's all soft, receiving energy even when she's being sassy. He's something else entirely. Something dark and deviant, something that pushes and pulls me until I'm right where he wants.

I've always preferred to be the more dominant partner. It's why I fucking love dominating Lou. But with Dirk, it's… different.

"Do yeh wanna come, Wolf?" he growls into my skin. A sharp nip along my collarbone pulls my wolf to the surface.

I lift my head and stare at him, bringing my forehead to his. "Yes."

"Say please." He pinches the tip of my cock until I whine and cry out.

I've never said please in the bedroom. Never asked someone for something. I'm always the one in charge. The word feels weird on my tongue.

"Say it," he demands, gripping my rigid length and stroking. His fingers are cool but rough, pulling heat through me as I fight not to come too fast. His stroking becomes faster, more insistent as I fight against rising pleasure.

"Wolf," he teases, "let yer handsome mate hear how much yeh'd like to come in his hand."

"Please," I grunt out.

"Please what?"

Does he want me to say what I think he does? That he's my mate? That I suspect he's right because my interest in him is becoming an obsession?

"Please, mate," I whisper.

Shock courses through me, realization slapping me at how good it feels to call him that. It feels right. *He* feels right. Even without Lou here between us.

Dirk drops to his knees and yanks my jeans down. In one swift move, he lurches forward and takes my entire cock in his mouth. I hit the back of his throat and keep going as desperate sounds leave my lips. Planting both hands on the tree behind him, I pant as I watch his cheeks hollow around my thickness. Pretty dark lashes flutter against his blue-freckled cheeks, highlighting his long, elegant features. Goddess, he's beautiful.

He pops off my dick and suckles at the tip, playing and licking as seed fills my sack until I feel like I'll explode.

"Dirk," I grunt. "Please."

He grins and takes me into his mouth until his nose touches my stomach. When he growls, the low vibration hits me so hard, I lose control. I cry out in pleasure as orgasm rushes through me, my entire body stiffening as heat and bliss radiate from my core outward. Hot seed barrels down my shaft, exploding down his throat as he hums around my throbbing length.

He swallows every fucking drop as I wheeze and heave and try not to pass out from how fucking good his mouth is. But he doesn't stop there. As soon as my orgasm fades, he drops lower and sucks one of my balls into his mouth, pulling gently. My softening cock grows hard again when he strokes between my ass cheeks with his fingers. It's just the hint, just the tease, and it reminds me we haven't talked about sexual preferences between the two of us. But I can't find words to even have that conversation as he tugs on my balls and circles my back hole with cool, wet fingers.

He's going to put his finger into my ass. I know that as he plays with it. And I'm going to let him because this feels too damn good to stop. Stepping my feet wide, I pant as I slide my fingers into his hair and grip.

The sudden sound of crashing reaches my ears, and I jerk my head around.

Dirk's mouth pops off my nut, and he looks up at me. "What is it?"

I turn as he rises.

"What do yeh hear?"

A slight rustling reaches me as I twitch an ear. "Something crashed through the underbrush," I whisper.

"Och, some asshole messing up my sexy plans." He scowls up at me, but there's a thoughtful look on his face.

"I don't know," I say. "Let's check it out."

He whines, "Fine, but I need to finish what I was doin' later, Wolf."

"Deal," I say breathlessly.

"Good. I wanna do it in front of our woman and watch her lose her mind."

Goddess. Heat flares through me at imagining Dirk's lips wrapped around my cock while she watches. I want it. I need it.

But faint rustling still reaches me, and my instinct has always been good. My wolf's at the front of my mind, focused on the direction the sound came from.

Rounding a bend, I pause at a half dozen ferns lying trampled across my usual path. Stopping, I drop to a knee and pick one up. It's coated in a sticky dark substance. When I bring it close, my nose scrunches.

Merfolk blood. It has an unusual undercurrent to it, like… berries or…I can't place it.

My hackles rise as I examine the crushed vegetation. That's when I notice a foot sticking out into the path a dozen paces ahead.

Oh shit.

Sprinting forward, I slide to a stop with Dirk by my side.

A female mermaid in human form lies tumbled over a mossy fallen tree, her arms askew and face hidden by masses of multi-hued dark hair. There's no visible blood at a quick glance, but I scent it in the air. My nostrils flaring, I look around, but there's no sign of someone else coming or going.

"Who's this?" Dirk steps over the log to brush the mermaid's blue hair away from her face. Her temple is bloody, a stream of it dribbling from a wound at her hairline.

"Amatheia," I press the back of my hand to her skin, "King Caralorn's eldest daughter. She's cold as ice."

Dirk lifts his comm watch. "I'll call Slade."

I nod, staring at the mermaid as he calls for help.

That done, he returns to where I've paused next to Amatheia's prone form.

"Her skin doesn't look right." Dirk drops to a knee and runs his fingers over her cheek. "It's mottled black. That's not a mermaid thing, as I remember."

"No." I frown.

Lifting my comm, I call Richard to let him know what's going on. He'll rally the full set of troops so we can figure out what happened. Whoever did this to Amatheia is out there somewhere.

A groan drifts up from the fallen mermaid, her fingertips twitching. Dirk strokes her hair away from her mouth and nose as she sputters, blinking wide azure eyes at him.

"I—I, where am I?" Her tone is urgent.

Dirk croons, "Shh there, lovely girl. We found yeh fallen in the woods, and yeh're bleeding from a wound at the temple."

"I need to go," she gasps, choking on the last word. A cough blasts from her throat, followed by a black viscous liquid that coats her chest and stomach.

"Get her on her knees," Dirk barks, shifting his hands under her armpits and rolling her onto her side.

I grip her hips until she's stable on her knees, face down in the dirt as she coughs up more dark, sticky-looking liquid.

Dirk reaches for Amatheia's hair and holds it out of the way as the mermaid chokes and coughs, spitting black liquid into the dirt below. She doesn't try to speak again.

"Have you ever seen anything like this?" I stare at Dirk. He's traveled so much more than I have, and has probably seen things I could scarcely imagine.

He shakes his head, holding the mermaid in place as she coughs and spits.

Just then, shouts echo through the forest.

I call out for the others. Dirk's worried eyes meet mine as Amatheia heaves and a pool of black liquid splashes into the dirt.

Lush ferns part, and Slade runs through, sliding to a stop next to us. "Roll her onto her side," he directs.

Dirk and I carefully roll the mermaid to her left side.

Slade takes quick stock of her, noting the wound at her temple. Black fingers come to Amatheia's mouth, and he opens it, feeling around inside.

She chokes again, sputtering as more liquid spews from her. Goddess, how much can she hold?

Slade frowns, rubbing the fluid between two fingers. When Amatheia groans and spits up more of it, he looks at Dirk and me. "Pick her up, bring her to my cottage immediately. I need to take a look at her and run some tests."

"I'll fly her." Dirk drops down and picks the mermaid up in his arms.

"No," Slade barks, his long black horns straightening behind his head. "You'll shock her, and we don't know what that'll do."

"I won't go windy," Dirk says, pulling Amatheia tightly to his chest.

"What do you mean?" Slade cocks his head to the side, but Dirk pushes off the ground and disappears between the trees, carrying Amatheia.

Slade's mouth drops open. He whirls around to me. "Did he just fly without shifting into his element?"

I'm too surprised by the events of the last ten minutes to process Slade's shock.

Slade shakes his head. "A mystery for another day. Let's go." Without further comment, he takes off the way he came, back toward downtown.

Fifteen minutes later, I'm coated in sweat as I walk through Doc Slade's front door, through the front room and into the giant examination room at the back. When we enter, Dirk and my alpha, Richard, stand with Arkan, staring down at Amatheia, who lies in a bathtub full of water. Her lower half has morphed back into a long blue and turquoise tail, her single fin draping over the porcelain tub edge. Her head lolls over the opposite side, arms draped over the curved surface.

Richard gives me a look. "You haven't missed anything. She passed out on the way here, according to Dirk, and hasn't woken up."

"She's not vomiting any longer," Slade murmurs from his spot next to the tub. He's got some sort of implement inserted partially into her ear, listening to it. We fall silent as Slade continues to examine the mermaid.

Dirk backs up next to me. "I called Louanna on the way over and asked her to meet us. I dinnae want her hearing this through the grapevine."

I crush down a sense of helplessness as I nod.

This is bad enough and I'm drowning in sorrow for the injured woman in the tub in front of us. But there's something deeper and more terrifying there.

It could just as easily have been Lou who was hurt.

CHAPTER TWENTY-TWO
LOU

I fly through Slade's front door and skid to a halt in the giant atrium examining room. Dirk and Connall reach for me at the same time. Dirk bends down and quietly updates me as I watch Slade hover over a bedraggled, dirt-smudged mermaid female.

The tension in the room is enough to choke on. Seeing the beautiful blue-hued monster lying in the tub brings me back to when the evil warlock Wesley possessed me. When he stabbed Leighton in the heart and used my hands to do it. I'll never forget watching my arm slice up through the air, or the wet sensation of sinking a blade deep into Leighton's chest.

All of that rushes back as Slade examines his patient. I force myself to stay still, even though the desire to flee the room is high. At the end of the day, I want to know what happened. Were Dirk and Connall close to whoever did this? I'm desperate for Slade to confirm this is not somehow my fault. How could it be? I've been at work!

We're all silent as he moves around the mermaid, seeming to examine every iridescent scale, every fibrous inch of her singular turquoise fin. I wonder what happened to the other one? All of the mermaids in the lake look like…well, fairytale mermaids with the traditional long tail and two matching fins that split into feet.

Slade moves back up her other side until he reaches the wound at her temple again. He must have cleaned it before I arrived. There's no blood, but the area is puffy and swollen like a bee sting. Finally, Slade sighs and looks up at Arkan and Richard. "I don't know what this is."

The two leaders exchange a concerned look as Slade continues, "The wound at her head seems superficial, likely from falling and hitting it on the way down. But the expulsion of this liquid?" He points at the floor where black goopy-looking tar has pooled. "I've never seen anything like it. I think we should call Vikand."

Richard runs a hand down his face, stroking his beard.

Vikand. The new Everton is something of a scholar. Kind of a nerd, actually. He wears glasses, vests and ties, and he's always so distracted because his nose is stuck in a book. But he's a wealth of information about a lot of things.

Most notably, the darker magics.

A chill skates like fingers down my spine, warning me. The need to flee rises again, so I shift my weight to my other foot and wrap my arms tighter around my torso. Connall glances over at me, his bright green eyes full of concern, auburn brows scrunched together in the middle. He looks so worried. And that kills me.

Leighton was his friend. I killed Leighton. And now we're staring at another mystery that's hurting someone.

I don't think I can take it anymore. "You should call Morgan too. Maybe she can heal this."

"Of course," Slade's pitch-black eyes move to me, "but before Morgan heals her, I'd like to understand how this came to be. From the head wound, it seems like she was attacked."

"Attacked." The word hangs tensely in the air.

Richard and Connall share another look before the new

Keeper speaks. His horse tail swishes from side to side as he stares down at the shifter alpha.

"We need to call Morgan and alert the merking." He looks at Richard. "I don't know the mermaids well, but I believe Amatheia is the king's eldest daughter?"

"That's right," Connall says as his alpha nods.

My fingers twitch against my sides. "I'm gonna get some air," I mutter to nobody in particular, turning from the room and heading through Slade's small cottage to the front door. Muffled voices float after me, but I ignore them even as I fling the door open and jog out into the street. Stars twinkle overhead, the light from Main Street warm and inviting despite what's going on in Slade's examining room.

I bend over and put both hands on my knees, sucking in slow, steady breaths. I'm sure Dirk'll be here at any moment to—

"Lou?"

It's Connall's deep voice that breaks through my thoughts. I attempt to get it together as I turn and give him a half-hearted smile.

Connall stands on Slade's front porch, the singular light illuminating him from behind. Like this, he seems a million feet tall and just as broad. Some invisible tether pulls me, making me run to his comforting presence and bury my face in his chest.

Will he be okay with that when he's in Second mode?

He says my name again, so I drag my eyes up to his. They're such a shocking green color, indicating that his wolf is present and focused on me. Gods, I'd love for him to shift into his wolf right now, let me crawl up on his big, comfy back, and ride off into the sunset and away from this mess.

The intense look deepens as I get lost in his shining gaze. "Did you say something?"

He frowns. "I can't imagine how difficult this is for you. Do you want to talk about it?"

Oh gods, he's therapizing me. Is that even a word?

I straighten my shoulders. "I'll be fine, thank you."

He stalks off the porch and places a finger under my chin, tilting my face up, up, up into his gaze. "It's okay not to be, Lou. You don't have to be strong all the time, even though I know you pride yourself on that. Talk to me, Sweetheart."

I fight not to pull my chin from his finger as the weight of my life hits me like a truck. I'm surrounded by grief's claws, scratching and tearing at me to pull me into an abyss of sadness. But I fucking refuse to go.

Something flashes through Connall's gaze. "With wolves, when someone's upset, we like to hug and purr, maybe even rub our cheeks together. Shall we try that?"

I nod because I can't think of a single word to say.

A big, warm hand slides up my back to grip my neck, his eyes never moving from mine. Do I imagine the color flaring in intensity? He uses that grip to pull my body flush with his. He's so tall, my head comes to his chest, but that's perfect, because he wraps his other arm around me.

When a deep rumble starts up from within his body, I sink into the touch, pressing my forehead between his pecs. He's like hugging a giant vibrating teddy bear with pecs like a bodybuilder. The purr starts soft but picks up in intensity, coming and going in rolling waves. I swear I feel them all the way to my bones and back.

I don't know how long we stand like that, but Connall's silent the whole time. When he pulls away, dropping his grip on my neck, I nearly cry over the loss.

"Aww, don't mind me, alpha," Dirk says from somewhere to my right. "I was havin' a fine time watchin'. Louanna, my sweet, are you alright?"

I worry that Connall will pull away, but instead his purr deepens, going a little rougher.

Glancing over at Dirk, I force a smile. "I'm...okay. I could stand like that all night, I think. Purr's nice."

Something flashes in Connall's gaze as I look up at him. "Of course, Lou. It's not a cure for grief, but in the moment, it helps."

Dirk comes closer, stroking a stray hair over my shoulder. "I'm sure Connall'd be happy to purr for you any time, my love. Or anything else you want that might make yeh feel better."

Connall reaches for my shoulder and rubs the backs of his thick fingers along my skin. "I need to go back inside," he says. "Dirk, you'll make sure she gets home safe, right? Unless you both want to come back in?"

"O'course, alpha," Dirk says, "But I wanted to—"

Movement catches my eye in the forest to the left of Slade's cottage. I cock my head to the side as ferns rustle and shift on an invisible breeze.

Dirk says something else, but I don't hear a fucking thing, because a figure steps out of the darkness to stand under a streetlight. The light illuminates his sharp features from above, casting eerie, ominous shadows over him.

I suck in a gasping breath.

Leighton.

CHAPTER TWENTY-THREE
CONNALL

Lou hisses in a breath, amber eyes flashing wide as her focus jerks from Dirk and me to something behind me. I spin to where she's looking and see...nothing. An empty sidewalk and tons of trees.

When I turn back to her, she's white as a sheet, her muscles quivering. "Leighton," she whispers. "Oh my gods."

Ice fills my veins as I turn again. Dirk comes to Lou's side as he scans the forest. "What?"

"He's right there," she hisses, pointing toward the sidewalk, "standing under the streetlight! What do you mean you can't see him?"

Pain and worry stab me in equal measure. Staring hard, I try to see what she's talking about, but there's no one. The sidewalk is empty.

I take a step forward, but Lou clamps a hand around my wrist. "Don't, Connall. Something's not right."

I'm a believer in following one's instincts—all wolves are. It's drilled into us from puphood. My wolf presses to the front of our consciousness, scanning for anything amiss. The idea that my longtime but dead friend is standing in front of me, and I can't see him? I don't know how to handle that.

Dirk gives Lou a look. "I'm gonna shift into my other form tae try and see what yer seein'."

"Please don't," Lou begs, her voice trembling. "He's right there, grinning at us."

"What else is he doin'?" Dirk questions.

Lou huffs. "Nothing, he's just standing there, staring. How are you not seeing this?" She glances between us, but when Dirk and I share a confused look, she darts forward, running to the spot where she claims to have seen Leighton. Dirk and I rush after her, but when she steps into the circle of light, she spins in place.

"He's gone! He was just here! What the fuck?"

Unease fills me, my wolf whining into our shared space. I look at Lou and Dirk. "We need to tell Richard and Arkan immediately."

My first thought is that this is connected to her thrall bites, and something's finally happening with those. The threat of that steals the breath from my lungs.

Dirk sighs as he watches Lou staring around her, seemingly perplexed about how a male could have been there and vanished in a moment.

"Yeah," he says eventually. "Yer right, alpha."

"Stay with her," I command as I head back into Slade's cottage. I go to the back room where Richard's still talking with Slade and the rest. Touching his elbow, I give him a meaningful look. He reads it and tells the others he'll be back.

My pack alpha follows me outside, his concern a near tangible thing behind me. When we exit, Lou still stands under the streetlight, looking around.

Dirk shoots us a wry smile. "Och, Richard, I dinnae know how to say this so I'll jest blurt it out. Louanna just saw Leighton right there under that light."

Richard's eyes go wide, dark brows sliding upward as he looks to me, then over to Lou, then back to me.

She scoffs and crosses her arms, walking over to join us. Her brows furrow in the middle. "I know that sounds crazy, Richard, and Dirk and Connall couldn't see him. But I saw him as clear as day. I'm telling you, he was *right there.*"

Richard stalks toward the streetlight, sniffing and looking around. Lou looks up at me with a distressed expression.

And it occurs to me that things might get worse for her before they get better. Because this? This isn't normal.

Richard rejoins us, both hands on his muscular hips as he shakes his head. "I'm not going out of town, not with this going on. I'll send Lola and join her as soon as we figure it out. But I can't leave this for you to deal with alone."

I pull Lou toward me, wrapping her in my arms and squeezing her tight. I just want to protect her from everyone and everything, and the idea that she can see something I can't makes me feel like I won't be able to do my job and keep her safe.

And I have to keep her safe. I fucking *have* to.

∼

"I've never seen anything like it." Slade flips another page from one of Vikand's books the following morning.

Books are stacked floor to ceiling in seeming disarray, random papers hanging out of their pages. Vikand, Arkan's father, stands at a tall wooden desk in the back, poring over a book as thick as my leg. His horse tail swishes slowly from side to side, long black hair rustling against his onyx coat.

He sighs, pushing wire-framed glasses to the end of his nose to look over them at me. "I've got two dozen more books to look through, but I can already tell you that Morgan won't be able to heal that girl."

Ice freezes in my veins as I stand from my spot, fists clenching.

Vikand closes the book and crosses muscular arms over his broad chest. "It's black magic."

I frown. "Morgan's a black witch."

He shakes his head. "But she's a *good* black witch. She's not dabbling in the dark arts. Well, I don't think she is. I can't see Abemet allowing that, but I digress. I examined the mermaid this morning. I'm certain that's what it is. Although what spell was used is hard to say."

My frown deepens as I place both hands on Vikand's desk, willing my muscles to relax. "Is now a good time to mention that Lou thought she saw Leighton last night?"

One of Vikand's pitch-black brows travels upward. "Oh?"

"I couldn't see anything. Dirk was there too, and he also couldn't see anything."

"Leighton's dead," Vikand reminds me, his tone gentle.

"I know." I can barely get the words out. "Could this be connected?"

Vikand considers that for a moment, but eventually shakes his head. "I don't think so. Leighton became a thrall, so even if he hadn't been cremated in the way of your people, if he was reanimated in some way, he'd be in his final form. And he's not a wraith, or he'd be drawn to Hel Motel, and they'd notify us of a new attendant."

I muddle my way through everything he just said. I can't fault the logic in any of that, but I lay awake all night worrying about Lou and wondering how it's possible she saw my dead friend when Dirk and I saw nothing.

"Alright," I finish lamely, lost in memory as I pinch the bridge of my nose with two fingers.

Vikand goes back to his book, seeming to forget Slade and I are there. His pale eyes, the same eyes as his son, Arkan, move hungrily over the page, one finger following the lines as he reads.

"Are you onto something or just reading for fun?" I cock my head to the side and shift forward, reminding him I'm there.

"Simply immersed in the book, it seems," echoes a female voice from the front.

I turn with a half smile. "Catherine."

If Arkan is Ever's Keeper, much like a human mayor, then Catherine is undoubtedly the haven's mother.

She sails gracefully between the stacks, her curvaceous figure highlighted in a dress that wraps around her body and ties in the front. A basket in one hand smells of tomatoes and cheese.

Gray eyes flash at me, pink-painted lips pulling into a soft frown. "How are you holding up, Connall? Richard told me about Amatheia."

I roll my shoulders to dissipate tension as I heave in a slow, steadying breath. "Not great," I finally admit. Jerking my head toward Vikand and Slade, I plant both hands on my hips. "Vikand is pretty certain it's black magic."

Catherine nods, a small sigh escaping her lips. Vikand still hasn't looked up from his book.

"Ever has always been so peaceful," she says in a soft tone. "But, my goodness, it's been a whirlwind the last few months."

"You can say that again," I mutter. Then a thought occurs to me. "Did you talk with Lou when she got back to the Annabelle last night?"

Dirk walked her home. I had to go back into Slade's with Richard. I'd have insisted on staying at the Annabelle to keep watch, but Dirk told me he keeps watch on her most nights. Something about that warms me to the core.

Catherine nods, dragging my thoughts back to the present. "I did. She mentioned seeing Leighton, although we all know that shouldn't be possible." Her brow furrows. "I'm worried she's becoming lost to her grief over his death, so much so that she's manufacturing visions of him. Perhaps the stress of seeing Amatheia injured brought this about." She sucks at her teeth. "But at the same time, I don't want to discount a woman who knows her mind. I'm torn because, while I don't understand how it's possible, I've certainly seen enough inexplicable things in my life to never assume I know it all."

I mull that over, my senses pinging with the need to do something. This is why Dirk has asked me to offer therapy sessions to Lou many times before I agreed. I'll never forget the night he told me that every time I saw her and knew she was hurting, I'd be called to help.

He's right. I am. Not that our first session was anything even remotely resembling therapy. The rest of the sessions I have in mind for her are decidedly more therapy-like.

"I'm going to talk to her," I murmur, more to myself than anyone.

"That's an excellent idea," Catherine says softly. "She trusts you. Lou carries the weight of her family on her shoulders. She's always been like a sister to the Hector triplets, but she steps in as their mother too. She's fiercely protective of them and their happiness, forgetting her own in the meantime."

"It's not uncommon." I glance at Vikand—still reading—then back to Catherine. I'm not sure if she's aware of the few dates Lou and I have been on. Goddess, the need to run to Lou right now is near overpowering. If I can wrap her in my arms, she'll be safe. I have to believe that, to tether myself to the idea of it, or I'll go crazy with worry.

"Good," Catherine says, pale eyes drifting to Vikand. A delighted, devious sparkle flashes through her gaze. "If you don't need anything, I've come to deliver Vikand a little lunch, then I'm heading home to check in with the triplets and Lou."

"Is that so?" Catherine making romantic overtures? I never thought I'd see the day.

Catherine returns her focus to me and lifts her chin. "It's always a good idea to be neighborly."

I think back to my arrival in town. "You never delivered me lunch. Or wine," I tack on, scenting the air around the box.

"Get out," she says playfully, slapping my shoulder with the back of her hand. "I'm on a mission." She looks at Slade. "You too."

The dark elf skirts past me with a devious wink at Catherine.

"I can see that," I say with a snort, looking at Vikand, who has ignored this entire conversation. "Best of luck breaking through…that."

Catherine laughs, the sound tinkling off the chunky wood-beam ceiling. "Don't fret, Connall. I'm a succubus. This is literally what I'm made for."

I smile at her before taking my leave.

Outside, Richard leans against the front wall. He smiles when I appear from inside. "Wanted to chat with you, but it gets a little stuffy in there."

"Not to mention Catherine's agenda," I say with a wry grin.

He chuckles as he shakes his head, glancing through the front door. "Never thought I'd see the day."

Like always, I sense my alpha's intention without him needing to use full sentences. "What's happened?"

He sighs and crosses his arms. "Walk with me to the post office. I'm picking up some packages for Lola, and I could use your arms. She's sent a bunch of clippings from plants in Santa Alaya for the gnome garden. She's going to offer them to Bellami to see if he'd like to incorporate them."

I turn to walk up the sidewalk with him. "What else?"

His second sigh goes deeper. "This one's more of a probe into your life. You've been quiet lately. Are you alright? I know you and Lou went on a date, but I'm getting that as hearsay. It was a mistake for me not to tell you about Lola and me early on. Please don't make the same one with me. I want to be here to support you, however I can."

A smile tugs my lips upward as the post office comes into view. "The date was wonderful. But it wasn't just Lou and me."

"Oh?" Richard's brows head skyward. "Do tell…"

I suspect if he's heard the gossip, he already knows what I'm about to say, but still…

"Well…" I run both hands through my hair, considering how best to break the news. I'm about to tell someone I'm dating a male, when I've never dated males in my entire life. "Dirk was there too."

Richard smiles. "Mmm."

I shoot him a quizzical look since he doesn't seem shocked in the slightest. "How could you possibly know? *I* didn't even know he was interested in me in that way."

Richard's smile goes thoughtful. "I've been around a long time, Connall. And I sensed it was a realization you needed to come to on your own. But I've been watching Dirk for a while, even before you told me of your interest in Lou. He's always watched you, always been distracted by your presence. He's not as secretive as he probably thinks."

"So much for my ability to read people well," I gruff out. Moons above.

"You were distracted too," he jokes, grabbing the door to the post office. "And I'm gonna make my woman pay up the second we get home, although as much time as she spends with the girls I suspect she already knows about all of this…" his voice trails off at a huge pile of boxes in the corner of the post office.

A harried-looking pegasus clerk waves at the huge pile. "All you, Richard. Sign here please and get these out of my post office! They've been here all day, and more keep coming!"

I laugh, staring at the pile. My queen certainly doesn't do anything by half measures.

Neither do I. Which is how I know what my next step is in this mess with Amatheia. Once I drop these boxes off at Richard and Lola's, I need to see Dirk and Lou.

CHAPTER TWENTY-FOUR
LOU

That evening, I'm sitting in my room at the Annabelle examining my nearly healed thrall bites when a soft knock breaks through my thoughts. I wave when I see Catherine standing in the doorway. She smiles, but it doesn't reach her eyes as she pushes the door open. Dirk and Connall stand behind her, wearing matching worried expressions.

I shift off the bed and pad toward them. Catherine enters the room and steps to the side to make way for…well, I guess, my boyfriends? Gods, I forgot to tell them I told her about us over breakfast yesterday, so she has the full scoop.

"What's going on?" I look between the trio, a suspicious tingle traveling down the backs of my legs.

Connall takes another step forward, reaching out to brush his knuckles along my jawline. "I want you and Dirk to move into my place until we figure out what's going on."

I glance at Dirk, then around at Catherine, and finally back at Connall. "Surely that's not necessary. I mean—"

Dirk joins Connall, wrapping one arm around my waist. "We want tae keep you safe, my beauty. We'd both feel better having you at Connall's place where one of us can stand guard."

I snort and cross my arms. "Stand guard? For real?" I glance around the males at Catherine, but the look on her face tells me she agrees.

She tucks her hands in the long sleeves of her dress. "It makes sense to me, Lou, if you're comfortable. Please don't feel that I want you to leave Annabelle and me, but—"

"I want you safe," Connall growls. "I *need* you safe, Lou. If something happened to you, I...I..." He purses his lips, a muscle twitching in his jaw.

"Okay." This is important to them; that much is clear. I look at them both. "Are you sure this won't feel weird to you, like we're rushing something?"

"I'll sleep on the sofa, if you like." Connall pulls me into his arms. "But if you stay here, I'll lie awake all night worrying about your safety." He glances up at the ceiling as the inn lets out a terrible noise. "No offense, Annabelle."

Home. Nothing has felt like home to me since Caroline died. Everything has felt out of place. She was my big sister and best friend. My heart kicks and stutters.

"I'll pack a bag now." Turning from them, I squeeze Catherine's forearm. "Will you feel okay here by yourself?"

"I asked her to come too," Connall says.

Catherine shakes her head, looking around the room at the inn. "Between Alo next door and the Annabelle, I feel quite comfortable, thank you." She smiles weakly at me. "This is probably a good idea, darling girl."

I nod, because I can't think of anything else to say about our situation.

The next half hour is a blur. Reality sinks in hard. Something dark is here in Ever, *inside* the magical wards meant to keep us safe. Danger lurks, and I can't help but feel like I'm somehow involved.

The guys help me pack, and it's not until Dirk grabs the box of letters I write at night to Catherine that I stop in place, staring. He takes my pen and tucks it carefully into a bag, along with the stack of blank paper. My heart clenches watching him with the letters. He knows how special that box is because he's been damn spying on me since I arrived, but somehow, it doesn't upset me.

Being there, being constant, I think that's Dirk's love language. Or maybe it's stalking. I should write the dude who wrote that love languages book and let him know he missed one.

Dirk turns to face me, a half-smile curving his beautiful lips. Slinging the bag strap over his shoulder, he stalks across the room to me. He pulls me into his arms, bends down and places a tender kiss on my forehead. "I couldnae be more excited for this, Louanna, despite the circumstances. It's a silver lining, if there's one tae be found."

I smirk. "If I didn't know you wouldn't attack someone, I'd almost think you'd organized a reason for us to have to live under one roof."

He feigns being offended. "Och, Louanna. 'Twas Connall's idea. I was perfectly happy floating around in the air to keep watch."

A warm body presses to my back, a hand sliding around my side and up my front to rest between my breasts. Dirk's eyes flash with hunger as he looks over my shoulder.

Connall presses me harder to Dirk. "Let's get her home and settled." Steel threads his tone as I remember something Lola told me Richard once said about Connall.

He's a lover, not a fighter, but he'll fight tooth and nail for those he loves.

I can see that in the way he's handling this. Not that I think he loves me, not yet, but his need to protect runs deep.

I glance up at Connall. "What about my nieces? What about the rest of town?"

He strokes my jawline, his teeth tightly grit. He looks stressed as fuck.

"I suspect your nieces will want to be with their mates, but your family is always welcome in my home."

I consider that, looking between the two males. Nipping the edge of my lip, I nod.

"You're right, they won't want to leave their mates. But when we get to your place, I want to call them anyhow."

"Of course," Dirk says. "Anything you need, my sweet."

We leave the Annabelle and head for Shifter Hollow, the guys refusing to let me carry any bags. When we get to Connall's place, he's already got dinner started—lasagna's cooking in the oven. Cheesy, tomatoey smells fill the main living area.

"I'm putting you in my room," he declares, stalking toward his bedroom with two bags over his broad shoulders.

"Oh, are you finally allowing me to see it?" I tease as Dirk and I trail after him.

He pushes the door open and deposits my bags just inside. Looking up, he crooks his finger at me. "Last night, I lay awake thinking about you all night. And then today, it occurred to me that you could stay here. And I got more and more riled up until having you here overtook all other conscious thought. Come here, Lou."

I obey until I'm close enough to touch him.

He plays with a long strand of my hair. "Call your nieces, if you like, and then Dirk and I can help you unpack. Whatever you need. I just…" His voice trails off as he rubs my arms with his big, warm hands. Bright green eyes flick to mine. "If I can keep you hidden away in my home, Dirk and I can keep you safe. I have to believe that. And I *have* to keep you safe, I have to. Do—"

I slide both hands up his chest and rub. "I understand, Connall. I'm safe here with you two…right?"

Dirk comes to my back, resting one of his hands over Connall's on my arm. "Call your nieces, my sweet. You're here, you're in one piece. Now we've got to make sure you're comfortable."

I rest my head on Dirk's chest and glance up, shooting him a wry look. "Right here? You two gonna let me go, or should I make the calls from this sandwichey spot?"

Dirk grins down at me. "I've no intentions of moving, Louanna. Go on." His blue eyes flick to Connall, then back to me. "Err, unless you need space, my sweet. In which case I'll fuck off to the corner, then zip back like a magnet once yer done."

The mental vision pulls a laugh from me as I lift my watch and comm first Morgan, then Thea and Wren. True to their word, the guys don't leave. Connall stares at me, stroking my hair and Dirk plays with the end of my braid.

My girls are safe with their mates, which is all I care about. I make them promise not to go anywhere alone and to check in several times a day. As long as I know they're not wandering around somewhere by themselves, I won't worry my head off.

When I hang up, I'm still smashed between two big bodies, and Connall looks…overwhelmed. His bright eyes drift over my face, down my head and neck, over my shoulder to Dirk, then back again.

"We're okay, Connall," I say, rubbing his chest. "We're gonna be fine."

One of his hands comes to the back of my neck and grips me tightly. "You'd be safer in my arms, Lou. The closer the better."

I'm grateful for the opening, so I waggle my brows at him. "Good thing there's a bed behind ya."

His dark lashes flutter, but he steps backward, pulling me with him. As we sink onto the bed, Dirk joins us at my back, his hands sliding down the outside of my thighs.

"What do you need, Lou?" Connall's voice is low and commanding but somehow thoughtful at the same time.

"Dickstraction," I sass. "My girls are safe. You two are safe. And I need to not think about the darkness for a while."

The barest hint of smile appears at the edges of his mouth.

"You've always joked about Dirk making anything sensual, Sweetheart, but I'm beginning to think you're as bad as he is."

From behind, a hand wraps around my braid and pulls my head back so cool lips can nip at my neck. "He means that in the best of ways, Louanna."

A moan tumbles from my throat as Dirk nips and nuzzles. At my front, Connall's all hard planes and heat. We've teased and played, but I can't imagine what it would be like to have sex with them both.

I'm imagining it now, though, desperate to focus on something other than the bullshit that went down yesterday. When Connall growls low under his breath, dipping to lick a rough path up the front of my neck, I jolt in Dirk's arms and press my palms to Connall's broad chest. My fingers move of their own accord as both males kiss and bite and tease. Every inch of me winds up tight, a dam ready to break loose, and I have far, far too many clothes on.

"Too many clothes," Dirk growls, making me wonder—not for the first time—if he can read minds. He rips my shirt over my head and pushes me against Connall's big frame.

I barely get a chance to notice the room, all dark colors and manly accents, because Connall and Dirk stand at the foot of the bed, staring at me. Connall's chest heaves, his wolf's shade flashing through his eyes. His fists are slightly balled, a sizable erection visible through his jeans. Even so, he glances around the room, pulling my focus to the side table.

"There's a spot for your letter box there, if you like." He rounds the bed and drops to both knees, opening the drawer of his side table. "Candles and lighter here plus a glass for water. I wasn't sure what else you'd need."

"Spot for the letter box was my idea," Dirk says, joining Connall. They stare at me, my wild, windy sylph and my perfect, strong wolf.

In that moment, I feel like I'm not fighting alone. Like I can be vulnerable, because if I fall, Dirk and Connall will catch me. Worry and emotion rushes back, but some semblance of peace comes with it as I look at them.

Connall points to a remote tucked in the corner of the drawer. "That controls the windows above the bed. You can darken them or call for different weather. Sometimes, when I sleep, I like to set it to rain." He smiles softly. "It reminds me of Arcadia."

"Thank you," I whisper, pulling my knees to my chest as I stare at them. "Thank you for this."

Connall nods, dark eyes roving over my body. He tenses, chest rising and falling fast. He looks like a man on the edge.

Next to him, Dirk wears a smirk as his eyes travel down my upper body.

"We're supposed to be thinking about safety, and we are, but godsdamn seeing you in his bed does things to me. Those fookin' tits are gonna be the death of me, Louanna. "

Grateful for the change of subject back to something lighter, I lean against the headboard. "Everything past the tits is pretty great too."

Connall lurches toward me just as a timer rings out from the kitchen, echoing down the hall and halting his progress across the bed. "Fuck," he grunts, rising and jogging out of the room.

"Och, poor riled-up wolf has to tend to the dinner," Dirk teases. "But I don't." He drops to his knees and reaches for my pants, blue eyes coming to mine. "I need to taste yeh, Louanna, the way he did. I need yeh to come on my tongue before we feed yeh. And then I'll show yeh where I suggested he put a bottle of lube. We're gonna need that, pretty girl."

I help him pull my pants down my legs. He tosses them aside and grabs my leg by the ankle, nipping just above it. Jolting, I pant as his cool lips and tongue make their way up my lower leg to the inside of my knee. He pauses there, playing, nipping, sucking at my skin until my clit throbs with the need to know what his mouth feels like.

He trails a teasing path of light kisses up my inner thigh and over my mound through my panties. Seeing him bent between my thighs is enough to light me on fire. But watching him worship my clit through the lace is too much tease. Not enough of that soft-looking devilish tongue.

"Dirk," I pant. "I need more than that."

"Och, Louanna," he murmurs into my pussy. "The best orgasms come after intense teasing. I wanna eat yeh for a while, my beauty."

"Nooo," I wail, flopping back in frustration.

So it surprises me when he rips the crotch of my panties out with his hands and buries his tongue in my channel. At the same time, his upper lip rubs over my clit. A scream tumbles from my throat. He's soft and wet and cool, and I don't even know where to focus as his left hand snakes up my body to pinch my nipple. I jerk, back arching as heat spears through me. A cramp starts low in my belly, my toes curling as a growl from the door pulls my attention.

Connall stands in the doorway, both hands gripping the frame above his head. His wolf's color shines through, their focus fully on me as I arch again. I can't take much more of this heat. I'm gonna come so hard and so fast. He doesn't enter the room, though. He stands there as Dirk thrusts his tongue in and out of me, curling it to rub my G-spot until I'm panting and squirming, my body locked up tight.

Before I realize what's happening, Connall's across the room, sliding onto his knees beside the bed. He dips his head between my thighs and sucks my clit into his mouth as Dirk continues his slow, torturous licking further down.

Bliss hits like a hurricane, battering me as I thrash and scream and claw at the sheets. But they don't stop. They lick and suck until I'm so sensitive, I start shoving them away.

When I do, Dirk gives Connall a devious look. "Shall we continue what we started earlier, Wolf?"

Connall looks at me, grins, and then looks back at Dirk. "Let's make her wait."

"What?" I sit up in the bed. "What happened earlier?"

Dirk boops me on the nose. "Wouldn't yeh like to know, my sweet?"

Connall crawls over top of me, flattening me to the bed as thick legs straddle my body. He brings one hand to my braid and fists it, pulling my head backward as he buries his mouth in my neck. Heat builds again as I rub my body against his like a cat in heat. He's so hot, so hard, so intensely masculine.

Rough lips nip at my shoulder, my neck, my ear. Then he sucks in a ragged, deep breath. "We played in the forest, Sweetheart. Our sylph is a filthy, filthy animal."

My eyes pop open as I look for Dirk. He's standing at the foot of the bed watching us, wearing a triumphant smile.

Connall licks and nips a path down my neck, up the front of my throat to my chin. Finally, he takes my mouth with slow, deep kisses. He rolls us and pulls me to straddle his waist. He's so damn big, I barely fit, spread wide around his muscular hips. We kiss again, and the bed dips when Dirk climbs onto it. He comes behind us, notching his hips against my ass as both hands stroke down my back under my tee.

"Och, yes, mates. I want us like this, Lou riding that knot while I take her ass."

Connall's answering growl has me both terrified and absolutely certain I want to try that. Breaking the kiss, I sit up and press my upper body to Dirk's.

He bends down and kisses the side of my neck, sharp teeth trailing a path to my shoulder. His hips roll against mine as his hands roam around my front, up to my tee. He pulls it over my head and deposits it on the bed next to us.

Immediately, Connall picks up the tee and brings it to his

nose, sucking in a deep breath. He groans and drops the shirt to his chest as I watch in fascination. Shifting onto his elbows, he gives Dirk and me a lazy grin.

"I brought you here for protection, Lou," he growls. "But I'm gonna fuck you tonight if you're a sweet girl. After dinner, though."

My bratty side rears her head immediately at the notion that I have to be good to get off.

Dirk brings his mouth to my ear. "Yer wolf is mighty inclined to feed yeh before we go too far. What say we let him do the housely duties and tease the fook out of him while he's doing it? How far could we go before he loses his mind, do yeh think?"

I chuckle. "Done."

Dirk shifts away from me and stands. Next thing I know, I'm being pulled into his arms and whisked from the room. I expect Connall to make sad sounds when we leave, but he pushes off the bed, muscles popping as he presses to a stand and stalks after us. I can't help staring at the way his jeans hang low on his hips, an obvious erection straining the fabric.

When we get to the kitchen, Connall heads to the oven and pulls out a lasagna, depositing it on the countertop to cool. He turns to where Dirk and I stand on the opposite side of the island.

"Dinner's done. Now what about all that teasing you promised me?"

"Uhhh." Dirk looks at me and snorts out a laugh. "Thought we had a solid half hour to be naughty on the sofa while you, I dunno, shredded cheese or something."

Connall stands tall and grins. "One thing you should learn about me, Sylph—I'm always prepared."

Those words shouldn't be so hot. But something about how Connall's always so thoughtful, always so ready for anything, always so steady and kind…it gives me something I haven't had since Caroline died. She was my rock. My best friend. And her daughters are my best friends now.

I never knew how to recapture that feeling of safety and security that I lost when she passed. But looking at Connall standing in the kitchen with dinner ready brings that feeling back.

His smirk falls, and he rounds the island, bright green eyes scanning my face. "Your scent changed, sweetheart. What's wrong?"

Dirk holds me tighter.

"My sister was like you," I admit. "Always prepared. Always mothering me because I was so much younger than her. She always brought me snacks, always remembered when my dance concerts were. I was a flighty kid; I—"

Words fail me. I don't know how to explain that feeling of home I get being here with them, don't know how to admit all of that aloud when this is still so new. It's a struggle to remind myself that monsters often move far faster than humans do when it comes to relationships. Maybe they won't find my rush of emotion weird.

Connall pulls his shirt over his head, revealing a broad chest covered in fine hair. Wolfish tattoos cover both pecs and scroll down both arms to his hands. He presses himself against me, his skin burning hot. Being sandwiched between them is my new favorite place in the world. Dirk's lightning streaks across his skin, gathering where our bodies touch. And Connall's a furnace, a deep purr rumbling from him.

"I didn't mean to get all sappy," I admit.

Connall strokes my jawline, his eyes morphing to full green as his wolf comes forward to look at me.

"We're gonna eat, Sweetheart. And we're gonna talk about what's going on. And then we're going to bed, alright? If you're in my arms, I can keep you safe. I have to believe that."

I can't muster up any response other than a quick nod, not

when Connall's like this. It's easy to let him take charge, especially with Dirk a quiet, steady presence at my back.

Connall turns from us and goes back to the island. He cuts the lasagna as Dirk and I join, sitting on the tall stools on the other side. Dirk shifts his chair close, laying an arm on the back of mine as Connall brings our plates to us.

Dirk rubs my shoulder in soft circles. "Louanna, what do you think about seeing Leighton? Yeh've had a day to consider it. What do you think is going on?"

Connall's eyes flash a brighter color as he lays his palms flat on the island and stares at me.

I pick at the lasagna.

"I don't know. I think it's odd that we found Amatheia hurt and then I see someone we know is dead. Not just dead, but cremated. It makes no sense."

Connall straightens and turns, walking across the room. He grabs the communication disk from his wall and returns, setting it on the countertop.

He looks over at Dirk and me. "I had an idea while Lou was just talking. I've got a contact at Shadowsurf. He might have insight."

I force myself to eat a bite of the lasagna even though my blood runs cold at what he just said. When I manage to swallow it, I look up at him. "You think this has something to do with my mental state?"

Connall blanches and shakes his head.

"I don't know, Lou. But it's significant that you're the only one who sees Leighton. Given that Slade doesn't know what happened and Morgan can't heal Amatheia, I think it makes sense to explore another avenue where we might find information. That's all I mean."

I chew another bite of lasagna as I consider his words. He's right. If there's any way we can find out what's going on, we should explore that. I shove my initial hurt feelings aside and nod.

"We should definitely call. Want to do it while we eat?"

Connall nods and depresses a button on top of the round disk. "Call Ezekiel Blackwater."

Blackwater. The same last name as Connall. I wonder if—

A hologram of a handsome, auburn-haired male rises from the disk. Blue eyes crinkle at the corners when he sees Connall. He could be Connall's brother, honestly. They've got the same hair and their features are similar. The other male is slightly lankier, his jawline and nose sharper. He's handsome.

Dirk's fingers curl around my shoulder.

"Cousin, you're looking well," Mr. Hologram says.

Connall smiles and crosses his arms. "Zeke, it's good to see you." He jerks his head toward us. "Meet Lou and Dirk."

Zeke turns and takes us in, his lips curling into a little smirk. "Hello Dirk and Lou." He looks back to Connall. "I haven't seen you in an age. Is everything okay?"

Connall rubs at the back of his neck. "Well, we've had an odd incident here and I'm wondering if you've ever heard anything similar from the Shadowsurf residents." He glances at me. "Lou, do you want to explain it in your own words?"

Zeke turns to me with a curious look.

I clear my throat and sit up a little straighter. "I saw a person who's supposed to be dead, a shifter from here, in Ever."

Zeke cocks his head to the side. "Supposed to be dead?"

"Definitely dead," Connall says, his tone mournful. "We cremated him. I was there. He's gone. But Lou saw him last night. Dirk and I were with her, and we saw nothing. I'm just wondering if you've heard of anything like that?"

Zeke grits his jaw. "What else was happening at the time? Anything?"

"A woman had been attacked," I say. "We can't figure out

what's wrong with her. But as our doctor was examining her, I saw Leighton when nobody else could."

Zeke's eyes spring wide open, and he looks around at all three of us before shaking his head.

Finally, he levels Connall with a serious look. "It's not uncommon for those of us who have been through trauma to see visions, to see monsters. But it tends to happen during sleep or when we're alone." He glances at me, brows furrowed. "It's not common to happen around others or to be connected to real world violence like this. Although, I suppose it's possible that the trauma of finding someone attacked could lead to visions."

I resist the urge to yell at him. What I saw was as real as the nose on my face.

A rolling purr rises up from Zeke's hologram chest.

"Easy, darlin', I don't mean to discredit what you saw." He shoots me a half smile. "You saw something that can't be explained, and that's important. I'm just sharing what I've seen in my years of running the Shadowsurf program. But if I've learned anything in all that time, it's to never assume I know the answer."

"Thanks, cousin," Connall says. "Mind doing me a favor and asking around a bit more, just to be sure? We've got an injured mermaid and what Lou saw. I don't want to leave any stone unturned."

Zeke agrees to do that and signs off. The kitchen is quiet, too quiet. I dig into the lasagna, mulling over what he shared.

"I'm not surprised he didn't have answers for us," Dirk says. "You're unique, Louanna."

I snort out a laugh. "You can say that again."

"I'm serious." Dirk rubs the back of my arm with the thrall bites. "You're different, my sweet. You've already done things no one can explain. Why should this be any different?"

He makes a good point. Doc Slade couldn't explain my thrall bites healing either. But still, the idea of all these things being connected to me is slightly terrifying.

We finish eating and Dirk mercifully changes the subject to skyball for a few minutes. The guys talk and I listen, trying to focus but continuing to come back to all the things we don't know right now. I know myself well enough to know that it'll consume me if I let it.

"Hey," I break in when there's a pause in the skyball chatter. "I'm anxious and feeling weirdly sappy about all this shit going on; I think we all are. But maybe we can set that aside for a little while."

Connall rounds the island, grabs the end of my braid, and pulls the hair tie from it. His fingers comb through the strands, undoing it. "It's not sappy to share your feelings and emotions. I want you both to do that, always. Never hold back from me, or each other. The only way to navigate something potentially complex is to be honest."

Good, I think. *Because I'm about to take this in an entirely different direction.*

I lift my chin. "I want to see what you guys did earlier."

Dirk chuckles.

Connall looks at him, his wolf's focus flashing through his irises as a muscle works overtime in his jaw. For a long moment, he seems to weigh the options, and I think he might actually say no.

But after a moment, his nostrils flare. "Get on the couch," he commands, waving us toward the giant pit sofa that might as well be a bed. He grins at Dirk. "Take your clothes off, Sylph."

I hold back a moan as Dirk's smile grows broad. He pulls his gem off and sets it on the edge of the sofa. Reaching down, he shoves tight jeans down his muscular legs, revealing a partially hard cock bobbing against his thigh. His dick is as beautiful as the rest of him, long and thick with heavy balls nestled beneath. He's hairless, but it just accentuates how chiseled he is.

"Sit against the back of the sofa," Connall says to Dirk. As Dirk obeys, Connall turns to me. "I want you to watch, Lou.

Watch and know we did this earlier. And we wanted you to see, to be part of it."

"Okay," is all I can manage as he unbuttons his jeans and steps out of them, kicking them onto the floor. His cock swings free, the bulbous section at the base swollen. I gulp as I stare at how huge it is, and I know it'll swell bigger, locking us in place during sex.

This is a much, much better idea than focusing on all the things I can't figure out tonight. Go me.

Then I imagine him and Dirk playing around. Would he put that giant knot inside Dirk? Or maybe ask Dirk to ride him? Heat flushes through me as Connall joins us on the sofa, crawling to the back to rest on his knees in front of Dirk.

He glances over his shoulder at us. "Come, Lou. Sit right next to him, Sweetheart."

I scramble to Dirk's side, tucking my knees to my chest as I rest against the low sofa back and stare at our wolf.

Green eyes flash at Dirk, swirling with emerald as his wolf presses to the surface. "I want to taste you the way you tasted me, but I need you to guide me. I haven't done this."

Dirk brings his foot flat, letting his right knee fall to the side as his cock spears the air, pointing toward Connall. "Och, Wolf. I'll like anything yeh do, but dinnae worry. I'm an excellent teacher."

My pussy tightens and clenches. They did this earlier? Gods, it's so hot, I can't bear it.

Connall drops onto all fours and brings his nose to the inside of Dirk's right knee, breathing in softly. He follows a trail down Dirk's thigh, dragging his fangs along Dirk's skin. Dirk is silent, watchful as his lightning streaks across his skin and sunbursts out from every point Connall touches.

By the time Connall's mouth nears Dirk's cock, Dirk's already dripping creamy white precum from his flushed tip. I ache to lean over and capture it, to lick him and suck, to find out how to make him fall apart. I want to see Dirk in the throes of ecstasy when he's not scheming, conniving and planning.

Connall's right hand comes to Dirk's sack, and he kneads it gently, tugging and pulling as Dirk lets out a soft moan. "Feels nice, Wolf," he croons, "but not as sensitive as my shaft."

Connall grins at me. "Same, but I was interested in what's back here." He slides his fingers behind Dirk's sack and rubs. I can't see anything more than that, but Dirk's cheeks flush a darker blue, his jaw tightening.

"Back there is so sensitive," he murmurs. "Needs lube though. Perhaps our Louanna can help us there."

I struggle to swallow. My mouth is dry as a desert. "I suggest spitting in your hand, Dirk."

At my suggestion, he rumbles out a seductive growl and holds an open palm out toward me. "You first, my sweet."

I lean forward and spit into his palm, but my eyes never leave his.

"Again," he demands. "I need more than that, Louanna."

I spit three more times before he's happy. Connall watches us in silence, but his muscles tremble slightly when Dirk takes the spit and coats the tip of his dick with it, rubbing it into his skin with a soft moan.

Connall bends forward and licks a stripe up the underside of Dirk's cock. It jolts, going rigid and slapping Connall in the face. Both males groan as I wipe a bead of sweat from my forehead.

"More, Wolf," Dirk demands. "Suck on it. Taste our Louanna."

Connall drags his tongue up Dirk's cock and then opens wide, closing his mouth around Dirk's cockhead. When he hollows his cheeks and sucks, Dirk's hips jerk. He grabs at my thigh, squeezing as his head falls back.

"Fuck, Wolf. Yer mouth is so hot, so wet."

Connall's responding growl sends Dirk into a panting frenzy, his chest heaving as Connall surges forward, taking all of Dirk's length into his mouth. Damn, I'm jealous. Deep-throating is an art, and he's making it look fucking easy. I want in on this action.

"Louanna," Dirk groans, "need yer mouth, princess."

I glance at Connall, but his eyes are hooded with lust as he drags his open mouth down one side of Dirk's cock. I don't wait for permission that won't come. My wolf is too lost to the heat. So I lean over and join him, sucking on the tip of Dirk's dick as he groans, threading his fingers through my loose hair.

Connall joins me, exploring Dirk with our mouths. We lick down to the base of his shaft and back up, taking turns sucking on him. Precum drips steadily from him as his hips roll nonstop.

Connall surges forward and takes my mouth in a deep, searing kiss that unleashes something inside me. Breaking the kiss, I take as much of Dirk as I can between my lips, sucking and licking as I pop off him.

He cries out, "More, Louanna."

I take him to the back of my throat as Connall dips below me and pulls one of Dirk's balls into his mouth.

The first spurt of cum hits my tongue as Dirk's hips vibrate with intensity. His lightning flashes to the base of his cock and spirals out from there, skating over his skin as he pants and cries out.

"He's about to come," Connall growls. His mouth replaces mine, taking Dirk to the base as I reach between his thighs and roll his heavy sack in one hand.

Dirk's eyes glaze over, his focus moving between us as his mouth opens and cheeks flush a darker shade of blue. Then his eyes roll into his head, lips pulling back into a snarl as his hips jerk with steady, fast movements.

He fucks Connall's face while I stare at them both in absolute wonder. This is mine. They are mine.

And then he explodes, his body going rigid as every muscle tenses. He arches backward, clawing at my thigh and the back of the sofa as he rams his cock into Connall's mouth with shallow, rapid thrusts. His panting becomes a roar, his lips curled back as he stiffens and grabs at Connall's hair with the hand not touching me.

Lust and need overtake me as I watch his dick disappear between Connall's lips. Strings of sticky cum drip from Connall's mouth, but as Dirk sags back to the couch with a gasping moan, Connall licks him clean. He laps at Dirk's slit and crown and all the way down both sides of his cock. It falls, spent, to Dirk's belly, his lightning returning to its usual lazy river state.

"That was…I have no words," my sylph moans, reaching down to drag his fingertips along Connall's jaw. He squeezes my knee with his other hand, reminding me that no matter what's happening in his life, part of him is always focused on me.

He always has been.

Connall glances over. "I can't wait for you both to do that to me."

"How about now?" I demand. "I wanna do it now."

He shakes his head and crawls up Dirk's body, taking his mouth in a deep, hot kiss that sears me to my core. When they part, he leans over and brings his mouth to Dirk's ear, saying something low.

Dirk's eyes flash and move to mine, his lips pulling into a wicked grin. "Yes, Wolf. Yes, we do."

Oh fuck. They're talking about me. But I'm a brat, so I scooch toward the end of the sofa. "If you two are busy telling secrets, I'll just—"

A big, warm arm yanks me back, my body hitting Connall's. The impact knocks the breath from my lungs as he brings his mouth to my neck and bites. Pain and shock war with pleasure as he follows the bite by suckling at my skin.

"My bratty woman," he growls into my ear, "you're going nowhere until that pussy gets a taste of me."

He dwarfs me like this, his huge body a furnace at my back. His chest hair tickles my skin as he reaches between my thighs and pulls his cock through them. He's so damn big, the tip of his dick sticks out between my legs. But then he rocks his body, hips slamming against my ass as his shaft rubs my clit and pussy.

"Fuck," I grunt out. He feels so damn good, so hot and hard, and I'm dripping like a damn faucet.

When Dirk crawls around to my front with a devious look, I can't pull my eyes from him, even as orgasm builds deep in my belly. All this teasing, all the watching, it's got me ready to combust.

So when Dirk leans down and sucks at my clit, I arch and claw at his head and Connall's big forearm. My muscles tremble as sweat breaks out over my skin. But then the touch disappears. When I look down, Dirk has Connall's cock in his mouth, lapping at the slit. Behind me, Connall lets out a low, needy moan.

I'm not gonna last another minute. Dirk reaches between my thighs and palms Connall's shaft, stroking him as our wolf bucks against me in hard, slow motions. The noises coming from him are nearly enough to get me off, but I'm not quite there.

"Louanna needs more," Dirk says. "She needs that knot, Wolf."

Oh gods. I've seen Connall's knot, and I'm half convinced it'd break me. But I'm more curious to try.

Connall moves from behind me but pulls me with him. "Turn around, sweetheart. Straddle me. I'm big, but we'll take this slow and Dirk'll help, alright?" There's a rustling noise and he brings his mouth to my ear. "I just put on a contraceptive ring, in case you see it. We should be careful, Sweetheart."

Heat streaks down my spine, along with nerves that pull goosebumps to the surface of my skin. Preparedness is so hot, and it feels so unbelievable that I'm here with them both. I slide a leg on either side of Connall, his cock a rigid bar pressed to his stomach. Just like he said, a large flesh-colored ring surrounds the base of his knot.

Dirk comes behind me, reaching around to grip Connall and

stroke. My wolf's eyes go hooded, lips curling back into a snarl. He's never looked like more of a predator than he does now, dominant like this.

Big hands come to my hips and lift me up. Behind me, Dirk guides Connall between my thighs until the head of his cock is notched against my pussy.

I'm trembling, focused on what we're about to do when Connall's warm fingers come to my clit and rub soft, gentle circles. Heat swirls as Dirk's hands come to my ass. He helps me lower down as Connall's cockhead fills me. I gasp at how big he is, how hard. I don't think this is gonna work. He fills and rubs every inch of my channel, my pussy clamping and fluttering around a dick that's too big but feels too fucking good.

"Not gonna let my knot lock you up tonight," Connall says. "It's an intense level of connection we haven't discussed, but I can't wait to do that with you, Sweetheart."

As Connall pushes deeper inside, rational thought disappears. There's only the sensation of being split around a cock that feels like it's the size of my damn arm.

But the brush of his fingers and filthy praise from Dirk help me drop down a few inches. My legs tremble even as Dirk holds me up. But then he drops me another inch lower, and I hit Connall's knot.

"There's no fucking way," I blurt out, falling forward onto my wolf's chest. "It's too damn big."

"You feel amazing, Sweetheart," he says with a growl. "This pussy was made for me, made to take me, to be knotted by me. Let me do the work. Let me keep you safe. Let me keep you *sated*, Lou."

Nearly sobbing at the stretch of him, I will my muscles to relax as I rest my cheek on Connall's chest. His hands come just below my ass cheeks as he begins to thrust with shallow, slow movements. The edges of his knot begin to push inside me as I pant and cry out. I don't know if there's enough lube in the world for this to work.

But then a warm tongue circles my back hole, and I scream and clench. Connall gasps and jerks his hips, and his knot fills me with a pop. I pant around the absolute fill of him. I'm stretched to the point of pain, but heat's building anyways, swirling with the first telltale signs of impending orgasm. I moan, because that's all I can do as Connall's dick flexes inside me, rubbing against... everything.

He groans again, but I don't feel Dirk, so—

"Fuck me, your tongue is amazing," Connall groans.

Oh gods, what's Dirk doing? I'm desperate to know.

Connall pulls me forward, capturing my lips as his cock slides out of me, dragging along my G-spot as I pant into the kiss.

Then Dirk's tongue licks a stripe from my pussy to my ass and back again. Connall and I groan together as he slides back in, his knot playing at the edges of my channel.

The second time he slips it inside me, it's easier.

The third time is easier still.

Until my wolf fucks up into me with hard, steady movements. Dirk teases and taunts us, his hands roaming my body and Connall's until I explode around the thickest cock I've ever seen. When orgasm hits me, Connall grunts out a string of expletives, and Dirk lets out a maniacal, pleased laugh. I'm too fucking far gone in the pleasure to comprehend anything but the way bliss radiates from my core, my eyes rolling back as I clench rhythmically around Connall's knot.

When pleasure finally fades, I slump forward and listen to Connall's steady heartbeat. It's a little faster than usual, his big chest heaving. Dirk curls over me from behind, kissing and stroking my back and Connall's side.

Before I even realize it, I'm falling asleep.

CHAPTER TWENTY-FIVE
DIRK

Lou is the first to fall asleep, her head tucked against Connall's muscular pecs. He strokes her back, green eyes on me while I touch both her and him. She's still perched on his knot, but it sits pressed to her pussy lips rather than buried deep inside her.

"Is this really our life?" he whispers as he rubs Lou's back and plays with her hair.

"Messy and beautiful and delightful. Yeah, this is our real life." I lean over him and kiss all over my Louanna's back. I want her to wake so I can tell her how perfect this feels, having her between us. Cherishing her. Worshipping her. How her commanding me in the bedroom almost sent me over the edge.

"You were right to bring her here." I look up to meet Connall's intense gaze. "The idea of something happening to her is gonna make me crazy."

He grinds his teeth. "We won't let that happen. I don't know how, but if we don't let her out of our sight…" His voice trails off and I'm sure he's thinking what I'm thinking. That we can't fight a foe we can't see. He closes his eyes and buries his face in her hair, tightening his arms around her.

Watching them together makes my cock harden again. I want her. I want them. But the heaviness of the day hangs around my neck now that she's resting peacefully, tucked into Connall's steady embrace. My Louanna's a sarcastic soul, but there's a sensitive edge to her, a delicateness that needs tending. We can be her safe place. Somehow. With all the power I have at my disposal, surely I can keep her safe.

Connall's eyes close as he touches her. I sense my wolf could use some rest too. When I push off the sofa and cross the room to the kitchen, I feel his eyes on me. I open cupboards, looking for something to cover the rest of the lasagna with.

"Above the stove," he calls out quietly from across the room.

I grab tin foil from the cabinet, cover the lasagna and put it into the fridge. Then I return to the sofa and find the nearest blanket. I crawl next to my mates and cover Lou.

"Get some rest," I tell Connall. "I'll keep watch."

"Not a cuddler?" His smile teases me.

"Och, Wolf. I love tae cuddle. But after today's events, I feel compelled to protect yeh both. So sleep."

He smiles and pulls Lou higher in his arms, burying his face in her hair once more. He opens his eyes long enough to look at me. "Is it possible to fall in love this quickly?"

My throat constricts because he's saying something I've been feeling for so long. But I want to tell them how much I love them when they're both awake. I can't share that for the first time without her. I won't.

I stroke mussed hair away from her cheek, tucking it over her back. Connall takes the long strands and plays with them, sighing contentedly.

"It is," I confirm, choking around the words. "Get some rest, mate."

Auburn lashes flutter over his freckled cheeks as he rests his face against the top of Louanna's head. It seems like mere moments later that soft snores ring through the treehouse.

I don't need sleep; the elements sustain me. I don't even need food, for that matter, although I can enjoy it. So I stand watch in the corner of the room while my family rests. In the wee hours of morning, Connall stirs, his beautiful cock bobbing against his thigh. His hands roam Lou's body, pinching her nipples, stroking between her thighs.

She moans and curls away from him, face in the blankets. He chuckles and sits up, looking at me. Rising to a stand, he crosses the room and grabs my hand. I can't pull my eyes from how hard he is, dick swinging heavy between his thighs. I want it so badly, my mouth goes dry. But my eyes move to our Louanna.

Connall's mouth comes to my neck. "Shower with me, Dirk. I'll leave the door open so we can keep an eye on her."

As long as I can watch her from a few feet away, I'm willing. So I allow my big mate to pull me into the bathroom, swinging the door wide. The entire back wall is a giant shower made of black pebbles. Black stone walls soar high. It's like stepping into a sexy, cavernous dragon's keep. Heat swirls between my thighs, cock stiffening as Connall turns the shower on. I glance at Louanna.

"If you're unsure, we can do this one at a time." He rests against the wall.

I've got a clear view of her from the bathroom, though, so I turn a bright smile on him. "This is perfect, Wolf."

"Good," he growls, pulling me into the shower. He lifts my hands high on the glass front. "Watch her while I bathe you."

My feral grin pulls a chuckle from my big mate. Part of me thought there might be unevenness in our relationship. That perhaps he'd never care for me the way he so obviously cares for her. But now that we're in it, that worry is gone.

I've dreamed of this for so long. Made the moves and arrangements so we could be in this spot at this time. Can it be this easy? I knew I could convince Louanna, but I thought Connall might have reservations, certain as I was that he's mine.

But when he brings big, warm hands to my back, lathering my skin with soap, I suspect he feels the connection like I do. He massages my skin, his touch reverent even as he glances over my shoulder at our woman. He's not rushed as his hands move up my neck and down both arms. His touch moves to my front, soapy hands coming to my cock and stroking.

"Connall," I moan. "Fook, that feels good."

My head falls back as his left hand strokes upward on the back of my leg. When warm fingers part my arse cheeks to stroke my back hole, I relax.

"Just where I want yeh, Wolf," I murmur.

He touches, running his fingers around the tight ring as his mouth comes to my ear. "You want me touching you here? Or you want to touch me here?"

Ah, I see what he's asking. I glance at him as he dips the barest hint of a finger inside me. "I'll touch yeh however yeh want, Wolf. But I need yeh on top of me sometimes, the rougher the better."

His low growl raises the hair on my nape, power building under my skin as he palms my cock and prods my arse. Sensations too numerous to catalog build and swirl at him touching me like this. He returns to my back, nudging at my back hole with the head of his cock.

"I've never done this," he says. "But I want to. And I don't know if I'd want it done to me, but we can try."

My focus flicks to our Louanna. She stirs in the bed. Safe. She's safe in our home. She has to be, because the alternative is too terrible to consider.

I glance over my shoulder at him. "We need lube, mate. Louanna's waking. Shall we put on a show for her?"

Connall bends and plants a kiss on my shoulder. It morphs into an open-mouthed bite. He bites again and again up my trap to my neck, which receives the same rough treatment. His dick is a hard bar between us, resting between my arse cheeks as he rocks his big hips against mine.

"The moment she's up, I want her with us," he growls into my skin. "I *need* her with us."

I know what he means. The masculine urge to have her in my arms and never set her down nearly chokes me. Even being this far away feels like torture. But if she needs anything right now, it's sleep. *Good* sleep.

He steps out of the shower long enough to root around in a cabinet and withdraw, handily, a bottle of lube. When he returns, I give him a wry look. "Just happened to have that there, did yeh?"

He smiles, and it's breathtaking. "I've been doing some research since you made your interest known. There's lube stashed all around the house." He rubs my side. "For that matter, there's a hook by the front door for your gem, if it's ever more comfortable for you to hang it there rather than wearing it at home."

Something about that statement flays me open. That I told him what he is to me and he did research to prepare. That he didn't run from the attraction. That, despite never dating a man or touching a man like this, he made arrangements.

My wicked smile must fall, because he steps back into the shower and places the lube on a small shelf. Returning to me, he spins me to face him and slants his mouth over mine until we're breathing the same air.

"My lack of experience with men says nothing about my level of interest in you."

"I know," I whisper.

"You'll be my first," he growls.

"And only."

His breathing goes ragged as he grabs one of my hands and guides it down to his cock. He's impossibly hard, covered in thick veins and that gorgeous wolfy knot. He wraps my fingers around his length and pulls rhythmically.

"This is for you," he murmurs into my mouth. "The evidence

of my attraction. I never expected this, Dirk, but you are captivating."

I grip him harder and run my fingers around his cockhead, pulling gently at the stretched length of skin running underneath the crown.

Connall snarls and grips my throat. "Lou bit me there, that day we played with the paints. It felt so good."

"Och, don't tease me," I grouse. "If I hadn't made a promise to stop spying on you, I'd have been there watching."

"Ask for her consent," he says on a growl. "But you can spy on me any time I'm not in session, or if I'm with her and she consents."

I stop stroking, eyes wide. "Seriously?"

"If she agrees," he clarifies. "The thought of you watching us makes me hot."

"It'll be important for yeh to have time alone with her," I offer.

"Of course."

"And me."

Connall's grin grows big as he palms my sack and strokes behind it. "Naturally."

He spins me again. "We're a team, protecting her. So watch our woman, look at how beautiful she is while I fuck this ass with my fingers."

A groan leaves me as the lube cap snaps open. Chilly fingers prod at my back hole, one slipping inside. It stretches as he thrusts, but it's not enough to get me off. Just a warmup as my lightning skates over my skin, tingling. But when he adds a second finger and strokes, heat builds between my thighs, my cock going rigid as a tree between my legs. I press my forehead to the glass and stare at Louanna as she sits upright, rubbing at her eyes.

There's a moment she looks around, concerned, but I groan to pull her attention to me. Amber eyes flash my direction and widen as Connall presses me hard to the glass, two fingers working in and out of my arse. But when he curls them, nudging at my prostate, I yip and grunt and make unintelligible noises.

Lou crawls out of bed, nipping at her bottom lip as she comes to the doorway. My mouth falls open as Connall explores me, figuring out what movements make me pant.

"Louanna, come," I plead, brows furrowing as the pleasure builds. The chill of the glass at my front is a harsh contrast to the searing hot alpha male at my back. I need Louanna's softness.

"Are you sure?" she asks, eyes flicking from me to Connall and back again.

"Come here, Sweetheart," he encourages.

His alpha tone hits us both. I groan, and Lou scurries into the shower, stepping around us into the water. I pull out of Connall's grasp just long enough to angle the shower head against the wall. Then I reach for my woman and haul her into my arms, pressing her back to the wall and ensuring the stream of water covers us so she doesn't grow cold.

Burying my face in her neck, I step my feet wide as Connall rejoins us. He kisses Lou over my shoulder, a tender slant of his mouth over hers, his tongue licking into her. When they part, he nuzzles her nose. "Good morning."

She stares up at him in wonder just as he removes his fingers from my arse. Next, he notches his enormous cockhead against my hole and pushes. I arch my back, fingers tightening on the backs of Louanna's legs.

At the first gentle thrust, I fall apart. My hole swallows Connall like it was made for his dick, and it was, I suppose. But nothing prepared me for the sensation of being filled by something so big and hot.

I groan into Louanna's neck, planting desperate kisses on her skin as Connall presses further in. He and I let out matching ragged groans.

"So fucking tight," he gasps.

"Give me more," I demand, lifting my head long enough to bring my mouth to my woman's.

She's panting, eyes hooded as she stares at us.

With a slow, steady drive of his hips, Connall fills me, dick pulsing in my channel as my lips peel back into a snarl. I've been with males before, always comfortable with a fluid sexual drive that calls me to people regardless of their gender. It's the spirit that attracts me, and my mates have spirit in spades.

Connall grips my hips and pulls out. When he enters me for the second time, my legs begin to tremble, grip tightening until Louanna grunts. But the scent of her arousal floods the small shower area as my dick rubs against her wet pussy. The shower head streams water on us as Connall thrusts harder, rocking me against our mate as her nipples pebble to diamond-hard points.

I want her to feel this pleasure the same as I am, but it's harder to maneuver her in the shower. But that thought spurs another, and I grin at my woman. Lifting her, I settle her higher against the wall, even as pleasure swirls through my core. Rational thought is about to flee my brain, so I wrap Louanna's legs over my shoulders and bury my face in her glistening pussy.

She curls over my head at the first pass of my tongue through her soaked pussy lips. Sweet cream coats my tongue as I grunt. Connall fills me, the slap of his hips on mine harder, rougher as he begins to lose control. Knowing I make him feel good, that he's on the verge of coming, has me arching my back to meet him thrust for thrust. My cock slaps against the tiled wall with every bounce of Connall's hips.

I suck at Louanna's clit, holding her pleasure between my lips as her thighs begin to tremble. She gasps as Connall snarls behind me, one hand coming to her thigh to use it as leverage. His big body arcs against mine, his thrusts hard and rough as a stream of growls fills the shower.

Lou groans, looking to where our wolf fucks me near senseless.

"You're taking him so well, Sylph," she murmurs. "My good boy. You're making him feel so good."

Oh fooooook. We need to play with *that* dynamic a whole fook of a lot more.

I cry out with need as I surge between her thighs again, covering her pussy with my mouth and sucking. She grits out a string of curse words and comes, exploding with pleasure that sparks my orgasm. It builds and swirls out from my guts, sending white-hot shards of ecstasy radiating through my system. I roar between her legs as I jolt.

Connall's movements go choppy and fast until he comes on a snarl, filling my arse with creamy cum. It drips down my thighs, prolonging my orgasm. Louanna's hips rock against my mouth as her bliss fades.

When we come down, panting and huddled together, I know I'll do anything, anything, to keep them by my side.

CHAPTER TWENTY-SIX
LOU

There's nothing hotter in this world than watching the two males you're obsessed with be obsessed with each other. Obsessed isn't even the right word for this. I'm falling in love and it happened so fast.

Was it like this for my nieces? One minute you're meeting a hot gargoyle and the next—*bam*—you want his babies?

I suspect they feel exactly the same way, too. It's clear in the way Connall looks at Dirk, and Dirk has always been so up front about his feelings. He slides me off his shoulders, beaming at me. But my focus moves to Connall, to the way he pulls out of Dirk and stares in wonder.

"You okay?" I ask, hoping I'm reading the look on his face right.

He runs both hands through wet, dark hair, but smiles, looking a little surprised. "Better than okay. I...That was nearly indescribable. Having you both like this."

Dirk glances over his shoulder with a wicked, knowing smile. After a moment, he looks back at me. "Louanna, I..."

His voice trails off as he closes his mouth, swallowing whatever he was going to say next. He glances from Connall to me, his expression tender, almost desperate.

"Woman, I wanted to tell yeh—"

The alarm on his comm watch pings, and he groans. "I've a meeting with Arkan that I'm likely to be late for, but I've got something for yeh both."

He bends down and kisses the tip of my nose. "Let me dry yeh off, Louanna. Then feed yeh a bit of Connall's food."

I give him a quizzical look. "Wasn't there something about how you're already late?"

Connall steps out of the shower and grabs a towel, wrapping it around his waist. I gulp as his thick cock disappears from view. Damn, I want that again.

"I'll give it to you later," he growls, "as long as you're a good girl, Sweetheart."

Dirk and I groan together. I slap his arm. "What are you groaning about? You already got dicked down, and I bet it felt so good."

"So good," Dirk confirms. "The fookin' best."

They're going to be such teases together; I can already tell.

Dirk pulls me out of the shower, and then I get the oddest experience of being hand-dried by two gorgeous males who refuse to let me do it myself. But when Connall drops to his knees, claiming he needs to tongue-bathe me, honestly? I let him.

Who would say no to that?

A delicious, orgasmic quarter-hour later, I'm dressed and standing in the kitchen as Connall cooks some sort of breakfast hash with potatoes and sausage. Dirk joins us in the kitchen, leaning against the island where I'm sitting, staring at Connall's ass while he cooks.

"Gods, it's beautiful," he muses. "I can see why yeh picked this spot, Louanna."

I shoot him a gleeful look. "It's just so bubbly and round. I mean, look at it!"

Connall turns, pink dusting his cheeks. He's still only wearing the towel from before. An enormous erection now tents the front of it.

I drop my eyes to stare at it, mouth watering before I'm able to pull my gaze back up. "You should definitely cook naked. There's no need for a towel. It's just me and Dirk here."

His blush grows deeper, spreading down his neck and chest as Dirk leans against the counter with both elbows. Connall reaches down and opens the towel, tossing it onto the counter next to us.

"Much better," I whisper. Now I've got a perfect view of that gorgeous cock and a knot that still seems too big to fit inside me. But it did, and then I came so hard, I nearly passed out.

"Yeh need a blow job," Dirk says on a growl. "And I would suck yeh off right now if I didn't have to show up before this fookin' meeting ends." He looks at me. "Perhaps Louanna can do something about that."

"I need to feed you both," Connall corrects, waving his spatula at Dirk. "Enough sex. We've got shit to do."

"Listen," Dirk teases, grabbing the spatula from Connall. "I've one rule in this relationship, and it's a sexy one." He winks at me. "Are yeh ready to hear it?"

Connall leans against the counter and crosses his enormous arms. "Let's hear it, Sylph."

"As many times as yeh can get it up, mate, we'll work tae get it back down."

I snort and cover my mouth as the corners of Connall's lips twitch upward.

Dirk reaches into his pocket and withdraws something, taking a step closer to Connall. "In all seriousness, Wolf, I told yeh I had presents, and I do." He opens his hand to reveal an etched silver cuff. The top is flat but becomes round as it encloses the circle. There's enough of a gap for someone to fit their wrist through.

My mouth goes dry watching my males together. Connall's dark lashes flutter against freckled cheeks. "You got me jewelry?"

"Och," Dirk laughs softly, "'tis the wolfish way, is it not? To gift your intended with jewels until they shine like the moon?"

"It is," Connall says quietly, holding his wrist out. His hand trembles, and tears fill my eyes. This feels somehow momentous, this gift.

Dirk slips the thin cuff over Connall's wrist and spins it, flat side up. Connall lifts it to examine the markings, stepping closer to show me.

"Silver is a traditional gift," he says. "But I've never seen a cuff quite like this."

"I had it custom-made." Dirk joins us, running his fingers over the surface.

"That takes a long time," Connall muses, looking over at Dirk.

"Almost two months," Dirk confirms.

Connall's green eyes go wide. "That means you ordered it—"

"The moment we met." Dirk lifts his chin, his expression more serious than I've ever seen it. He reaches out and places a hand on my thigh, squeezing, his fingers shaky as he looks between us.

I can't look away from either of them.

Connall lurches forward and slams his mouth against Dirk's. It's so quick and rough that I gasp, but Dirk just snarls and shoves Connall against the countertop, their kiss ragged and desperate. My body is molten lava watching them. Dirk's hand never leaves my thigh. I could reach out and touch either of them, or both of them.

Their kiss slows to a tender, thorough exploration, and moments later, they part. Connall pulls me close to them and takes my mouth with the same attention he gave Dirk. His lips are soft and hot. But then Dirk grips the back of my neck and steals me from Connall, slamming his mouth against mine as he bends me backward into our wolf. This kiss is harder, needier, with an almost desperate edge. And he kisses me until I'm breathless.

When we part, Dirk dips to Connall's neck and places a tender kiss over a spot where his neck and shoulder meet.

Gods, I think he's about to profess his love. Or maybe I just hope he does. Because watching them fall for one another might be the best thing I've ever had the privilege to witness.

After kissing Connall, he turns to me, removing something else from his pocket. He moves and parts my thighs, slipping his big body between them. Opening his hand, he reveals a tiny round orb on a long, thin silver chain. The orb is clear glass, and inside, blue mist swirls like it's alive.

"Tis a bit of my magic, Louanna," he shares. "A very traditional air elemental gift. Because you're mine, it'll bring yeh peace and joy when I'm not around. Just rub it, and the magic'll react to yeh, following your fingertip around the orb."

I fully expect a bit of snark, because that's how Dirk delivers all news. But none comes.

Instead, he lifts my chin with a forefinger. "It would be my greatest honor if yeh'd wear this, my beauty."

I can't find words, so I take the tiny orb and slip the chain over my neck. It lands level with my heart, something I suspect he planned. Because, if nothing else, Dirk is an insane planner.

"It's beautiful," I whisper, tears springing unbidden to my eyes.

He presses forward and brings his cool lips to mine. "Yeh deserve the world, Louanna. And Connall and I will strive to give that to yeh every fookin' day. Do yeh hear me? This world and every other that exists, mate." He kisses the tip of my nose. "We'll be worthy of a box full of letters to Caroline."

I gulp around words that choke me. I'm still figuring out this dynamic and what it means, and I—

But Dirk banishes those thoughts from my mind when he

slants his mouth over mine, his tongue dipping in to taste me. A soft moan from him has me rocking my hips against his.

When Connall's big hands slide up the back of my neck, holding my head while Dirk kisses me, I decide I'm going to beg them both to stay home today. No matter that we all have work to do.

But when Dirk's comm watch pings, we part. He looks at Arkan's name hovering over the band and groans.

"I've got tae go." His voice is mournful, so I suspect he's feeling the same thing as I am.

Connall grips my neck and turns me to face him. "Are you working today?"

I nod. "Yeah, my shift starts in an hour."

His expression goes soft. "I'd like to walk you to work, if Dirk is leaving. And maybe take you to lunch after you're done?"

It's on the tip of my tongue to snark about not needing someone to walk me the five minutes to Alkemi, but when I think back to what happened with Amatheia, I decide not to.

"Sounds good," I agree. "To both."

"Och, Louanna's tryin' not tae sass yeh," Dirk says on a laugh. "She thought about it; I could see it in her face."

Connall's grip tightens as he presses his body to my thigh. "Let's play with that sass a little bit tonight."

Heat spears through me, and I squirm on the countertop. Gods, I love Connall in dominant mode.

Eventually, we can't delay any longer, and Dirk disappears on a lazy gust of wind.

Connall and I dress, and then he stands in the doorway and stares at me while I braid my hair.

As I loop the elastic around the end, he joins me in the bathroom, wrapping the braid around his fist. Green eyes roam over the strands before meeting mine in the mirror.

"Would you teach me how to do this sometime? The idea of braiding your hair is appealing."

I raise a brow. "Appealing, huh?"

He comes to stand behind me, pressing me to the sink as we stare at one another in the mirror. His big hand comes to mine, and he guides it to his heart, green eyes locked onto mine.

"Appealing, Lou," he says to our reflections. "Because I want to be part of every moment of your day. The big moments, the smaller ones." He twirls my hair around his fingertip. "I want to take care of you, sweet girl, just like Dirk does."

"I've been thinking about that," I admit.

"And?"

"I'd like us to plan something special for Dirk." I lean back against Connall's chest, lifting my head to look up at him. "He's this crazy master planner when it comes to us, and I don't want him to feel like it always has to be him. What we're doing, it's… new. But in his mind, it's been all about us since he met us."

"What do you have in mind?" Connall's voice goes deep, his wolf's sheen swirling through his irises as a hand snakes around my front to rest between my breasts.

"Not sure," I admit. "Think about it, and we can make a plan over lunch?"

"Done," Connall whispers into my hair, kissing the top of my forehead.

When we leave his place, he reaches a hand out for me. It hangs there in the air, expectant, hopeful. But the look on his face is downright pleased.

I slip my fingers through his, reveling at how warm and rough they are. We talk about his childhood and his parents, who still live in Arcadia.

We get the occasional stare and whisper as we pass through town. I wonder how the pack feels about their Second dating? Are they excited for him? Feel weird because I have no wolf? I wonder…

But he pays them no mind, focused on me from door to door.

When we get to Alkemi, I struggle to untwine my fingers from his. I don't want to let him go.

Eventually, after a couple parting kisses, I manage to get myself in the door. But I miss him.

I miss them both.

And I'm falling in love. I'm definitely falling in love.

～

"Okay, so you want to plan something special for Dirk?" Malik glances down at me as we arrange a new window display of aragonite crystals. I stare at the gorgeous yellowy-amber color, musing about how, if I had any sort of power, these crystals would help to channel it. But I don't, and they are completely wasted on me.

"Yeah." I glance up at Malik. "Is it weird to talk about me dating two males?"

He snorts and turns the largest crystal in the display, angling it so the sunlight outside filters through the crystal to cast yellow light on the whole tabletop.

"Not hardly, Lou. Many monsters mate in throuples or even in groups. Are humans not the same?"

"Some." I shrug. "For a long time, I think it's something people did behind closed doors and simply whispered about. Nowadays, it's more common and accepted, but you still can't marry multiple people."

He cocks his head to the side. "Who would keep you from your mates? What do you mean?"

"I mean in a legal sense." I stare up at him. "Does Hearth HQ not have rules about mating?"

He shakes his head, stomping one foreleg. "Hardly. There are so many species of monster, it would be impossible for them to capture the nuance of mating habits. Plus, they differ all around the world. The Hearth is more focused on the haven system itself, and its administration, less so on individual monsters and their customs."

"I guess that makes sense."

Malik reaches into a box and withdraws the next large crystal. "Well, if you wanted to plan something fun for Dirk, you could always take home a couple of the enhancing potions we just got in."

I stare up at my boss. "You haven't explained those to me yet. What exactly do they enhance?" I give him a meaningful look.

A pink blush steals over his pale cheeks. "Not physical enhancement. It's a mental stimulant. They make sensations feel more...well, more powerful. Every touch, every look is enhanced. They were originally designed by a pegasus warlock like me who mated a human. Because of the size difference, things were challenging."

I laugh as I retrieve another crystal from the box between us. "Do you mean challenging in that he had a giant dong, and she was my size?"

Malik clears his throat and chuckles as he blushes scarlet. "Something like that, yes."

I focus on setting the crystal carefully down. "My niece Wren used something like that when she and Ohken mated."

He shakes his head. "Ah. That's different. That's a traditional troll potion and wouldn't be something you could buy in a store. It has to be brewed by the troll for his or her intended."

"Right, right. How does one use this enhancer potion?"

Malik's grin grows wicked. "Massage it into the skin, of course."

I grin as I mull that idea over. I'm definitely liking the idea of this.

Three hours later, my shift is over and nothing notable has happened. I leave Alkemi and head toward the gnome village to check on how it's coming along. Bellami hasn't asked for more help, which makes me wonder if we irritated him too badly with all the flirting on the job.

When I arrive, the village is bustling. I glance around but don't see my grouchy, bossy friend.

"Lou!" One of the other gnomes jogs up. "Need something?"

"Well, I was going to find Bellami and see if you guys need any more help."

He smiles at me, maybe the first smile I've ever seen one of the gnomes give. "He went to mark more logs. I believe he was planning to find you tomorrow to schedule more time. Why don't you head up the path and check with him now?"

Nerves prickle across my skin. Connall will be here any second for lunch, and I don't think I should go into the woods alone. That's how horror movies start, and I'm not a dumbass.

But I feel comfy striding to the back of the gnome village, craning my neck for any sign of Bellami. Nothing but crickets.

Then a figure stalks through the trees, eyes lit white from the darkness of the forest.

Leighton.

I gasp, hand flying to my mouth.

Leighton's mouth stretches wide, teeth black as he opens his mouth and lets out a soundless cackle.

Oh gods, oh gods, oh gods.

Leighton dissipates into nothing as I stare in shock at the spot where he was. Suddenly, nothing can hold me back as I dash up the path, roaring Bellami's name. Surprised shouting drifts behind me as I tear around a corner and into the verdant green.

Not ten seconds later, I spot Bellami's small figure prone in the pathway. Sliding to my knees, I stare at him. And then I start screaming for help, even though I can already hear footsteps and rushed shouting.

Bellami's skin is mottled black, eyes staring at the sky. He's muttering, but no words leave his lips.

The gnomes rush around the corner and into view, Connall

right behind them. He sprints toward me and drops by my side, glancing around with his eyes narrowed. He takes one look at Bellami and lifts his wrist to comm Richard, then Arkan. The gnomes mill around as I pick up Bellami's tiny hand and hold it.

Why is this happening?

And why do we all seem powerless to stop it?

CHAPTER TWENTY-SEVEN
CONNALL

I was just arriving to meet Lou for lunch when she took off up the path into the woods. Terror filled me watching her, wondering if she was seeing Leighton. I'm not allowed in the gnome village, though, so I sprinted through Alkemi and out the back door as terror filled me.

I've never known fear like that, watching her run toward danger and being unable to be by her side in a moment.

Now, Lou shuts down, holding the gnome's hand as I comm first my Alpha, then Arkan. The gnomes talk in low tones for the five minutes it takes Richard, Arkan, and Doc Slade to arrive. We had just parted to head home after a day of meetings about haven planning.

But now all I can think about is how another monster's been hurt, and how my mate has gone catatonic by his feet. She was close to whoever did this. *Again.*

I long to comfort her, but the need to protect rides me harder. I stalk the sides of the path, looking for anything that could have done this to the tiny gnome. There's nothing. Just the same beautiful forest there's always been.

Lifting my comm watch, I direct it to call Dirk.

"Wolf," he murmurs throatily when he picks up. "Tell me yeh've called to have delicious phone se—"

"We need you," I say. "Behind the gnome village."

His voice goes steely. "I'm coming." He signs off without another word, and less than a minute later, he pops into view in front of me. Intelligent eyes survey the scene, filling with sorrow when they land once more on me.

He drops to his knees by Lou and lifts her chin. "Louanna."

When a tear streams down her cheek, he pulls her into his embrace.

Slade asks the gnomes' permission to lift Bellami, and we jog back to downtown.

An hour later, the verdict is the same as before. Whatever happened to Amatheia happened to Bellami too. He's stiff as a board, muttering something unintelligible. Morgan arrived shortly after we did. She's had her hand over Bellami's stomach for the last few minutes.

She turns to us with a shake of the head. "I can't fix him either, whatever it is. It's dark and I can usually feel that. I mean…I knew I could touch Wesley's black magic when I killed him. But whatever this is? I can't get near it. It's almost like it's hiding from me."

Lou hasn't said a word since we left Shifter Hollow.

"I need to call a town hall meeting," Arkan says, big arms crossed over his broad chest.

Richard and I nod. My alpha looks to Slade. "Given that this is the second incident, and we're still no closer to figuring out what happened, any idea how we can recommend monsters proceed? Simply stay indoors? Since both victims were found outside?"

Slade reaches up and tugs at one end of a long, curved horn. "The only other similarity is that they were both found in Shifter Hollow and not in downtown Ever or near the gas station. I'm wondering if we should move everyone—"

"I saw Leighton again," Lou says out of nowhere. "It was him. He did this."

A hush falls over the room. Richard and I exchange looks.

Lou steps to the table where Bellami lies, stroking the backs of her fingers along his jawline. "I know you all probably think I'm crazy, that I'm seeing things because I killed Leighton. But I'm telling you, I saw him after Amatheia was hurt, and I saw him again tonight. It can't be a coincidence."

The therapist in me wonders if she's seeing connections where none lie, but since we have no other theories, I can't brush her concerns aside to give her any other answer.

Dirk joins her, slipping an arm around her waist but facing us. "We should go to the wraith motel. Their magic comes from a darker place. And given what Lou's seen, they might have insight."

Arkan blows a loud breath out from his dark lips. "They won't love being interrupted at night."

"I know," Dirk says with a grimace. "Cannae be helped, though."

Richard looks at Arkan. "Let's take my truck. Won't be comfy, but you can ride in the back."

"Done," Arkan says with a grim look.

Richard turns to Dirk and me. "Does one of you want to take Lou back home?"

"Oh, she's got tae come." Dirk tightens his arm around her. "They'll want to speak with her." He glances down at Lou. "Assuming you feel up to this, my beauty."

"Of course." Her voice is pure steel as she turns from Bellami, fists balled at her sides. "Let's go." She leaves Bellami's side and heads for the door, hard footsteps echoing around the cavernous room.

I risk a glance at Dirk as he watches her leave. His brows are furrowed, eyes wide as a muscle works overtime in his jaw. I've never seen Dirk worried.

But he's worried now.

The ride to Hel Motel is quiet. I don't think anyone has an idea what to say. The idea that Leighton is somehow involved is too horrible to consider. He's gone. We burned him on the traditional pyre, gifted his ashes to his parents, and mourned him. We're *still* mourning him.

By the time we pull up in front of the motel, uncharacteristic anxiety prickles my skin, my heart racing uncomfortably in my chest. In the front seat, Lou's completely silent, her figure stiff. The need to protect her forces breath back into my lungs. First the thrall bites and now she's seeing a dead monster? What if those things are connected and she's getting sick?

I can't imagine anything more terrifying in this world than something happening to her. Forcing air into my lungs, I concentrate on steadying my wolf and myself so we can be supportive to Lou.

I get out of the car the moment we stop and open her door. Holding a hand out for her, I stare deeply into her eyes as she takes it.

"I'm here, Sweetheart," I promise. "Right by your side, okay?"

She nods as I pull her to my chest, purring and wrapping my arms all the way around her. Dirk joins us, gripping the back of her neck and leaning in to kiss the top of her head. If my Alpha, Arkan, or Slade are at all surprised to see us both comfort Lou, they don't show it. Richard's face is grim when our gazes meet.

"Hello, Keeper and othersss…" a hissed whisper of a voice floats toward us from the direction of the motel.

Lou extricates herself from my embrace enough to glance around me. Her eyes go wide, then move up to mine.

"I'm right here," I reiterate, bending down to rub my cheek along hers, purring in her ear.

Turning, she threads her fingers through my hand and reaches for Dirk. He slips an arm around her waist, his fingers in the pocket of her jeans.

A single wraith floats at the base of the black stone stairs leading into Hel Motel.

"Welcommme to Hellllll…" he rasps. "May I cheeeeck you into a rooommm?" His voice is hollow, like shouting into a void. I can't imagine a being that seems less suited to host travelers, but wraiths are famous system-wide for their hospitality. It's why every single haven has at least one wraith motel.

"No thank you, Zevrial," Arkan says confidently. "We're here to ask for your help with a security issue."

The wraith, Zevrial, seems to stiffen, even though he's floating off the ground, his long black cloak fluttering in the air around him. "Weeee are not responsible for ssssecurity, Keeper."

"I know," Arkan returns gently. "But two Evertons have been…well, we think they've been attacked. They lie catatonic in Doc Slade's office."

Slade steps forward and nods his confirmation before Arkan continues.

"Both times, Lou," he points to her, "saw a vision of someone who recently died here in town. Leighton, from Shifter Hollow."

I stiffen at hearing it described that way. Very few monsters know of Lou's involvement in Leighton's death. It's a level of secrecy Leighton's parents insisted on after they learned the full story.

Lou unthreads her fingers from mine and steps forward. "I don't know how much you know about Leighton's death, or Wesley's involvement, but—"

The wraith raises his hand. "Weeee knowwwww, Louanna of Shifter Hollllllow. Commmme insiiiiide." Without another word, the wraith turns and floats up the black stairs. Double glass-paned front doors swing open wide, and he disappears through them.

Arkan glances at us, mouth pursing into a flat line. Our group hesitates. Shifters, in particular, are wary of wraiths, preferring to stay with local packs rather than at wraith motels when we travel. There's something about their aura that rubs me the wrong way, my wolf focused and unsettled, growling under his breath.

"We need answers," Lou says, glancing over her shoulder. Without waiting for a response, she heads for the stairs and begins to ascend them.

Dirk and I are right behind her. I'd marvel at how exceedingly brave she is if I wasn't sick to death about what's going on. She doesn't need this, any of this. Not when she's trying to heal from trauma. She needs therapy, love, snacks, a good dicking down at the end of the day. She needs comfort and safety. And a nest. A big gigantic nest where I can lavish her with attention. A nest where I can keep her safely within the cocoon of my arms.

But the world seems determined to throw Lou obstacle after obstacle.

When we enter the motel lobby, she halts and stares around in wonder, mouth dropped wide open.

Arkan clip-clops through the door with Richard and Slade by his side. He looks down at Lou and smiles. "Hardly similar to the human version of a motel, hmm?"

"Hardly," she murmurs.

I try to see Hel from her perspective, and I don't know what human motels are like.

"Motel is the closest translation of the wraith word for these sorts of buildings," Arkan offers, waving at our surroundings.

"Uh, this is a mansion," Lou corrects with a snort. She points to the giant crystal chandelier hanging from the ceiling. "Mansion." Textured black wallpaper and black and white checkered tiles lend the entryway an elegant look. Her finger moves to a beautifully etched black wood table in the center of the circular entry. A black vase is filled with black, red and white flowers. It's stunning.

"Mansion," she whispers. "You haven't seen a motel if you think that's what this is."

A wraith appears behind the table, floating up over it to stand in front of Louanna. "Motelsssss are the lowesssst-levellll offer-rrinnnng in our porrrrtfoliiooo of residencesssss. Hennnce the naming connnnventionn. Ourrrr version of a bed and break-fasssst isss quite luxurrriousss."

Lou's mouth drops open. "You don't find this luxurious?"

The wraith shakes his head, the dark mask where his face should be obscured by a flowy black hood. "I dooooo noooooot. Commmme to theeeee officccce." He turns again and disappears through the flower vase, reappearing on the other side.

"Go on," Arkan encourages, seeming at ease with this place.

My wolf whines and stands forward in our shared mental space, focused on both Lou and our surroundings. Dirk is a tense presence at my side as we trail the wraith around the table and between two giant curved black staircases that lead to the motel's second floor.

Everything in a wraith motel is opulent. It's why, despite how otherworldly they seem, most monsters opt to stay in wraith motels when they travel.

Our group is silent, save for the sound of Arkan's hooves, as we follow the wraith through dark hallways, past the open doors of a ballroom, past a bustling kitchen where more wraiths flit quietly around, cooking. Eventually, we come to black double doors that swing open for us. The room within is lit faintly by the blue light that emanates from all wraiths, their soul auras.

Lou walks into the room as if there's nothing at all unusual about this. But from what I've learned about humans from other monsters over the years, and past human residents, it's that the wraith are usually considered "creepy."

Yet my woman isn't afraid.

As a therapist, that tugs at my instinct, because I worry she'd willingly put herself in harm's way to keep someone from being hurt again. And as her mate, I simply worry she has more shit to deal with, shit I'm at a loss to fix.

The moment I enter the office, I step behind Lou, hoping she'll feel my presence like a warm hug. Dirk joins us, pressing his body to hers. But her focus is entirely on the scene before us.

A half circle of identical wraiths float in the air around a black wooden desk. The entire room is sophisticated but dark. Rows of black books line every wall to the ceiling. Thick black curtains hang in front of the room's only window, which doesn't seem to show the outdoors. It's all black too.

At the desk sits another wraith, this one larger than the rest. The only discernible difference between him and the others is his size and a sparkling black star-shaped pendant clipped to the front of his cloak.

The manager.

Ghostly dark hands are half-tucked into the wide sleeves of his cloak, but he removes them, setting his palms flat on his desk when our full group is inside the room. "Whaaat bringgss yyyyyou here, Keeperrrr?

The ethereal hiss of his voice causes my wolf to growl. I choke it back, masking it under a cough as Dirk glances up at me with a quizzical expression. He slips a hand around my waist, his other hand moving to Lou's hip. The touch comforts me, and my wolf settles.

Arkan steps slightly forward of our group. "Jezbelah, we have a problem in town. Two monsters have been stricken with, well," he waves a hand through the air, "I'm not sure what. Doc Slade has examined both patients, but they are simply catatonic. At first, they..." His voice trails off as the manager, Jezbelah, turns from him and glances at the wraith to his left.

All the wraiths start murmuring under their breath, looking at one another. Ultimately, they return their gazes to the manager.

Arkan plants his hand on his hip. "What am I missing?"

The manager stands, easily towering over the other wraiths. "We have sssssssensed a dark presencccce in the foresssst around the motel, but have been unable to traaaack it downnnn. However, if whaaaat yyyyou are sayinnnng is corr—"

"It is," Slade says. "I've examined the victims myself. I've never seen anything like this in all my centuries as a healer."

"—ect," Jezbelah finishes his word, ignoring Slade, "thennnn I thinnnnk we knoooow what weeee've been ssssensing." He slips both hands back into his sleeves. "Yyyou have a revenannnnt on your handsssss."

Lou steps out of our embrace before I can stop her, stalking across the office. She plants her hands on the manager's desk and leans over it, her body stiff.

"What the fuck is a revenant?"

CHAPTER TWENTY-EIGHT
LOU

I stare up into a hooded face with no visible features, willing answers to spill from the wraith's mouth. "I've seen him twice," I continue. "Right after he hurt Amatheia and Bellami."

"Marrrrked," the wraith grits out. "Iffff you can seeee himmm, you are marrrrked by the rrrrrevenant."

And here we are again. Somehow I'm the center of this dark magic bullshit despite not having an ounce of magic in my veins. Somehow, this is my fault. My shoulders stiffen.

The manager rounds the desk and stands next to me, removing his hands from his wide sleeves. He's huge like this, probably twelve feet tall. He has to curl in half to bring his face to my level.

"Mayyyy I touch your foreheaaaaad?"

I nod, gulping around a knot in my throat. "I'm gonna need some answers, though, please. What's a revenant? What does it mean to be marked? Why couldn't my niece, Morgan, heal the victims if she's a black witch?"

He reaches forward and places the tip of his thumb between my brows. For a long moment, I don't breathe; I don't think; all I can focus on is the scattered drumbeat of my heart. It feels like it'll explode out of my chest. My friends, my males, stand frozen across the room.

The wraith sighs and straightens, floating backward a foot or two before he addresses our group. "Revenantssss are not evillll by nature. Typically, theyyyy are protectorssss of wayward, lossst souls. But the warlock Wessslllley's magic bounnnnd Leighton heeeere in pain. Louanna was marrrked by Leighton in his finnnnal moments. Onnnnly sheee will seeeee him."

Of fucking course.

Of. Fucking. Course!

"How do we unbind him?" I snip.

"Releassseeee him with the same black magic that bound him…"

Relief fills me. "Okay, so we get Morgan." I turn to the group. "Maybe Vikand can help us research how to do th—"

"Nooot Morgannnn Hectorrrr," the wraith interrupts. "Sheeee isss a goood blaaaack witch… Sheeee isss a healllerrrr. Heeee musssst beee releasssed. Not heeeallled."

Arkan speaks up, "That's blue magic. There are no blue witches anywhere in the haven system."

I spin and look at Dirk, my genius mate on all things hunt-y. "Dirk, have you heard of this? Got any ideas?"

His gaze falls, eyes flitting from side to side as he thinks. Eventually, he lifts his focus back to us. "I jest might, Louanna. Arkan and I can put our heads together."

"Can you help us?"

Arkan's question surprises me, and I turn to the wraith. The big monster shakes his head, slipping his hands back into his sleeves. "Nooot with darrrrk magiiiic, Keeperrrr. Sorrrryyyyy." With that, he returns around his desk and reseats himself. The half moon of wraith surrounding him float through the walls and ceiling and disappear.

"Let's go," Arkan says grimly.

I turn to follow. Dirk and Connall sandwich me between them as we leave, and I'd almost chuckle, except there's nothing funny about this. They can't see Leighton, can't sense him or do anything about him. I feel…hopeless, like there's a weight crushing my chest and refusing to allow air into my lungs.

By the time we get back to Richard's truck, I'm in full fight-or-flight mode. How the hells are we gonna fix this?

"Eyes on me, Lou." Connall's directive snaps my focus to him. Green eyes are wide and concerned as he brings a hand to my throat and wraps his fingers around it. "We'll figure this out, alright? Dirk has contacts all over the place, probably even some he shouldn't, if my intuition is right." He glances at Dirk. "Am I right? If anyone was hiding blue witch knowledge in their back pocket it would be you."

Dirk rubs a hand over the back of his neck, looking sheepish. "Well, I was a bit of a fright as a younger man, so yeh. I might know a few folks dabbling in other magics. I'll call 'em."

Arkan joins us. "Same. I was a horrible teenager, and I've kept up with some of those contacts. I didn't want to share that so publicly, but I might know someone."

I must give him an incredulous look, because his shoulders rise to his ears as he shrugs guiltily. "What? They were a lot of fun! I was a kid!"

"How are we going to fix this?" I whisper.

Richard joins us and claps a hand on Connall's shoulder, staring grimly at his Second. "I don't know, but we will. We have to, before anyone else gets hurt."

I clench my jaw as I resolve to be part of the solution.

Hours later, I'm reorganizing the Alkemi checkout area with Malik. I insisted on going back to work, and Dirk and Connall insisted on Malik staying with me throughout my shift. They don't want me to be alone at all, and while I appreciate the thought behind the mandate, it rankles too. I want to do more. I wish I could.

They're working with Arkan and haven leadership to spread the word about what's happened. The official recommendation is for monsters to remain inside, especially those in Shifter Hollow. I know it's hard, though, because all the bigger monsters live here. Many of them spend a majority of their day outside their homes.

Still, fierce danger is within Ever's wards. We can't be too safe.

I've seen Leighton twice. Both times, he interacted with me but didn't try to hurt me. Somehow, I think he either doesn't intend to hurt me, or perhaps can't. Because, surely, given my role in his death, he'd do that if he could?

I'm mulling that over when Malik taps me on the shoulder. When I turn, his eyes crinkle in the corners, his lips flat. He looks so worried.

"I won't let him hurt you," I state, straightening. I don't know how I'm going to make good on that promise, but somehow, through sheer grit and moxie, I'll make it happen.

Malik scoffs. "I'm hardly worried for myself, Lou. I'm worried about you, and Alba, of course, although she insisted, if I hovered, she'd kick me in the leg."

I hold back a bitter laugh, because I can picture Alba pointing a long finger at Malik and shouting about being coddled.

"I'll be fine. I've been through shit before. I'll get through this shit now."

He makes a disapproving sound under his breath and pulls me close to his body. Like this, my face is pretty much pressed to his belly button, but I'm going to pretend that's not weird. He curls over and rubs the top of my back. It's nice, and I appreciate it, but I—

Shadows at the edges of the room flicker and shift, a display lamp turning off and cloaking that section of the wall display in darkness. Malik releases me as I stiffen and pull out of his embrace. The lamp blinks repeatedly, and then a dark figure steps out of the shadows.

Leighton.

I ball my fists as he sneers at me, that same oversized sneer that would have been too much when he was alive. It seems to stretch across his entire face.

Malik touches my shoulder. "Lou, what's going on? You're so tense."

Leighton's glowing eyes flick over my shoulder to Malik, and he smiles, shoving both hands into his pockets.

"Don't do it," I hiss, taking another step forward.

Leighton's smile goes cruel, distorting his once-handsome features. He lifts his hand and crooks a finger, indicating I should follow. Then he strides toward the back of the shop and disappears through the wall.

I dash after him, Malik at my back shouting for me to stop.

But I can't, because Leighton's going to hurt someone. I feel it in my bones.

Malik's hand grips my shoulder, and he spins me in place, an urgent expression on his face. "What are you doing, Lou?"

"It's Leighton," I bark, yanking out of his hold. "He's going to hurt someone. I have to stop him!"

"You don't know how!" Malik shouts as I sprint for the back door and bash my way through it. When I emerge behind the building, Leighton stands at the corner, waiting.

I stomp up to him and look way up into his face. He was tall and built in real life. He's just as tall and built in revenant form. Glaring up at him, I point a finger.

"I don't know why you're doing this, but I need you to stop. I'll find a way to release you, but give me time. Don't hurt anyone!" It's a plea more than anything, despite the steel in my voice.

Malik rushes out the door behind me and stares around, but it's obvious he can't see Leighton.

Leighton glances at him again, then back at me, and the smile falls. He turns and strides up the alleyway toward Sycamore Street. When I go to jog after him, Malik stops me.

"Stop, Lou," he shouts. "We need help for this. You can't tackle Leighton on your own!"

"Let go!" I yank out of his hold a second time and dash up the street to find Leighton. He's there at the corner, waiting for me. Heat and ice sizzle through me in equal measures. Even my skin feels alive with energy. I can't allow him to hurt someone. Malik's right. I don't know how to fix this, and I'll do everything in my power to find a way, but I can't stand by while Leighton stalks into the darkness and hurts another monster.

Not on my watch.

I follow him, Malik a silent, upset presence at my back. But he doesn't stop me.

Leighton heads up the street and disappears into the alley that leads to Richard and Lola's treehouse. All the heat in my skin turns to rock-hard ice as he looks at me, then vanishes into the staircase.

Dirk and Connall are upstairs with the rest of haven leadership, discussing how to find someone who knows the right kind of blue magic to dispel Leighton's energy.

I move without rational thought, flying up the stairs and shoving my way through the door. Every head jerks up to face me. My mates. Richard. Arkan. Alo. Shepherd. Ohken. Catherine. Even the former Keeper, Abemet. They're all here.

"Lou?" Connall stands, a confused expression on his face.

Leighton floats across the room as I watch in horror.

"No…" My command is barely above a whisper as Leighton stops next to Connall. He eyes my mate up and down. Then he glances over his shoulder at me, and that awful smile returns.

CHAPTER TWENTY-NINE
CONNALL

Leighton's here; he must be. Or Lou thinks he is. She wouldn't barge into a meeting like this, looking harried and smelling like a mix of fear and anger. Her fists are balled, body vibrating with tension. My wolf sits up and growls, immediately alert for whatever's got her beautiful eyes open so wide.

The air smells of dread as haven leadership rises and looks around. But we're helpless against Leighton, if the wraiths are to be believed.

But then Lou launches herself across the room, screaming as she rushes an enemy I can't see. I reach for her, but she jumps into thin air and hangs there, like she's clinging onto someone's neck, but there's no visible body. A blast propels her backward, and she lands on top of Richard's dining table.

We all look around but there's nothing, there's no one. But she attacked *something*.

She leaps upright, standing on the table as she stares at something to my right.

"No," she snarls so viciously it raises my hackles, and my wolf shoves forward, desperate to protect her. Blue appears in the depths of Lou's eyes, spiraling outward until they glow otherworldly bright. She lifts her hands, and in both palms, pale blue flames flicker and sputter.

"Lou," I gasp, reaching for her. But when I touch her, she's an immovable rock, like she suddenly weighs a thousand pounds. "Dirk, help me," I bark.

He reaches for her, and we both pull, but she's locked in place. I drop my hands. I don't know what to do. Glancing at Richard, I find him as shocked as I feel, staring at Lou like he can't understand what he's seeing.

Lou's face screws up in anger, nose scrunching as she stares over my shoulder. Her muscles tense. I don't know what's happening, but whatever's behind me must be about to move. I tense too, unsure if shifting and attacking will just make this worse.

But then she roars, and the flames in her palms transfer to her clothing, her hair, to everything, flickering and jerking and dancing with blue light. Even her hair is on fire.

"Beautiful," Dirk murmurs.

It's on the tip of my tongue to shout at how he can comment on her beauty, when I realize he means her power. Because that's what this is. It has to be.

She snarls, lets out an ethereal growl, then stalks to the end of the table. The moment she reaches it, she shrieks again. There's a rushing whoosh of air that whips her hair up into a pile of blue flame on top of her head.

Then, she collapses to the table in a heap, all the flames gone.

I rush to the edge and pull her into my arms. She's limp and coated in sweat, babbling nonsensically with her eyes closed.

"She's a blue witch." Dirk rounds the table and presses a kiss to Lou's forehead as he addresses the room, "We need help fast. This is a battle magic."

I turn to face the room, only to see a group of matching shocked expressions.

"I don't remember the last time I met a blue witch," Abemet murmurs as I sweep Lou into my arms. He places a hand on her forehead, feeling her temperature as he turns to Arkan. "Were there any blue witches at HQ after my time there?"

"No," Arkan confirms. "Not even among the hunters. Most blue witches don't want to be officially labeled, as they don't want tae be forced to work with the Hearth. I might know someone who knows someone. I'll make a few calls through unofficial channels."

"Need to get her home." I look at the catatonic woman in my arms. "Lou first. We'll figure the rest of this shit out later." I head for the door without waiting for an answer, and nobody stops me.

Ten minutes later, the treehouse swings the doors open as Dirk and I sail through.

"I'll run a bath," he offers, jogging toward the bathroom.

I set Lou on the couch and undress her. Her entire body is covered in tiny smoke smudges. When I run my fingers over the black streaks, flickering blue flames follow.

I don't know what this means. Blue magic is so rare, I've never even met a blue witch. It's said to be a blessing, but I don't know how much is known about it. And why Lou?

She needs time and space and love to heal. She doesn't need *this* burden. Because that's what it'll be when the Hearth finds out she has this power. Blue witches can crush armies and flatten cities. And they're basically an endangered species.

Worry for her fills me, and I hold her to my chest. She still hasn't woken up.

Dirk comes back, squeezing my shoulder lightly. "Bath's ready, mate."

His easy normalcy spurs me into action. I stand and turn with him, heading for the bathroom. When I enter, the tub's running, and bubbles are beginning to form.

Dirk shucks his gem and pants off, glancing at me. "I'd like tae go in with her, if it's alright with you."

"Of course." I set Lou carefully in the tub, and he crawls in behind her. When he sits down and pulls her back to his chest, it steals my breath. Seeing them together like this, I don't think I could want anything more in this world.

"I love you," I whisper, glancing at Dirk. "And I love her. And it happened so fast, but, goddess, I really do."

Fuck. This isn't the right time for this admission. I realize that now the words are out of my mouth.

But Dirk's lips split into a wicked grin, eyes bright as one brow curls upward. "Och, you love me then? Jest as I hoped you would. Good." He reaches down and strokes Lou's arm for a moment, then looks back up at me. "I thought we could keep her safe, mate, but instead, it's Louanna doing the protecting."

Dropping to my knees next to the tub, I cover his hand with mine, squeezing Lou's arm as I consider how fucking hard and fast I fell. That's not uncommon for shifters; I just never realized it would be so endless, so complete. Leaning over the tub, I rest my cheek on my forearm as I stare at my beautiful mates.

I reach into the water and stroke up Lou's belly and along the front of her neck. I want her to wake up. I need to hear her sass, to know she's fine and that she'll *be* fine. I desperately want to talk to her about what happened tonight.

Lou groans and shifts in Dirk's arms.

Thank the goddess, oh thank fuck she's coming to.

"She's waking," he says, grabbing a washcloth and dabbing at the smudges on her forehead. "We're here, my sweet, you're safe."

She groans and sits upright, clutching her forehead. Then she slumps against Dirk, looking up over her shoulder at him. "What happened?"

"Yeh gave us a shock, Louanna," Dirk murmurs into her ear. "Finally let us in on yer huge secret, my love?"

"What *happened?*" she croaks.

I resist the need to shudder, but goosebumps coat my skin thinking back to how the flames enveloped her. "You're a blue witch, sweetheart. Your power scared...whatever was in the room. And it left, we think. We couldn't see it."

She blinks, expression blank. "I was tested for magic in Rainbow. It was negative."

"Yeh cannae test for blue magic, Louanna," Dirk offers. "It's too rare."

She lifts her palms and looks at them, eyeing the scorch marks.

"It was glorious," he whispers.

She grunts but looks at me. "Is this real? I'm a blue witch?"

"Absolutely real," I whisper. "You were amazing, Lou. You protected us; I—"

Blue flames flicker in her eyes, her nostrils flaring as her gaze roves over me. The look on her face is appreciative, almost sultry. But I'd be shocked if she was feeling anything close to sensual after what just happened.

A tiny smile lifts the edges of her mouth.

"Take me to bed," she commands, rising from the tub like a godsdamned queen. "Right now."

CHAPTER THIRTY
LOU

The world is cloaked in blue, everything around me reduced to slashes of shadow. The only thing I can focus on, the only thing that still looks real, are the two males who belong to me. The two males I'd do fucking *anything* to protect.

Fire slicks along my skin as Connall rises from the tub, lifting his hands.

"You need rest, Lou, absolutely, but—"

"No," I state simply, stepping out of the tub. I look at Dirk. "Go to the bed, Dirk. Now."

His eyes go wide, and he looks to Connall.

Bits of reality filter through the blue haze. Little niggling thoughts eat up space in my brain, reminding me that I should call my nieces and check on them, make sure they're safe. And I should ask more questions about what the fuck happened in that room with Leighton. Was anyone hurt? Did I do anything crazy? The last thing I remember is screaming at Leighton, his eyes going wide, and then…nothing

But somehow, I can't focus on that. When I try, the thoughts just slip away, and all that's left is heat and need and desperation.

And the flames. Fuck me, the flames. I'm burning from the inside out, the world reduced again to blue shadows. I don't know if I'm riding a high from the magic or what, but I need my men.

Right now. With a desperation that's drowning me in lust.

Connall helps me out of the tub and tosses me over his shoulder, where I get a great view of his bubbly, round ass. Then he reaches for Dirk, who steps elegantly out of the water, suds sluicing down his muscular frame.

Dirk threads his fingers through Connall's, but his focus is on me. His usual smirk is missing, his eyes slightly hooded, lips parted. His tongue comes out to run along his lower lip as I prop my chin in my hand, elbow against Connall's back.

"I'll take you to bed, woman," Connall says in a tone laced with his wolf's depth. "But you're resting."

I don't bother to agree as our wolf returns to the main room and hooks a left, down a long hall to his bedroom. Our bedroom, I suppose. Because we haven't said we're all moving in together, but all my shit is here, and I can't imagine either of them allowing me to leave. Not that I'd want to.

Not that either of them would even let me go. I know that deep in my heart.

Dirk's navy eyes never leave mine as Connall sets me on the bed. I scoot to the headboard and watch in rapt fascination as my men stand at the foot, staring at me like they don't understand me.

Laying both arms over the pillows, I step my legs outward. My pussy's wet, soaked, actually. And the blue covering my vision is starting to overtake Dirk and Connall, too. Everything blue. Every possible shade.

Magic.

"Touch each other," I command. "And then fuck me."

Connall sputters, running both hands through his hair. "Lou, this is…You need *rest*. I'm serious. You just—"

"She needs this," Dirk says, staring at me as a look of understanding passes over his elegant, angular features. "She knows her mind, Connall, and this is what she needs."

I wave a hand at him. "Thank you, Dirk. I *do* know my mind. And my mind wants to see you touch. Go on." I flick my gaze to Connall, who still looks shell shocked.

He stands straighter and pulls Dirk in front of him, one hand gripping Dirk's throat and the other sliding lazily down Dirk's abs. Connall's fingers trail a soft path along Dirk's hard cock as Dirk grits his jaw and stares at me like a man possessed.

"What do you want to see us do, Lou?"

Connall's question has my empty pussy clenching with need.

"Bite him," I demand. "Stroke him. Then let me take him."

Dirk gasps, head falling back against Connall's shoulder.

Connall strikes with predatory intensity, sinking his fangs into Dirk's neck. The effect is instant. Dirk barks out a curse, but lets his head fall to the side as I watch. Connall wraps his enormous hand around Dirk's hardening length and tugs slowly, pinching the tip with soft, familiar strokes.

"That's it," I praise. "Make a mess of him, then let him free."

"Louanna," Dirk all but begs. My sweet but conniving sylph looks ready to lose his mind.

Connall releases the bite and pushes Dirk onto the bed. "Go, sylph. I want to watch you." His eyes meet mine. "I'm going to sit next to the bed while he takes you for the first time."

Dirk glances up at our mate. "And then yeh'll join us." It's not really a question; it's more of a statement.

Connall grins, reaching down to stroke his thick, hard cock. "Maybe."

Dirk groans and looks back at me, licking his lips. "Oh, Louanna. I've waited so long, my love. So patiently."

I snort. "Patient, my ass."

His grin goes full feral. "If I'd have done what I wanted to when I first saw yeh, yeh'd be locked up in a cave wearing nothing, chained to my bed for me to have whenever I wanted. It was hard not to steal you away, Louanna." Lightning flashes over his skin, straining toward me.

"I'd have escaped." I cross my arms and my legs at the ankle, taunting him. "You couldn't have held me there."

Dirk's nostrils flare. He lurches across the bed, grabbing my ankles and yanking them farther apart. Cool hands slide up my inner thighs and press outward at my knees. Dirk's casual perusal of my pussy has me tightening, desperate to touch him despite the commands I just gave him.

I'm all talk, I swear. The truth is that when my sylph wants something, he takes it. He is the literal definition of persistence. But something inside me says that's not exactly right. That I need to command him. That it pleases me.

That I should do it more.

Connall rounds the bed to my right and grabs an armchair from the corner. He drags it to the side of the bed and sits with an ankle on his knee. He's still clothed, but it'd be hard to miss the enormous erection pressed to his zipper.

"Eyes on him, Lou," my wolf commands.

Groaning, I debate sassing him. I love sassing him. And he loves to *be* sassed.

But a feral growl from Dirk pulls my attention back to him.

"I'm gonna take yeh, Louanna," he growls, biting at my inner thighs as his grip tightens. "And I don't want yeh to look away from me. Not for a second. No matter what our wolf does. Do yeh understand?"

Chest heaving, I nod as I watch his thin lips trail a prickly line up my leg. He bites, then swirls his tongue over the indentions of his teeth. The pain of his bites and soft pleasure of his tongue have me ready to fly apart at the seams.

It's been so long that we've danced around this. So long that I pushed him away and told myself I wasn't ready. Maybe I'm not. Or maybe it doesn't matter, because these two love me so hard, I can't find a reason not to give in to them.

"Dirk, be a good boy," I say, reaching for him with both hands. "Just give me what I want."

He lifts his head, eyes flashing as his lightning zips faster across his skin. It entrances me, all that delicious blue flame. I've never been able to look away when it goes all erratic like it is now.

Because I'm a blue witch.

Holy gods. Realization hits me like a ton of bricks, and I shoot upright in the bed, staring at the way Dirk's lightning zips and jags over his skin.

I press my hand to his chest. "Did you know?" My voice is impossibly soft.

He pauses, rubbing the stubble of his chin along my inner thigh.

"Did you know I was a blue witch?" I demand. "Come up here and tell me right now, you—"

A big hand grips my throat, his thumb running roughly over my lower lip. "Scoundrel?" His tone is dark and devious. It's easy to see how he got in trouble as a younger male. "Menace? Deviant? I am all of those things, Louanna," he growls. "I didn't *know* yeh were a blue witch, mate, but I had an inkling."

Connall shifts forward on the seat. "And you didn't mention this before?"

Dirk squeezes my throat and nips at my lower lip, his talented fingers coming to my pussy and slipping inside. He curls them and strokes my G-spot as I pant and gasp.

"Och, don't be upset. I'm an air elemental. She's a battle witch. And yer our blue moon wolf. What do blue moons signify in yer culture, Connall?"

Connall sits back in his chair with a look of incredulity. "Growth, wisdom, love."

"And when were yeh born, my sweet wolf?" Dirk's voice is lower than I've ever heard it.

"During a blue moon," Connall whispers.

I glance between them.

Dirk dips down and bites my nipple, sucking hard at the bud and swirling his tongue over it as I cry out. Gods, I'm going to come already. This is too much, this revelation.

"Yeh were both fated to be mine from the moment yeh arrived on this planet. Mine as ordained by the shifter gods." He smiles at Connall, then looks up at me. "Mine as ordained by the witchling gods and goddesses." Then he places his hand over his chest where his gem normally lies. "And mine according to all the lore of my people. Yeh couldn't be any more mine if I'd written our story myself."

I stare at him in shock, but he returns to my other breast, biting and sucking. "It's always been you," he whispers into my skin. "I didnae tell yeh about the witch guess because I didn't want the pressure that'd inevitably come from that. I could've been wrong. There are so few blue witches who publicly admit their power. But I've met enough to guess at yeh bein' one…"

I huff. "I don't know whether to slap you or deny you this sweet, sweet pussy."

Sweat breaks out over my skin, rolling down my back as my muscles tremble. Blue overtakes the world again, lust radiating out from between my thighs in giant sunbursts that have me ready to explode.

"Neither, Louanna." He flops onto his back in the pillows, then pulls me on top of him and notches his cock between my pussy lips. Using his grip on my thighs, he rubs me up and down his length. "Tell me yeh don't want more of this, that yeh haven't dreamed of what it might feel like to do this."

"I haven't," I snark, even as I shunt my hips rhythmically, taking pleasure from his thick, veiny cock. Gods, it's perfect. But when lightning streaks down it, sending tiny vibrations into my skin, I shudder.

"That's right, witch," Dirk croons. "It'll be inside yeh too."

I plant both hands on his chest and use that leverage to thrust harder. "Maybe I'll come all over you and leave you hanging," I taunt.

"Don't think so," he growls.

"I'm getting close," I gasp. Every drag of my hips along his length sends tiny zaps of lightning to my clit. I'm going to tease my bratty sylph by—

One moment I'm on top of him, and the next we're lurching across the bed. Dirk lands next to it, standing with me in front of him, legs parted around his midsection.

"What the fuck?" I blurt out. "How?"

"Yeh might've noticed I don't always move like others do." He yanks me to the edge of the bed, his heavy cock resting over my pussy and lower belly. "Yeh're soaking wet, Louanna. It's time, my sweet."

I'm not ready when he grips his cock and notches it at my pussy. A teasing thrust later, electricity shoots through me as he works his way inside. He slides out, eyes locked onto mine.

"Don't look away, Louanna," he reminds me. His grip on the backs of my legs tightens, and he presses into me on a slow, measured stroke. His dark eyes fall to where we're connected as Connall starts purring beside the bed. I can't help thrusting to meet Dirk, but he laughs and pulls back out, leaving me empty and frustrated.

"Och, Louanna," he sighs, "yeh'll be the death of me, but yeh need a tease, woman. If I know anything about yeh, it's that I cannae give yeh everything yeh want the moment yeh want it."

Growling, I rock my hips again, impaling myself on the very tip of his cock. His body's not hot like Connall's, but that fucking lightning zips and teases at my entrance like a damn vibrator.

Except it zags and streaks outward from my core and along my limbs, causing my muscles to tense and tighten.

"Fuck her," Connall commands. "Hard and slow, Sylph."

I glance over. I can't help myself. I love Connall in command mode.

The moment I do, Dirk grips my throat and forces my gaze back to his flashing eyes. "Dinnae look away, woman," he snarls. With a quick rock of his hips, he thrusts all the way inside, filling me to the brim as I scream and arch around his fullness. Flutters of lightning bounce around, making him feel even bigger as I gasp around the intensity.

He pulls out and then rocks his hips, plunging back inside me until he takes up a slow and steady pace, driving into me and then withdrawing. Every pass drags his cock along my G-spot, his grip on my throat tightening as blue darkens his cheeks.

"Godsdamn, Louanna," he rumbles. "I've never felt anything so tight, so hot. Yer pussy swallows me up, woman. How does it feel?"

But I'm too caught up in the slow, intense build of this electrical storm to answer. I wrap my fingers in the sheets to center myself as I try not to come too fast. But my muscles tremble as heat builds in my core, my pussy tightening around Dirk every time he thrusts into me.

"Faster," Connall commands. "Make her come, then start over again, and I'll join you."

Fuck, oh fuck, the idea of being between them, of being taken by them both, overwhelms me, and I start shoving my hips up to meet Dirk. Or trying to, but his grip on the backs of my legs tightens as he moves faster. Low, masculine grunts erupt from him. He's as close to losing his mind as I am.

"Fuck me harder," I say darkly, shifting onto my elbows to watch his cock slip deep inside me.

"Fuck, Louanna," he moans.

"That's it, Dirk," I purr, "give me that thick cock until I come. I need to feel you explode inside me, mate."

His rhythm goes jagged and desperate.

The right side of the bed dips, and Connall crawls to my side. He wears a knowing smirk as he unzips his pants and pulls out his cock.

"I see what you're doing, Lou. So I'll give you something else to do with that pretty, sassy mouth." He grabs his cock by the base as Dirk's rhythm steadies. Scooting slightly forward, he rubs the tip of his dick along my lips. "Open wide, sweetheart. You still owe me a few inches."

Lightning skates over my skin and zings up the length of Connall's cock. My wolf bellows and tenses, back arching as his nipples pebble. I don't know when he took his shirt off, but thank the gods for that. Watching Dirk's power streak over Connall's skin and back down to mine, circling my clit, is enough to toss me to the very edge of sanity.

Crying out, I surge forward and take as much of Connall as I can.

Dirk groans, low and ragged, a masculine sound that has me on the edge of coming. But when Connall wraps a fist around my braid and uses it as leverage to fuck my mouth, I lose it. It's too much.

The first moments of my orgasm are an intense fluttering wave, like riding to the top of the rollercoaster. And then I tip over the edge into bliss, flying apart at the seams as I fall to my back and scream. My toes curl as everything goes silent. And Dirk never stops fucking me with hard strokes that pull my orgasm along until it strengthens and radiates out from my core, my body imploding around him.

Ecstasy batters me for years, it feels like. When it finally recedes to lap lazily at the edges of my consciousness, my eyes flutter open to look at my males. Dirk stands between my thighs with his lips slightly parted, eyes hooded. He's coated in a thin sheen of sweat, blue flames licking up his skin, chasing his lightning playfully.

He looks delicious.

Kneeling by my side, Connall plays with the end of my braid, lips tilted into a smile. "You still owe me inches, Lou. Let's try that again."

I lift a brow. "Come take them, Wolf."

CHAPTER THIRTY-ONE
DIRK

In the early hours of dawn, I'm watching over my mates while they sleep. A soft noise outside draws my attention from them. There's rustling at the door. I shake Connall awake. He shifts and curls protectively around Lou, alert. I creep to the front door and yank it open.

Vikand stands outside with a pile of books in his hand. When I throw the door open wide, he yelps and drops the pile of books, his glasses falling off his nose.

"Gods almighty, Vikand," I hiss, "what the hells are yeh doin'?"

He puts a hand over his heart and waves at the books on the ground. "Well, this is everything I have on blue witches. I was up late finding the books and I figured I'd drop them by. I didn't mean to wake you." His dark eyes flick to the books then back down at me. "There's a lot of good information in there. Start with the book on top. It was written by a blue witch. It's an old book, but it should be helpful."

He glances around, then grimaces. "Sorry to wake you. Come by my office if you have questions." With that, he turns and trots up the street into the darkness.

Grumbling at the fright he just gave me and Connall, I restack the books and carry them inside. Connall remains curled protectively around Louanna, although his wolf's claws tip his fingers.

I bring the stack of books to the sofa and hand him the one Vikand mentioned. "I'm guessing you heard what Vikand said. That's the book written by another blue witch."

Connall takes it with a sigh, stroking Lou's hair away from her face. "I don't think I'll be able to go back to sleep now. Want to stay up with me and read this so we can figure out how best to support her?"

Nodding, I tuck myself against his bigger body. Louanna throws a leg and arm over him, and he pulls her in close.

Safe.

The title on the book says "A Blue Witch's Accounting of Blue Magic".

"Here we go," I murmur as I flip the book open to the first page.

Hours later, Connall and I are nearly halfway through the book, and we've learned a lot. But I need my Louanna to wake so we can share this with her. He nuzzles her neck and shoulders as he wakes, one hand roving over her body. But she's a sound sleeper, our Louanna. An early morning sex kitten, she's not.

Laughing at the idea of it, I head for the kitchen. Grabbing bacon and eggs from the fridge, I start the makings of breakfast. My wolf needs a lot of calories to maintain that huge frame. He'll be hungry soon. And Louanna will wake up, well, whenever the fook she wants to.

Once the bacon begins to sizzle in the pan, Connall's soft footfalls drift up the hallway. He smiles as he rounds the corner. Joining me, he presses his warm, naked body to mine, one hand braced on the countertop and the other running under my arm and up my chest.

"Mmm," he growls in my ear, kissing just below it. "You smell good, mate."

"Yer smellin' the bacon, Wolf," I tease, cocking my head to the side to grant him better access.

Rough lips and teeth trail a path down to my shoulder as the hard bar of his cock nestles between my arse cheeks. "Keep that up, and I'm gonna forget about the bacon, Connall," I warn.

He bites my shoulder muscle hard, then licks over it with a wet, soft tongue. "Fine."

He's all tease as he turns from me and heads to the bathroom. As he goes, I stare at the tight, round bubbles of his arse cheeks. He's so damn big and muscular. The sound of running water echoes moments later. Anticipation prickles through me. Louanna's a sound sleeper, and my wolf has a crazy high libido. He is very *much* a morning sex kitten.

Yet given what happened, I'm reticent to stray any farther from Louanna than absolutely needed.

Ten minutes later, I've got a plate piled high with toast, and another with bacon and eggs. Connall emerges from the bathroom with a towel around his waist. It does nothing to hide the erection masting the fabric. My mouth goes dry. I want to drop to both knees and worship him, my blue moon wolf.

He crosses the room and cages me against the island, his body still damp from the shower. "You should have told us about your witch theory." He bends down to kiss the tip of my nose. "If for no reason other than it's important."

"She'd have felt pressured," I remind him. "Responsible to fix things."

Connall slides a hand up the back of my neck and strokes. "And how do you think she feels now?"

I pause, considering that.

When I say nothing, he brushes his lips over my mouth. "She still feels that pressure, but now it's combined with the niggling sense that you didn't think she could handle the news."

"That's not it," I declare. "You know that's not it."

He strokes my side. "If you *had* told us, we could have worked through it together and told no one else. She might have felt extra pressure, but she'd have felt it with us firmly in her corner."

Surprise snakes uneasily through me, along with something I don't usually feel.

Guilt.

I run both hands through my hair. "I need to talk to her. Yer right, o' course. I—"

Connall's thumb brushes over my lower lip. "You can talk to her when she's up. She's in desperate need of good rest. You're mine right now." He reaches down between us and grips my cock in one hand and his in the other. Stepping closer, he brings my cock flat to his and wraps his fingers around the both of us.

I grunt when his big, rough palm strokes our lengths. He's so hot, turning my electricity into a storm of pleasure. I sag against the countertop as heat swirls through my sack. My cock bobs and drips under his ministrations. My wolf is quiet, focused, eyes gone full emerald as he watches what he's doing.

His cheeks flush red, mouth dropping open as he rubs our cockheads together.

"Imagine these both inside her sweet pussy," he murmurs. "I want that sometime. To feel you like this, but inside her."

"She's so tiny," I groan, head falling back.

"We'll fit," he says with a growl.

The warmth of his cock disappears, pulling a whine from my throat. But when I look down, he's playing with the thick skin around the base of his cockhead.

"Hold yourself steady for me," he commands, not looking up.

Enthralled, I grip my dick by the base. He moves forward until his cockhead touches mine, our precum slippery as sensation amps. Connall pulls and stretches his foreskin, slipping it over my dick as I gasp at the feel of tight, hot pressure around my crown.

"Where'd yeh learn this?" I grunt when he grips our cocks together and begins to rub.

"I'm a thorough researcher," he offers, "and, goddess, the research has been fun."

I grunt at the idea of him in his office, reading books on how to fuck a man.

Reaching down, I replace his hand with mine and jack us together. We're dripping steadily, creating suction every time I move his foreskin over my cock. He's hard and getting harder by the second. We won't be able to do this for long. Moaning softly, I rub our plump heads together as precum drips to the floor below us. Connall growls and reaches between us, palming my sack and playing behind it with his fingers.

Soft footsteps echo up the hall. Louanna joins us, eyes wide as she takes in the scene playing out in the kitchen.

"Louanna," I murmur. "Join us, mate."

Connall pulls away, his foreskin pulling my cock, sucking on it like the tightest mouth I've ever felt. When we pop free, I groan at how dark and swollen my tip is, covered in Connall's pleasure.

My wolf reaches for Louanna, dropping them both to the floor by my feet. He's rocked back on his knees with her seated in his lap. He wraps a muscular arm around her waist, sliding his hand to grip her neck. He brings his mouth just below her ear and nibbles.

"Let's have breakfast, Lou." Reaching up, he grabs my cock and shifts her upward until my tip hits her lips. Like the sweetest of girls, she opens up and swallows me as far as she can.

I hiss at the pleasure that explodes between my thighs. I was already so amped up, and the feel of Connall's fingers wrapped around my cock while she sucks is almost too much.

"Fook," I manage, sagging to the countertop. Lou alternates swirling her tongue and sucking on my tip. When she moves to the underneath and nibbles at the stretched, taut skin, I nearly blow my load. But then a harder mouth replaces hers, a big, rough tongue licking over my crown. Louanna's lips slide down the side of my cock as Connall sucks the head of it.

Glancing down, I marvel at the sight of my mates blowing me together. It's everything I can do to hold back the ecstasy. I place a hand on Lou's head, reveling in the feel of her soft lips moving up and down my length. When she drops lower and pulls one of my nuts into her mouth, sucking, I grunt, knees nearly giving out. It's when Connall lurches forward, swallowing me down, that I finally lose it.

Bliss hits me with all the force of a hurricane, hot seed barreling down my shaft as I thrust and groan, hips rolling to meet their mouths. Connall swallows hard around me as Lou laps and sucks at my sack, her tongue drawing out the pleasure until I arch with a keening wail, flailing as I try to catch my bearings. It's too much, too hot, too damn perfect.

They are mine and I'd do anything to keep them safe. I'd murder, maim, topple buildings or level havens. I hope to the gods I don't ever have to, because I truly would.

CHAPTER THIRTY-TWO
LOU

Once we manage to untangle ourselves, Dirk reaches for me with a smile.

"My sweet, Vikand dropped some books by for you. They're all about blue magic, one written by a blue witch." He pulls my hair toward his nose and sucks in a deep breath, eyes rolling into his head. "Glorious," he murmurs. Blue eyes drift to mine. "Connall and I started reading while yeh were sleepin', Louanna. There's a lot to be learned."

Connall joins us, setting three cups of coffee on the long skinny table behind his sofa. He takes a sip, looking thoughtful. "According to the only book written by another actual blue witch, you're incredibly hard to kill." He pulls in a deep breath, like it pained him to even say that sentence. His wolf presses to the front of his mind, his eyes going full emerald. "The book hasn't specifically mentioned thralls, but I bet that's why you didn't turn when they bit you."

I look from him to Dirk and back again, mouth going dry.

"And I'm sorry I didnae share my suspicions with you, my sweet. I thought to protect you." He looks sorrowfully between Connall and me. "'Twas the wrong thing to do. Forgive me?"

I snuggle against him even as I toss a saucy look up over my shoulder at him. "See me after class, Mister Zefferus. It'll be detention for you on account of extremely poor behavior."

He groans and buries his face in my neck, laughing even as he sighs.

"I'm being serious, my sweet," he manages, chuckling into my skin.

"Me too." I nudge him in the belly with my elbow. "Can I see this book, please?"

"Of course." Connall rises gracefully and grabs a book from the kitchen island. Somehow I didn't notice the stack sitting there, what with the fuckery and all. He paces back to us and hands me the book. "Dirk and I got about halfway through it. There's a lot there."

I take it, running my fingers over the worn cover.

And then I lose myself for hours, devouring every scrap of information in its pages. Connall leaves to meet Richard, but Dirk stays with me. He's silent while I read, stroking my hair and rubbing my back. Eventually, he leaves to clean up the bedroom and kitchen. I've got a lunch date at the Green Bean, but I read right up until it's time to go. What I learn is fucking fascinating.

Dirk appears from the hallway, pulling fresh jeans on. Blue eyes flash at me, wrinkling in the corners as he smiles. "What is it my sweet? That look on your face tells me yeh've got to the part where blue witches need to sexually recharge after an expulsion of magic. Am I right?"

"Yeah." I stare at him, gobsmacked. "But that explains why after I passed out I couldn't wait to drag you both into the bedroom. I'm like a giant sex battery. A solar sex battery."

Dirk laughs. "Well, I'm pleased as punch tae be the thing you need to recharge yeh, Louanna. Swear tae the gods I didnae plan that one, but when I say they made us to fit together, I'm right."

I snort out a laugh and return to the book.

The blue witch who wrote it shares stories of blue witches

decimating entire armies and leveling cities to the ground. It's terrifying...and exhilarating.

But by the time we need to leave for the diner, I still haven't found any mention of revenants.

"Damn," I curse as I close the book, glancing at my watch.

Dirk holds a hand out for me. "Come, my sweet. Yer burgers await..."

Despite how serious and shocking this whole situation is, I love how he can still find a way to laugh. I take his hand, and we disappear into the wind.

～

"I'll be fine," I reassure Dirk for the millionth time, pointing at not only my nieces, but all three of their mates as well. "I'm in good hands."

Dirk's dark eyes move around the booth at the Galloping Green Bean.

"I'll comm you if anything remotely suspicious occurs," Abemet croons in his silky, deep voice, crimson eyes flashing with mirth.

Morgan smiles as she rubs his thigh.

Dirk lifts his chin at the former Keeper's promise. "If I didn't have to meet with yer mother right now, I'd not be leaving my woman, but..."

"It's fine," I repeat. He hasn't talked much about work. Technically, he's still on paid leave, finally using up the days he's been accruing for the last ninety years.

Dirk bends down and presses his lips to mine, slinging his arm around my waist. "If yeh see him, dinnae try to stop him, love."

"I don't know if I can agree to that," I whisper, lifting a palm for him to see. The tiniest of blue flames flickers there, and I can feel it now. That sense of otherworldly power. I should probably be terrified about this entire thing with Leighton. But somehow, now, I'm not. I'm far more terrified at the idea he'll hurt someone else than worried for myself. I think if he wanted to hurt me, he would have.

Dirk grits his jaw. "I'll be back soon, my beauty." Without waiting for an answer, he slaps his gem and disappears on a gust of wind.

I take a seat next to Morgan and snatch a fry off her plate. She shoves the whole thing toward me with a wry smile. I've always been a food stealer. I've been stealing the triplets' extras since we were kids together.

When Ohken, Wren's big troll mate, gives me a funny little smile, I shrug. "What? It's called the snack tax. Because I've watched over these girls their whole life, I get to tax their snacks until death do us part."

I blanch a little after saying "death," but Ohken grins, one auburn brow traveling toward his hairline. He glances at Wren, squeezing her hip. "Snack tax sounds like something I need to incorporate in our home."

Wren snorts. "You've got me, honey, so you've already got the whole-ass snack, okay?"

His smile goes bigger, and my heart melts. My girls have found the most perfect mates, and I couldn't be happier for them.

Shepherd leans over the booth table and shoves my hand away, snatching a fry.

When I growl, he winks at me. "You literally just taught us about the snack tax, and Alo and I are protecting everybody all the time. I need to catch up on back tax snack tax."

I snort, then Wren follows suit, and everybody but Abemet laughs. And seeing the ever-stern look on his face as he watches us laugh makes me laugh harder. Finally, finally, he cracks the barest of smiles.

When our group's laughter dies, I kick Shepherd under the table. "I want to go back to the wraith motel today. I've got questions for them after reading some books that Vikand dropped off. Are you guys up for a little adventure?"

Morgan glances at her mate. "That's safe, right?"

"Safe as anywhere within the wards, my darling." He strokes a stray bang back behind her ear. His eyes flick toward the door and narrow. He glances back at me with the hint of a smile. "But, actually, Arkan and I reached out to an old friend, a blue witch, to see if she might be willing to help. And she's just walked in the door, so..."

We all whirl around in our seats to see who he's talking about. A stunning, pale vampire female stands in the doorway, talking with Taylor, the centaur host. She's got a smile like a true predator, all vicious intensity. Stark white hair is drawn back and up into a loose, effortlessly messy bun. She's hot, and she looks like a badass. Even her outfit is awesome—tight black leather leggings and a red collared shirt with a fitted black leather vest. She's a sexy vampiric schoolmarm, and suddenly I'm wondering how the guys might feel about a foursome.

"Jesus, she's hot," Thea mutters.

I spin back around and squirm in my seat, looking at Abe. "That hot vampire is the blue witch?"

He grins at me. But as he opens his mouth to speak, a gust of wind ruffles my hair, and the hot vampire lady appears to my left. She plants both hands on her hips and beams at me, twin fangs poking her bottom lip.

Oh fuck. I forgot that vampires can slip quickly over short distances.

"Name's Laerith," she says confidently. "And, yes, I'm the blue witch. And a vampire like Abemet here, so my hearing is quite excellent."

"Fuck," Thea and I mutter at the same time.

"No thanks," she chirps. "But I'm told you need to learn blue magic quickly, so let's go."

I cough. "Now?!" It seems dangerous to take off with a woman I just met, given everything that's going on right now.

"You're safe with Laerith," Abe says. "I've known her for centuries. Probably safer than anywhere else, to be honest."

"We'll come with you," Morgan states, rising from her seat.

"You won't," Laerith says, her tone brooking no argument. I bristle, knowing Morgan won't let it go.

But somehow, she does. I bet fifty bucks Abe is squeezing her thigh under the table.

"Come on, Witch," Laerith says, heading for the door. She doesn't look back to see if I'm coming. I stare around at my girls, who all look a little worried. Except for Wren, who, like always, wears a knowing smile on her face.

"You'll be fine, Auntie," she says quietly. "Go learn about your power, alright?"

That comment gets me moving. I rise and reach for my wallet in my back pocket, but Shepherd stays my hand. "Go on, Lou," he says kindly. "We've got this."

I thank them, gulping as I head for the exit.

I really, really hope I've got this.

My mind wanders to Caroline. If she were here, she'd tell me I've got this, too. She'd tell me I deserve to learn about my power, to see what it can do. Maybe she'd even tell me that she was a witch too, and she knew about this mystical, magical world beyond the human one I remember from my childhood.

I'm certain of one thing. She'd say that I should take a chance on Laerith.

Plus, Abe wouldn't tell me it was safe if it wasn't.

Outside the door, the hot vampire stands with her hands on her hips. When I emerge, she jerks her head up Sycamore Street. "Let's head for the woods in Shifter Hollow. We need peace and quiet and to not have onlookers."

I resist the urge to ask if I can call my mates. I think she'd say no. And this female is crazy intimidating. Still, the bratty side of my nature that sometimes doesn't know what's good for me rears her head. When I open my mouth to say something, Laerith's elegant nostrils flare.

"You asked me here, Witch. Well, Abe and Arkan on your behalf. Do you want help or not? Or would you like to handle a revenant all on your own?"

Shock courses through me. "You know about revenants?"

"You don't know the half of it, sister," she mutters. Then she spins on her heel and strides quickly up Sycamore toward Shifter Hollow.

"Wait, how is all of this gonna work?" I shout up the street after her.

When she doesn't pause or answer, I jog to catch up.

She glances down, smirking as I struggle to keep pace. "We'll toss you right into the deep end, Witch. Few things you need to know about me. First, I'm here as a favor to Abe. If it weren't for him, I wouldn't step foot in a haven at all. Second, if you mention one word of my involvement to Evenia, I will come for you, rip your innards out through your pussy and leave you for the ravens to pick apart."

"Oof, sounds shitty," I blurt out, sucking in deep breaths as I hustle to keep up.

"Listen," she says with a snort, waving one long black-nailed finger at my face. "I don't fuck with that bitch, and I don't come to the haven system because I don't want her siccing hunters on me to force me into service. You'd do well to hide this magic from her because she'll do the same thing to you."

"Err, is it gonna be a problem that one of my mates is a hunter?"

Laerith grabs my shoulder and halts me in the street. "Your mate is a hunter?"

I nod. "One of them. The other's a—"

"Don't care," Laerith all but shouts, her crimson eyes wide as her fangs grow longer. She glances around, like super-secret hunter spies might be around every corner. "Don't like this."

I'm pretty sure she's talking to herself.

"Laerith, I need this help," I press. "My hunter's not a rule follower. I swear on my life he won't tell Evenia about you. People are getting hurt. Doc Slade can't fix it. And my family is at risk. I—"

Her frown turns into a feral smile. "Did you say Doc Slade? As in the dark elf with those gorgeous long horns?"

I shake my head, confused. "I guess? Tall, thin, he's been here a long time, I think."

"Since Ever's beginning," she muses, tapping her chin with her forefinger. "Hmm. Very interesting. Okay, little blue, let's go. My first rules still apply, and as long as you're good with that, I'll stick around long enough to give you a primer. You should be able to pick up the rest on your own, once you can feel the magic well."

I take off at a jog to keep up with her, but when she darts off into the underbrush, disappearing behind two ferns, I stop and stare. This is ridiculous. Am I really about to follow a woman I just met into the exact type of situation where the guys found Amatheia?

Laerith pops back out from behind the ferns with a wry expression. "Your inability to follow basic instructions does not inspire confidence." She shoots me a haughty look and then disappears, and I think of my old mantra about how it takes a bitch to know a bitch.

So I follow my new bitchy teacher because I see a little bit of myself in her.

Pushing through the ferns, I follow her trail, barely keeping up with her. I jog, shoving plants and shit out of my face, until I run right through a spiderweb she must have somehow dodged. Or else I'm going totally the wrong way. When I shout, sputter and whirl around to wipe the web off my face, Laerith appears in my side view, sighing exasperatedly.

"Gods, you're a mess, girl." Without further ado, she steps forward, picks me bodily up and throws me over her shoulder like a sack of potatoes, grumbling under her breath the whole time.

"Put me down!" I shout. "Or I'm calling Abe!"

"Please do," she sasses, spanking me on the ass.

I'm embarrassed at how hot I find it to be hauled off into the woods by a gorgeous vampire. If my mates could see me now, I think they'd laugh and enjoy this view. Even so, my power bristles and surges to the tips of my fingers.

"Call Abemet," her hand tightly grips my upper ass, "because I have quite a few questions for him, my little dumpling."

"Dumpling?" I shriek. "What on ea—"

I'm promptly dumped onto the ground in a heap, and before I can even track movement, Laerith stands across a small clearing, leaning against a tree as she picks at her long black nails.

I rise and bend over my knees, sucking in harsh breaths as I glare at her. "Come over here so I can slap you."

She grins and stalks to the middle of the clearing. "I like you." She waves a hand toward my entire body. "I like everything about you. But you don't know shit about your power, and we need to change that fast."

Get it together, Lou, I shout at myself.

Rising to my full, short height, I match her stance. "I'm ready, Obi Wan."

"Don't quote *Star Wars* to me, girl," she snarks.

I'm so shocked she got the reference, my mouth drops open.

Laerith continues right on as if she didn't just "get" a human reference. Nobody gets them here.

"You know *Star Wars*?" I blurt out.

She pinches the bridge of her nose. "Didn't I already say that I don't live within the haven system?" She narrows crimson eyes at me. "So, if we use our incredible powers of deduction, where might I live, if *not* within the system?"

This lady's got attitude by the bucketload.

I wonder if that's a blue witch thing?

"Noted," I bark. "Let's get going, then."

She sighs again, returning her hands to her hips, where they seem to be a majority of the time. Then she begins muttering to herself about what a bad idea this all is. It's on the tip of my tongue to be sassy, but people's lives are at stake—my mates, my girls, my friends.

"Please," I say quietly, "I don't want anyone else to get hurt if I can potentially stop him."

Laerith stops in her tracks and turns to me. She stares for a long moment, crimson gaze dropping to my feet and coming back up. It's a lazy perusal, but I stand tall and lift my chin. It feels like she's assessing my soul, and I don't want her to find it lacking.

"Fine," she says, crossing her arms. "Blue magic is so rare that most of us have just learned by *doing* over the years. But there are a few basic tenets that can be taught."

"How many of us are there?"

She snorts. "Within the haven system? I can't think of any. It's well known Evenia wants one to become her personal guard dog, so most of us stay out of the havens, lest our power show itself. The stronger you get with the power, the more frequently it'll come out, and nothing screams blue witch like blue flames licking up your hands."

"That happened to me," I admit. "Leighton, the revenant, threatened one of my mates, and I burst into flame."

Laerith's brows rise. "And then?"

"It shocked him, I guess, and he left."

"You're lucky, and strong. But I'm guessing you have no idea how to recreate what you did?"

"I don't," I admit. "Or how to use it if I could create it. Well, I've read part of one book."

"Blue power is primarily born from the fire elements, meaning it works like fire. But you can guide and direct your flames into weapons of almost any sort. Wait," she stalks closer, "you know it's battle magic, right? Do I need to start at the very beginning?"

I grin. "I knew that much, thank you. I started that book about it to try to figure things out."

"Written by blue witches?" Laerith looks skeptical.

"One was," I manage.

She shakes her head. "Let's move along. Nothing better than working with your magic. The magic arrives through the power of belief and need. Needing to help someone, believing that you can, those things are the crux of your power. Like this."

She focuses over my shoulder, lifting a palm. Blue flames crackle, and then they spin and morph into a long sword that looks like it's made of glowing blue glass.

"I'm going to throw this," she murmurs. "Watch what happens." She never takes her eyes off whatever she's looking at.

I walk to her side, and she tosses the spear with a grunt. It slices through the closest tree and embeds deep into the tree behind it. Blue flames lick up the tree and begin to catch fire to the lower limbs.

I gasp, staring at the spot where the spear's lodged.

Laerith stalks past me. Grabbing the spear, she pulls it from the tree and swirls her hand in the air. All the flames rush to her and disappear into her skin as I watch in amazement.

A slow clap echoes through the air. I whirl around to see my mates standing about twenty feet away. Dirk comes closer, looking at the spear in Laerith's hand.

She bristles. "Don't know who you are, but we're in the middle of something here. Get lost." She flips the spear, and it disappears into nothing.

Connall follows Dirk into the clearing, coming to my side and rubbing his cheek along mine. "You alright? Abe got us up to speed, but Dirk felt compelled to make sure you were okay…"

I smile and tickle his chin. "I'm fine." Turning to Laerith, I offer a smile. "Laerith, these are my mates, Connall and Dirk." Holy shit. I introduced them as my mates. And it didn't even feel weird. No, it felt good. I felt proud to introduce them.

Laerith doesn't bat an eye, instead giving Dirk a once-over. She looks at me. "We need space to work, girl."

I give my mates an imploring look. "I'll be home soon, I promise."

Laerith snorts. "She'll be home when I think she's learned something."

Dirk visibly bristles.

What is going on here?

Laerith snorts and points lazily at him. "Got to love air elemental posturing. You must be the hunter. Go puff yourself, boy."

Dirk grins like he's about to blast her to smithereens, but comes to me and wraps an arm around my neck, pulling me to his chest. He peppers me with kisses all over the side of my face.

"What's gotten into you?" I try to extricate myself from his cool embrace.

"Air and fire are opposites on the elemental spectrum," Laerith coos. "We pretty much always hate each other." She barks out a harsh laugh. "Tell me, hunter, has Evenia got your nuts in a vice like the rest of your kind?"

Oh okay. Elemental drama. Dirk stiffens but holds me tight.

"But those elements can also be incredible partners," Connall breaks in evenly, sparing us from whatever Dirk's answer was about to be. "Air can bolster fire, help it to burn hotter by providing oxygen to the flames. And fire can turn air deadly."

"Or suck it out of a room," Laerith snaps.

Dirk growls, something I've never heard him do, and glares at Laerith.

"Okay, this is getting a little too much for me." I push out of Dirk's hold. "Why don't you two go so I can learn something that might help us?"

"Sounds like a plan." Connall kisses my forehead. "Kick ass, Sweetheart." He turns to Laerith. "And I'd like you to come for dinner, please. I'm making chicken marsala."

Dirk's still an irritated looking, frozen popsicle by my side. "Be good to my woman," he barks.

Laerith grins. "Maybe. Now scurry along, males."

Connall smiles despite her insult. I push Dirk toward him. Threading his fingers through Dirk's hand, he pulls my sylph toward the road.

When they've gone, I stare at Laerith. "What gives?"

She frowns. "What do you mean?"

I point at the direction my mates left in. "With Dirk. Why would you take an immediate dislike to him, and he to you? Is it just because he's a hunter? It was his idea to *find* you."

She rears back and laughs. She laughs so long and hard, I start thinking maybe she's a little nuts. When the laughter begins to fade, she wipes tears from her eyes.

"Not to worry, little blue, your mates seem quite lovely. Elementals and those with elemental gifts often posture like that. Elements work together, as your wolf mentioned. Most of us can be strengthened through partnership with another. But talking shit is in our nature. Prepare yourself for a dinner full of insults."

"Gods, you're all weird," I mutter. "I might be the only normal one."

Laerith points at me. "Call your flames, Lou. I'm very hungry, and now that your mate mentioned food, I'd like to get this first session done."

Laughing, I focus on the power but can't feel it at all. I felt it earlier when I was angry-ish about the ass grabbing, though.

"Think how you felt when you thought he'd attack your males," Laerith says quietly.

Normally I try to dispel bad thoughts, not keep them and focus on them. But I allow myself to do it now because, if I have the power to help people, I will. I remember how terrified I was when Leighton entered that room and stood behind Connall. An electric zing travels through me. When I look down, my palms are full of blue flames.

A sudden thought occurs to me and I stare up at Laerith as the flames disappear.

"Why didn't this power come to me when I was possessed by a warlock? That would have been a really fucking convenient time."

She cocks her head to the side, looking thoughtful. "Blue magic often goes undiscovered for a long time. No one is truly clear on what causes it to appear. But one thing *is* clear—it's a battle magic so it's typically used in service of *others*." She crosses her arms. "As a younger one, I could certainly have used my blue magic to protect myself against…things." She shudders. "But it didn't come in for me until I needed it to protect someone else, and then it came in like a fuckin' hurricane."

Before I get a chance to ask her about that, she waves dismissively at me. "Call the power again."

When I do it with ease, Laerith grins wickedly. "Well done, little blue, well done."

CHAPTER THIRTY-THREE
DIRK

I'm slicing bread at Connall's behest when the treehouse door flies open and Louanna rushes through.

"Dirk! I caught a tree on fire with my flames! It was amazing!"

I round the island and catch her when she throws herself into my arms. Seating her on the island top, I press my forehead to hers. "Tell me everything, my sweet. How did it feel?"

"Your mate is strong," the vampire's voice drifts from the doorway. "Bound and determined. She'll make a fine blue."

Connall enters the kitchen with a smile and a bottle of wine in one hand. "You have our eternal thanks. It's Laerith, right? Abemet told us, but I wasn't sure I remembered correctly."

She grins at him, flaring her nostrils.

"Dinnae think about his blood," I snap. "Not a drop fer you."

"Aww, come on," she croons. "I can make it feel nice. It'll only pinch a little." She grins at me. "You can watch, sylph."

Lou grumbles and attempts to slide out of my arms. She waves a hand around at all three of us. "Are you gonna be like this all night? Or can we get along?"

"'Tis just posturing, my love," I offer, but Lou shrugs.

"Well, I'm in desperate need of a shower, so I'm gonna do that."

"Need any help scrubbing?" Laerith asks, eyes dropping down my mate's body.

To my surprise, when I press my mouth to Lou's neck, her scent is strong. Och, my Louanna finds the idea of Laerith touching her intriguing. I hold back a chuckle, my competitive nature rearing forward.

"Mine," I rumble, sucking at Louanna's skin as she squirms.

Laerith rolls her eyes, and Connall watches our standoff with a bemused smile.

Tension is thick in the room. Elemental monsters from opposing elements are always like this…nitpicking and arguing. It's part of why my being teased as a child was such a big deal. I lived with air elementals. It shouldn't have happened to the degree it did. It should have been surface level, playful.

I'm lost in thought about that when Louanna shoves out of my arms. She turns and kisses my lips roughly. Then, with a grumble, she heads down the hall, leaving Connall and me alone with Laerith.

"Laerith, can I make you a drink?" Connall rounds the bar to stand beside me, slipping one hand up between my shoulders to grip the back of my neck. His touch is possessive and reassuring all at once. He's telling everyone I'm his, while still being accommodating.

Laerith watches us with a thoughtful smile, then crosses her arms. "Anything you've got that's strong."

"Excellent." Connall heads for the bar area and grabs an assortment of bottles. Laerith and I stare at one another as if in challenge.

And it continues like that as my mate makes her a drink. She snips, and I respond until I suspect Connall wants to crack our heads together.

Ten fraught minutes later, faint footsteps echoing up the hall tell me my beautiful mate is out of the shower.

Connall can deal with the vampire for a moment. I need to reconnect with my woman, and she's naked under that towel.

She laughs when I jog after her into the bedroom. Grabbing the edge of the towel, I rip it from her and drop it to the floor. She spins to face me, eyes flashing and glorious long hair all mussed. Heavy, round breasts sway, glistening with droplets from the shower.

"Yeh need to be tongue-bathed dry, Louanna," I murmur.

She grabs a long strand of wet hair. "What I need is a hair dryer. Think you can do that for me, Mister Zefferus?"

Grunting, I fall to both knees and grip her hips, pulling her to me. I sit back on my haunches and kiss my way up her belly. "Gladly, my sweet."

Louanna's gaze goes thoughtful, her smirk falling. She stares at me, a multitude of emotions passing through her elegant features.

"I love you," she whispers. "So damn much."

I rise, emotion overwhelming me as my heart rate kicks into overdrive. Slipping my fingers into her hair, I tilt her face upward. For once, I'm speechless. Hearing her say those words after hoping for so long... Pressing my lips to hers, I kiss her, knowing I've finally, *finally*, broken down the walls. That she trusts me enough to let me in.

She loves me.

She loves *me*.

"Louanna," I gasp. "I love you too. I always have, I—"

She silences me with the press of her lips to mine. When we part, she runs both hands up my chest, resting them over my heart.

"I pushed you away for so long, and I'm sorry for that."

I crush her to me, determination rushing through me. "Never apologize for that, my sweet. You weren't ready until you were.

Thank you for taking a chance on a wild, rule-breaking elemental. I cannae promise that everything will always be perfect and safe, but I promise you a life full of love, fun and, och, yes, likely a bit of danger too."

"Good thing I'm a blue witch, then." She nips at my chin. "Laerith told me once I'm strong enough, I'll be able to pick you up with my power and toss you around like a ragdoll."

I run my hands down her plump arse, slipping my fingers between her cheeks to tease at her back hole. "I cannae wait for that. I've got to taste yeh, Louanna, and then I'll happily dry all that glorious hair."

I don't wait for an answer. Instead, I slide my tongue between her pussy lips and circle her clit as she grumbles about the guest in our living room. Yet her scent explodes around us, so I grip her ass cheeks harder and hold her open for me. I'm so amped from another elemental power being in our home that my licking goes rough and ragged. But Lou groans, bringing both hands to my hair and threading her fingers through.

The pinch of her grip drives my lust higher as I sling one of her legs over my shoulder. Growling, I call my lightning and direct it to my tongue, where little zaps along her pussy have her moaning and asking for more.

When she comes, she chokes the sounds back as she floods my tongue with sweet honey.

"Louanna," I groan, "give me more, my sweet." I keep going as her legs tremble, knees buckling. But I hold her steady. I'll always hold her steady.

She pants and gasps as her orgasm prolongs, my tongue slipping over her mound and back to her clit. Eventually, her bliss fades, and I press tender kisses to both thighs and up to her bellybutton.

"Beautiful."

"I love you," she whispers again, eyes closed as she steadies her breathing. "So much."

I smile. "Did yeh tell Caroline that yeh wanted me before you admitted it to me?"

Her eyes flash wide. "Did you spy *and* read my letters?!"

I shake my head. "Never. 'Twas only a guess based on watching you write them. I promise I've not read them."

She slaps my chest playfully. "We can read them together sometime, but, yes, I told her about you, and Connall. Although I haven't written to her since the two of you bowled me over with your advances."

"Och, Louanna," I moan, feigning hurt. "Perhaps you should write to tell her all about getting dicked down by two handsome males, then."

She laughs, but her eyes flick to the door. "You left Connall with Laerith, and we're being rude. We better get out there."

"Fine," I agree. I'm not ready to leave this room, but she's right. We cannae leave Connall to host the blue witch either. "Let me do yer hair, then."

When my woman nods, I slap my gem and dissipate. I swirl lazily through her long strands at first, pulling moisture from them. Then I strengthen until I'm brushing fast through her hair. In a minute, I've got it dry and braided, and I'm having the time of my life. I could play with her hair for ages.

I return to my human form and tug the end of her braid back over her shoulder, holding it up so she can wrap a hair band around it.

"Holy shit," she breathes, grabbing the dry braid and staring at it in shock. "Best blow dryer ever, all the stars, no notes, highly recommend."

"I'm great at blowin' things," I say with a wink.

Her smile goes big and wicked. "Yeah, you are. Speaking of which, shall we rescue our mate?"

Our mate.

"Yes, Louanna," I agree. "Let's."

CHAPTER THIRTY-FOUR
LOU

Dirk and I help Connall plate the chicken marsala and bring it to the table. Laerith sits at the head with her arms folded across her chest, a toothpick hanging from the corner of her mouth. Ruby eyes glitter as I set the plate of food down in front of her.

She reaches up and pats the side of my ass, then gives it a little squeeze. "I like it when you serve me, little blue."

Dirk lets out an honest to gods growl and grabs his knife as he sits down to Laerith's right. "Hands off my woman."

"Begads!" She says with a mocking sneer. "A woman has hit on *my* woman! Whatever will I do? My manliness is affronted!" She follows the mockery up by sticking out her tongue.

When Dirk rises with the knife in his hand, I shoot them both accusatory looks.

I swat Laerith's hand off my ass and wag my finger in her face. "You, stop teasing my mate." Turning to Dirk, I shoot a meaningful glance at the knife in his hand. "And you, put that down because she's our guest."

He opens his mouth to say something, but Connall grabs him

by the shoulders and directs him to the next seat over—farthest from our dinner guest.

Laerith smirks like she's just won. Blue flames dance in her eyes as she grins down the table toward Dirk. "Good thing your handsome mate put you there so I didn't have to do it myself." Her fangs glint in the low light.

Rolling my eyes, I walk to the far end of the table and pick the opposite head chair with Dirk to my right. As I sit, I bat my lashes at Laerith, whose smile becomes a scowl.

Connall offers Laerith a bowl of salad, indicating she should go first. "We can't thank you enough for working with Lou. The appearance of her power was a real shock for two of us."

"You can say that again," I mutter as I dig into the perfectly cooked chicken.

Dirk scooches his chair closer, squeezing my thigh under the table as he smirks.

Laerith looks between us. "Tell me what you've learned from this *book* you mentioned earlier. We'll go from there."

For the next quarter hour we share everything we've read about. Admittedly, we're still just halfway through. But even that much knowledge has made me feel so much more empowered. Or maybe I'm still in shock. That's possible too.

"One thing you mentioned that I cannot stress enough is what her needs will be after expulsions of power. Even after our sessions." She wags her brows at me, then returns her focus to my mates. "If she fights this Leighton character, she'll need you afterward in a way she hasn't needed you before. As in, drink plenty of water and call in sick for a few days."

Connall's eyes spring wide, and he runs a hand over his mouth, looking at me. "It almost sounds like an omega's heat."

Laerith makes a pleased sound. "Build her a nest, if you like, alpha. Her sexual need will be *precisely* like a heat."

They're just casually discussing my sexual intensity like it's regular ole dinner conversation. This is so…weird. Except that the look on Connall's face tells me he couldn't be more excited by the prospect of sharing something like a heat together.

I take another bite of marsala and chew around buttery, mushroomy deliciousness. "What else, Laerith? What do I have to know before you skedaddle out of here?"

"Yer welcome to run along any time," Dirk says playfully, batting his lashes as he smiles. "Wouldn't want your knickers in a twist if Evenia randomly shows up to town. Her son lives here, yeh know."

Laerith's red eyes narrow, and she takes an aggressive bite of her marsala.

I sigh. This is gonna be a long dinner with all of this elemental posturing back and forth.

But I kinda think I love it.

~

"Tell me about these Evertons," Laerith demands, crossing her muscular arms over her chest.

We're standing with Morgan at Doc Slade's the morning after dinner. No idea where Slade is, but we let ourselves in, and now I'm staring at Bellami's softly rising chest, even though he's facing the ceiling, completely catatonic.

I reach down and straighten his hat. I remember him telling me once that it's highly inappropriate for anyone to see a gnome's hair, and his hat seems to be in danger of falling off.

"This is my friend Bellami," I say. "He tasked me with helping the gnomes build their new village, and—"

Laerith snorts. "A witch in a gnome village? You must be mistaken."

Morgan huffs out an irritated-sounding noise. "Why is it so unbelievable to everyone that Lou would get invited to help the gnomes? They fucking love her. Everybody loves her. There's not a better person to help them."

"Why'd they ask you?" Laerith turns and drops her hands casually to her sides, although she widens her stance.

I'm ready when blue flame shoots from one hand and forms a long, wicked curved blade. Hissing, I call my power and shove it toward her in a rush of blue flame. At the last minute, it dissipates around her blade and dies a quick death.

"Aww, godsdamnit," I huff, returning my focus to Bellami and Amatheia.

"This is new," Morgan reminds me for the millionth time. "You're kicking ass, Auntie. Go easy on yourself, okay?"

It's Laerith's turn to huff. "Or ignore your niece's stupid advice because a revenant is attacking your friends, and maybe your family could be next. Use that impending tragedy as fuel for your fire."

"That's too much pressure!" Morgan grabs my hand and pulls me close to her, wrapping an arm around my shoulder.

I snake my arm around her waist. She's about to go into mama bear mode, which is funny because usually that's me about my nieces. But since they all mated monsters, they've taken a more motherly approach to me, and I find that sort of hilarious.

"She's right, Mor," I whisper to my niece, pinching her muscular hip. "I've got to be ready."

"Ready, sure," Morgan barks. "But you're not gonna learn everything in a fucking week." She raises an arm and points one angry finger at Laerith. "Chill out, lady."

Laerith shrugs and jerks her head toward Amatheia. "Tell me about that one."

"The merking's eldest daughter, Amatheia" I whisper. "My mates found her in human form in the woods."

Laerith drops to a knee beside the giant tub Doc Slade hauled in for Amatheia to rest in. The mermaid's tail hangs over the edge.

"Just one fin." She looks up. "So, in human form, she's got just one foot?"

"Half of one leg," I confirm. "Not sure why that matters."

"Maybe it doesn't," the vampire croons. "Maybe it does. He seems to have attacked those who'd be least suited to defend themselves." She glances around the room as if it'll help her think. After a long moment, she heads for the door, calling out to us over her shoulder, "Come along, my little humies. Now that we've recentered on why this work matters, let's get serious."

"Humies," Morgan grunts. "Haven't been called that since the first week we arrived. And we're not even human; we're witches!"

I sigh. "Let's go, though. If I don't follow quickly, she'll make me run laps and I already did that all morning. And while I'm down with tossing flames at garbage bags, ya girl is not down with running, okay?"

Morgan laughs and heads for the door. As she goes, I turn to look at our fallen friends.

Reaching out, I give Bellami's tiny hand a squeeze.

"I'll fix this," I promise him. "I'll get you back to Penn soon. No matter what."

~

The next two days of working with Laerith have my mind blank and fired up all at the same time. She's a taskmaster, demanding I not work at Alkemi while she's here so we can spend every minute together.

"Focus, Lou," she snaps, breaking through my thoughts.

"Why can't we just go *look* for him?" I whine for the millionth time.

Laerith plants her hands on her hips and sighs, staring up into the sky. She mutters something I can't quite make out, but I'm pretty sure I hear the words "asshole" and "reprieve".

I stare at the side of Higher Grounds, focusing on a bag of trash that I've been trying to light on fire for the last ten minutes. Conversation from Main Street distracts me, and I turn to see.

"Lou," Laerith sighs, rubbing her face with both hands. "You won't always have the benefit of a quiet forest to use your power in. Focus, girl. Must I repeat myself a thousand times?"

"Pretty sure it's already been two thousand," I mutter.

Laerith stalks closer, bringing her lips to my ear. "If it's three thousand before you get this, I will begin to question my skills as a teacher."

"Noted," I grumble. "Scoot, you're distracting me. You're too hot."

She slaps my ass before stalking a few feet away. When I glare over at her, she grins. "Didn't *mean* to distract, Lou."

Riiight. I'm beginning to internalize more of what I learned about blue witches and sexuality. I've always loved sex and had a healthy sex life, whether dating or not. But there's something about the magic that amplifies all of that. I can barely keep my hands to myself when I'm around Connall and Dirk. It was like that from the very beginning. Laerith told us last night that most blue witches take multiple mates to deal with their sexual demands.

"I know exactly what you're thinking about," she croons, slipping across the space between us. She leans down and moans in my ear, sounding like she's getting off right here. Her moans go rough and ragged as she pants into my ear. "Laerith, right there, please. Oh fuckkkk!"

"Stop it," I hiss, slapping her boob. She's all talk.

"And so," she snaps. "You gonna wait all day? Or can we commence with the training? Or perhaps you need further distraction..." She slings an arm around my waist and hauls me against her taller figure so our boobs mash together.

"Maybe." I bat my lashes playfully just as something appears out of the corner of my eye.

Shadows blur by the trash can. I freeze in place as they twist and form into a now familiar shape.

"Leighton," I breathe, begging my lungs to fill with oxygen. I shove my way out of Laerith's arms.

Has he already hurt someone? Is he about to?

Blue flames leap from my fingertips, curling up my arms.

Laerith spins to my side, alert in a moment. She looks where I'm looking, but I know she can't see him. They're not bound together like he and I are.

"You see him right now?"

Balling my fists, I nod. Laerith straightens next to me, matching my stance.

"Do as we discussed, Lou," she instructs. "Focus on imagining your power as a weapon. We must release Leighton from his revenant form so his soul can return to his goddess."

In my mind's eye, I picture the glowing, long sphere she taught me to think about. It's blue, because of course.

My blue moon wolf.

My blue lightning sylph.

The tiny blue flames licking over my palms.

Leighton sneers at me and hover-walks backward toward Main Street. I jolt forward to follow him as Laerith snatches at my arm but misses. I hear her comm'ing Arkan, but everything past that blurs as Leighton's figure backs toward Main.

Despite Arkan's public warning about what happened to Amatheia and Bellami, Main Street is busy. I recognize a dozen familiar faces as Leighton moves into the crowd, looking around like he's picking his next victim.

A tiny voice shouts my name. Leighton and I spin at the same time to see Iggy barreling through the air toward me, his wings flapping chaotically at his back. Time slows. Leighton and I look at one another. His half-smile turns into a wicked grin, and he moves toward Iggy.

I scream Iggy's name and shout for him to run. But all he does is pause, confused, in the middle of Main, staring at me.

Desperation rising, I claw my way toward him, but Laerith gets there first, snatching Iggy out of thin air. She slips with impossible speed to the opposite side of the street as relief floods me.

Leighton turns to me with a snarl, both fists balled as I pause in front of him. Around us, monsters stop and turn to look, confused at what's going on. Murmurs rustle through the crowd. Leighton looks around, and for a moment, I think I see fear and terror on his handsome features.

I've got to get him out of there.

"Let me help you, Leighton," I say calmly. In my mind's eye, I picture the glowing blue spear.

He turns to me and growls, that same deep wolfy growl Connall sometimes does when he's riled up. It lifts the hair on my nape. It's easy to imagine the shifters as predators seeing Leighton right now.

A horrible thought occurs to me. Can he shift into his wolf like this? I gulp around the idea of that.

Iggy raises a racket across the street. Out of the corner of my eye, I make out Laerith holding him on her muscular shoulder, even though he's squawking and throwing an absolute fit.

Leighton's eyes follow the noise, and his smirk returns. I sense he's about to move just moments before he does. We run in parallel toward Iggy, and the moment Laerith sees us coming, she slips up the street with the young gargoyle. But Iggy's losing his mind, stabbing at her face with his tail spade and shrieking like he's possessed.

I scream the moment she loses her hold on him, and he spins, executing a perfect flip in thin air and slicing toward me. Leighton disappears and reappears behind Iggy, raising both hands, his mouth open on a long, loud wail.

Envisioning the spear piercing Leighton through the heart, just like Laerith taught me, I cup my hands together and push the magic away from me, begging it to protect Iggy as he flaps wildly toward me. A stream of blue flames shoots out of my palms, and Iggy squeaks, darting around them.

He lands on top of my head and slings himself around my neck, choking me half to death with his chubby frame in front of my face.

"Ig, fuck!" I shout, trying to shake him away just enough to see.

Focus. Focus. Focus.

I picture the spear entering Leighton's heart. A loud thud and a grunt break my concentration. Reaching up, I tear Iggy from over my face and jam him on my shoulder, looking at where Leighton stood.

He was a solid ten feet away, and now he stands inches from Iggy and me. Like this, he towers over us. Iggy roars, likely sensing something's wrong. It's a deep battle cry that nearly ruptures my eardrums as he yanks at my hair, unable to see the threat.

Leighton glares at me, his features twisted into a sneer. His eyes drop down to his chest, where just the blue-jeweled hilt of my spear protrudes. He clutches at it, tugging as Laerith appears by my side. She reaches for Iggy, but he's stabbing wildly in front of us, trying to dispel an enemy he can't see.

"Think about releasing him," Laerith whispers, reaching down to rest her hand in the middle of my back.

"Lou! Lou!" I hear my mates even though I can't tear my focus from Leighton, who's still grabbing at the weapon lodged all the way through him.

"Quiet!" Laerith hisses over my head.

A crowd has gathered around us, staring, but I pay them no mind.

Laerith pats Iggy's haunch. "You cannot see the revenant, young one, but simply lend Lou your comfort and support. That will be the greatest help you can give, young one."

Iggy presses tighter to my head until I'm practically wearing a gargoyle hat, but when he wraps a hand around my head to hold my ear, and his spade slips into my shirt to rest over my heart, I pull in a deep, steadying breath.

I think about my mates. I think about Leighton, and that terrible time I wasn't in control of my body. And then I pray for him to return to Alaya, the patron goddess of all shifters.

"You can go, Leighton," I whisper, focusing on the spear, willing it to spread battle magic throughout the twisted, dark form holding him captive.

Blue flames form a circle where the spear's stuck, radiating outward like fire burning a sheet of paper. Leighton claws and scratches at it, terror taking over his features as he steps backward.

Iggy rubs soft circles over my heart, and Laerith presses her hand higher up my back.

Then, out of nowhere, my nieces join us, their hands finding spots near Laerith's as tears fill my eyes. Connall and Dirk come next, steady presences as Connall's arm slips around my waist. Dirk's there in elemental form, sending a cool breeze over my cheeks, telling me he loves me with action.

The strength of my love and devotion to my family surges through me. I can't allow them to be hurt, and I can't allow Leighton to be like this, not if I have an ounce of power that could change the outcome for him.

"I'm sorry," I whisper as the fiery circle spreads outward. Gasps go up around us, murmurs as the Evertons begin to see Leighton for the first time. By the time the blue flames reach his extremities, his whole figure is cloaked in a blue tint, all the way to his eyelashes.

He glances around, looking shocked and unaware.

"I release you," I say a little louder. "I release you from this prison, Leighton. I'm so sorry, but you're free."

Dark eyes rove the crowd, the spear seemingly forgotten.

They land on Connall and soften, then return to me. "Louuuuu Heeeectorrrr," he murmurs.

"You remember me." It's a statement. I know he does. It's always been us bound up in this horrible magical contract that led to innocent monsters being hurt.

"I'm sorry," I repeat. "I had no control over what happened to you then or now, and I'm *still* sorry."

He halts a moment, then lifts a hand to look at it. The tips of his fingers seem to blur and move, and then they disappear into tiny blue dots that float away on the evening breeze. More and more of him disappears until he has no hands.

He looks up at me. "I don't blame you, Lou Hector," he says calmly. "I'm happy for you."

Grief chokes me as I watch more of him disappear, using my magic to coax his soul out of the earthly binding. Power builds and builds under my skin, blue flames sluicing along my hands as Leighton disappears faster and faster.

"Easy, Lou," Laerith whispers.

Leighton looks at me with a soft smile. "Goodbye, and thank you…" He closes his eyes and breathes slowly, his head falling back as he lifts what's left of his arms.

Flames swirl up my fingers to my elbows as magic builds and sparks. My vision goes blue until all of downtown is cloaked in the same hue as Leighton. Every heartbeat is like a blue flare within each monster. I become aware of them, of their life forces.

Of the control I have over those life forces, if I wanted it.

"Easy, girl," Laerith hisses. "Don't let it go to your head!"

"You've got this," Connall purrs, the sound vibrating up my back.

Magic stings its way along my skin as Leighton disappears from view, and then it barrels through me, exploding out of my fingertips. I'm barely aware of the sounds of glass breaking and monsters shrieking.

And then it's lights out for ya girl Lou.

CHAPTER THIRTY-FIVE
CONNALL

Main Street explodes into blue flames, every glass window shattering outward and lighting on fire. Monsters duck and run, screaming, but all I can focus on is Lou, who collapses into my arms. Iggy doesn't let go, falling against me with his body still wrapped around her head.

"Iggy, give her a sec to breathe," Wren says calmly, reaching for the small gargoyle.

He ignores her and slaps Lou's cheek. "Wake up, Lou! We did it—well, you did it! Wake up!"

I'm barely aware of Alo dropping out of the sky and reaching for his son. But Iggy won't leave Lou any more than I will.

Dirk returns to his physical form and helps me guide Lou carefully to the ground. She's surrounded by her sisters and Laerith, who stands on the sidewalk with a smug grin.

"Couldn't quite control it in the end," she quips, "but, damn, that was quite the fireworks show."

It's chaos after that, as town leadership arrives and checks on anyone who was injured by the glass. There's nothing major, but Doc Slade rushes from monster to monster as I hold Lou in my arms.

By the time he gets to us, he's covered in sweat, looking a bit harried. He blanches when he sees Laerith. "Erm, hello again," he blurts out, going from harried to totally frazzled.

"Hello, Doctor," Laerith purrs. I'd swear she tossed a little extra depth into her voice.

Slade gulps and drops to a knee next to Lou, mumbling something about vampires low under his breath. He checks Lou over as I stroke her face and neck. I should be worried. No, I should be freaking the fuck out at my mate on the ground. But my wolf is calm. He's just waiting for her to return to us. Somehow, some damn way, I know she's fine. That she just needs a quick reset because of her power.

I still don't know much about blue magic, but I'm bound and determined to learn as fast as possible so I can support her. But I sense her, like I've always sensed her. I want to take her home, put her in a nest, and service her until she's done with me.

It's what she needs and I know that now.

Chocolate lashes flutter against her freckled skin. She lifts her chin and glances up at me. "Did we do it? Is he released?"

"He's gone, my love," I whisper. "You worked a miracle."

Grief wars with the sense of victory inside me. My friend is dead, but now he's truly gone in the *right* way of our people. And she accomplished putting him to rest.

Slade feels her forehead, then looks inside her ear. "I think you're going to be just fine, Lou. I don't see any damage from the explosion."

She shoots upright, ripping out of my arms and stalking to the center of the street. She throws both hands on top of her head and spins circles, looking utterly horrified. "Oh my gods, I did this?"

Laerith steps off the sidewalk toward Lou. Dirk moves to follow her, but I place a hand on his chest.

"She needs a minute." My mate looks at me, confusion swirling in his beautiful eyes. So I bend down and bring my lips to his ear. "She needs guidance, mentorship, friendship from Laerith. She gets other things from us."

He rubs his stubbly cheek against my mouth, huffing under his breath. Poor, sweet sylph. Dirk is so used to control. It's hard for him not to have it.

Dirk and I stand together, arms around one another's waists as Laerith and Lou talk in low tones. Eventually, Lou stops looking so distressed, and her scent returns to normal. When a bright, hopeful smile overtakes her delicate features, I pull Dirk into the street to join the girls. The triplets quietly follow.

When we surround Lou, she looks at each of us in turn.

"Laerith thinks Amatheia and Bellami might be awake now that Leighton's been released. We're going to check. They'll be afraid if they wake up at the doc's office, and he's here."

"You were amazing, Lou," Morgan says, reaching for her aunt. She pulls Lou into her arms and rests her head on top of my mate's. "Absofuckinglutely terrifying, but that was amazing."

"I did smash all the windows, though," Lou grumbles, her sass returning.

"I can fix those, honey." Morgan smiles. "Black witch, remember?"

Lou lifts her gaze to Morgan's and smiles. "Oh, thank fuck! I was worried all the buildings were going to hate me forever."

"Maybe the movie theater won't let you drink soda anymore, just like me!" Iggy shouts, fluttering into the circle and squeezing his way between Lou and Morgan. He plants his feet on Morgan's chest and pushes, shoving him and Lou away from her. When the girls laugh and part, he snuggles up with his head under Lou's chin, his tail draped up and over her shoulder.

"You did such a good job, Iggy," she whispers to the tiny gargoyle. "That battle cry nearly blew out my eardrums."

He nuzzles her neck. "I'm really tired now, though. But I wasn't afraid. I tried to be brave like Dad and Uncle Shepherd."

"And we need to do a post-attack family meeting to assess

what happened," Alo's deep voice breaks through the group as he joins, smiling proudly at his son.

Iggy looks up at his father with big blue eyes, pouting a little. "Do we have to do it now? Lou was gonna take me to Slade's to check on the fallen monsters."

Lou snorts and lightly spanks his thigh. "And was I also carrying you the whole way?"

He mimics her snort and slaps her shoulder lightly with his tail. "Of course, Lou. You need comforting. Gargoyles are good at that. Miriam always says it's the best feeling in the world to hold me."

"It is," Lou whispers, but her eyes flash as she finds Dirk and me.

Heat snakes down my spine at the look in her eyes. She's ready to recharge. I can feel it in the way she's staring. Blue flames dance in her irises, tiny flecks of fire skirting along her skin.

We aren't coming out of the bedroom for days, if those books are right.

I'll need to prep for that with Richard, make sure he feels okay on his own without me around...Laerith warned us about this, but Richard and I need to have the conversation.

Lou looks at all of us around her and smiles. "Shall we go?"

The triplets opt to stay on Main and clean up a bit. Lou waffles about leaving, but they insist she go with Slade to check on Amatheia and Bellami.

The walk to Slade's cottage takes just a minute. When Slade opens the door, voices echo faintly from within. He takes off at a sprint through his front room, past the kitchen and down the long hall to the room where Bellami and Amatheia have been staying.

When Lou takes off after him, Dirk and I exchange smiles. Relief fills me as shouted exclamations drift up the back room. We follow Lou, Iggy, Slade and Laerith into the room. Inside,

Amatheia clutches the edges of the tub, staring at us as we enter.

"What's going on here? What happened? I don't remember..." Her voice is tremulous, luminescent blue eyes wide.

Slade drops to a knee between Amatheia's tub and the small table Bellami was on. He looks between them both, smiles, and recounts the story of what just happened. By the end of it, they both look shocked, but Bellami sits up and gives Lou a wry grin.

"So you were our savior, huh? Why am I not surprised?" He crosses both arms.

Lou matches his stance, stalking across the room and picking him up by both shoulders. She brings him right to her face, and I prep myself for the snark she's inevitably going to deliver. But my mate surprises me.

"I'm glad you're okay, Bellami," she whispers. "I had no idea how we were going to fix things, and gnome village wouldn't be the same without you."

He reaches for her, and she pulls him to her cheek, squeezing him tight. He hugs her back. I watch in shocked silence. Gnomes can only be described as brusque and surly. I've never seen a gnome display *any* sort of affection.

Bellami kisses Lou's cheek, then bends toward her ear, whispering loud enough that I'm able to hear him, "Don't think any of this gets you out of helping us, Lou. We need you, okay? It'll go so much faster if—"

"I get it," she says with a huffy laugh. "Jesus, I can't believe that's your first thought after being knocked out for ages."

He tips his head at her, then blushes and looks around. "Err, where's my hat? It's highly inappropriate for you to see my whole head."

Slade appears with a tiny red hat between his fingers, handing it to Bellami.

The gnome takes the hat and places it on his head. Then he

wriggles out of Lou's hands. She sighs as he trots up her arm and slides down her side, using her clothing.

Amber eyes flash to Dirk and me. "I'm getting used to males being all over me all the time."

Heat. Lust. They sizzle through me as Dirk takes a step closer to me and slides his hand up the back of my shirt.

Lou's eyes move to the tub, and she smiles softly. "Amatheia, we haven't met, but I'm Lou. My mates and I found you when you were hurt, and we brought you here."

The mermaid shifts upright, long dark hair falling over her exposed breasts. "You have a lifetime of my thanks."

"And of course we'll return you to the lake the moment you're ready," Slade offers, his eyes softening.

Amatheia hunches over, tucking wet hair behind her long, tapered ear as she flattens them to her head. "I'd like to stay here a bit longer, if you don't mind. I still feel…weak."

"Of course, Sweetheart," Slade says gently.

Laerith makes a strangled noise at the back of her throat, and I turn to see. But her fierce gaze is focused on Slade and the way he's staring thoughtfully at the woman in the water.

Oh moons.

"I'd be happy to help you get home," Laerith croons. I don't know if it's the predator in me that senses an innate deviance in Laerith's tone, but Amatheia doesn't seem to mind.

She smiles brightly at the female vampire. "Give me a day to luxuriate in this tub and figure out what I'm going to tell my father, and then I'll take you up on your offer."

"I can speak with him," Slade says, "if you'd find it helpful."

Amatheia blushes, dark blue tinting her high cheeks. "That won't be necessary, Doctor. King Caralorn doesn't come to the surface."

"Richard and I would be happy to assist," I offer. "And I'm sure Arkan or Abemet would too."

Mermaid society is incredibly structured and rigid. Caralorn's word is law, and I suspect he won't be pleased that his daughter disappeared without a word, even though she was attacked.

"Maybe Richard could speak with him," Amatheia says softly. "He might listen to Richard."

I nod. "Consider it done. When you're ready to go home, we'll deliver you there and request an audience with your father."

She smiles, but there's no joy in it. She sinks further into the water until all that's visible is her wide eyes and the tops of her pointy, flared ears.

I glance at Dirk. "I'm ready to take our mate home. She's probably exhausted."

"No!" Lou shouts, lifting a hand. "I've got to go clean up Main Street! I made a hellsuva mess, you guys."

"Absolutely not," Dirk says with a snort. "Morgan can fix it in moments with her magic. It's probably already done."

Lou shakes her head. "I'm not leaving a mess for someone else to clean up. I want to see for myself that it's all fine before we go home."

My grin is so big, it hurts my cheeks. This woman, moons. She is everything to me.

CHAPTER THIRTY-SIX
DIRK

One minute we're standing on Main, and Morgan's reassuring us she's taken care of the buildings, and the next I'm swooping my mates into my arms. I dissolve us into pure air and whisk them up to the wards. I dance along the sleek surface, finding the fastest path back home. This day has taken us on a wild ride, and I need them alone.

I need to talk with them. What Connall said earlier about working with them instead of planning everything myself has been bothering me. Lou just saved *everyone*, but this whole thing with her power could've been easier if I'd been forthright with my suspicion.

There's something else I haven't told them, something I kept from them so they didn't have to worry until I knew exactly what was happening. But I need to tell them now, because he's right—they deserve truth, partnership. I'm no longer the male pushing them across a chessboard to ensure we end up together. We're together now. I can't think about things the same way.

My secret consumes me as I swirl us through the back door and into the living room. I drop my mates gently on the sofa.

They cling to each other, laughing as Louanna buries her face in Connall's neck. They chuckle and snuggle as I watch.

I love their love.

I love *our* love.

And I'm still learning how to love them the way they deserve.

"I need to talk to you both," I say as they settle down.

Connall shifts upright, pulling Lou into his lap. She nestles between his thighs, resting a hand on both of his knees with a wicked grin at me.

"Go on, mate," he encourages, bringing his lips to Louanna's neck. His eyes flash emerald as his wolf pushes forward to be with us. When he nuzzles her and nips, my body flushes with heat. I pant as I watch his mouth trail a path over her skin, kissing every freckle, worshiping every inch. By the time he gets to her shoulder, sliding her tee down for better access, I'm desperate.

"It's serious!" I blurt out.

Connall stops on a dime and returns Louanna's shirt to its original position. Her smile falls. As they stare at me, uncharacteristic nerves stab my belly. I don't get nervous. I'm a hunter. This is...terrible.

"There's something I've been dealing with regarding work that I didn't want to burden you both with because I don't know what the outcome will be. But Connall suggested that, when something's wrong, I need to talk to you both. So, this is me talking, because I want to be a good mate, and..." My voice trails off. I look back at them. I didn't even realize I'd looked away when I started speaking. "I love you and I don't know what I'm doing."

Connall's eyes are soft at the corners, a smile tugging his lips upward. Lou looks dead serious as she rises from his lap. She reaches for me with both hands and pulls me onto the sofa next to them. We fall into a pile with her on top of me and Connall by our side. Their presence soothes me.

I pull in a steadying breath, my upper half resting in the pillows. Lou's lying on my chest, staring up at me.

Forcing air to fill my lungs, I focus on them. "I'm probably going tae be sacked soon for my part in helping Richard and Lola reunite. Evenia's not mentioned what I did, hasn't even revoked my portal access. But I suspect she's waiting fer a time when she can embarrass me publicly. I don't know what'll happen after that. I'm a hunter, but if I cannae go back to work, I'm not sure what I'll do. And I don't know if I even want tae go back, because it requires so much travel…" My words trail off again. I glance at my mates. "What do you think?"

Lou sits upright and trails her fingertips over my chest to my jewel. When she strokes it, all my lightning zings toward her and sends pleasure searing outward from my chest.

"I think Evenia can go fuck herself, per usual, and if she fires you, it'll be her loss. You don't need that job because you have us. But if you *want* that job, or any other job, I'm in full support of you."

"Och, Louanna." I rub her forearm as she strokes me.

"I couldn't agree more," Connall says quietly. "Lou's right. Evenia can go to hells for all I care, although I don't want her to publicly embarrass you."

"Might not be that." I give them both a wry look. "I could simply get a summons to appear at Belcastle Prison."

"What?" Lou gasps, her fingers curling into my skin. "She'd imprison you?"

"It's possible," I say. "Unlikely, but nothing surprises me about my boss at this point. I broke quite a few laws, if yeh remember."

Blue flames curl up Lou's forearms, snaking up into her hair as it begins to float around her head. Blue shines from her eyes.

"Easy, Sweetheart," Connall murmurs. "We'll figure this out."

"There's a lot tae figure out," I admit. "Because I don't know that we can hide what happened with Leighton from her. If she finds out yer a blue witch, Louanna, she'll want to press yeh into service for Hearth Headquarters."

Louanna scrunches her nose. "She can try, but I'm not beholden to her."

Connall twirls the end of Lou's braid. "There's a reason most blue witches don't live within the haven system. Dirk is right… Evenia will do everything in her power to get you to work for HQ."

"Then maybe I will," Louanna says cautiously. "Dirk and I can hunt baddies together."

Connall visibly pales, mopping at his brow. "I'm going to need therapy if you two take on those roles and travel all the time."

Lou shimmies against him and looks up, the back of her head resting on his broad chest. "I'm kidding, my love. I've had enough drama to last me a lifetime. All I want is time alone with you two."

"We'll get that," I say more to myself than anyone. Whatever I have to do, I'll make sure we do.

A ringing sound echoes from the wall.

Connall's communication disk.

We share a look as he rises and grabs it off the wall. Evenia's name hovers above it, flashing insistently.

"You've got to be shitting me," Lou gasps.

"Well, here goes nothing," I mutter, directing the disk to answer my boss as I pray for her to be lenient for once in her fookin' life. I set the disk down next to my mates as a life-sized Evenia hologram rises up from the piece of tech.

Haughty as ever, she looks from me to a neutral Connall and scowling Lou, then back again.

"I think you know why I'm calling, Mister Zefferus."

"Och, a bit early for a check in, isn't it?" I keep my voice steady. "I've not used up all my vacay days yet, boss."

She sighs. "You used your security clearance to override the shifter king's shutdown code for the Santa Alaya portal. Deny it, I dare you."

I look at my mates. Connall's expression is impressively neutral, but Lou's chest rises and falls rapidly, blue flames flickering from her fingertips.

Easy, I mouth at her.

"I did," I confirm. "To save a life. It was a judgment call."

"I've always liked you, Dirk," Evenia says with a beleaguered sigh. "But I consider this not only a fireable offense but a personal affront. I headhunted you. You've worked for me for a very long time, my best hunter. Even so, I can't be lenient. Not even for you. Report to Belcastle Prison in two days' time and do not even *think* of running."

"Prison?" Lou shouts, rising from Connall's lap to glare at Evenia. Blue flames rise from her skin, her hair lifting as fire envelopes most of her body.

"Shit," Connall murmurs, pulling Lou toward him as he attempts to cover her with his much larger frame.

"How fucking *dare* you!" Lou screeches, shoving away from Connall to point a finger right at Evenia's face. "Leave him alone you heinous bi—"

Evenia lets out a joyous laugh, crimson eyes locked onto Louanna's flames. "A blue…finally. Well, well, well, Louanna Hector. This *is* interesting." Dark eyes flick to me. "It doesn't change what Dirk did and I can't let other monsters think abiding by our laws is optional."

Lou's expression falls, morphing into something desperate. "Leave him alone and I'll consider helping you on occasion."

"Lou!" Connall barks.

"Easy, my sweet," I caution. There's no fookin' way I'm getting out of Evenia's sentence.

Lou's expression grows fierce again. "I'm serious, Evenia. Leave him alone."

Evenia smirks, not deigning to answer. She looks back at me.

"We've got a lot to discuss, Dirk. Report to Belcastle in two days or else."

She doesn't wait for me to respond, signing off with a click. Her hologram disappears into the disk as I stare across the space at my mates.

Lou's eyes well with tears as Connall slumps and pulls her into his arms.

She rests her head against his chest as she stares at me, the first tears falling. "What are we going to do, Dirk? I refuse to let you go."

Crawling over to them, I straddle Connall's legs and crush her between us.

"'Twill be fine, my sweet. I'll do this, because the sooner I go, the sooner I can return to you both." I look from Lou to Connall and back again, drinking them in. "I *promise* I'll be back."

CHAPTER THIRTY-SEVEN
CONNALL

Six weeks later

I stride through the back door onto the porch, holding a tray of martinis for Lou and her nieces. The triplets have been visiting a ton since Dirk left for his stint at Belcastle. We've been inundated with visitors—Richard, Lola, half the pack. Even Amatheia and Bellami have come by a few times, bringing gifts and thanking Lou over and over.

The fact that Evenia forced Dirk to do time nearly crushed Lou and me. We've tried pulling every string we could, but as far as I can tell, nothing has worked to get him out.

Dirk being gone is the worst feeling. I love having time with Lou, but it was always meant to be all three of us. Him not being here leaves us hollow and empty. I've been keeping us busy. We've been having lots of conversations about the things she's gone through, and how she's feeling. She calls it therapy lite.

It's definitely still not therapy.

"Damn, Connall," Thea says. "You make a mean martini, sir."

I smile as Lou's eyes meet mine, then swirl blue. They do that a lot lately. But according to everything we've read about blue magic, it'll continue to compound and grow inside her until she's strong enough to fight off armies.

Not that I'd ever want that for her.

Morgan looks at me, then Lou. "Have you heard from Evenia about your magic? It sucks that we couldn't keep it a secret."

"Arkan tried," Lou sighs. "His official report didn't mention my magic but I fucked up when Evenia called and I kinda revealed it. I was just so mad about Belcastle. But Evenia's a real piece of work, and Leighton's release was public, so I'm not surprised. I offered to do the occasional favor for her if she let Dirk come home, but she didn't budge, that bitch."

"Well," Wren says evenly, "maybe if Dirk goes back to work as a hunter, you can join him as a badass blue witch and banish evil all over the place."

I make a choked sound in the back of my throat. The last thing I want is for my mates to be running around looking for danger and criminals. The idea's come up a few times since Dirk left.

Wren blanches. "Sorry, Connall. That's probably not my best suggestion, huh?"

"Part of me feels called to that the more I think about it," Lou admits, looking from her nieces to me. "But ninety-five percent of me wants to hole up here with my mates and enjoy life for a while. I want to hang out with you girls, too. And let's not forget Iggy."

Thea laughs. "He told us at family dinner the other night that he was super proud he'd been able to come over every single day." Her brows travel upward. "Aren't you lucky?"

"He's great, actually," Lou says with a laugh. "I taught him how to braid my hair, and he got into it, so now he comes over and just plays with my hair for hours. It's fab."

I grin and return to the kitchen, thinking about how cute Iggy and Lou are together. A breeze follows me, rustling my hair and brushing cold touches over my cheeks. Dirk's not out for another sixteen weeks, but I swear I feel him in the wind. I've been spending a lot of time outside, closing my eyes and letting the air dance around me. When he returns, Lou and I have gifts for him—a silver cuff from me and a wedding band from her.

Returning my focus to the dinner in front of me, I reach for a knife to cut veggies when there's a soft pop, and a cool presence at my back.

Elegant blue fingers slide along my forearm to my wrist, encircling it as my mate presses his big body to me. "Och, Wolf, how I've missed yeh."

I flip my wrist and grab him, yanking him to me and placing him on the countertop. Grabbing his knees, I shove them wide and stand between them, drinking him greedily in. The stubble on Dirk's jawline's thicker, and he's a little thinner than when he left, his cheeks gaunt. But that same blue sparkle is in his eyes. Nobody can dim Dirk, no matter what they do to him.

"You're home early." I grip his throat and stroke his lower lip. "How?"

"Good behavior, my love," he says with a wry chuckle. "Tae be honest, I think Abemet called in a favor. Betmal himself showed up to retrieve me."

"Good. I'll thank them later." I push forward to slant my mouth over his. It's a desperate kiss, the kiss of a male who's missed his mate so much, it hurt. I devour him, clutching him to me like I can't ever let him go. We part long enough for him to gasp out Lou's name.

"Outside," I manage. "With the triplets."

"Let's surprise her," he whispers into my lips.

I need to know what happened while he was in there. Is he okay? Was he hurt? I need to feed him. Now that he's back, I want everybody gone. I need my mates naked. Under me. Over me. Coming long and hard.

Protect. Feed. Love. Those motivations ride me as I look from him to the back porch. Lou needs to be with us.

Now.

A million to-dos flow through my mind as I stalk to the back door and lean into the doorway. Four pairs of eyes flick to me.

"Lou, can I see you for a moment in the kitchen?"

She gives the triplets a quizzical look, and Thea sips loudly at her martini. But my mate joins me in the doorway. I grab her around the waist and pull her around me, her back to my chest.

Dirk sits on the edge of the island, leaning back on both hands with a wide grin. His lightning flashes erratically. "Hello, Louanna, my beauty."

Lou lets out a strangled gasp and runs for him, leaping into his arms. They fall off the counter, but Dirk manages to stand. She wraps her legs around his waist and kisses him.

The triplets join us, but upon seeing Lou and Dirk clutched together, they say goodbye and head for the door.

"We'll make up dinner sometime later," I promise as they go.

"No need," Morgan says with a smile. "This reunion is more than worth it. Lou is worth it; she's worth anything."

I smile, returning my gaze to watch Dirk devour our woman. She's right. She's worth all the blue moons in the sky.

CHAPTER THIRTY-EIGHT
DIRK

I kiss my Louanna until I can barely breathe, and when the kiss goes languid and deep, Connall joins us.

"How are you out?!" Lou practically shouts, tears streaming down her freckled cheeks.

"Good behavior and Abemet, I think," I say with a laugh.

Louanna's amber eyes rove my face. "I can't believe you're home."

Connall strokes my side, his fingers warm and rough. "Dirk, are you hungry? Can we feed you?"

"Och, Wolf, I'll be fine in a few days," I respond. "My cell was in the dungeon. Naught for fresh air down there. But a few days in glorious Ever, and I'll be right as rain." I look at Lou and grin. "What I could really use is being buried inside our woman." I glance at him. "With you buried inside me. Everything else later. I need to touch yeh both."

Connall's cheeks go pink even as he smiles.

I wrap Louanna's braid around my fist, dipping her head back to kiss my way up her neck. "Make me the meat in a mate sammie, please."

Louanna chuckles and grinds her hips against mine, arms still around my neck.

I stop kissing her skin long enough to stare deeply into those stunning, incredible eyes. "Tell me all about the sex you had while I was gone. Try anything new?"

"You haven't changed." Connall huffs, pressing us to the countertop with Lou in between. He brings his mouth to the side of her neck and licks, causing her to shiver in my arms. "Not so much new as nonstop. We fucked all the time, mate. In my office, in the woods, in the hot tub, on the deck and every surface of this home."

I shudder at the mental visions filling my mind as he speaks. "Wish I could've watched all that."

Connall bends over Lou's shoulder and brings his mouth to mine. Lou moans when my hands tighten around her ass cheeks. Connall's kiss is slow but rough, just a windup of what's to come. I sense my mate's need for dominance.

"I want to watch you," Lou says. "Let me, please."

We part long enough for Connall to growl and take her mouth. She's quivering in my arms, lust driven sky-high by the idea of us together.

"Bedroom," I whine. "I want our bedroom. Then I want to catch up on everything I missed."

Connall bends down and picks us both up in his arms. Lou laughs at the awkward position, but as he stalks to the bedroom, she falls quiet.

"I missed you so much," I admit. "All I thought about was you."

"She's never taking you from us again," Lou barks, her brows furrowing as blue flames erupt across her skin. Her eyes flash blue with heat, and I laugh.

"My sassy blue witch." I stroke her cheek. "I was half surprised you didn't show up at Belcastle to blast me out of there, my sweet."

She positively scowls, crossing her arms. "I threatened to, but

Connall convinced me that I'd make it worse, and it might keep you from us for longer."

We enter the bedroom, and Lou leaps out of Connall's arms. "I'll grab the lube!" She runs for the bathroom and disappears as he slides me down to a stand. The thick bar of his cock brushes my front as my brain scrambles.

Big hands come to my chest straps and stroke. "May I remove this?"

I choke up hard, and all I can do is nod. I'm home. *Home.*

Lou returns and jumps onto the bed, setting a bottle of lube on our nightstand. She settles into the pillows as Connall slips a hand underneath my gem. He depresses the button to release it. As the straps fall from my chest, I look up at him. Green eyes flash with the brighter shade as his wolf pushes forward to look at me.

Their interest is palpable. I stand before them, letting them look their fill. Connall's green-swirled eyes drift down my neck and over my chest before dropping lower. He jerks his head toward my pants.

"Off."

The single command hits me the way his deep voice always hits me—right in the damn guts until I can scarcely think around the need.

A sweet scent distracts me, and when I look to the left, Lou's cheeks are flushed, her mouth dropped open and eyes hooded as she watches us. I grin.

"You're so beautiful," I whisper.

"All yours." She fans at her face and pulls her knees to her chest.

Connall brings his hands to my jeans and shoves them roughly down my thighs. "I said off, Sylph. She and I fought a lot in the bedroom. Sexy fighting. But we need you between us."

"Our plaything," she says with a seductive purr.

His dominance raises the hair on the back of my neck as I

scramble to step out of my jeans. The moment I do, he grips my hips and shoves me onto the bed, falling behind me. Big body curled over mine, he thrusts his hips and pushes me forward until I'm hovering over Louanna, breathing the same air as her.

"Stay," he purrs.

I look over my shoulder, but all I see is my big wolf as he runs both hands over my arse and up my lower back. His eyes are full, bright green, focused on me. When he scoots backward and bends farther down to run his tongue up and over one arse cheek, my eyes roll into my head, and I fall forward to Louanna's neck, burying my face into her soft comfort.

She squirms and pants, threading her fingers through my hair.

Connall growls and bites his way along my arse to the back of my thigh, bringing his thumb to my back pucker at the same time. I moan when he presses against it. His rough fingers are a sharp contrast to pointy teeth and a hot, soft tongue. He licks and nips at my thighs until he's close, so close to that stripe of skin between my sack and my hole.

When he runs his tongue between my nuts and up to my pucker, I gasp and nip at Louanna.

"Oh fuck," she cries out. "Don't stop, Connall."

His growl turns into a rolling purr that vibrates my cock as it hangs heavy between my thighs. Wet heat swirls over my taut skin, teasing and taunting me. I need so much more than this. But Connall drops lower and sucks the globe of one ball into his mouth, pulling it tight between his hot lips.

I cry out into Lou's neck when his other hand comes to my cock and strokes roughly. His touch is the practiced, firm grip he knows I love best. He rubs me hard but slow, pinching the tip of my dick with each pass until I'm rocking back, desperate to get more, to get closer.

But he's in control, always in control.

He releases my sack and moves his attention to my arse,

licking and nipping until I'm a sweaty, squirming mess. Louanna's scent envelops me as our play stokes her arousal. Her breasts heave close, so close to my mouth.

"Are you ready to come, my sweet?" she says playfully, running her hands through my hair.

"Shirt off," I beg. "Let me touch you."

She shifts forward and rips it over her head just as Connall moves his hand to the base of my dick and squeezes hard. His tongue spears my back hole at the same time, and I cry out, arching. When I bring my face back down, Louanna's wearing naught but black lace, her pink nipples visible through the lace's thin pattern.

With utter desperation, I lean forward and bite her peaked breast, even as I try not to come from how good Connall's teeth, lips and tongue feel. My wolf goes wild, biting and licking in great big stripes up and down the cleft of my arse, to my sack and back again.

I whine as Lou's panting becomes soft, mewling cries. Her scent explodes around the room, driving Connall and me higher as her hips begin to roll, touching nothing. I dive lower, burying my face between her thighs.

"Too much lace," I growl, reaching forward to slip it to the side. She's wet, soaked, in fact, and I—

Connall grabs the bottle of lube, dripping it into my crack as his cock nudes at my back hole, halting rational thought. My eyes roll back into my head as he pushes forward slowly, steadily. Fuck me, it's been too long since I've taken him like this. It's like sitting on a log of firewood, but, gods, that stretch.

"More," I moan.

Louanna's pussy glistens with arousal, distracting me from the feel of my mate filling me to the brim with his thick, delicious length.

"More," I gasp. I dunno who I'm even talking to at this point, so I surge forward and suck at my mate's swollen clit, desperately swirling my tongue over the hood as she grunts and collapses to one side, thighs falling open for me.

"Yes." I grab her thigh and hold it down as Connall's dick nudges my prostate, the broad hood dragging along that sensitive spot inside me. Heat overtakes me as I attack Louanna with my lips, tongue and mouth.

Connall runs a hand up my back to grip my neck. "Eat her fast and hard," he commands. "Make her come at least once before you do."

I obey, gods, do I obey. And I have my pretty little witch coming in moments. She grips my hair hard as she screeches, hips thrusting to get my tongue deeper between her legs. Every desperate sound that leaves her mouth sends my electricity haywire, until it's dancing over her skin and down the length of my cock and zapping at my nipples.

Connall grunts as his rhythm goes harder, deeper, his hips slapping my arse as he rails into me with measured, heavy strokes.

But when Louanna rolls under me and takes the tip of my cock between her lips, I lose control. I explode, clenching tightly around Connall, which tips him over the edge. He roars, lining my arse with cum as I spurt all over my pretty mate's face. Every sense muffles and disappears until there's nothing but the insane pleasure of my mates. Bliss batters me, fire licking up my body, igniting with my lightning until my woman sucks every last drop of cum from my shaft.

As my senses return, I slump forward, hauling my woman with me. Connall's still lodged inside me, his knot pushing at the edges.

Louanna snuggles into my neck, burrowing beneath my chin with a happy little hum. She's covered in my seed but seems not to care in the slightest. I stroke her hair as Connall pulls out of me, his cock rubbing my prostate and sending heat flaring through me, my dick bobbing against Louanna's legs.

Connall falls to his side behind me, reaching over me to place a hand on her hip. He plays with the string of her lace panties as he kisses my back. "She'll need more shortly. She's insatiable since her power came in more fully."

"Och, I think I'm up to the task," I say quietly. Louanna's snoring softly in my arms already. "She fell asleep." I glance over my shoulder at my big mate. "Did we not do enough to keep her interest, yeh think?"

He smiles and kisses the tip of my nose. "Cat naps are suddenly a thing she needs. See if you feel the same way after she gets two minutes of rest. Wherever you are, she'll tackle you to the ground and take what she wants. We've been having a lot of fun playing with dominance. She's the brattiest woman on the planet, I think."

"Godsdamnit," I mutter. "I need to spend a little spy time, watch the two of yeh when yeh're alone. I need to see her manhandle you, mate."

"Mhm," he says with a laugh. "I let her tie me up last week so we could play around with teasing. She made me lose my damn mind, and I broke the headboard to get at her, little minx."

"I can hear you, you know," my sweet little mate says wryly, sitting up to pretend-glare at us.

"Yeh were just snoring, my love," I offer, twisting her braid around my finger.

"Well…" She dips toward my lap and sucks my swollen, aching cock between her lips. Her tongue swirls around it as I arch against Connall. "I'm not asleep anymore."

But I have no words as she starts everything over again. I don't think words exist in the universe to accurately describe how much I love them.

How much I will *always* love them.

CHAPTER THIRTY-NINE
LOU

As I stack crystals on a new table in Alkemi's front window, I consider how much my life has changed in the last few months. From the triplets' first text message about finding Ever, to the thrall attack, to Leighton's death and everything since… It's been a whirlwind.

Some days I still think about Leighton and want to cry. He was a victim more so than me. Connall would tell me that's not true, that I'm equally blameless, but I still struggle with it. Even the process to release him felt violent and awful to me, although Leighton seemed peaceful at the very end.

Laerith stayed an extra week and talked me through some of the mindset shift that comes with being a blue witch. Now we have weekly chats to keep in touch about my power as it grows. I can call my flames easily now, but that desire to serve, to help, to protect is growing along with it. I don't know what will come of that, but somehow I'll find a way to channel all that energy into something *good*.

Connall and Richard traveled to the haven where Leighton's parents moved to let them know what happened in the end. I didn't go. I thought it might be harder for them to see me, knowing my role in Leighton's death.

But I know Connall would also tell me that healing isn't a linear path. That I have to be gentle with myself and let the emotions flow. Experience them, let them have their moment, then allow them to move on.

"Great job, Lou." Malik joins me to admire the window display.

"I've got a knack for displays," I say with a laugh.

"Honestly, that's a whole job you could travel around and do. Some of the other havens are pretty damn swanky, and stores pay a lot of money to designers for their window displays."

I shrug. "I don't think that pace of life is for me."

Malik sighs. "Do you think you'll have a choice?"

I set down a crystal and turn, resting against the moss-covered wall. "Evenia's comm'd me three times this week. I haven't answered, but I won't be able to avoid her forever. And, truly, I feel called to help with my magic." I consider a future where I travel around to help keep havens safe.

"I think I'd like to help, but on my terms," I say finally.

"I'll miss you here," Malik says quietly. "Although Alba has agreed to come help me from time to time."

I grin wickedly up at my boss as pale sunlight filters through the glass and highlights his elegant features. The sign painted on the front door catches my attention.

"You know what?" I look up at him with a grin. "Maybe I was always meant to be here. Alchemy is the study of turning normal things to gold through chemical processes, and that's pretty much what happened to me here. I turned from a regular human sad girl into a blue witch. That's worth something, right?"

Malik snorts and swishes his tail lazily. "You were always pure gold to me, Lou. You've been golden since the beginning, my friend. You were a treasure the day you stepped in here with

Richard and inquired about the job, and you are equally a treasure now."

My heart is full to the brim with love—for Malik, for Ever, for my nieces and my found family. For the mates I can't get enough of.

"Lou, get your ass out here!"

The harsh command makes my magic bristle, spikes of fire emerging along my skin. I whip around to where the voice came from, only to find Bellami standing on top of a mushroom on the mushroom display in the center of the store. He taps one foot, then lifts his hand and looks dramatically at his tiny watch.

"You were supposed to be in the gnome village five minutes ago, girl. Shirking your duties already now that you're a blue witch? Typical." He crosses his arms.

I stalk to the tiny gnome, bending down to get in his face. "Bellami, I told you I had to finish this display today."

He waves my comment away. "And I'd like to have a new home to bring our bride to. So can we go or what?"

A bride? A bride?? I've never even seen a female gnome. Gods, I have so many questions. Plus, I saw him kissing Penn?!

"Well." I turn to Malik, but he just smiles and gestures for me to go. "Fine," I say to Bellami. "But now that I'm a blue witch, you're gonna need to be less bossy, or I might do something crazy."

Malik shoves me out the door with a kiss on the cheek. Outside, Dirk and Connall stand holding hands. Dirk's new wedding band flashes bright in the sunlight. It matches the band I designed for Connall that should be arriving any day now with a ring he picked out from a jeweler back home in Arcadia.

Connall reaches for me when I exit, but Bellami tsks at him.

"No, sir! She's with us tonight!"

I shrug and give my mates a wink. "Sorry, boys, it's all mushies for me for the next couple hours. Why don't you grab a drink, and I'll meet you at Biergarten for a late dinner?"

They grin broadly, and Dirk smiles up at Connall. "Oh, I dunno. What do yeh think, Wolf? Shall we manhandle wood for our Louanna? I'm not sure I can bear to be parted from her at the moment."

"Yeah," Connall rumbles with a lascivious drop of his eyes down my body. "Me neither."

Heat flares through me as his eyes go full wolfy emerald.

"Ugh," Bellami snorts. "Can we get going or what?"

I toss my braid over my shoulder and stick my tongue out at my mates. "Don't forget to leave some wood for me!" I call out as they chuckle and follow.

On to the next adventure. I can't wait.

THE END

++

**Ready for Amatheia's happily ever after with Betmal, the Keeper's father?
Preorder Making Out With Mermaids now!**

BONUS CONTENT:

Wanna know what happens when Connall takes Lou and Dirk home to Arcadia to meet the family? Sign up for my newsletter to access the spicy but sweet bonus epilogue to Slaying With Sylphs!

CHAPTER ONE - MAKING OUT WITH MERMAIDS

BETMAL (unedited)

Smiling, I straighten my fitted vest and step through the glittering green portal surface and into the translucent hallway that'll take me straight to Ever. It's the last of many trips, I hope, as I leave the haven that's been my home for so long.

The reality is that I won't miss much about Hearth Headquarters. I lived here only because my mates lived and worked here.

If I can even call them mates. I certainly don't think of them that way, not after everything that's happened over the last thousand or so years.

Focusing to relax the automatic tension in my jaw when I think of Evenia and Aberen, I release the agitation and stride confidently through the portal hall, emerging on the other side in Ever haven's portal station.

The first two monsters I see are my son, Abemet, and his wife, Morgan.

"Betmal!" she shouts, lurching forward to fling herself into my arms. She squeezes my neck until I can barely breathe, laughing and making happy noises as my son watches silently. A tiny smile tips his lips upward.

I return Morgan's hug, but eventually I set her down.

She steps back and grins at me. "Please tell me Evenia caused some sort of a scene on the way out, and you got to verbally bitch slap her in front of all of HQ? Please tell me it happened because I've been having dreams about it."

A laugh bubbles from my throat, but I shake my head. "Sorry to disappoint, darling girl, but she did not show." I glance at Abemet, trying to decide if I should speak ill of his mother and other father. Ultimately, I decide it's fine. We all know whose son Abe truly is. I return Morgan's feral grin. "Aberen did see fit to send me a gorgeous bouquet of poisoned blood roses."

Morgan gasps, and Abe snorts out an amused laugh.

Gray eyes narrowing in fury, Morgan crosses her arms, one foot tapping on the tiled floor of Ever's beautiful portal station. "He poisoned you?"

"Purely symbolic," I assure her. "A last, 'fuck you', if you will. He would never expect me to fall for the trick and actually be poisoned."

"I swear to gods," she huffs, "if either of them show their face in Ever, I'm gonna get Lou to run them through with her blue magic. She could do it, too."

"But a blue witch never would," I remind my daughter in law. "Spiteful as Lou might feel on my behalf, she's born to protect."

The noise that erupts from Morgan is half irritated and half conniving. I've gotten the chance to know my son's witchy mate well, and if I've learned one thing, it's that she will hold a grudge until the day she dies.

Abe clears his throat. "I've already made it clear that Evenia and Aberen are not welcome in Ever, not for any reason." He shrugs and reaches for my bag. "It won't stop Mother from coming if she sees something to crow about, but barring that, they're not likely to show up any time soon." He tosses my bag over his muscular shoulder and jerks his head toward the exit. "Shall we? A lovely cottage popped up on the edge of town. Something tells me it has your name on it."

Morgan's fierce look morphs into a smile as she tosses her sheet of auburn hair over her shoulder. "It's adorable, too. We hope you love it! We're just so glad you're finally here for good." She glances up at me, batting her lashes coyly. "Maybe now that you're here and…unencumbered, you might find a lovely monstress to date who likes you for you."

I chuckle as she slips her arm through mine, holding onto my biceps as I guide her to follow Abe. "I'm not worried about that in the slightest, darling. Entanglements happen when and where they want to, but it's not my focus." Resting my hand over the one she has wrapped around my arm, I grin more broadly. "I want to spend time with you two and reconnect with friends who live here. I couldn't be more excited for that."

She squeezes me tighter as we exit the cavernous portal station and emerge deep inside the forest in what's known as Shifter Hollow, the part of Ever reserved for shifters, centaurs and pegasi. For the next half hour, Morgan regales me with tales of the shifter queen and her mate who rule from the Hollow. Apparently, the queen is now on a musical tour, being a literal as well as figurative rock star.

"She's the coolest monster I've ever met," Morgan gushes, glancing at Abe with a quick nip of her lower lip. "Besides Abe, of course."

I look at my son as he strides confidently up the street a pace ahead of us. My intuitive gift pings. Abe's happy. More than happy. He's at peace. He's got Morgan after hundreds of years of wanting her. He waited for so long. I love that the read I get on him now is peaceful comfort.

"There it is," he says now, pointing toward a curve in Sycamore Street.

I bring my hand to my forehead, shading my eyes from Ever's

bright sun as I focus up the road a bit. At the edge of the street's curve, I can just see a gravel driveway.

Abe pauses as Morgan and I stop next to him. He looks at me with all his characteristic seriousness. "I think you'll be pleased, Father. The home is gorgeous. Gothic yet modern. I had a hand in a bit of the design, although Ever does what she wants when homes pop up, as you know."

Ah, that little bit of magic is something I insisted on when monster leadership designed the haven system all those centuries ago. It's a compatibility spell of sorts, ensuring that those who belong in specific havens are given every reason to stay. Magical houses popping up out of nowhere certainly does make one want to remain.

Excitement warms me from the inside. I clap my son on the shoulder. "Thank you, Abemet. I can't wait to see what you and Ever have cooked up."

His lips tilt upward. It's been a long time since he worked as an architect, and these days he's all but retired. But I know my son, and I know it won't be long until he gets the itch to work again. Although I suppose spending his time keeping up with his brilliant, fierce mate is perhaps all he has time for.

He takes off again, leading us to the curve in the road. Once we arrive at the driveway, I see my new home for the first time. Pride rushes through me, knowing that the town itself built this home for me, but that Abe had a hand in her design.

Morgan jogs ahead to catch up with her mate, clinging to his arm as they walk peacefully up the driveway with my luggage. I follow, admiring the bones of the home.

Wide black stone steps lead to a curved arch with a recessed front door. The entryway section of the house is built of pale gray stone with black trimmed windows and doors. To the right of the entryway, two giant sections arch like church windows. Intricately scrolled details give the entire house a gothic, yet modern, vibe. Even the roof tiles are black. Through expansive windows across the home's front, interior lights shine pale yellow light on modern furnishings.

"It's beautiful," I murmur, knowing my son can hear the praise even from far away, good as vampire hearing is.

Abe spins and walks slowly backward, opening his arms wide. "I've imported quite a few furnishings for you but the house is well aware that you might choose to change some things. And I left the entire backyard alone, although I get the sense she might try to put a workshop of sorts back there." His smile grows bigger. "I suppose that'll be up to you."

A workshop. He knows I love having a separate working space from my home. When he was a child, he often joined me in seeking solace from Evenia and Aberen. My workshop in the castle he grew up in was our little hideaway. Most of my fond memories from his childhood are times we spent together playing, working magic, learning about our innate vampiric abilities.

He flew for the first time by jumping off the workshop roof with me.

I absolutely must have a workshop here. But he's right...it's best if I create it in partnership with the house.

Abe and Morgan swing matching glossy black doors open.

"Welcome home, Betmal," Morgan says quietly, her smile soft as I enter the house.

"Home, indeed," I murmur, turning to stroke the matte black wallpaper covering every inch of the front entryway. Nearly all of the furnishings are dark, the entryway punctuated by just a singular modern concrete entry table. Glittering ornate lamps sit on either end, a giant bowl in the middle is full of stones.

I turn to Abe with a surprised look, pointing to the bowl. "Good luck stones from home? However did you manage that?"

For the first time, his grin is as feral as his mate's can be. "Turns out the castle workshop still holds me in high regard. I was able to snatch these from the river while Evenia and Aberen were at work one day."

A laugh bubbles out of my throat. Our former home was notoriously prickly and always loved my mates far more than it loved me. I always assumed that's why the workshop popped up for Abe and me—that was *our* home, our place, our sanctuary away from the rest of the world.

Not that the world didn't catch up with my son eventually. But thankfully, we're past that these days.

"Now listen," Morgan starts, striding into the entryway as she jerks a thumb toward the back of the home. "We thought it might be nice to cook you dinner, but I also recognize that you might want time to yourself. Please kick us out if you'd rather be al—"

"Alone?" I cut in. "Never. I moved here to spend time with the two of you and I have no other priorities. I don't even have a job anymore now that I extricated myself from my former partnership. But, allow me to do the cooking, please."

She laughs. "As long as it's not Abe. Cooking is not his forté."

Abe pinches her playfully on the side. "You've never complained all that much about my cooking."

"It's awful, honey," she says with a playful laugh. "Did you think I took over just 'cause I love it?"

I clear my throat, drawing my daughter in law's attention. "Do you have a dish in mind for tonight?"

She nods. "Yeah, I was going to test a lemon peel pesto on you. And then, of course, we stocked the fridge with imported blood from a place Abe says you like." She falls silent. It's an awkward topic. I should have sustained myself on my mates' blood. But it's been nearly a thousand years since I touched or drank from them. Still, I would never betray our bond, either, so I've been purchasing donated blood for that whole time, unwilling to hunt as my ancestors once did.

It's uncouth, and if I had any other family still alive, they'd abhor it. But as they're mostly all dead or so far removed that we never speak, I'm not fussed over the habit.

"That was generous, thank you," I offer.

Pink tinges Morgan's cheeks.

Pacing past her, I tuck my hands at my back and admire room after room of gorgeous gothic architecture with modern touches. Abe gets his love of this style from me, and over all the years I've lived, gothic modern remains my favorite type of design.

Eventually, we make our way to the kitchen, which sits at the back of the house. Black plated windows line the back wall and half of the ceiling, bringing in an incredible view of a clearing. Dense forest lies beyond that. A stack of wood sits in the clearing, a singular box of nails and a hammer on top of it.

Turning to Abe, I chuckle. "I see what you mean about the workshop. She's ready to add on, clearly."

He pats the countertop in a friendly way, and the house shudders, making her agreement known.

Morgan gets to work on dinner as Abe crafts elegant cocktails from a gorgeous bar inlaid into one wall of the kitchen. When he brings beautiful etched glass cocktail glasses from the bar, I sigh.

"You've thought of everything, darling."

He fills my glass, then slides it across the black concrete bar to me. "Well, I learned from the best. Preparation is key, is it not?"

"Tis," I agree, clinking my glass to his.

Dinner is delightful. Morgan has me in stitches, and Abe even laughs a time or two. It's not in his nature to be outright joyful—his career training stole that from him—but he finds obvious pleasure in Morgan's exuberance.

The meal is over far too soon, and my guests retire for the evening. If they're anything like I was when I was newly mated, they can't wait to get home and rip one another's clothes off.

I'd be lying if I didn't admit to missing those days, when my mates and I seemed to live perpetually in a tangle of limbs, blood splattered across the sheets, our bodies reduced to live wires of pleasure. It's been so long since then, I can scarcely remember what it feels like to be in love.

No. I fell out of love as quickly as I fell into it. If not for Abe and my desire to protect him from a harsh mother and an absentee second father, I wouldn't have stayed as long as I did. Even then, I wasn't able to fully protect him as Evenia became the most powerful monster in our world. I wasn't there when she forced Abe to go through Keeper training and the painful ritual that stripped him of much of his innate personality, rewiring his brain to think in terms of pure logic.

I'll never forgive myself for not seeing that coming, for not being there to save him from her. Even so, it worked out alright for him eventually. I have the gods to thank for that.

Night falls and I sit in front of the pale stone fireplace in my room. Arches soar up and cross the ceiling, giving the entire bedroom a vaguely churchlike feel. I've been alive since before the first church was ever built, but there's something absolutely titillating about the idea of fucking in one.

Not that I moved to Ever to find physical pleasure. But I'm old enough to know that sometimes, the moments you're *not* looking for something are the perfect moments to find it.

BOOKS BY ANNA FURY (MY OTHER PEN NAME)

DARK FANTASY SHIFTER OMEGAVERSE

Temple Maze Series

NOIRE | JET | TENEBRIS

DYSTOPIAN OMEGAVERSE

Alpha Compound Series

THE ALPHA AWAKENS | WAKE UP, ALPHA | WIDE AWAKE | SLEEPWALK | AWAKE AT LAST

Northern Rejects Series

ROCK HARD REJECT | HEARTLESS HEATHEN | PRETTY LITTLE SINNER

Scan the QR code to access all my books, socials, current deals and more!

@annafuryauthor
liinks.co/annafuryauthor

ABOUT THE AUTHOR

Hazel Mack is the sweet alter-ego of Anna Fury, a North Carolina native fluent in snark and sarcasm, tiki decor, and an aficionado of phallic plants. Visit her on Instagram for a glimpse of the sexiest wiener wallpaper you've ever seen. #ifyouknowyouknow

She writes any time she has a free minute—walking the dogs, in the shower, ON THE TOILET. The voices in her head wait for no one. When she's not furiously hen-pecking at her computer, she loves to hike and bike and get out in nature.

She currently lives in Raleigh, North Carolina, with her Mr. Right, a tiny tornado, and two sassy dogs. Hazel LOVES to connect with readers, so visit her on social or email her at author@annafury.com.

Printed in Great Britain
by Amazon